CW01494733

KEITH MARSHALL

A Rufus Tremayne Investigation.

Out of the Dunes.

To
Vicki and Joe
For all their help with this book.

1

A Jaguar, whose colour was indeterminate under the sodium streetlamps, was parked up by the kerbside. Its engine purred softly. It was a cold night, but inside the car the heater filled the cab with warm air. The two occupants sat in silence as they watched the entrance of the *Wild Orchid* club further along the street. The club's brightly illuminated sign flashed red and blue in turn, announcing that it was still open for business. It was just after midnight.

Inside the club the music blasted out, making it almost too loud to hear yourself think. The club was occupied almost exclusively by young thirty-something men. The bar area was busy with groups of them, shouting to be heard above the music as they ordered drinks. Many just stood in silence and made gestures to their mates, as they watched the girls on the low stage going through their pole dancing routines. Cheers and shouts of encouragement for the girls to remove yet another item of their scanty clothing, with more cheers echoing around the room as they did; increasing the noise level to an ear-bursting crescendo.

One man sat alone. He was perched on a stool at the end of the long bar. He neither watched the girls performing nor engaged anyone in conversation. He just held his pint of strong lager in front of him; the glass was almost full. Gerry the barman asked him jokingly if he was making love to it, but he didn't answer, nor did he look up. He wasn't in the mood for drinking, socially that is, but it hadn't stopped him downing several pints. He peered intently into the lager as if hoping that some thought provoking inspiration might suddenly well into his mind as if by osmosis.

He looked worried; occasionally he would suddenly sit upright and look along the bar. Sometimes, he would stand on the stool's cross bar, craning his neck to look above the heads across the crowded room. Who was he looking for, his girlfriend; a drinking mate? At that end of the bar it was marginally quieter. Gerry asked him on more than one occasion if he was all right. Each time he just looked at him and in a monotone, downcast voice said 'yeah.' He took a long draught from his glass, belching the gas build-up from his gut. He then resumed his peering deeply into the lager. Eventually he finished it. He called for a refill by holding the glass up and shaking it from side to side. He then recommenced his deep thinking and peering. *I'll go and talk to 'im, he's a reasonable bloke; we've sorted things in the past. Yeah, it'll be alright, no worries.* He kept telling himself this, reassuring himself that his problems could easily be put right.

Outside the club, the two men continued their watch. The place had closed. The show was over for yet another night. The punters had gone, but the man at the end of the bar had not moved. Gerry cleaned up around him; only the club's working-lights remained on providing just enough light by which to do the routine jobs before going home.

'I'm going to have to ask you to leave now Mickey, time to call it a night and I need my sleep.' Gerry said. Mickey looked up at him.

'Okay mate, I'm off.' Mickey Edwards drained his glass 'G'night then Gerry' his words slurred as he climbed down from the bar stool where he'd spent the last seven hours. He steadied himself, his hand holding the edge of the bar. He took his bearings and headed for the door. It was now two o'clock in the morning.

Mickey Edwards stood in the shadow of the club's doorway; its neon signs and lights had gone out long ago. He looked up and down the poorly lit street. He noticed a car; he squinted at it, trying to focus through his tired, bleary eyes. He couldn't make out whether anyone was in it or not, nor could he tell that its engine was running. He left his doorway shelter and moved along the street away from the club and the car. Keeping to the shadows he moved as quickly as he could, hoping not to be seen. His plan failed.

The man in the passenger seat of the car, smartly dressed, slim and athletic, touched his partner's elbow. Without a word he lifted his hand and pointed towards the shadowy figure slinking quickly along the street, as close to the wall as he could manage. Mickey had gone no more than a hundred metres, when the car pulled up in front of him. The door immediately opened. Mickey backed away from the car, hitting the wall behind him hard. He looked intently at the face staring back at him. He tried to focus his beery-blurred eyes, he recognised the face. Then he ran as fast as he could. The car pulled ahead of him again, this time it slewed across the footpath, coming to a halt, blocking his way. Mickey stopped, he began to run in the opposite direction, but the lager had got the better of him, he came to a halt, bent double, panting, out of breath, spewing on his shoes. The athletic man was out of the car before Mickey had a chance to realise what was happening. The driver jumped out of the car, firing a single shot from a small pistol. The bullet ricocheted off the wall just in front of Mickey. He froze momentarily, for a fraction of a second, before turning and continuing to run again.

The athletic man was quickly on him. Mickey was hauled back to the car where the driver stood menacingly by the open boot. They bundled Mickey into the waiting boot. The lid was slammed shut. The Jaguar sped away into the night.

The boot lid was at last opened and Mickey was unceremoniously hauled out. He screwed up his eyes against the light from a powerful lantern being shone into his face. He squinted against the light, while trying to make out where he was. The rough journey and the effects of the strong lager, had taken their effect. The athletic man looked into the boot, and then angrily at Mickey Edwards, but he said nothing. He nodded to the big man who hauled Mickey inside the building. Mickey made out that he was in some kind of workshop; old machinery, rusted and broken lay testament to the industry that once took place there. Boxes and crates that had never been moved for years were stacked against the walls. Almost every window was broken and Mickey could feel the cold wind blowing through them. Chairs and filing cabinets covered in dust and pigeon shit lay in desolate heaps. The workshop had obviously used by local kids for bashes, empty and crushed beer cans and broken Vodka bottles were strewn about along with the odd discarded condom. The big man dragged Mickey into an old office. Facing him as he entered the room, a table stood centrally; a chair had been placed on each side of it.

Mickey was forced into the chair facing the athletic man. The big man stood just behind Mickey. Mickey shifted slightly to try and see him, but was cuffed on the side of his head for his trouble.

'Mickey Edwards,' said the athletic man. His voice level and even, not aggressive. 'I believe you are in possession of some things that don't belong to you?' He waited for Mickey to answer.

'Things, what things, belonging to who?'

'Come on Mickey don't be silly now. You just tell us where you've got this stuff and you'll walk out of here free as a bird. What do you say eh?'

'I don't know what you're talking about…what stuff. If you tell me what it is, I might be able to help you.'

The big man hit Mickey a hard striking blow to the side of his head. It sent Mickey lurching to one side. He cried out, his eyes blurred, and his hand instinctively went to the spot where contact had been made. It left Mickey screaming. The athletic man in mock sympathy continued.

'Now Mickey, Mickey…be sensible. We don't want to get nasty…really we don't. All I want to know is where you've put this stuff that you took on one of your little night-time jaunts. Now tell us where it is and you can go and Reggie here won't have to resort to…' The athletic man gave Mickey a half smile. 'Well we don't want to think about that now do we?'

Time passed, Mickey was still maintaining that he knew nothing. The athletic man was getting more irritated and threatening as the seconds ticked by. Mickey held out for as long as the pain allowed. He thought he would tell them anything just as long as they stopped the beating.

'Okay…okay' he spluttered, blood spitting from his mouth onto the table and the floor as he spoke. 'Okay. so I picked up some jewels and stuff, but I can't remember which house. It was one I just picked at random; it looked a well-off place. I didn't know whose place it was, honest. I put them in…'

The ringing of the athletic man's mobile phone interrupted the proceedings. He stood and took the phone from his pocket. Walking away from the table, putting the phone to his ear he listened, but said nothing for a minute.

'Okay, as you wish.' He said finally, finishing the call. He sat down again and faced Mickey.

'You were saying…well never mind Mickey. It doesn't matter anymore.

Mickey Edwards was never seen again, well not alive anyway.

2

Detective Chief Inspector Rufus Tremayne and his French partner and forensic pathologist Sophie Bouvier were enjoying each other's company in one of their favourite restaurants. The place was full. There was a steady buzz of chatter from contented diners. The tables were covered with crisp white cloths, on which was an array of cutlery and fine crystal glassware that might confuse many diners. However it also indicated the restaurant's style. Black-suited waiters with pristine white aprons moved expertly around the room. Their skills in placing the diner's choice before them was a cut above what you might call a typical restaurant. Every movement was done with precision, unhurried yet sharp. The walls were adorned with a mix of antique mirrors and period oil paintings, and crystal chandeliers hung from the decorated ceiling throwing their light onto the richly embossed plasterwork. Some would call it a throw-back to another time. Over-elaborate and fussy.

Rufus and Sophie enjoyed eating out, trying different styles of food. It didn't really matter what sort of restaurant it was, just as long as the food was tasty and well served. They had been sitting in silence for a minute and his thoughts drifted to his relationship with Sophie, he was very happy with how things were, but it worried him sometimes. He had seen it all too often, break-ups between people, between police officers. He put it down to the job, a vocation that got into the blood. To many an officer, the job is everything. It's not a conscious decision, it's just that things happen and you have to do something about it. A phone call, an incident, a response is required. *You can't pick and choose.* He could hear himself telling raw recruits. He loved Sophie very much, but if I asked her to marry me how would that change things. *I must get to grips, stop dithering man, and do something positive.*

Rufus ordered a glass of Kir for each of them and he also asked Thomas, the sommelier, to send a bottle of his current favourite, a red wine from the southwest of France called Madiran. Thomas had pre-empted Tremayne's choice.

'I have taken the liberty...' he said. He had known Tremayne was dining that evening and had, rightly or wrongly, anticipated his choice and had opened a bottle some time earlier, giving it chance to breath. Much to Tremayne's delight the wine appeared no sooner than he'd asked for it.

Thomas poured a little of it into the bottom of the over-large glass. Tremayne often thought they were too large; nonetheless, he took the glass by its stem and swirled the wine round a little. He lifted, tilting the glass and stared into the deep red liquid before putting it under his nose, appreciating its bouquet before finally sipping. It was a wine heavy in tannins, the type Tremayne liked, fortunately so did Sophie. He thought that its strong heaviness would go well with his beef.

'Thank you Thomas, excellent as usual.'

Rufus and Sophie chatted about nothing in particular; Sophie was saying that she was thinking she might have their apartment redecorated. She talked about a colour scheme, but Rufus was of the opinion that whatever she wanted was fine by him. He had confidence in her interior design ability.

'We need something...something warm...like golds and reds, a hint of yellow maybe. Abigail likes all white, but I think everything white is a bit...well...clinical, don't you think so Rufus?'

Rufus replied 'Yes, that sounds just fine. You know I have every faith in your ability to choose whatever's right. You know I'm no good at visualizing colours. Maybe Abigail is the same, so she thinks that white is a pretty safe colour.'

'Oh come on Rufus you must be able to come up with some ideas...' She began, but then thought the better of it and went on to another topic of conversation.

As they chatted, with the menus resting on their laps, unread; they sipped the last of their Kir. Rufus had just lifted his menu and opened it when a young waiter arrived at their table and asked, in a hushed tone that was hardly discernable above the constant chatter around them,

'Excuse me Sir, might I enquire if you and your guest are ready to order?'

'Oh! Sorry' Tremayne said 'Give us a few more minutes could you?'

'Certainly Sir.' The waiter disappeared into the room, but he kept an eye on his charges from a distance, until he thought they were ready. They studied their menus. Overlarge, leather embossed things, and quite heavy too. After a minutes reading, he asked Sophie what she might like. But she just shrugged her shoulders and turned the corners of her mouth down, in an expression of bewilderment at the choice on offer.

'Well,' said Tremayne at last 'I'm just going to have a nice grilled fillet steak, cooked slightly underdone and some of their excellent fries…maybe a side salad, nice and simple tonight I think.'

'Oh Rufus! Be a little more adventurous…er…how about the Navarin d'agneau…or here, there's a nice Sole bonne femme…or, there's a…'

Tremayne cut her short,

'Sophie, never mind all the French stuff. I'll enjoy the steak thank you. Now you have whatever you like, but tonight I just feel like a simple fillet steak, possibly with a little béarnaise sauce.'

'Shall we have hors d'oeuvre? I think I'll have the charcuterie.'

'Umm…yes that sounds good; yes I'll have the same.'

The waiter approached them again; he took their order and disappeared into the business of the restaurant.

As they were chatting, Tremayne became aware of a presence behind him; two men were approaching the table. Tremayne swivelled round in his seat. The lead man was the Maître d'hôtel, he could not quite see the face of the man following him; and then his heart sank when he did recognise the other man. Redfern Sutcliffe, an American and a private investigator who spent his time working on both sides of the Atlantic. Tremayne had a professional, sort of love-hate relationship with Redfern Sutcliffe.

They could from time to time use one another's expertise. Each in their everyday work came across things that on occasions helped the other. Sutcliffe was certainly not an informer, Tremayne considered him, a sort of ally, an associate. He had contacts on both sides of the Atlantic, some in high places, many on low places. Tremayne was not fully cognizant of Sutcliffe's CV; but they trusted each other's judgement.

'This gentleman insists on speaking with you Mr Tremayne.' The Maitre d'hôtel began. 'I'm dreadfully sorry for the interruption.'

'That's all right Olivier, he won't be staying long.' Tremayne said eyeing Sutcliffe with displeasure, and thinking. *This had better be good, interrupting my evening.*

The Maître d'hôtel bowed slightly, eyed the intruder with suspicion, he left them alone. Sutcliffe said nothing; he pulled a chair over from the adjacent table and sat down.

'What do you want Redfern, could this not wait until morning?' Tremayne asked; a little irritated at being disturbed.

He did not answer. He reached across to the table from where he'd taken the chair and removed a glass, and then he poured himself some wine from Tremayne's bottle.

'I asked, what do you want?' Tremayne repeated impatiently.

'What is this?' Sutcliffe questioned after tasting the wine, he picked up the bottle and read the label. 'Madiran…umm…don't know it…bit tanniny for my liking.'

'Redfern, I don't give a damn whether you like it or don't like it, and I never offered it in the first place. Anyway…for the third time what do you want?'

'I'm sorry Rufus, but I'm flying back to New York early a.m. I had to bring you this.' He took an envelope from the inside pocket of his overcoat and handed it across to Tremayne. 'I know you like a little mystery Rufus, a challenge even. I was given this by…well, never mind, it's not important just now. But I know that you'll know what to do with it.' He took another sip of the wine, grimaced, and put the glass down. 'I'm sorry to have disturbed your meal ma'am, my apologies. But I thought that this might intrigue our friend here.' He got up saying 'Good evening to you both and *Bon Apertit.*

'Good night Redfern; you've delivered it, now you can leave us in peace. If I need to speak to you I know where you are.'

'I take it you're not going to invite me to dine? Well that's okay; I know a good fish and chip shop.' Sutcliffe said with mock disappointment.

'Yes, well you know how it is…eh; goodnight Redfern.'
Redfern Sutcliffe turned away from them and walked out of the restaurant. The waiter hurried over to the table, quickly replacing the chair and a clean wine glass on the adjacent table before removing the one Sutcliffe had used from Tremayne's table; uttering that he was sorry about the interruption.

'What is that?' Sophie asked when Sutcliffe had gone.

'I don't know.' He said pulling the envelope open and peering inside, it contained some newspaper cuttings, and he pulled them out. The first was a report about a murder, so was the second one.

'They are old newspaper cuttings about a couple of murder cases.' He looked puzzled. He looked at the dates on the top of the pages. 'This one dates from the war, and…this one's the 1960s. Well, what am I…' He scanned the two pages. 'Both found in the dunes…twenty odd years apart. Interesting but I don't know what I'm supposed to do about them?' He

sensed the waiter hovering and he pushed them back into their envelope. He folded it and asked Sophie to put it in her handbag. 'Right, let's enjoy the rest of our evening. Hopefully undisturbed.'
The young waiter sensed that they were ready and began to serve them.

Tremayne woke early. He made himself a pot of coffee. He sat down at the breakfast bar and began to read through the contents of the envelope, in detail. He had just scanned though the contents when Sophie ambled into the kitchen, wearing a full-length silk kimono by Agent Provocateur; graduated blue-grey to plum red from the shoulder down, and nothing else. Rufus looked up and smiled. She walked over to him, 'Good morning.' she said leaning over and kissing him; his hands instinctively held her waist. The feel of her soft body through the silk sent a shiver of desire through him, but he resisted the temptation, saying to himself that he had work to do.

'Good morning.' He said, kissing her on her lips. 'I didn't want to wake you at this hour. I just thought I'd take a look though these before I go in. They are old newspaper cuttings from the Liverpool Echo.'

'Good morning' she repeated softly, stretching her arms and yawning. 'What are they all about?'

'They are talking about a couple of murders. This one,' He said holding it out to her. '…is about a young naval officer, a Chief Petty Officer. Simon Carter was his name. He was found dead in the sand dunes way back in nineteen forty-four; the fourteenth of October to be precise.

'Nineteen forty-four?' Sophie repeated, sounding very surprised. 'I'm sorry carry on.'

'And this one,' He handed Sophie the second cutting. '…this is dated almost twenty years later…nineteen sixty-three. It talks about another body being found in the dunes as well. It says that his name was Richard Gilbert Mason aged fifty five. Which means he was born, what, in er…nineteen oh-eight?' Sophie agreed with his maths. 'Both had been beaten…with the usual blunt instrument and they were both buried in an attempt to hide them.'

'So what are you going to do about it?'

'To be honest Sophie, I haven't the faintest. But it's interesting, don't you think?'

'To you maybe. But what does Redfern expect you to do; find out a bit more about them?

'Yeah, I suppose he does. He didn't really say, did he?'

'No.'

'Anyway I'll see what I can dig up.'

'If you get too busy with this new case, it might be a good idea to ask your journalist friend Tony Clayton. He's on the Echo, isn't he? He could do a bit of digging in the archive. If he can't, he might know someone who could have a look…might throw some light on the subject. But, I'm still puzzled…why do you suppose Redfern gave them to you in the first place? He could have done it all himself, couldn't he?'

'I don't know, I suppose he could have. Maybe he thinks I can find something in our archive, anyway I'll work on it.'

Tremayne drove into the police station's car park. He parked his electric blue Alfa Romeo 159 and was just pressing the flip key as Detective Constable Clive Fraser was walking away from his silver Peugeot 308.

'That's some motor you have there, boss…one of these days….yeah very smart.' Clive said admiringly nodding his head.

'Nice to hear you have some ambitions in life DC Fraser. But I hope it's a little more than admiring my car?'

'Yes boss, sergeant's exams in a couple of weeks.'

'Glad to hear it Clive, shall we get inside and you can achieve another one of your ambitions and begin to learn a bit more about policing.' They both laughed and walked into the building.

The incident room was a buzz of activity as Tremayne walked into the large open-plan office. Brief greetings were exchanged. He entered his own small side-office. He looked with dismay at the pile of papers that had been laid on his desk. He stared at it all and shook his head as he sat down heavily into his chair. Almost immediately the phone rang, with its annoying trill.

'Tremayne…' He answered putting the phone to his ear. 'Ah! Good morning Sir.'

Chief Superintendent Derek Pearsall was Tremayne's superior officer. He was the sort of senior police officer who was always expecting quick results in all things. He was also the type who kept a keen eye on the books, the budget books especially and scrutinized every minute of overtime.

'We are on top of things Sir.' He lied. 'Yes Sir I'll be up straight away.' He said putting the phone down, Tremayne looked into the outer office and waved his hand to attract Detective Sergeant Helen Machin.

She acknowledged him, left her desk and walked into his office. As soon as the door opened he asked. 'He wants to know what progress you've made.' pointing a finger at the ceiling towards the super's office above. Helen took the empty seat opposite Tremayne, she could tell him, nothing he didn't already know and that there was nothing new. Tremayne got up from behind his desk and walked to the incident board Helen followed him. He stood in front of the board. The incident board was a large, magnetic white board that was fastened to and covered the whole of an end wall. In large block-capital letters above everything else was written **DUNES INCIDENT**. Attached to the board with little coloured magnets was a map of the area, various photographs of the scene of crime. Several showed the position of the body from various angles. The body was that of a man, one photograph showed him half buried in the sand. Two lines were drawn from the photos. One to the words – **NAME – UNKNOWN,** some joker has scribbled below *as yet*. The other line was to the map of the area showing the location of the body.

'As mysterious as ever, I see.'

'Yes Sir.' Replied Helen.

'Okay…so let me go through this again before I go and see the chief super'. So this guy…whoever he is.' Tremayne said tapping his finger on the photo of the dead man 'was found in the sand dunes here,' He tapped his finger on the map. '…the wind had blown the sand and uncovered him. A woman walking her dog found him…yeah.'

'Yes Sir.'

'So what have else have we got; a name perhaps?'

'No Sir, no name, no ID on him at all. He's been badly beaten, not easy to recognise and his fingertips were burnt. There were a few coins in his pocket, nothing really, about sixty pence that's all.'

'Was anything found near the body?'

'No…nothing.'

'It goes without saying…we have looked?' Tremayne held his hands and arms open in a pleading posture, hoping for some positive response. 'Have we dug around per-chance, eh?'

'Yes sir, we've had a preliminary look round, but not as yet a thorough search.'

'Yes get that sorted…if that's not too much trouble Detective sergeant.'

She felt angered at the remark, but said nothing. She turned on her heels and checked through an A4 sized notebook marked DUNE INCIDENT LOG.

'During the prelim look round the site Sir, nothing was found. A proper search will be carried out later today, it's being set up as we speak.' Helen said returning to where Tremayne was still standing in front of the incident board.

'You know Helen; this case reminds me of another one. I don't know why it should, the other was years ago. But there's something familiar about this one.'

'Something you've read recently perhaps, or spoken to someone about.'

'Yes, it's the same as a couple of other cases, in some ways. But I don't know why it should be, sheer coincidence.' He said shaking his head. Tremayne was interrupted by the phone ringing and Clive Fraser calling him.

'Yes Sir, I'll remind him.' He replaced the receiver. 'Boss, the Chief Superintendent wants to know where you are.'

'Oh shit…I forgot about him; organise that search Sergeant.' Tremayne said as he hurried out of the office.

Tremayne heard Chief Superintendent Pearsall's voice as knocked on his office door, sounding like a man under pressure 'COME…' Tremayne pushed the door open. 'There you are Tremayne, what kept you. If you think I've got nothing better to do that chase after you…sit.'

'I'm sorry Sir; I was just checking on…developments.'

'Well.'

'The body found in the sand dunes has not been identified…as yet. There was nothing in his pockets to tell us who he is. We've given the area a check over; a thorough search is now underway. The preliminary forensic report indicates that the body was deliberately beaten, around the torso and especially around the head and face, and the finger tips have been burned. We must assume that was done to make it difficult for us to identify him, as a deliberate act to slow us down as least.'

'Well, someone has gone to a lot of trouble there Tremayne. Do you suspect major gangland involvement here involving drugs perhaps?

'I don't know Sir, early days. We're still waiting for the post mortem report that might tell us something more. It should be ready by lunchtime. I'm hoping we might find something where we found him. Obviously we need to find out who he is…but until then…well?'

'All right Tremayne, keep me posted…that's all.'

It was difficult to get vehicles close to the crime scene. They had to park their vans and cars on the beach, as close as possible to the scene of crime. They then had to carry whatever they needed into the dunes. Through the soft sand, up the steep inclines; taking one step forward and two back as they struggled to get purchase. After several trips their calf muscles were letting everyone know that they didn't like this struggling through soft sugary sand.

The area around where the body of the unknown man had been found was now taped off with bright yellow tape fastened to metal stakes driven into the sand. A temporary tent, like a picnic gazebo, had been erected over the site; it was anchored down as best as could be to prevent it taking-off along the beach in the strong wind. Sand was constantly being blown around. It made it uncomfortable for those there, it stung their faces and after a while they were grinding it in their teeth. Inside, two forensic officers, one being Sophie Bouvier, were painstakingly trying to move the sand from one place to another. The job was made more difficult as the soft dry sand ran back into any space as quickly as it was moved.

Tremayne poked his head through the flap. He smiled at Sophie and asked, but didn't expect a sensible answer, if they had found anything.

'Nice collection of shells.' Alan Stephens answered without lifting his head. 'We'll let you know Rufus.' Sophie said. 'But don't bank on quick results. We're going to have to put the sand through a sieve, it's impossible to scrape away as we would normally do.'

'Thank you.' He said with a half laugh. 'I'll leave you in peace. See you later Sophie. Bye for now.'

Tremayne walked away from the tent. He stood on the top of an adjacent dune and looked over the surrounding area. All he saw was bare patches of sand, with swathes of marram grass, used to hold the dunes together, bent over by the wind. Inland was greener, with established vegetation and low scrubby bushes. He noticed the odd bit of litter and a few rusted empty drink cans, left by last summer's picnicers. The whole area was pock-marked where people had walked, even though it was some distance from the beach entrance where vehicles had to park. He remembered back to a time when you could drive along the beach. But that had been stopped and the beach closed to vehicles for conservation reasons. He remembered, when he was a boy, being taken by his father for a pleasure flight in a biplane that used the beach as an aerodrome; and his grandfather telling him of competitions for racing cars and motor bikes and of land speed trials in the 1920s. He had turned full circle now, and looking towards the tent and the uniformed policemen huddled against the wind and driving sand, it brought him back to reality and his questions. *A forensic nightmare. What're they going to find there, only sea shells as Alan said; unless someone was clumsy enough to drop anything, which I doubt. Was he killed elsewhere and brought here? And who the hell is he and why was he killed and why was he disfigured? And why does Redfern Sutcliffe want me to look into old cases?*

He left his lofty position and joined Helen on the beach. 'We'll go and have a word with Dr Winterton. I've had enough of the seaside for one day.'

They trudged back to where the cars were parked, away from the soft sand at the edge of the dunes. Tremayne opened the car door, but stopped momentarily to look up and down the beach. He said nothing and got into the car, slamming the door and telling the driver to take them back to the pub car park where he'd left his Alfa.

They found Doctor Ruth Winterton writing reports in her office, she looked up as they entered, saying…

'Ah, Rufus, I was just about to call you. You've saved me the cost of a phone call; need to save all the money I can,' She said grinning. '…you know what it is with cutbacks, all the scrimping and saving we need to do these days.' By now she was rolling her hands together in a Uriah Heap interpretation; still laughing.

'Yeah…tell me about it. It's ol' fungus face's favourite hobby. I could tell him how to save money…by not sending out dozens of memos, that'd save paper, and someone ought to send him one about all his meetings at HQ every other day.' He complained, shaking his head. 'Ah well! Never mind, enough of my ranting. So what have you got for me?'

'You'll get the full written report in due course, after the full PM has been carried out. This is Sophie's case and as you know she's on site, just now. But I can tell you that he may have been in the dunes for some time. The dryness of the sand and where he was buried, on the lee side of the hill, has sort of mummified him in a way. Well not really, but he has certainly not decomposed as quickly as if it were damper and with more insect activity. I'd say he'd been dead for a month, several weeks at least.

16

I think originally he was buried much deeper and with the scarcity of flies and the usual soil living detritivores, which are not present in the calcareous environment, the body stayed intact longer. Then due to the wind and people's feet, he's now come to the surface.' She looked at Tremayne, who appeared puzzled.

'What?' she asked.

'I need a dictionary every time I come in here. Detriti what?'

Alright, detritivores are organisms that help to…eat up any dead matter in the soil and calcareous relates to chalky or limestoney soil or in this case shelly, basically shells are limestone.

'Okay Ruth thanks for the science lesson. So, how did he die?'

'He was beaten, quite badly in fact by someone using their fists most likely, must have been a powerful man. But then they worked on his fingertips. I don't understand that, was he part of some gang Rufus?'

He shook his head. 'We might determine that when we discover who he is. How old would you say he was?'

'Well judging by the teeth, and his general condition. I'd say he had a reasonably good diet. His age…well I'd say he was in his late twenties or early thirties; certainly not middle aged. I would have said he was in his prime, fit-ish, but certainly no athlete, judging by his beer belly.'

'Okay Ruth thanks very much. I know what you'll say, but he's had a thorough going over?

'We are professional around here Rufus. As I've said, Sophie is dealing with this case and she'll give you a full report…'

Tremayne held his hand up in submission. 'Okay, sorry, I'll try to be patient.' He said as he left the office.'

'Yeah, I'll hold you to that Rufus.' She called as the door closed behind him.

It had been a frustrating day for them all. There had been no developments what-so-ever. Pearsall had vented his frustration at the lack of progress. Tremayne was now sitting in The Golden Lion with his colleagues

'What's that wine you're drinking boss?' Allie asked.

'.It's an Argentinean Malbec, try it.'

'I've tried red wine; I'm not sure I really like it; bit…er.' She said, turning her mouth down showing her dislike.

Tremayne described the wine, the experts say it's like drinking blackberries, cherries, plums and chocolate all rolled into one, but I'm not entirely sure of that, but I like it. Maybe it I drink enough of it.' He laughed. He offered her the glass, she hesitated. 'Try it…It's all right I'll get another.' he told her to hold her nose in the glass, inhale slowly, fill your head with the aroma. She was not sure whether he was joking or not. Allie took a sip, but said she couldn't really taste chocolate, and said she thought it a bit strong. Tremayne told her to work on it, and perhaps try something less heavy, a Cote du Rhone perhaps.'

'I'll stick to my usual though.' Allie said.

Tremayne smiled then checked his watch, took his mobile from his pocket and called Sophie.

'Hello everyone.' Sophie said as she arrived in the pub ten minutes later, a beaming smile on her face. 'How are you all?' Rufus poured her a glass of his Malbec, which she sipped and nodded her approval. Rufus asked her how the PM was going. She told him that the test results and report would be ready in due course. Tremayne felt frustrated, but didn't push it. Sophie turned and chatted to Martin.

'Julia and I have just booked a camping holiday in France.' Martin told her enthusiastically. 'It should be nice, we're not in tents; we're in what they call a mobile home. To tell you the truth it looks like a big caravan to me, but it's got everything in it including a shower. So there'll be no walking over to the communal block anymore.'

'Sounds nice,' replied Sophie, 'Where in France is it?'

'Brittany, it's a big site near a place called Dol de Bretagne, lots for children to do, children's pool, games club, and it's not too far from the beaches and Mont St Michel. I think Briony will love it.'

'Yes I know the area well; I was born not too far away in Combourg. I think you'll enjoy it, well I certainly hope you do. Dol is a very old town dating back to the Roman period, lots of lovely old buildings from the middle ages with wood on the outside.'

Martin and Sophie continued to chat about Brittany. With Sophie suggesting places that Martin and his family should go and see. Rufus and Nick Chandler were sitting in the corner chatting quietly.

'So…' Nick said 'What's this theory of yours that there's a connection between this guy we've found in the dunes and the one you say was found back in nineteen forty something?'

'Nineteen forty four, yeah, it's only tenuous though. Just now the only link is the sand dunes. Back in late forty four, the war hadn't too long to go, not that they knew that. They came across the body in October forty four. The newspaper article suggested that he had been out drinking,

18

but he was found miles away from the nearest pub. There had been a bit of a storm and the wind had blown the sand, exposing the body.'

'Just like our guy?'

'Yeah exactly, I contacted Tony Clayton; I'm waiting for him to get back to me. I asked him to do a bit of digging in their archive for me.'

'Do you think there'll have reported it in the papers? There was heavy censorship then…so there might not be much detail.'

'Yes there was censorship, to keep up morale and all that, but I'm not so sure it would have included crimes.' Tremayne said, not sounding too sure of his facts.

'You planning on checking through the police records? They's probably something knocking about somewhere, but I don't know when you're going to find the time; during your holidays perhaps?' Nick laughed.

'Oh yes.' Tremayne said smiling and nodding towards Sophie. 'It's on the to-do list, when I get around to it.'

3

Tremayne had a sleepless night; his mind in turmoil; tossing and turning, much to Sophie's annoyance. Eventually he got up. He looked at the clock shining out in the dark; its red figures glowed four thirty. Without turning on the lights he crept out of the bedroom, and by instinct he found his dressing gown on his way out. He settled himself in the kitchen with a mug of coffee.

Three deaths and all the bodies found in the dunes, more or less in the same place. Is there a link or is it just too much of a coincidence. And what's Sutcliffe's interest in them? Has he been paid by someone to find out something, and he's getting me to delve into police records – well tough, Pal. I'm busy. He pondered for some time, he made more coffee and waited for the dawn, or inspiration or both. Dawn broke and the sky lightened. But the light of inspiration didn't even flicker. The sun eventually broke the darkness, its orange glow building over the hills in the dark distance. Eventually, the sun shone in through the kitchen window, bringing in the new day.

Sophie walked into the kitchen, turning off the lights. She asked him what he was doing up so early and what time he had got up. Explaining that he couldn't sleep, he said he'd been there for a couple of hours or more.

'I've been sitting here drinking coffee and thinking about these three murders.' He said to her. 'Maybe I'm just taking on a wild goose chase with these newspaper reports that Sutcliffe gave me. How on earth can three deaths spanning forty odd years possibly be linked?'

'I couldn't begin to think of a theory, but you never know there might be something encouraging waiting for you when you get in.' Sophie said trying to be positive.

'Yeah,' He sighed. 'You never know your luck. But to be realistic, they must be totally separate, unconnected events…haven't they?' He finished his coffee, banged his fists lightly on the counter. 'Be positive, you never know what we'll uncover. And you'll have my report soon eh?' He smiled and went off to shower, dress and go to work.

Tremayne phoned Tony Clayton the minute he got to his desk, despite the dozens of   hand-written and e-mail messages waiting there for him. He picked up the top memo as he listened to the ringing of Clayton's phone.

Does that man never go home? Is he here all night writing memos to all and sundry? Rufus tossed it back onto the pile having read;

Memo from: DCS. D Pearsall;

To: DCI. W Tremayne:

Speak to me ASAP today.

It had been dated and timed at 20:00hrs. Tremayne snorted, *Yeah right, when I get a minute*. He was then drawn back to reality as Tony Clayton answered the call.

'Good morning Tony, have you got anything for me?'

'Morning Rufus. Sorry, not really, I've had a quick look but I can't really give any time to it. But, the good news is that I do have someone who can. Her name is Frankie Bolton; she's pretty and she's efficient, and she likes to get her teeth into a bit of research. She'll dig something up I've no doubt; and if she can get a story from it...'

'Good that's what I like to hear. I'll look forward to meeting her. Thanks for this – I own you one Tony...and there may be a story in there somewhere for her.'

'Now that's what I like to hear from you Rufus. See you soon, bye.' Tony said with a chuckle in his voice.

Tremayne put the phone down and considered the pile of messages facing him. *Ah sod it*, he said to himself, and walked into the incident room. Some of the officers glanced up at him as he walked over to the large board that took up most of one wall. His hands went into his trouser pockets and he stared at it. Little was written on it. A few photos and a map of the crime scene adorned it, but that was all, nothing new, apart from the name, address and phone number of the dog walker who had found the unknown corpse.

'What did this dog walker have to say?' He said, to no one in particular.

'Only that she walks along that part of the beach every day. She said she was shocked to find him.'

'Yeah, I bet she was.' said Tremayne as an aside.

'Yeah...her dog went mad having got a whiff of him then it ran off into the dunes. She ran after it, shouting its name. She got to the dog and found it barking and scratching around the body.' Helen said, who had now come to stand next to him.

'I take it we still don't know who he is?'

'No, we don't, not yet anyway.'

'What about post mortem results?'

'Nothing yet.' Tremayne let out a deep sigh, his cheeks inflating as he breathed out.

'Okay, we need to get this moving or ol' beardy chops will be having words with me…again.' Tremayne walked away from the board and headed back into his office, he turned at its door, looked at Helen.

'Get yourself down to that path lab and see what they've found, I need some guidance here. I need some answers.'

'Right boss.' Replied Helen. She walked over to her desk and grabbed her coat from the back of her chair. She was just pulling the door open when Tremayne shouted.

'Oh, and ask them about dental records too. We need to know who this guy is…yesterday if possible. And ask Ruth Winterton about facial recon, travelling back in time…anything and everything…' Helen watched him for a minute, thinking he was going to follow on with something, but all he said was.

'And don't come back empty handed…right off you go then.' Tremayne turned, slamming his office door, he sat down heavily into his chair; it creaked and groaned as usual, objecting to such treatment. He mumbled obscenities under his breath, thinking it would collapse under him one day. *There's no money for furniture* he could hear Pearsall bemoaning. He picked up a pen and began tapping it on the desk, biting his lower lip in deep thought. He grabbed the top memo.

Helen turned right into the hospital campus. She paused to study the huge sign that indicated all the various departments of the district hospital. As she scanned it looking for pathology, the car behind hooted its horn angrily. She didn't even look in her mirror she just lifted her arm and put up two fingers. Muttering, *you just bloody wait mate.* She spotted Pathology, and just as she thought, it was right round the back of the building, tucked out of the way. She paused again, before pulling out to let an ambulance pass. The car that had blown its horn hurried forwards behind it. Helen shook her head at the driver who just smirked at her.

'For two pins I'd nick you, you impatient bugger.' She shouted, but unheard.

She followed them for fifty metres the ambulance turned into A&E, the car pulled into the public car park, Helen drove on.

'DS Machin,' she announced herself 'I'm looking for Dr Winterton.'

'She's in her office' said the young girl on reception, smiling. '…it's just along the corridor along there, third door on the right.' Helen thanked the girl, found the office and knocked, entering at the beckoning from within.

'Hello…' said Helen 'I'm Detective Sergeant Machin…' Dr Winterton smiled at her and indicated for her to take a seat, as she finished writing something on the sheet of paper in front of her.

'Ah!' she said knowingly, as she put her pen down. 'Rufus sent you to chase us up no doubt. Very impatient that man?'

'Yes…I suppose. He wanted to know…'

'Oh yes I know what he wants, about the man from the dunes.' Dr Winterton said, interrupting Helen. 'I'm surprised he hasn't been in and out of here himself, but things have to run their course. I organised the facial reconstruction straight away. It might be ready later today; it takes the computer some time to work through all the data.'

'Well yes, I suppose it would take time.' Helen said 'I know what it is, but I don't know much about, how it's all done. Where do you start with facial reconstruction, that is; it all seems very complicated if you ask me. Tell me, out of interest. How do you get to reconstruct a face?' Helen asked sounding rather puzzled.   'In simple terms, it's based on the fact that there is a relationship between the skull and the overlying soft tissue. We know how the face is built up and what the muscles do. So we are able now to build up a face from a skull, if that's not too damaged. We do a lot of work for archaeological research. Do you know we built up a face last year of an eleven hundred year old Saxon king…amazing. Sometimes we use a computer programme and sometime a model is built up using clay.'

'The computer is quickest though?' Helen speculated.

'Yes, but it still takes time. There's never an exact copy made, only a likeness that would resemble the true face, but it's near enough for your purposes. One can usually recognise the person from the finished model.'

'How long before we get a result with this one?'

Ruth Winterton picked up the phone saying 'Let me check.' she listened a moment and asked Helen's question. 'Okay.' she said putting the phone down.

'They're almost there.' she said, getting up from her chair. 'Come on we'll go and take a look.'

Helen followed Ruth out of the office, along the corridor and up a single flight of stairs. The door at the top opened out into a huge room that was subdivided into sections. People in white coats sat at long tables, high shelves above them with glassware, strange to Helen's eyes. Machines stood on the long tables and on benches that ran the full length of the lab. Some people were peering at computer screens, others down microscopes. They walked over to a young woman. She was leaning back on her stool, watching the monitor. She swung round when she realised someone was behind her.

'Ah, Dr Winterton Bonjour.'

'Helen, this is Sophie Bouvier; she's been working on your chap. Detective Sergeant Helen Machin.' Dr Winterton said introducing the two women. Helen knew Sophie and greeted her warmly.

'Of course you know each other…Rufus, yes I should have realised.'

'How's it coming?' asked Helen

'Oh fine, we'll be there soon. The face was very badly damaged; it took us some time to sort it out. I think half an hour or so will do it.'

'Thanks Sophie, we'll be in my office. Would you bring it down as soon as you've got something?'

Ruth and Helen sat in soft comfy chairs sipping coffee and chatting. It was less than half an hour when a knock on the door made them stir. Ruth called 'come in.' and Sophie walked in with a folder in her hand.

'Here he is.' she said holding the folder towards Dr Winterton.

'Thank you Sophie. Coffee?'

'Non merci' she said 'I've a few things to do, thank you, see you later maybe Helen. Bye.'

Yes' said Helen 'Bye for now.' Dr Winterton took the images from the envelope and spread them out on the table. The two women looked at them.

'Wow, these are amazing, I saw him in the mortuary a couple of days ago; I'd never have thought…' Helen said.

'Do you know who he is?' asked Ruth, as Helen studied the images.

'No…'fraid not.' Replied Helen shaking her head 'Maybe the boss will.' She gathered the images together replacing them into the folder. 'Well thank you for all your help. I'll see you again no doubt.'

Clive Fraser held the phone up at arms-length and waved it, 'Boss…' he shouted 'there's a Frankie Bolton on the line for you.'

'Oh good, put it though here Clive…' he shouted and pointed towards his office; he hurried in and grabbed the phone. Clive transferred the call.

'Hello Frankie, Rufus Tremayne here, it's nice to talk to you at last…have you managed to find anything?'

'Well, I've got a bit on the Chief Petty Officer Simon Carter, but the bank manager Richard Mason I've got nothing more than what I've read in the papers of the time. The write-up mentions the bank where he worked, but it's one that's been swallowed up by one of the big banks. So I'm going to poke around, and see what I can find. '

'Okay, so what about Simon Carter then?'

'Well, he served on-board several ships during the Second World War. Then a few months before his death, he went on a mission to Norway. He was part of a team made up of both naval men and commandos. Well, I found out that they had to go there to pick up some Norwegian resistance men and bring them back to England. They also had to search a house used by the Germans, but I don't know much about that. I think they had to look for any useful documents.'

'I don't suppose you found out what those documents were about or who the Norwegians were?'

'No I didn't. My next line of research is through the National Archive at Kew in London and the Naval Archive. I'll see what I can find out about missions to Norway.'

'Anything else?'

'Oh yes, and I'm really excited about this. I've found out that two of the group are still alive and they live here…in the northwest. One's in Preston, and the other's in Southport. So I've made arrangements to go and talk to them.'

'That's good…nice work. Let me know what you find out. Sorry, but I'll have to go, I'll speak with you soon Bye.'

Helen stood by the door of Tremayne's office waiting for him to finish his phone call. She placed the folder of images in front of him. He looked up and asked 'What's this?'

'Er…it's what you've been waiting for. I've been to the path lab…facial recon'' She replied looking at him questioningly.

'Oh, Right! Sorry…miles away.' He took the envelope and emptied its contents onto the desk. He continued talking as he arranged them. 'That was Frankie Bolton; colleague of Tony Clayton. She's been researching those newspaper cuttings I had.' He looked at the pictures for only a second. 'Bloody hell…well I'll be damned…Mickey Edwards,' he said with a whisper, but Helen caught the astonishment in his voice. '…now what were you up to, to end up like this?' He pushed himself out of his seat and called into the incident room 'Nick come and take a look at these; Facial recon pics of our man in the dunes.' Nick Chandler took one brief look at the images on the desk and gasped. 'Well I never, Mickey Edwards…what's he been up to then?'

'That's exactly what I said Nick. Why don't you to go and talk to his mates.' Tremayne said.

'Has he got any?' Chandler replied laughing.

'By the look of him over there…' he said pointing to the incident board. 'I'd say no.'

'Do you know where he usually hung out?'

'Yeah, we'll go and chat with the natives.'

Chandler walked back into the incident room. 'Good news folks, we've got ID on the guy found in the sand dunes.' Everyone looked up in hushed anticipation. 'He is one Michael Paul Edwards; some of you may know him as he's got a long record,' a couple of them nodded knowingly. Nick acknowledged them. 'Yeah, we've known him a long time, he started his career way back in his teens. He's been up for shoplifting, burglary, nicking cars. He fancies himself, sorry fancied himself as a driver. He was suspected of being the driver for a post office job a few years ago but he was never convicted. Anyway we need to find out what he's been doing lately. So, we'll split up and go and have a talk to known associates.'

Clive Fraser walked up to the incident board and wrote – MICHAEL PAUL EDWARDS alongside the new images, which he stuck up next to the photo of his beaten body.

'Okay, Allie you're with me. Clive, you're with Martin.' As they headed off to meet the local lowlife. They swept past Chief Superintendent

Pearsall as he walked into the incident room. He called to Tremayne and demanded to know where they were going in such a hurry.

'We've got a name for the guy that was found in the dunes Sir.' Tremayne said 'Do you remember a Michael Paul Edwards, known as Mickey, petty villain, small time burglary and such.'
Pearsall thought a minute, and then said.

'Yes, I remember him, the little sod. So someone has finally caught up with his carryings-on have they?' Pearsall paused. 'But why would a tosser like Edwards end up like that?' He said pointing to his pictures on the incident board.

'I don't know sir, it does seem a bit extreme, to deal with the likes of him. I can only think he got mixed up with something way out of his depth; drugs maybe? Possibly, whoever did this to him, had to some sort of deal going; then he tried to cross them.'

'More than likely.' said Pearsall 'You'll need to track his movements over the last few months.'

'Yes Sir, just what I was thinking. That's what Nick's onto now. He and the others were just going to chat up some of his mates as you came in.'

'Good…rattle a few cages. Right Tremayne, keep me informed.' Tremayne looked up at the wall clock; three thirty. 'Helen, give Nick a call, tell him we're going to have a word with Tony Franklin.' Helen spoke to him, passing on Rufus' message. 'He says good luck with that boss.' As she put the phone back into her coat pocket, Tremayne laughed

'Come on then Helen, let's go and see what he has to say for himself.'

They sat in Tremayne's Alfa Romeo 159, and parked just along the road from the *Wild Orchid* club. For a while they watched men going in and coming out, even though it was the middle of the afternoon, it had a steady stream of customers. Eventually Tremayne said he'd go in and see Franklin.

'See that doorman…that's Heavy-handed Harry.' He said as he got out of the car. 'Keep your eye on him and anyone that he seems to talk to seriously, take their photo. He's the eyes and ears round here.' He closed the car door and walked slowly up to the entrance of the club. The doorman greeted him 'Good afternoon Mr Tremayne.'

'Is Tony in, Harry?'
'In the office I should think.'

Tremayne walked into the semi-darkened room, the music thumped out, the base tone's deep rhythmic and almost primeval beat reached every part of the brain. Tremayne could feel it in the pit of his stomach. Two tall slim and well-shaped girls gyrated topless on a small stage that jutted out into the centre of the room. Some men stood nearby, ogling the girls and drooling into their lager at their provocative actions. Several others stood leaning on the bar. They seemed to be more interested in their lagers that the sexy girls. Tremayne stopped and watched them briefly. They smiled at him, danced towards him and pushed their breasts forward, hoping he'd put a couple of tenners into their G-strings so as encourage them into something more provocative.

When he just smiled back and shrugged his shoulders and headed towards the office door they blew him a kiss before continuing with their gyrating to the bawdy calls from the guys sitting close to the stage.

Another of Franklin's goons was standing by the office door. He eyed Tremayne suspiciously as he approached. He half turned and knocked on the door and opened it when he recognised who he was.

Tremayne walked into a rather stylish office. It was furnished with deep-buttoned, red leather Chesterfield chairs. A large TV screen silently played the floor show from the club; another showed channel four's horse racing coverage from Cheltenham or somewhere. Anthony Donald Franklin or Tony to his friends was watching the racing from his over-large leather chair behind an equally large partners' desk. He rose, and came out from behind the desk to greet Tremayne like a long-lost buddy. This behaviour always sickened Tremayne; thinking as he shook hands, *I'll have you, you bastard one of these days.* Tremayne noticed someone else, standing quietly to one side, and out of the way was Malcolm Smith or Trendy, as he was known because of his appetite for tailored, fashionable clothes and hair styles. Trendy was Franklin's gopher. He was never very far away and always at his beck an' call. But, Trendy was more than just a gopher, he was someone whom you didn't want to get on the wrong side of, and especially if you upset Franklin for any reason. Trendy was dangerous.

'With what do I owe this pleasure, Mr Tremayne?' he said offering his hand. Tremayne didn't reciprocate the gesture. Franklin shook his head in mock insult '…always a pleasure to see you Mr Tremayne,' Smiling rather unconvincingly. 'Please take a seat. Trendy, drinks for our guest.' He simply nodded and opened a tall wooden cabinet that to Tremayne's eyes looked like an antique piece. He took two crystal flutes down from the upper shelf, and then opened the lower cupboard door to reveal a small refrigerator, from where he took a bottle of champagne. Tremayne sank into one of the Chesterfields.

'Very nice.' He said as he made himself comfortable in the soft leather.

'Yes aren't they, I can get you a good price…look very stylish in your office Mr Tremayne.'

'Most likely they would, but my boss would no doubt disapprove of such extravagance. We're not made of money in the public sector you know.'

'I suppose not. You should come and work in the private sector Mr Tremayne, many more lucrative business opportunities.' Tremayne eyed him with contempt. *Smug little bugger* he thought, *I am going to have you one of these days.*

'Now what brings you here this fine afternoon?'

'Mickey Edwards.' Tremayne said straight to the point. '…seen him lately?'

'Edwards…Mickey Edwards?' Franklin said slowly, appearing to dredge up the name from the dark recesses of his mind. 'Am I supposed to know the gentleman?'

'Yes…and he's no gentleman…as you very well know.'
Trendy arrived with the two glasses and a bottle of champagne, which he poured and offered.

'Trendy, do you know anyone called Mickey…er, what did you say his last name was Mr Tremayne, ah yes, Edwards?' Tremayne nodded, but said nothing, knowing Franklin was evading the subject. 'That's right Mickey Edwards. Have you heard of him Trendy?'

'No Mr Franklin; never heard of 'im.'

'All right Trendy you can go.' He left the office. 'Enjoy your champagne Mr Tremayne it's kosher, real good stuff direct from Reims in France.'

'Really?' said Tremayne as he took a sip and replaced the glass onto the table.

'Now come on Tony…you know as well as I do who Mickey Edwards is. So stop messing me about and tell me. When was the last time you saw him in here?'

'I can't be expected to remember everyone who comes in here Mr Tremayne; we are a very busy club, as you would have noticed when you came in. Why, what's he done?'

'What's he done, as if you didn't know? Suffice to say, over his lifetime he's accumulated a string of offences. But most recently, he's gone and got himself murdered. Now shall we start again? When was he last in here?'

'Honestly Mr Tremayne, I really can't say, as I've just said....'

'Yeah, yeah, you're very busy. Well what about heavy-handed Harry on the door then, would he know?'

'I've no idea; you'll have to ask him.'

'I'll do just that on the way out.' Tremayne took another sip of the champagne, 'Very nice. I'll be seeing you Tony.'

'Yes, it was nice chatting to you too Mr Tremayne.'

Trendy opened the door and closed it behind Tremayne. Franklin returned to his seat looking very annoyed, he gulped his glass of champagne and watched Tremayne on the monitor as he walked through the club towards the exit. He gave the two girls a smile as he passed them; they wriggled their breasts and smiled back.

Heavy-handed Harry was ushering out three young lads who had tried to get into the club. 'Don't try that again.' he hissed at them or I'll have to...' He didn't finish off when he noticed Tremayne standing behind him. 'Mr Tremayne I didn't see you there.'

'I guessed as much. Having a little bother are we?'

'No...no bother. Just a couple of young lads trying to get in to see a few tits, that's all.'

'Tell me Harry, when did you last see Mickey Edwards?'

'Mickey Edwards...Oh, not for a while.' He put his hand to his chin, still watching the young lads over Tremayne's shoulder. 'you know, come to think of it I've not seen Mickey for...must be a few weeks at least. He normally comes in more often. Why...did you want to talk to 'im?'

'Well that would be awkward Harry. You see...he's dead.'

'Dead! How, when?'

'He was found him in the sand dunes a few days ago. He'd been dead for a while. Been a bit roughed up too. We think someone tried to hide his identity, very nasty.'

'Why would anyone do that? It couldn't have been anyone from round 'ere, 'e was too well known.'

'Yeah I know, that's what's puzzling. So, if you hear of anything, you let me know, okay.' Tremayne slipped Harry a couple of twentys then walked back to his car. He didn't drive off straight away. He called Nick

30

Chandler, but got no reply. 'Where the bloody hell is he?' Helen shrugged her shoulders but made no suggestion.

Tremayne pulled into the station's car park; he noticed that there was no sign of Nick's car. *They must be having a whale of a time* he thought. They walked into the station and up to the incident room. Tremayne got into his office and sat heavily into his chair and as usual it creaked in protest. He leaned back in it and stared at the ceiling. The same old questions kept going round and round in his mind. What was that little bugger mixed up in for someone to treat him like that? Harry might be right; thinking whoever did it weren't from these parts. He was startled back into reality by a commotion coming from the incident room. He jumped up. '...the hells going on?' he shouted. Clive and Martin stood in the centre of the room.

'Of course he knows more than he's saying, and I know, he knows who Mickey's girl friend is. He's just a lying little toe rag. He's a compulsive liar. He's made an art of it.' Martin was saying, in a rather loud voice. He realised Tremayne was standing in his office doorway. 'Isn't that right boss? Tricky Dickey Bryant is a compulsive liar and can't be trusted to tell you the right time of day, even if the Liver building clock was in front of him.'

'I'm afraid so, don't be put off by anything Bryant tells you Clive. He does know stuff. If you press him long enough and buy him a couple of drinks he usually breaks. But even then you have to double check. It's just that he can't help himself. He's harmless really, but far from reliable.' Clive smiled, feeling rather defeated. But we did find out who his girlfriend was though. Someone called Angie. I know it's not much, but it's a start.'

'Angie?' Tremayne uttered under his breath. 'Ask Nick when he gets back, he knows all the nice people round here.'

4

Frankie Bolton sat at her desk and typed >national archives< into her search engine. She read the details featured on the home page. She then typed >royal navy archive< and read that home page. The newspaper was registered with many websites and that allowed her fast and easy access to help with research. In these days of the Freedom of Information Act, there were many derestricted official documents and these gave her a wealth of useful information. She busily scribbled brief notes.

Finding out about people who served on particular ships was easy enough, but finding out about particular missions, that proved more difficult for her and certainly time consuming. All she had was a name and rank; Chief Petty Officer Simon Carter. She didn't know the name of any ships he'd served on so she typed his name and rank then pressed search.

Clive Fraser stuck his head round Tremayne's office door. 'DI Chandler has just phoned in boss. They've found out where Mickey Edwards lived. It's a big old Victorian place divided into flats, number sixteen North Street.'

'Has he now? Well let's go and take a look-see shall we.' Getting up from his chair he grabbed his coat, at the same time, he called over to Helen. 'Nick's found Mickey's gaff. Let's go and take a look'

The Alfa Romeo pulled up behind Nick's Volvo. Tremayne and his team stood together on the footpath. They looked up at the old Victorian house. A curtain twitched in the ground floor window.

'The natives have seen us boss.' Allie commented, nodding towards the house. 'Ground floor window, to the right of the door.'

The old house looked a bit run down. It had certainly seen better days. The window frames certainly needed painting. The garden had all been paved over and the once grey flagstones were now black with tyre rubber and spotted with oil from the old cars parked there. Big commercial bins were lined against the side wall, filled to overflowing; several black bin sacks lay beside them. Some torn open by marauding dogs or cats or even the odd urban fox. 'Do these never get emptied?' commented Clive, 'God they hum a bit...must be swarming with vermin round here...I hate rats.'

'Which flat did he doss in Nick?'

'Number four…on the first floor.'

'Is there a caretaker on the premises?'

'Not sure boss, I shouldn't think so, looking at the state of the place.'

'Okay let's find out.'

Tremayne, followed by the others, walked up to the front door. He pushed it, it opened. Their noses were assaulted by the musty dampness of the place. The hallway had once had a highly-polished parquet floor, but the polish had long ago been worn off and now pieces of wood were missing. The rest was scratched and indented by numerous boots and things being dropped on it.

'Someone check number four. Check that flat there Nick, it's the one with the twitchy curtains. I bet they don't miss a trick.' Nick knocked on the door of flat number one, nothing happened, so he knocked again, a little louder. A voice answered 'I'm coming, I'm coming, just give me a mo.' The door was opened by an old man; thin grey hair, unshaven and with a very sallow complexion. 'Yes,' he said in a small croaky voice.

'I'm a police officer,' said Nick loudly, thinking also, that the old guy was deaf. 'Do you know Mr Edwards, Mickey Edwards from number four?' Nick continued, his finger pointing upstairs.

'We see 'im now and again.'

'You wouldn't happen to hold a key for him would you?'

'No, but the landlord does.'

'Right and where might we find him…the landlord?'

'Come in and I'll give you the address.'

'Allie, you go with him, and get some details off the old dears, they might know something.' He said, knowing full we they wouldn't.

Allie followed Nick and the old man into the flat. Her nose was immediately assaulted by a strong smell of cat. The said cat suddenly appeared and moved between her legs, rubbing its head on her calves. She tried to push it away but it wasn't having any. She pushed a little harder. Then she noticed the old woman sitting in front of the fire. 'Timmy likes you.' She said. Allie gave a half smile to the women and under her breath replied 'yes, doesn't he, flea bitten moggy.'

The old man busied himself in the drawer of a sideboard. 'Here it is.' He said as he handed Nick a sheet of paper. It was their rental agreement. He walked to the table and made a note of the address and phone number in his notebook.

'Thank you.' He said and disappeared, leaving Allie in the flat.

'Would you mind if I just asked you a few questions.' Allie asked.

'Yes, that'll be all right, won't it Alice.' Replied the man.

'May I just take your names please?'

'Yes, Mr and Mrs Fielding; Reg and Alice, and this is Timmy our old cat, he's very friendly.'

'Have you lived here long?' Allie asked, trying not to think of the cat, hoping to change the subject and hoping that someone would call her away. But no such luck.

'Oh yes thirty years or more, it was a nice house when we first moved in, but it's gone to the dogs a bit in recent years since new landlords took over. They don't look after the place like the old landlords did. They never paint the windows, or fix anything. Now you wouldn't think a few cans of paint would cost a fortune would you?'

'No' said Allie 'I noticed that, shame isn't it. Did you know Mr Edwards?' But before Mr Fielding could answer a voice shouted.

'Allie have you got everything you need in there?'

'My boss calling, but about Mr Edwards, did you see him at all?'

'No not very often, he would say hello if we passed that's all. I spoke to his girlfriend once, a nice girl. She said she was a dancer. She said her name was…Ann, Annie, something like that.'

'Angie?'

'Yes Angie that's it.'

'Do you know where she worked, or danced?'

'No sorry.' She thanked them, they smiled at her and she walked into the entrance hall.

'Thanks for the rescue boss. They did confirm though, that his girlfriend came here, said her name was Angie.'

'Good. Nick's gone to see who this mysterious landlord is and get the key for Mickey's flat off him.'

Tremayne stood at the foot of the stairs, looking up towards the first floor. Allie glanced back at the now closed door of the Fieldings' flat and gave an involuntary shiver; she couldn't get the smell of the Fieldings' cat out of her nostrils. Tremayne set off up the stairs, closely followed by Allie. Pausing on the landing he looked around. He took in the shabby appearance of the place, brown-painted and chipped doors, much worn threadbare carpet, and the mildewed smell, from the damp atmosphere of the unheated building. He moved towards the door of flat number four. He tried the handle; it was locked as he thought it would be. They turned and headed back downstairs. 'Try number three Allie.' Allie knocked on the door, she knocked a bit harder the second time, but there was still no answer. 'We need to find out who lives there?'

At the bottom of the stairs Tremayne turned towards number two 'See if anyone's at home?' He said to Allie who knocked on the door. After a minute the door slowly opened to the extent of the security chain. Tremayne and Allie flashed their warrant cards at the person peering out at them.

'Hello, I'm Detective Chief Inspector Tremayne, Merseyside CID and this is Detective constable Stewart. May we have a word?'

'What about?'

'We're making enquiries regarding your neighbour, Mr Edwards from number four. Do you know him by any chance?'

'Why…what's he done?'

'I'm afraid he's met with an accident, I'm trying to trace his movements over the last few days that's all.'

'Okay,' she said. The door closed and Tremayne could hear the chain being removed. The door opened fully, to reveal a young woman, a small child clinging to the hem of her flowery skirt. Tremayne made to enter. 'Hello' he said to the child, who moved behind his mother and looked up at the strangers coming into his home.

They were shown into the sitting room. The floor was littered with the child's toys, but otherwise it was clean and tidy. The girl hurriedly removed toys from a chair and offered it for Tremayne. Allie sat on an upright chair at the dining table. She took out her notebook and pen and jotted away as Tremayne asked the girl questions.

'Sarah…Sarah Griffith,' she replied to Tremayne's first question. 'and this is Tyler, he's three.' She smiled at the boy as he busily pushed a yellow tip-up truck around the floor. 'You said Mickey has met with an accident, is he all right, what happened?'

'I'm afraid, it wasn't an accident really, I'm sorry to tell you, but he's dead.'

The girl suddenly looked shocked; her hands instinctively went to her mouth. Through them she uttered

'Oh my God! What happened?'

'How well did you know Mr Edwards?' Tremayne continued without elaborating on how Mickey had met his end.

'Not very well really. I only met him in passing, coming and going, you know. I don't think he was…my type really. We never invited him in for a drink or anything like that. My partner didn't like him; said he was weird, thought he was up to something, but he wouldn't say what. You know what I mean?'

'And your partner's name is?'

'Kieran…Kieran Bailey. He's out at work just now.'

'Where does he work?'

'He's a chef at Benedict's restaurant. It's quite a fancy place. Do you know it?'

'Yes it's very good too. I must congratulate him on their food. Tell me, why do you say he didn't like Edwards?'

'I don't know really, it was just…the way he acted…as though he was up to something. He always seemed to be looking over his shoulder; you know what I mean, as though someone was after him.'

'So, can you remember, when was the last time you saw Mickey?'

'Well, it was…now you come to mention it…I've not seen him for a while…weeks, yeah. How did he die?'

'Sorry I can't say. If it's all right with you I'd like you to sign a statement to that effect, Constable Stewart will do that. It won't take a minute.'

'Okay, I don't mind.'

Tremayne thanked the girl for her help and left Allie to take down her statement. He walked out onto the street, where Martin and Clive waited.

'Where in hell's name is Nick, where's he gone for this key…Timbuktu?'

'Don't know boss, he didn't say.'

'How long's he been gone?'

'Well he shot off after he'd got the address from the Fieldings. It must be about twenty five minutes.'

Tremayne looked up at the building then walked up and down the street surveying the other houses.

'Might be worth a door to door.' He said to Martin and Clive. They said they'd get it sorted. They had now been joined by Allie. 'Someone in these fine residences might know our Mickey?' Tremayne laughed at the thought of fine residences in context with Mickey Edwards. As they looked up and down the street Tremayne was becoming more and more agitated waiting for Nick Chandler to return. Finally he said to Allie. 'Give him a bell and find out where the hell he is.' But just as she retrieved her phone from her bag, his car was seen pulling up outside number 16 North Street.

'What kept you?' asked Tremayne. Nick ignored his remark.

'You'll never believe who the landlord is?'

'Go on then, enlighten me.'

'I believe you were talking to him only a couple of hours ago…'

'No…not Tony bloody Franklin. Well I never! You've just been to the club then?'

'No, I went to an office. Trading under the name of Franklin Investments; it's a property management company.' said Nick.

'I'm sure he'll be pleased when he learns we've been round, more so, that we got the key instead of us using our own door opening method. After we've finished here I must have another word with him.'

'Yeah I'm sure he'll be over the moon to see you. Here it is.' He said waving the key. '…shall we?' and headed towards the door.

Entering Mickey's flat the same musty smell was present. The whole house seemed to be the same. 'It's been closed up for a while.' someone commented.

'Right, now without too much disturbance have a good look round. I'll call SOCO.'

'I'll bet most of this stuff's dodgy?' Allie commented cynically, laughing. 'More than likely.' replied Clive. The detectives worked their way around Mickey's flat, after donning latex gloves, they opened and closed drawers. They looked in cupboards, which were mostly bare, save for a few baked bean cans and opened packets of pasta. Allie moved into the bedroom, she dropped onto her knees and looked under the bed. From under it she pulled out and a brand new suitcase. '*Interesting.*' She thought and lifted it and dropped it onto the bed, where it bounced on the mattress. Clicking the catches back, she flipped open the lid. Inside there was a collection of shirts, trousers and other clothing all neatly folded.' *I think he must have been planning a little holiday by the looks of this lot.*' She said to herself, and began to carefully lift the clothes out; she stopped when Tremayne shouted.

'Okay folks, forensic guys are here, everyone out.'

She was about to drop the clothes she was holding back into the case, when her eye was drawn to something. She stared at it for a second, deciding whether to grab it or not. She put the clothes down and reached in, picking it up. It was a large leather bag, a toiletry bag with a silver fob hanging off the zip; it had been that she'd noticed. She walked out as Tremayne shouted again. The bag still in her hand.

'What's that?' Tremayne asked when he saw she was holding something.

'Oh, sorry boss, I had just picked it up when you called. It's a toiletry bag; I found it in a suitcase that was under the bed. It was all neatly packed; I think he might have been planning a little trip somewhere.'

'I wonder where to, and why? So…what's in the bag?'

'I don't know…haven't looked yet.'

'Well don't keep us in suspense.'

Allie zipped opened the bag; inverting it she tipped out the contents onto a small half-round hall table. By now everyone had crowded round to see what Allie had found. Their mouths dropped at what they saw.

'Whoa!' she gasped 'Would you look at this. Now this definitely has to be knock-off.'

'Right Allie, get this stuff back to the station. We can look at it later, after which, forensics can take a look. When you get back make a list of it all.'

Allie put the contents back into the bag and left. She got a patrol car to take her back to the station because she'd driven down with Clive in his car. Tremayne spoke with Nick Chandler, and nodding towards Clive and Martin, said. 'Get those two, to get hold of some uniformed officers and do a door to door up and down the street.'

Nick called them over. 'Get a couple of uniformed and check nearby houses. Ask if anyone knew Mickey Edwards, maybe they can recall any unusual activities in and out of here…you know the score. Even if it's only in passing, we want to know his movements. Someone might have seen him talking to someone in the street or being picked up by someone, see if they remember a car picking him up or dropping him off, even if it's only a taxi. Find something…anything. Clive you see to that. Martin, before you join them, go and ask the Fieldings if they know the occupant of number 3? Oh, and ask them if they know who he works for?'

More than an hour passed before forensics appeared outside the house where Tremayne was waiting, to say that they had done. Alan Stephens reported that there were two sets of identifiable prints. 'Most probably belonging to Edwards,' He said to Tremayne. '…the other set, mainly in the kitchen and bathroom might be a girlfriend. We found a bottle of DKNY perfume called Delicious Nights in the bathroom cabinet, along with a few other women's toiletries so he must have had a girl here.' Tremayne thanked him.

In the Fielding's flat Martin was being introduced to Timmy the cat. They were very interested in all the goings on.

'We've never had so much excitement in a long time.' said Mr Fielding. Mrs Fielding asked if he'd like a cup of tea, which he declined, saying he was busy and he couldn't stop.

'What I'd like to ask you is. Do you know the occupant of number 3?'

'Ah yes, that'd be Mr Brookes, Roger's his other name. Long distance lorry driver he is. Goes all over the continent too he does.' Said Mr Fielding.

'Do you know which firm he works for?'

'Now you're asking something. I think they are a Liverpool firm. He drives one of those great long things. He's usually away for weeks on end.'

'When was the last time you saw him?'

'Oh…I forget…how long's it been Alice?'

'Couple of weeks at least.'

'And you can't think who he works for, it's quite important?'

'I know…' said Alice suddenly, exclaiming loudly, and making the cat scatter, with a shriek, from where it was dozing. 'He gave us his mobile number, didn't he? It's in the phonebook.' She heaved herself up from her seat and shuffled over to a large brown dresser. She went through a couple of the drawers before returning with a rather tatty, dull red address book. 'It's in here somewhere.' She smiled at Martin before turning the pages one by one. Martin was by now beginning to feel impatient; he thought he'd be in there forever at this pace.

'Can I be of any assistance?' he asked.

'No I'm all right' she began. 'This is a private document.' she said earnestly. After what seemed like hours she finally said 'Ah…here it is. Have you got a pencil and paper? I'll read it to you.' Martin took out his notebook and Mrs Fielding read out Roger Brookes' mobile number. Martin thanked them for their time and left. He told Tremayne that he'd got Brookes' mobile number. 'I'll give him a bell?' Martin dialled the number. He let it ring for a few minutes before giving up. Shaking his head he said 'No answer boss.'

Okay…' replied Tremayne. 'There's a little job for you when we get back. Trace him. Find out who he works for.'

'There must be hundreds of haulage firms in Liverpool.'

'Is that a fact?' Tremayne said firmly, but with a rue smile. 'It'll keep you out of mischief.'

Frankie Bolton set her SATNAV with Davy Cox's post code. He lived in the centre of Preston; in a new apartment building overlooking the River Ribble. She started the engine of her Renault Clio and drove out of the newspaper office's car park. She was on her way to interview Davy Cox, the eighty-six year old ex-Royal Marine commando, who had served on the mission alongside Simon Carter. Frankie hoped that he might remember something about the raid to Norway. She also hoped that he'd remember something about CPO Carter too. He had told her that he did, when she'd phoned him the day before.

Martin Wilcox was a picture of frustration. He had the local yellow pages open in front of him, at the haulage section. He'd gone through the list once and highlighted all the local firms that did long distance. He'd then begun to phone each one in turn. He hated this part of police work, the dreary slog of trying to trace people. Still, he thought, at least it's warm in here. He took a sip from his already lukewarm tea…uttered 'yuk', shook his head and put it down. He dialled the next number. By now he'd asked almost thirty people the same question 'Do you employ a driver by the name of Roger Brookes?' and he had received thirty answers, all telling him 'Sorry, no we haven't.' He was beginning to feel depressed, and after another couple more calls he slammed the phone down, got up and made to leave the office. 'I need a break,' He said stretching and yawning. As he walked past Allie, he stopped to ask. 'How are you doing with your little hoard?'

'Yes good. This is really an expensive little lot; well it's not so little. Just look at all this stuff. There's diamond rings, gold necklaces and four gold watches with watch chains, and two with these…err, dangly things'

'The chain is called an Albert. Named after Prince Albert, you know Queen Victoria's husband' Martin said 'My grandfather had one, which he wore with his waistcoat and on the end of the watch chain he had a fob, that's these things.' He said picking one up to look at it more closely.

'Oh right,' said Allie, thanks. '…and look at these things, these little gold boxes. And this one, set with diamonds and other precious stones,' She enthused excitedly. 'I think these are rubies, and sapphires and emeralds. You know this little lot must be worth a small fortune.'

Martin gazed at it all, equally amazed. 'I wonder where he got it all?' he questioned himself. '...and as you said, it's all definitely been nicked. But where from, that's what I'd like to know?'

'Me too, I'm going to have to go through all the reported thefts of...what is all this, jewels, art treasure...what? And God knows how far I'll have to go back.' Allie sighed deeply at the thought. She picked up the phone as Martin continued on his journey out of the office. Allie spoke when she heard someone answer. 'Hi, DC Stewart here, could you send a photographer up to DCI Tremayne's office. I've got some jewellery and things that I need pictures of...' She listened 'Thanks I'll see him soon.' She collected all the jewellery together and locked it in her desk draw. She thought to herself, '*Where do I start?*' So she keyed into her police database >art theft< and began to search through all reported thefts beginning with the most recent.

Heavy-handed Harry greeted the two CID officers

'I didn't expect you back so soon Mr Tremayne...and Mr Chandler as well. How nice for Mr Franklin, he'll be ever so pleased to see you both.' The two detectives looked stony-faced at the doorman.

'I'm sure he will Harry, over the moon, no doubt about it.' Nick said, sneeringly. They walked past the doorman and into the club. Not slowing, they glanced at the girls on stage and marched up to Franklin's office. Nick glared at the big guy standing by the office door, the man knocked on it, opening it for them, announcing the two detectives.

'You seem to like my club Mr Tremayne,' Franklin said cynically '...would you both like to take out a membership. I can do it at discount for officers of the constabulary.' He smiled at the two men before him.

'I wouldn't be seen dead drinking in this fucking place.' snarled Nick.

'Now that's not very polite Mr Chandler; whatever have I done to offend you?'

'Do you want a list?'

'Now Nick. We're not here to cause trouble.' Tremayne shook his head, and pursed his lips indicating to Chandler to shut up. 'Alright Tony, the reason for our visit is that we've just found out that *you* own the house where Mickey Edwards lived. You never mentioned that during our last little tête-à-tête.'

'Well Mr Tremayne, you know how it is. I own many such houses. I'm a businessman…so you can't honestly expect me to remember all my tenants now can you? Anyway I don't bother myself with the letting. I have people who do that for me, my main concern is this club.'

'Businessman, ha! Yeah and we know what business that is, don't we Tony' snapped Nick. 'Now come on Tony, Mickey worked for you. So you must have known where he lived. Now you tell us what you know about Mickey Edwards. And what kind of work he did for you?'

'Yeah okay, yeah he's done a few odd jobs for me that's all, but nothing lately.'

'What sort of…odd jobs?' Nick said pointedly.

'Well you know…just little errands. Collecting rent, taking the girls home after a late night, you know that sort of thing. I'm sure the girls paid him well for that, he wasn't a bad looking lad. He ran me about on occasions, he liked driving'

'Yeah we've heard of his driving exploits.'

'I'm sure I don't know what you mean Mr Chandler.'

'Well, let me enlighten you…'

'Okay Nick.' Tremayne cut in. 'So Tony…these little jobs Mickey was involved in, was there any…rough stuff?'

'Mr Tremayne,' said Tony in mock shock. 'I'm sure I don't know what you're implying…rough stuff. I've told you, I'm a legitimate businessman.' He was holding the palms of his hands open, sort of pleading. 'I do not resort to violence of any kind. People do owe me money, I'll admit and…on occasions, mind, I may have to speak to them…shall I say…strongly. Put on a little pressure possibly. But never, I never resort to violence…it's bad for business. I want my customers to come back here and to my other clubs, where they part from their money and have a good time doing it.' He said seriously. 'Now that's all legit and above board. My establishments are no different from any other clubs Mr Tremayne.'

'So, what other work did Mickey get involved in? Did he work for anyone else for instance?'

'I've no idea Mr Tremayne. All I know is that he comes in here now and again and asks if I can help him out. He tells me he's short of money he needs a few quid, so I give him a few hours work. I pay him cash in hand and that's the end of it. What he gets up to when he's not in here I'm not interested.'

'Okay Tony, thanks for your time. See you around.'

Allie had just finished cataloguing the jewellery and the photographer had taken pictures of every piece. She called across to Martin to ask how he was doing tracing the lorry driver.

'You'd never believe just how many haulage firms there are round here. I've phoned fifty up to now and there's still no sign of Roger bloody Brookes and there doesn't seem to be any end to this damn list either.'

'Well, I've made my list.' Allie said cheerily.

'Well bully for you.' He replied snappily. But Allie ignored him.

'I cleared it with Helen and phoned one or two jewellers, just to ask them to take a look at them. Hopefully they'll be able to tell me what they are and give me a ball-park figure of how much they might be worth.'

'Well at least it'll get you out of here…enjoy.' He said feeling a bit dejected, after all the hours he'd spent looking at the list of haulage firms.

Just as Allie was walking across the car park Tremayne drove in. He pulled up alongside her, the window rolled down. He asked where she was going.

'Helen's ok'd it, I'm taking the jewels and things to get an expert to take a look. I've phoned a Mr Meyer, he's a jeweller in the High Street.'

'Okay' he said, 'but in the privacy of his office…Oh, and be discrete about where they came from, right?'

Allie said she would and jumped into her car and drove off. Tremayne and Nick Chandler marched into the station. 'How is it ol' beardy chops always appears when I've nothing to tell him?' Tremayne said quietly to Nick as Chief Superintendent Pearsall walked towards them.

'Sir,' they both said in unison, greeting him.

'Ah Tremayne, Chandler. How's it going…your investigation into this chap on the beach?'

'Nicely Sir, nicely…bit slow, but we're beginning to pick up some pieces. I wouldn't be surprised to find Tony Franklin involved somewhere along the line.'

'Franklin?' Superintendent Pearsall said sounding puzzled at first. 'Franklin, ah yes Tony Franklin. If you think we might find something to implicate him in this one? Now that would give us some brownie points.'

'Too early to say just now Sir, but you'll be the first to know when we do.' They both gave him a broad smile.

'Good…good.' Pearsall said disappearing down the corridor.

'You never mentioned the sparkly stuff?' Nick whispered conspiratorially.

'Certainly not, can't give him the juicy bits all at once, now can we?'

5.

Frankie Bolton pulled up in front of the smart modern apartment block. The view over-looking the river was, in her thoughts *cool, really nice.* The garden was well planted with flowers and shrubs. There was a well mown lawn surrounding the beds and benches were strategically positioned allowing the residents prime views across the river and gardens. Mature trees shaded some of the benches, providing a cool place to sit during the summer. She walked up to the front door; it had an intercom system as security. Frankie took out her iPhone and found Mr Cox's details. She keyed in his apartment number on the intercom. A few seconds passed, a voice answered 'Yes.' She replied. 'Hello Mr Cox, this is Frankie Bolton.' Soon she was being ushered into a very comfortable room. She noticed it had a view overlooking the river.

'It's good of you to see me. A wonderful view you have.' She said as he welcomed her.

'It's a pleasure, my dear; it's nice to have people around. I don't get many visitors these days; all my mates are dropping like flies.' Davy Cox got them both some tea and a plate of biscuits. Placing them on the low table between them, they settled down into two soft, easy chairs. Before Frankie began her questions, they sipped their tea and chatted for a few minutes.

'What I wanted to talk to you about,' she said as the conversation tailed off. '…was about your time in the marines, particularly concerning a mission to Norway and someone called Simon Carter, I believe he was a petty officer?'

'Do you think I've got the memory of an elephant, young lady? I was demobbed in nineteen forty five you know, at the end of the war.' He said teasingly, he smiled a great beaming smile. 'Only joking; I've got a few photos here and a few scribbled notes. I got my album out after you'd phoned. I thought you would want to see it. There's not many young people want to listen to old men reminiscing about the war nowadays.' Davy reached for the large dark blue album that sat on the low coffee table in front of them. He opened it at the page he'd marked with a strip of paper.

'Here we are Frankie,' he said 'This photo is the team that went to Norway.' Davy named all the men standing in a group, pointing to them in

45

turn. Some were navy; others were commandos wearing their distinctive woollen hats. 'Now that's him there, that's Simon Carter.'
Frankie leaned forward to get a closer look at the man she had been looking for.

'Do you think I could have a copy of that?'

'Yes of course, I've got a copier with my computer; it prints, copies and scans documents. I've got all the modern technology you know, computer, the internet, satellite TV, a SATNAV in my car and an MP3 player for when I go out walking.' He said laughing.

'Wow, that's cool.' Frankie said and thinking the old man really on the ball with modern technology. As she sipped her tea she asked. 'What sort of man was he, Simon Carter?'

'Well, it's hard to recall precisely after all this time. But I do remember he never seemed to mix with the lads. I know he was a CPO, but even so, most others had a word with the lads. But he kept himself above us poor ratings, although I don't recall that he was ever very aggressive or pushy, 'e was just, sort of…well, distant. He did his job and that was that.'
Frankie busily scribbled down notes as Davy chatted away. He paused periodically while he got his thoughts together, trying to remember the briefest of facts from sixty-six years earlier. 'I do seem to remember that we all thought, you know all the lads, that he was always after something. You know on the lookout for an easy buck, as the Yanks used to say. I don't know what it was; we always thought he looked a bit sneaky, if you know what I mean?'

'What do you recall about this mission you went on?'

'The one to Norway you mean?'

'Yeah.'

'We were all assembled in Scapa Flow in Orkney. We'd been training in the Highlands for a couple of weeks and off the north coast of Scotland. Getting used to the rough conditions, and they were tough too, what these youngsters call yomping now, they didn't invent it you know. We hiked over the moors, up mountains, climbing cliffs, boat handling and landings, out in all weathers. Aye, that was hard.' He paused again.
'We knew something was on, but we hadn't a clue what. Then we were ordered to report to our ship. We weren't told anything; only that we were going on a mission. No, we were never told what was goin' on…that was typical though, secrecy; walls have ears – you know…'

'Walls have ears?' Frankie repeated sounding puzzled.

'Yeah, sorry. During the war they were paranoid about spies. So a campaign was launched, there were posters all over the place about not speaking out of turn. They said, anyone could be listening and you didn't know who was who. So they said walls have ears, in other words don't gossip.'

'Oh, I understand.'

'So, we're in Scapa Flow, it's just after dinner time, we'd eaten and we were told to report to HMS Sandown at 2100hrs on the Monday night with full kit. We boarded her and a few hours later we shoved off into the blackness of the north Atlantic. We were told to bunk down and we would be briefed in due course. We sailed all that night, and next day and the following night. We were at sea a couple of days nearly, dodging about, avoiding the Germans. Eventually we were called into the mess room and we were briefed by the captain about our destination. Then our commando captain spoke to us about what we were going to be doing…'

Frankie interrupted saying 'How were you feeling at that time, were you not afraid?'

'Afraid? No not really we were concentrating on the job that had to be done. We listened to the captain. We had to remember every word, every detail, where we were supposed to be at any particular time. We had to know where to be and where our mates were, your lives depended on your mates, everyone doing their job properly. We knew from experience that it all had to run like clockwork or we were all dead or captured. But, no we weren't afraid…not at that time anyway. A lot of the lads felt it later, on the way back or even days after. They call it post-traumatic stress nowadays. In my day there was no such thing, sometimes they'd call it shell-shock if you'd been under fire. Poor bastards in the first war were shot for cowardice…' Davy shook his head and repeated 'poor bastards.' Davy carried on talking about the preparations and the journey over to Norway. They talked about life on board a frigate. They spoke for a long time before finally Davy got to the landing and all the sneaking about as he called it.

'We rendezvoused with the Norwegian resistance chaps, but not until we'd secured the place. We'd made our way up a steep path from the beach. We were heading for the house that was now being used by the Germans as some kind of HQ. Before the war a Norwegian family used it as their summer home, lucky sods, it looked a beautiful place to spend a summer. I thought I might go back there at one time, but I never did make the trip…shame really it was a beautiful place, I bet they had a boat and went fishing and sailing, what a life eh?' Anyway, that's where the shooting started. There were about a dozen or so Germans guarding the place. It was all over fairly quickly, I don't think they really expected to see us. Two of our chaps were wounded, not seriously, but they were taken back to the shore. The rest of us then rushed into the house, but there was no one there. CPO Carter was just behind me. After we'd entered the house, we began our search. The commando captain was after something in particular, so he ordered us to look for the red coloured box file. I remember the captain saying it might have the words '*Privat und vertraulich. Leider mitarbeiter muster nur.*' I found a piece of paper and a pencil to write it down, well I wrote Privat, he said it meant private, I didn't know any German, I looked it up later. If I remember correctly all it meant was private and confidential, senior staff eyes only. Eventually we found a strong room; a grenade sorted the door out, no problem. There was a stack of files locked away in there. As we were engaged in there, Carter was rooting about elsewhere in the house. I think we must have been in the strong-room for about twenty minutes, half an hour at most. We'd finished and the commando captain called everyone to assemble outside quickly. As we were moving out, Carter suddenly appeared from round the back of the house, he'd been outside. The captain asked him if he'd found anything. He said there was a cellar but there was nothing in it. But…there was something about the way he replied, I always thought that he had found something and kept it to himself. Whatever it was, he'd hidden it in his rucksack that was supposed to be for a few medical supplies. Could have been money, but what good were Reich Marks to anyone? Might have been Norwegian I suppose. Anyway we returned to the ship and got back to Scapa Flow. Soon after that we were all busy doing other jobs. I never heard of or saw Carter again. Not until you phoned and mentioned his name, I'd not even thought about him. So what's all this about then?'

Frankie reached into her bag and pulled out a yellow document file. She flipped it open and handed Davy a copy of the newspaper cutting.

'Have seen this before?' she asked.
Davy took the sheet of paper and read it. He glanced up at Frankie saying.

'You know, after you called, I began to wonder what happened to him. So, he was murdered was he? I'd bet my last shilling that he was mixed up in something fishy? Come to think of it, when he appeared from round the back of that house, I was sure he'd found something in there.

We were getting out of that place fast before anyone else turned up. There wasn't time to speak to him. We didn't know whether there was another German patrol about, we had to get out of there and we'd got what we'd gone for.

Frankie and Davy Cox chatted for some time before they parted company. Frankie asked him did he remember Jimmy Wall. He said he did, 'We're the same age.' he said, '…only lives down the road in Southport. We see one another from time to time.' But he wasn't sure whether he'd remember anything else about Carter or not.

Tremayne and Sophie had just finished eating. Tremayne cupped a glass of wine in both hands; he was staring into its depths, obviously deep in thought.

'Penny for them?' Sophie said quietly. He did not respond and she repeated 'Penny for them?' Only a little louder.

'Sorry Sophie, I was miles away. You know there's something puzzling me about this case. Mickey Edwards was a small-time crook, a petty thief, dealt in penny numbers and did odd jobs for the likes of Tony Franklin just to make ends meet, give him some beer money. So…why did he end up in the dunes viciously beaten like that? And where the hell did he get that jewellery?'

'Yes it was a vicious attack and without advances in facial reconstruction we'd never have found out who he was.' Rufus agreed. 'I think it must have something to do with those jewels. Tell me; have you discovered what that old concrete thing is they came across buried in the sand?' Sophie asked.

'Oh yes, it's a wartime anti-aircraft battery, there was a whole string of them protecting Liverpool and the near-by airfield. I don't know whether we need to uncover it or even go inside. If there's access, we might take a quick look, but it'll be full of sand…forty-years' worth.

'What have you done with those cuttings that Redfern Sutcliffe gave to you?'

'I handed them over to Tony Clayton and he's given the job of finding out about them to a young journalist called Frankie Bolton. She's apparently traipsing about all over the northwest interviewing people who knew the Chief Petty Officer. But where she's got with it I don't know. Tony thinks there might be a story at the end of it all, but…well there might be I suppose.'

'You've not thought to get back to Sutcliffe and ask him what the hell this is all about, have you?'

'Yes, I've thought about it, but I've not got round to it yet, to be honest I've not had much time. I'll wait and see what Frankie digs up then I'll give him a buzz.' Tremayne stretched out as he sat in his chair and gave a huge yawn.

'I'm beat,' he said stifling another yawn. 'Come on let's get off to bed. We've both got busy days ahead of us, I dare say.'

Allie Stewart pushed open the door to Meyer's, a long-established and reputable jeweller on the high street. The assistant greeted her with a cheery good morning.

'How can I help you madam?'

'Good morning, I'm Detective Constable Stewart. I telephoned you earlier; I'm here to speak with Mr Leonard Meyer.'
The young lady hurried off to fetch Mr Meyer, who appeared almost instantly from his office at the back of the shop.

'Good morning constable. How may I help you?'

'I have some items that I'd like you to look at. In private if you don't mind.'

'Of course, of course.' He said ushering Allie into his office and closing the door behind him. They sat opposite each other across a leather-topped antique desk. Mr Meyer opened a drawer and took out a velvet cloth, which he spread out over the desk-top.

'Now Constable Stewart, may we look at these items please.'
There was a knock on the door, it opened. It was Meyer's secretary asking if they would like coffee. She was told not just yet and that they were not to be disturbed until further notice. Allie passed the leather bag over to Meyer. Taking the items from the bag, he arranged them across the cloth. He said nothing at first. He took up each one in turn and turned it over in his hands, examining it with minute precision, he examined each piece through his loop; he said nothing, apart from the odd umm or arr. After twenty minutes he then sat back into his deep buttoned leather chair. He placed his hands together across his chest, his fingers interlocked. His eyes narrowed as he looked intensely at the jewels spread out before him. Allie watched him, in eager anticipation, but not daring to break his concentration. His demeanour was that of an emeritus professor in deep thought. At last he came into an upright sitting position. He placed his hands flat on the table and asked, quietly but firmly.

'May I ask where these came from Constable Stewart?'

'I'm sorry but I can't really say...as you'll appreciate.'

'I see...' He continued his scrutiny of the jewels. He picked some of them up again, studying each in its turn. 'Have you any idea what these are?' he asked '...or where they might have originated?'

'No I haven't' Allie answered truthfully. She assumed they were made of gold and that the stones were diamonds and other precious stones, apart from that she hadn't a clue.

Meyer merely answered by saying – 'I see.' Allie pushed the cuff of her sleeve back to look at her watch. She realised that she had now been sitting in this office, for more than an hour.

'Mr Meyer.' She began 'What can you tell me about these items. I get the feeling that there is something about them that you...recognise them perhaps.'

'Yes, yes...there is something about them. If I'm correct, I think they have had a chequered career. But for them to be in your hands, I assume they were recently stolen?'

'Well yes. We are assuming that they were stolen by the man in whose flat they were found.'

'Well constable, I believe these items originally came out of Europe, stolen there many years ago, and as you have confirmed they have been stolen again more recently.'

'I'm sorry, I don't follow?'

'Do you know from where they came prior to your discovery?'

No, that's why I came to you. Do you know what they are or where they originate?'

'I would need to verify my thinking.' Meyer paused for a minute, before continuing. 'Would it possible for me to keep hold of them for a day or so, just to verify their origin?'

'Oh, I don't know. I would need to speak with my superior officer. He would have to give permission. I'll give him a ring and check.'

'Yes of course. Would you like to use my phone?'

While Allie made her call to Tremayne, Meyer pushed a button on an intercom and asked for some coffee to be brought in. By the time Allie had finished the call, Meyer's secretary had arrived with a silver tray, on which was a silver coffee pot and matching cream jug and sugar bowl and two fine porcelain cups and saucers. Meyer poured out the coffee into the two cups, placing one in front of Allie who had by now finished her call and had taken her seat again.

'Thank you,' she said. '…and a silver coffee pot as well.'

'Yes, rather splendid isn't it.'

'Is it old?'

'Georgian, seventeen fifty eight, hallmarked London. That's George the second, seventeen twenty seven 'til seventeen sixty.' Allie put half a spoon of sugar into her cup, stirred and sipped the coffee. Umm, she muttered, very nice.'

'Tell me, what did your superior say…and his name?'

'Chief Inspector Tremayne. He said it would be all right for you to keep hold of them for a day or two, but I'll obviously need a signature.'

'Of course, I'll get my secretary to draft something and you can take that as security.' Allie's business was concluded and she thanked Meyer for his help and said that she looked forward to hearing from him.

Tremayne and Helen stood out on the vast expanse of windy beach; there was no sign of the sea only the undulations the waves had created on the sand. The sand dunes disappeared into the heavy, moisture-laden air in both directions. The marram grass was laying almost flat against the sand. A lone gull swept past them downwind at such a speed, its whole body twisting and manoeuvring testing its flying instinct to the full. Flocks of waders wheeled and flowed like smoke somewhere way out nearer the sea's edge. Tremayne watched the gull and wondered how it managed to fly and not to get its wings ripped off. The whole shore seemed to be on the move. The sand was being blown a foot high above the ground, moving visibly along the shore. After a minute or two they both walked into the dunes, the canvas shelter covering the scene of crime was itself taking a battering. 'I hope that's well fastened down?' He called to Helen, nodding at the wind-blown canvas. They entered the canvas tent; the constable looked up.

'Good morning Sir' he said, jumping quickly to his feet, embarrassed to be found inattentive.

'Alright Constable, what's happening?' Tremayne asked, giving an involuntary shiver against the cold biting wind. 'Have you come across anything yet?'

'No Sir. Mike is…er Constable Gerard is in there now Sir.'

'Give him a shout Helen; ask him if he's got anything.' Helen knelt alongside the square hatchway, and peered into the blackness. She could see the glow of the working lamps.

'Hello,' she shouted 'It's DS Machin. Have you got anything down there?'

'Yes, a pain in the backside.' Mike Gerard said, hoping he wasn't heard, Then Helen saw the light moving. Suddenly it shone into her face and she blinked as the light hit her eyes.

'Oh sorry sergeant,' the dismembered voice from the darkness said, as he redirected the torches beam.

'Have you found anything?'

'No not yet. There's a lot of sand in here. It's so dry you move it from one place to another and it just runs straight back. But something may show up.' An obvious sigh in his voice.

'Right, I'm coming down to look.' said Helen as she placed a foot on the top rung of the ladder. Constable Gerard handed her his torch. She panned it round, its beam breaking the darkness. Her torch beam hit the stark grey walls of nineteen forties concrete. Graffiti on the walls drawn by the soldiers stationed there spoke of their hatred of the Nazis. She moved through the three rooms and thought *is it worth excavating all this damn sand?*

'Okay Constable, give it a rest for the time being. I'm not sure it's worth digging all this out, it'll take forever. I'll have a word with the boss, see what he can come up with.'

She climbed out and spoke to Tremayne. He stood peering down through the square hatchway into the black hole. He walked away from the site and stood with his back to the wind, pulling his collar up to fend off its effect. Helen followed a minute later.

'What do you think boss?'

'To be honest Helen, I think we're wasting our time with all that sand down there. Pearsall will have a donkey fit at the cost if we have to remove it all. There might be something buried in there, who knows. We could sweep the whole place clean and in the end we have to ask ourselves is it worth it?' Silence reigned for a few minutes. Then he said, but not with any confidence. 'Get hold of a metal detector. It might show something up, and get hold of a couple of long metal pins; they can use them to poke through the sand, save digging. Get Gerard out of there and tell him what we're thinking. Get him to organise it.'

An hour later a police van pulled up on the beach with a metal detector and two metal pins. Gerard and his partner Alan Hunt climbed back down into the darkness once more and began their search.

6

Helen was tapping away with two fingers, at the keyboard of her computer when Nick Chandler passed her desk. He had just reached the door and pulled it open when Helen called to him.

'Oh Nick. Do you know a girl called Angie? We believe she's the girlfriend of Mickey Edwards.'

Nick slowly walked towards Helen, repeating the name to himself quietly.

'Angie, Angie, Angie…I don't suppose for a minute there's a surname?' answering his own question 'No, of course there isn't…there never is. How can these people operate with only one name? It's damn inconsiderate of the buggers. I'll have to think about it Helen. A friend of Mickey Edwards, you say, eh, I bet she's a nice girl?' Nick kept repeating the phrase softly under his breath as he walked back towards the office door. 'Okay, I'll see you later.' He called, and with that Nick left the office.

'What was that all about?' Allie asked.

'Girlfriend of Mickey Edwards, someone called Angie. I don't suppose…no of course not.'

'If she's a girlfriend of his, what do suppose she's likely to do…as a job I mean?'

'Yeah…I wonder? Well, she might be…on the game or … work as a hostess or…or she might be just a barmaid…in any one of a thousand pubs and clubs. Oh I don't know she could be doing anything, she might even be a nurse who tended to him one night after he'd wandered into A&E all covered in blood and vomit and Florence Nightingale cleaned him up and fell for him…God knows why. I'll bet there's a name for such a situation.'

'Well it was only a thought.'

'No it was good thinking Allie; it's just me the eternal cynic. It's the job you know; you'll be the same in a few years.' Helen laughed. 'But on second thoughts she might well be a stripper. Working in just the sort of club Mickey would frequent. Yeah, could well be. Fancy a trip round a few clubs?'

Martin Wilcox was not having too much luck in tracing the haulage company that Roger Brookes worked for. He had telephoned fifty companies or more all over the north-west of England. He was beginning to think that he wasn't a lorry driver at all. Knocking on Tremayne's office door, he entered and told Tremayne where he was and what he was thinking. Tremayne was ready to tell him to call it a day.

'Okay Martin, look we can't spend forever on this.' He checked his watch. 'Give it a couple more calls and then we'll have to move on. Perhaps go back to it later.'

Martin returned to his desk, a little happier at the thought of not having to endlessly phone people only to get the same answer. He checked his marks on the yellow pages; he was into the letter 'T'. The next likely company was called Transcontinental Logistics. He dialled; a woman telephonist answered with the usual God morning, this is…, my name is…, how can I help you?

'Good morning.' He began 'My name's Wilcox, Detective constable Wilcox Merseyside CID. Would you put me through to your personnel section please.'

'If it's about staff you'll want Human Resources Management, just a moment please. I'll put you through to Anne Barrett our HRM manager.' She said and immediately Martin was listening to yet another classical piece, this time Jupiter from Holst's Planets. He hadn't listened to it more than thirty seconds when his call was answered by an officious sounding female voice.

'Good morning, Anne Barrett. How may I help you?'

'Good Morning, I'm Detective Constable Martin Wilcox. I'm trying to trace someone whom we think is a lorry driver. His name is Roger Brookes. Could you check if he works for you?' Anne Barrett asked him to hold a second; she tapped away on her keyboard. Martin could hear the click of the keys as she searched in her database.

'Yes, we do have a Roger Brookes.'

'Ah good,' Martin said, very relieved. 'This Roger Brookes lives at 16 North Street, flat 3. Is that where your Mr Brookes lives?' Anne Barrett confirmed that it was the same address.   'Good, success at last. Can you tell me where he is now and how I can contact him?'

'I can't give out that information over the phone. You could be anyone.' She said quite sternly. 'You'll have to come in to the office.'

'Very well,' Martin replied snappily. 'I'll do that; I'll be round within the hour.'

Martin jumped up from his seat, almost dancing with joy. He entered Tremayne's office

'I've got him boss.'

'Who?'

'The lorry driver…Brookes, Roger Brookes, he works for a firm called Transcontinental Logistics, they're in Aintree. I'm going round there to get his details from them now. They wouldn't give them to me over the phone.'

'Nice work Martin. I'm not sure he can help us, but at least we'll be able to eliminate him from the case.'

Helen and Allie drove slowly along a street, notorious for kerb-crawlers. They pulled into a pub car park. The pub was called Cunard, a throw-back from days when the docks did more trade and when the shipping line of the same name had a big presence in the city; and this place was close to the docks. But now the pub was on its last legs, the whole place was close to being deserted. It had scratch-and-sniff carpets, peeling paintwork, boarded up windows and a surly barman too.

'God what a dump…' Helen said 'We'll catch something if we drink in here.' They approached the bar. The barman was talking to a couple of old men, who were the only customers in the place. Loud music blared a sixties hit.

'What can I do for you two…ladies then?' She flashed her warrant card, scowling at the man..

'I might have known.' He said sarcastically.

'Do you know a girl called Angie or someone called Mickey Edwards?'

'No, I don't think so.' said the barman unconcerned about their enquiry.

'Are you sure you've never heard of Mickey Edwards. He's a local lad.'

'Like I just said sweetheart, never heard of 'im.'

'Okay, thanks for your trouble.'

'Are you not even going to buy a drink?'

Allie exhaled noisily saying 'You must be joking. Huh' before walking out.

'Well, where now?' asked Allie when they got outside, 'I hope it's better than this dump.'

'We'll just have a walk round and have a talk to some of the girls round here. But nothing over the top or they'll clam up as tight as the proverbial duck's whatsit.'

They walked away from the pub. Turning right into a side street, they'd walked about twenty metres when a car slowed and drew up alongside them. The driver's window was open. A middle-aged man smirked at them.

'Hello darlings,' He said in hopeful anticipation. 'I've not made it with two before, how you fixed?'

Helen bent forward coming eye to eye with the driver.

'I'll tell you how we're fixed.' She said calmly. 'We're fixed to nick you for kerb-crawling.' Pushing her warrant card into the man's face. 'Out,' she ordered. The man shyly got out of the car and stood shame-faced watching the two women officers. 'Is this a favourite haunt of yours?'

'No.'

'Are you sure? Look...' said Helen 'We're looking for a girl called Angie. Do you know anyone of that name, she might...work around here?'

'No I'm sorry I don't know anyone called Angie.'

'Right, Well today, it's your lucky day. It's a good job for you we're not from vice. Now piss off and don't come back, okay?'

'Yes officer, right, just as you say. I'm going. Thanks.'

Martin Wilcox pulled into the yard of Transcontinental Logistics and parked in the visitor's space outside the office. He looked around at the various vans and lorries parked up, many being loaded. One or two men stopped and watched him for a moment. One of them was close, so Martin walked over to him.

'Hi, Martin Wilcox.' He said showing his warrant card. 'Would you know a driver, called Roger Brookes by any chance?'

'Yeah sure, he works here, but he's away just now. Not sure when he'll be back. Why what's he done.'

'Oh, nothing. He just lives in the same house as someone who died and we are trying to find a bit about the man. We'd just like to ask Mr Brookes about this guy, that's all.'

'Who was he...the guy who died?'

'His name's Mickey Edwards, you don't know him do you?'

'Mickey Edwards...and he lives in the same house as Roger?'

'Yeah; Mr Brookes is in flat three and Mickey was in flat four.'

'I don't think I know him. But you might try asking in the Wheatsheaf, it's a pub just round the corner from Roger's place, I've had the odd pint in there with him. Your man might have been a regular there.'

'Thanks, I'll give it a try later. And you are?'

'Ray Collins.'

'Okay thanks Ray.'

Martin entered the office building; he introduced himself and said he was there to speak with Anne Barrett. The receptionist showed him to the HRM office.

Anne Barrett sat behind a desk. Except for her laptop it was clear of clutter. She wore a dark blue tailored suit, a white blouse with a wine-red silk tie loosely fastened around her neck. She gave Martin the impression that she was not a woman to be trifled with. She put Martin's back up just to look at her, with her air of superiority.

'May I ask what this is all about Constable Wilcox?' she said in an authoritative tone.

'We just need to speak to Mr Brookes about a matter that he doesn't need to worry about, and it has no bearing on this company either.' He smiled at Anne Barrett, hoping it would alleviate her fears that it was about his driving or his lorry. Now if you could tell me how we might contact him, and when he will return from wherever he is, which is where by the way?'

'He has taken a load to Germany, Munich to be precise. Let me check with dispatch, they will know when he is due back.' Anne Barrett picked up her phone and pressed a number. 'Mr Jones, Ms Barrett. Could you please tell me when Roger Brookes is due back please? I have a police officer here and he is keen to speak with him.' There was a few moments silence. 'Thank you Mr Jones.' She replaced the telephone carefully on its cradle. 'Mr Jones our transport manager informs me that he is due back on the fifteenth which is next Thursday. He is due back into the depot at around three in the afternoon.'

'Do you have a contact number for him?'

'Yes, just a moment.' She tapped a few keys and read the screen. 'Here we are, I have his mobile number.' She took a notepad from a drawer and copied down the number, tearing out the page, she handed it to Martin.

'Thank you very much Anne.'

'Ms Bennett…if you don't mind.'

'Sorry…Ms Bennett. Thank you for your time. Goodbye.'

The doorman watched Helen and Allie guardedly as they walked purposefully towards the *Magnolia Club*.

'Good afternoon ladies.' He said. 'Can I help you?'

'You might,' Allie said producing her warrant card. 'We're looking for a girl called Angie. Anyone of that name work here?'

'Yeah, I think so. There's only four of the girls do the pm shift, but she's not one of 'em.'

'The manager in…per chance?' Helen said with a knowing wink.

'What at this time of day? Nah! They're bloody nocturnal aren't they.'

Helen turned to Allie as they walked away. 'It looks like a bit of nocturnal work for us too.'

'Is it worth trying a couple of the local pubs?'

'I don't see why not, I could do with a drink and a bite to eat though.'

'How about that place there?' Allie said nodding towards a smart-looking bar. 'Looks a bit girlie.'

'Yeah, I'll try anywhere.' The café bar was painted in pale shades of blue, its name was The Café Antoinette, 'Not a blokeish name is it?' commented Allie as they approached it. Two clipped box bushes in aluminium containers adorned the entrance, one either side of the door. The windows had been acid etched with a French phrase *Il faut vivre pour manger, et non pas manger pour vivre.* Many of the tables were occupied, with people dining, others simply enjoying a glass of wine. No one took any notice as Helen and Allie made their way towards the bar. The cheery waitress greeted them.

'Hi I'm Becky what can I get for you?' They ordered two glasses of Chardonnay. 'Take a seat and I'll bring them over to you in a sec'' she said.

They chose a table from where they could observe the comings and goings; not that there was much going on. Becky brought them their drinks and asked if they'd like anything to eat.

'We have a small menu, but everything is made fresh in our kitchen. I'd recommend the tomato Tarte Tatin with basil; it's a lovely, tasty snack.' She said enthusiastically.

Helen eyed Allie and nodded. 'Go on then we'll try it.' They sat quietly for a minute or two, sipping their wine and watching the other people in the café bar.

'Do you think our girl Angie would frequent a place like this? You don't think this is a bit too…up market for the likes of a stripper?'

'I don't know, it might be,' replied Helen 'how do I know what her tastes are?'

After about five minutes Becky brought their tomato Tarte Tatin. It was very expertly arranged with green leaves, shavings of parmesan and a drizzle of balsamic dressing. They asked for two more glasses of wine. When Becky returned with them Allie asked what the French phrase read on the window.

'Oh, that was Veronica's idea, she's the chef; we jointly own the place. It says something like, you live to eat, not eat to live. Anyway I think that's what it means. Enjoy your tatin.'

'Oh, before you go…' Helen said 'Do you know a girl called Angie. I think she comes in here? She works as a dancer in one of the local clubs. I don't know her last name. It's just that I thought you might get to know some of the local girls.'

'I do know someone called Angela, she has a friend Jacqueline. You don't suppose that might be her?'

'Yeah possibly, Angela to Angie, could well be? She's not in here now I don't suppose?'

Becky looked around the room, 'Yes, that's her there; sitting in the window with the girl in the yellow jumper.'

'Okay thanks.'

Becky leaned forward, conspiratorially, 'Are you police?' she whispered.

'Yes, but nothing's wrong. Anyway, we'll try your tarte now, it looks very delicious.'

'Oh, of course sorry, I hope you enjoy it. It's new on the menu.' Becky said before going to see to her other customers.

'We'll talk to her when we've eaten. This is nice though, umm, yes I like this.' Helen said licking her lips. The two detectives were busy enjoying their meal and didn't notice the girls leave. When they looked over toward the table again if was empty.

'Oh no! She's gone.' Allie said rather annoyed.

'She might have gone to the loo?' Helen suggested, Allie went to check.

'No one.' She said shaking her head.

'Damn,' she said angrily. '…back to square one.' When Becky came to clear their plates, Helen asked if she knew where Angie lived.

'No I don't, but she comes in here regularly.'

'Good. I'll leave you my card. Next time she comes in would you give this to her and ask here to give me a call. Say there's nothing to worry about, no one's in trouble we are just trying to tie up loose ends about someone she might know. We'll try to call in ourselves again, even if it's just for your tarte. That really was very good, compliments to the chef.'

On his return to the station, Martin Wilcox tried Roger Brookes' mobile number several times, but all he kept getting was a number unobtainable. Anyway, he said to himself, I'll catch him next Thursday when he gets back. Why won't he answer his phone?

Helen and Allie returned to the office later that afternoon. Allie found a telephone message sticker fastened to the screen of her computer.

> **Message from**: Mr Leonard Meyer.
> **Taken by**:   M Wilcox.
> **Time**:   16:08.
> **Message**: please contact him re: jewellery.

Oh good, Allie thought, I was beginning to wonder when he'd get back. Allie dialled his number. It was answered after the third ring.

'Good afternoon Meyer's jewellers, Carol speaking, how may I help you?'

'Hello,' Allie said 'I'm Detective Constable Stewart. Would you put me through to Mr Meyer please?' Allie was then entertained by a bit of Bach's Concerto No 1. But no sooner had it begun to play, Meyer answered.

'Good afternoon Constable Stewart, I have some news for you about the jewellery. Would it be possible for you to come into the shop today?'

'Yes of course. I'll come straight away, if that's all right. I can be there in say…twenty-five minutes.'

'Excellent, I'll look forward to seeing you. Goodbye for now.' The phone went dead, Allie shook her head at the somewhat abrupt ending. Ah well she thought I'll get some news soon. Eagerly she almost ran from the office and was soon in her car and heading for Meyer's shop.

Thirty minutes later she was sitting in Meyer's office, the jewels spread out on the velvet cloth in front of her. A tray with the silver coffee jug was also on the table and a delicious cup of Blue Mountain coffee in front of her.

'This *is* delicious coffee,' she enthused as she took a sip from the porcelain demitasse. 'But what can you tell me about these?' she continued pointing at the jewels.

Leonard Meyer sat upright in his leather chair, his back straight, his hands flat on the velvet cloth that covered the leather-topped desk. Speaking softly and slowly, like some eminent doctor, he began to tell Allie about the pieces.

'These are very interesting objects, yes very interesting indeed.' he began. 'They were probably, no, almost certainly made in Europe. In Moscow or even…. Paris. These were designed and made by a top class jeweller, a craftsman of the *highest* calibre and I mean the very best.' Meyer paused momentarily. 'Do you know the name Fabergé…Peter Carl Fabergé, master jewellery to the Russian court?'

'Fabergé Yes…he made…Easter eggs didn't he? Are you telling me these are made by him?'

'Some, undeniably so, but not all of them. These small boxes are.' Meyer picked up one of the boxes; he turned it over in his fingers. 'Yes, here…do you see these marks,' He turned the box so that Allie could see. These are written in Cyrillic letters, Russian letters. ФБЕРЖЕ, '…it reads Fabergé.' Allie nodded; she didn't know what to say. She was thinking, she knew the name and she knew also that these items would be worth a lot of money. But she avoided asking 'how much…'

'What were they made for?' She asked, hoping she would appear enthusiastic, wanting to know more about them and not just mercenary, wanting to know there value.

'This pretty little thing is called a *Bonboniére.* They were given as gifts, they contained small exquisite pieces of confectionery, sugared almonds that kind of thing. Can you imagine being given sweets in such a box?' Meyer paused again, just thinking of it. Slowly shaking his head as he did 'And this,' picking up the next piece. '…is a *Nécessaire* it was used to carry all those little things a lady may need, something that may be necessary to her during an evening…hence the name, French of course.' Allie looked bewildered. 'What things?' she asked. Meyer smiled. 'What do you carry in your handbag?' He opened the small box. 'See all these little compartments, they would be used to hold a pencil, or small scissors or tweezers, needles, a thimble and a length of thread, anything the lady thought…necessary to cover all eventualities.' Allie nodded. 'Yes I see.'

Meyer continued. 'This with the threaded screw is a parasol handle; beautiful, exquisite are they not? These other jewels are not his, but judging by the quality they were made by a fine craftsman.'

'When were they made, do you think?'

'I should say in the eighteen nineties judging by the style, perhaps a little later. They are all set in, what I would suggest is eighteen caret gold; they are not hall marked because they were not assayed in England. All the stones are of extremely high quality. Most as you can see are diamonds, the green stone is emerald, and these are sapphires and rubies too. They are truly exquisite. But tell me Constable Stewart, you said they were all stolen, yes?'

'Yes, they were found hidden in the house of a known burglar, who had a record for house breaking.'

'From where were they stolen do you think?'

'Ah well, to be honest with you Mr Meyer, we don't know. We have no record of any break-ins locally. No one has reported items such as these being stolen. We have gone through the police national database of stolen jewellery, art artefacts and so on and that drew a blank. There have been no museums or galleries reporting missing items, such as these. So really we are at a loss. Do...do you recognise them? Do you know of anyone who collects such items?'

'Yes, of course, but I would have heard something if anything like these had disappeared. All I can tell you, is that they were made in Moscow or Paris over a hundred years ago. And I think they spent their lives in Europe, obviously in a grand house. These jewels were the property of a wealthy person. More than likely, they were the property of more than one person. I would suggest that they were originally stolen sometime during the Second World War...by the Nazis. The families that originally owned these, were probably Jewish and sometime later they came into the hands of your thief. But how they got into this country and came into his hands, well, that's your job to discover I'm afraid.' Meyer said smiling.

'Well, thank you very much Mr Meyer, that's been most interesting. One last thing, could you tell me how much do you think these items are worth?'

'As individual pieces? Well that is difficult to say. In auction on the open market, I think they could possibly realise hundreds of thousands of pounds, maybe as much as a million or possibly more. I've really no idea; I've not seen jewels such as these come onto the open market for many years. But you can rest assured, that they would cost a buyer a small fortune.'

'Really, that's some money we're talking about. Well thanks once again Mr Meyer. My boss is never going to believe this.'

Frankie Bolton listened intently to Jimmy Wall as he spoke of his recollections in Norway, and of his shipmates, and what he'd done just prior to the Norway mission. He had been talking for some time before he really mentioned the man Frankie was interested in.

'He wasn't an honourable man, if you ask me. I served with him on a couple of ships just before the Norway raid. In Norway I was only part of the shore party. Our job was to keep the shore secure and get the others back to the ship as quickly as possible on their return. So I don't really know what he was up to in that house they went to look into.'

'I spoke to Davy Cox the other day and he told me that he felt he was up to something in there. He thought that maybe he'd found something, but what, he'd no idea.'

'Yes well Davy would know. He might have only been a corporal, but he had everybody sussed. He'd have made a good copper too, never missed a trick.'

Frankie chatted with Jimmy Wall for some time but she didn't learn much more than she already knew having spoken to Davy Cox. Later, relating her story to Tony Clayton; who listened intently before commenting that it was all very interesting.

'Why do you suppose he's interested in this wartime murder and assault anyway?' Frankie asked.

'To be honest Frankie I haven't the foggiest idea. Perhaps you ought to phone him. Go and ask him personally. Tell him what you've got so far and try and find out what the hell it's all about.'
Tony Clayton gave Frankie his number. Rufus arranged to meet her that evening in the Golden Lion. He said that he'd be there with the rest of his team around six thirty.

'We usually go for a drink just to wind down, you know. Don't worry about being amongst a load of coppers, they're quite house trained.' He laughed at his own joke, said bye for now and hung up.

Rufus Tremayne, along with Nick Chandler, Helen Machin, and Allie Stewart were assembled in the office of Chief Superintendent Derek Pearsall. The jewels were spread out on the table in front of them all. Allie had just finished explaining what the items were. They looked on in stunned silence, taking in their value.

At last Pearsall spoke. 'You might get the arts boys over, Tremayne, and let them take a look at these. They might have something but, as Constable Stewart has already stated, they were probably stolen by the Nazis from Jewish families during the war. Strictly speaking that doesn't involve us directly. However, a man has been found dead, and it has been verified that he was murdered and these were found in his flat. So they have become part of your investigation. What you have to determine now Tremayne is, how did Mickey Edwards get his grubby fingers on them?' Pearsall paused. 'And are you absolutely positive that no one has reported such items as these being stolen?'

'Yes Sir, DC Stewart has checked the national database and there is absolutely nothing on record.'

'Very well Tremayne, as long as you're sure.'

Tremayne looked as though he was about to speak again, but he remained silent. Pearsall was watching him, 'You have something else to comment Chief Inspector?'

'Well, not really Sir.' Tremayne paused briefly, before speaking again. 'There maybe something Sir. Just over a week ago I was given an envelope by a private investigator that I know. His name is Redfern Sutcliffe, an American.'

Pearsall interrupted 'And who might he be?'

'He takes on jobs tracing their stolen artefacts...pieces of art...well this kind of think mainly.' He said touching the items on the table. 'I was in a restaurant with Sophie when he interrupted our meal. He handed over the envelope. It contained old newspaper cuttings. They were reports about two old murder cases. I've checked and neither was solved, no one was brought to book. The first victim was a Chief Petty Officer in the Royal Navy, he was found buried in the sand dunes in October nineteen forty four. The second victim was a bank manager. He was also found in the dunes, in nineteen sixty three. The connecting factor is, they were all discovered in the dunes, which I accept is coincidental, however, I believe that there is a link, and that's what these are.'

'Yes, yes...so are you saying there's a link with these items and these three cases?'

'Yes Sir, I believe that these jewels are very much the factor that links these three cases.'

Silence stood heavily in that office for a long minute until Allie spoke up breaking the silence.

'I believe they are the link Sir.' Allie said nodding towards the jewels in front of them all. As Pearsall spoke, she wished she hadn't opened her mouth.

'How do you work that out constable?' Pearsall said with monotone bluntness, hoping to get another opinion regarding them.

'Well Sir, Mickey Edwards was found buried in the dunes, and I found these in his flat. The rest of the jewels were found close to where all three bodies were discovered.'

'Yes…I can see where you're coming from constable, but I feel it's all circumstantial. You're going to have to come up with something a bit more solid than that. Keep on it Tremayne. And get these into a safe. Very well, that's all, carry on.'

As soon as they'd arrived back into the office Martin announced that he'd finally made contact with Roger Brookes the lorry driver. He told me that his phone had been on the blink, but he hadn't swapped the chip over.'

'So, what has he got to say for himself then?' enquired Tremayne.

'Said he'd been out of the country for ten days and that he's due back next week; which is what I was told by Transcontinental Logistics.'

'Okay Martin, keep on it and as soon as he gets back have a quiet word with him. And…track down any calls he's made and contact them…just to verify things.'

7

The Golden Lion was busy; as it always was early evening; when office workers stopped off for a swift half before going home. There was a steady buzz of banter and laughter. Music played in the background; some complained to the barman that it was too loud to hold a sensible conversation. He would turn it down, but little by little the volume increased steadily over the next several minutes; it was like a game between them. People jostled trying to get the attention of any member of the bar staff. Helen commented to Allie that she thought it was unusually busy. Allie agreed, finally she got the attention of a barman and called for two glasses of chardonnay. They paid for their drinks and pushed their way through to where Rufus, Sophie and Nick were sitting. As they sat down Helen again mentioned how busy she thought it was.

'It'll clear soon; this is just the six o'clock office crowd. It's almost seven now, they'll be off any minute, you watch. Then we'll be able to hear ourselves think.' Nick shouted. 'He can turn that music down too.'

'Don't be so miserable Nick, enjoy yourself.' Helen called to him about it.

'I'm expecting Frankie Bolton soon,' Tremayne said, looking at his watch.

The conversation moved away from the music's volume to work and onto football and the forthcoming derby match, then onto what they'd watched on the telly last night.

'Chief Inspector Tremayne?' a silky voice broke their chatter dead, announcing the presence of a very pretty, blond-haired young woman. Bright blue eyes and a broad smile peered over the shoulder of Nick Chandler, who couldn't quite turn round far enough to see who had just arrived, despite him trying.

Tremayne got to his feet and said 'You must be Frankie?' as he held his hand out in greeting.

'Yes.' She replied.

'Make a place for her you lot,' A great deal of shuffling followed and another chair was pulled in for her. Clive asked her what she would like to drink and he shot off, to the now, much quieter bar. Tremayne introduced them all in turn by which time Clive had returned with the glass of rosé, which she had asked for. Clive then introduced himself and sat down next to her.

'So you're a journalist?' he said 'I bet that's interesting, meeting all sorts of people…like this lot for instance,' he said waving his hand towards the group sitting around the table, and laughing. 'Been doing that long have you?'

'Since I left Uni', about eighteen months that's all. I enjoy it very much. I've especially enjoyed researching those old cuttings Inspector.' she said moving away from Clive's chat-up lines and directing her last remark to Tremayne.

'Good, so what did you learn?' Clive shrugged, sat back and listened.

'I discovered that there were two men living locally and they were on the same mission to Norway as Chief Petty Officer Simon Carter, the man found in nineteen forty four.'

'Really,' Tremayne said rather surprised. '…that was a stroke of luck. They must be getting on a bit now. Were they able to throw any light on him?' Tremayne seemed very eager to know all about these mystery men.

'Oh, yes. I first spoke to Davy Cox; he was a Royal Marine commando. He lives in Preston and was with the landing party. I then spoke to Jimmy Wall, whom was in the Royal Navy. He had served with Carter on the mission to Norway and on other ships before that. He remained on the beach as security in case the Germans came.'

'So did the, er, the commando…'

'Davy Cox.'

'Davy Cox, yeah, was he able to tell you anything?'

'Yes. He told me that they'd gone to retrieve some documents or something and to pick up a group of Norwegian resistance people then bring them back to England. But he said Carter disappeared during the search of the house that they'd gone to. He said he only reappeared just as they were leaving, after the Captain had called for them all to reassemble outside and move back to the beach.'

'What do you suppose he was looking for?'

'Jimmy Wall told me that he thought Carter was always on the look-out for…easy pickings, something for nothing.'

'I know the type.' commented Nick Chandler. 'I'll bet you he was looking for a stash of cash or something valuable. Something he could sell on, a little nest-egg for after the war. When was this raid by the way?'

Frankie picked up her bag and fished out her shorthand notebook. She flipped through the pages before saying 'It was in July nineteen forty four.'

'The war only had about twelve months or so to go then. This raid was not long after D-day, but I don't suppose the officers knew anything about that. But I bet Carter was lining his pockets for the day that war ended and he would then have something to sell and make a lot of cash.'

Tremayne agreed with Nick's line of thought. No one would have known much about D-day prior to the event, not being directly involved. He couldn't possibly have known how much longer the war was going to go on for. For all anybody knew it might have gone on for as long as we have been fighting in Afghanistan. Tremayne thought that Nick was thinking as someone who saw all this as history, so didn't consider his comments as valuable.

'Oh, I nearly forgot,' Frankie said producing an envelope from her bag. 'This is him,' she said indicating the face that she'd circled. 'Davy gave me a copy of a group photograph with Simon Carter in it. That's the same man's face that was in the cutting that announced the discovery of his body in the sand dunes.'

'Yeah, that's him all right. So, the next question is why was he killed and then buried in the dunes?' Tremayne sat thinking, sipping his Chilean Merlot. The others had lost interest and were now chatting amongst themselves. Sophie leaned across and spoke softly into his ear. 'Where's all this going?' she asked. 'It's an old case, it's not only a cold case, it is frozen solid and no one cares about it. And anyway it's nothing to do with you.'

'Maybe, but Sutcliffe wants something from it. So there must be something in these stories…but I don't know what, there has to be something. Why else would Sutcliffe take the trouble of finding out where we were that night, then to make a special journey just to give me that package containing details of old murder cases, Eh? You tell me why?'

'I can't.' Sophie said. 'Maybe you ought to ask Sutcliffe.'

'Oh Yeah…I most certainly will.' He took a gulp of his wine.

Allie interrupted the conversation, seeing his glass empty she asked if anyone would like another drink. She collected the order and went off to the bar.

'What about the other guy; Frankie; the bank manager, have you managed to get anything on him yet?'

'He's my next job, unless Tony has something else for me that is, but I'll keep you posted.' Frankie looked at her watch, and excused herself, saying. 'I'll ring you when I get something.'

Tremayne lay on his back staring into the blackness of the bedroom. He could hear Sophie breathing gently beside him. He couldn't get rid of the idea that there was a link between Mickey Edwards and Simon Carter. Their murders, being sixty-six years apart could have no direct link, but he thought there was a link, indirect maybe, but something, somewhere would tie in. Was it something to do with that mission to Norway all those years ago? He rolled over and looked towards the clock. Its red figures glowed strongly in the dark; they told him that it was three forty five. He closed his eyes and tried to put murders out of his mind, at least for the time being, he tried to sleep. He must have dropped off because the alarm woke him with a start three hours later.

Over breakfast he said to Sophie that he hadn't slept much. That he'd been thinking of Sutcliffe and those damn newspaper cuttings.

'I'll see if I can get hold of him today.' He said, spreading butter and marmalade on his slice of toast and taking a bite out of it.

'I think that's a good idea.' She replied 'If there's one person who knows something it's him. I've been wondering too, if there's a connection between him and that Navy guy, what's his name er…Carter.'

'I don't know, possibly, probably, but I will find out sooner or later. Starting with a phone call to Redfern.'

Tremayne's morning briefing with Chief Superintendent Derek Pearsall had left him in no doubt as to the Chief Super's thinking. Pearsall had quizzed Tremayne about the newspaper cuttings and asked what made him think there was some kind of link. His words rang in Tremayne's ears, '…they were old, cold and long forgotten.' He emphasised, in no uncertain terms, the importance of the current case and told him to get that sorted. 'We need results on this – don't get side-tracked…' he had said almost shouting.

Tremayne arrived back in his office frustrated and angry. He tried to phone Redfern Sutcliffe, but without success, which didn't improve his mood. 'The man's a bloody enigma; you can never find him when you want him.' He complained to himself.

Clive picked up the phone, listened for a minute. Holding his hand over the speaker he called. 'Boss, PC Hunt from that site on the beach. Said he's found something. What do you want me to tell him?'

'Tell him I'll be there in…er; I don't know. Tell him I'm on my way.' He grabbed his coat from the chair back, on his way through the incident room he called to Helen. 'They've found something in that old gun emplacement. Let's go and see what they've got shall we?' Just as Tremayne reached the office door he turned and shouted to Clive Fraser. 'Get back onto Hunt and tell him to meet us with his car in The Beach Angler car park.' He turned to Helen, when he noticed her grin. 'I'm not taking my car onto that beach to get caked in sand and salt spray.'

'Right you are boss.' Clive said. Twenty minutes later they pulled into The Beach Angler pub car park and parked next to the police patrol car waiting for them, PC Alan Hunt jumped out, opening the rear door for Tremayne.

'Good morning Sir…Sergeant.'

'All right constable, let's go and see what you've got.'

They drove the couple of miles, and then walked into the dunes to where PC Mike Gerard stood waiting. He was standing on top of the slab of concrete that formed the roof of the wartime anti-aircraft gun emplacement.

'We haven't moved anything Sir. And we've got hold of a genny, so there's light in there now.'

PC Gerard led the way down into the concrete vault, followed by Tremayne and Helen Machin. Alan Hunt remained at the entrance, primarily to stop anyone coming close to see what was going on.

'Right constable, what have we got here?'

'This way Sir, it's in here.' Gerard showed them into another small room. He said they'd hit something metal with one of the probing rods, 'We had to shift a hell of a lot of sand,' He laughed. '…there seemed to be no end to the bloody stuff.' Gerard pointed towards a long, green metal box that sat in the corner of the room. All the sand had been cleared away from around it.

'Here we are Sir. It's an old ammo box.' He said. 'Do you think it's still full Sir?'

Tremayne said nothing at first, he moved towards it, and knelt down beside it, he reached out and took hold of the lid and attempted to open it.

71

'It seems to be rusted up, which is not surprising I suppose. Why would they leave a box full of ammunition for someone to find? No, I don't think they were that casual with live rounds. Do you have a screw driver with you Constable?'

'Yes Sir, I got one earlier, I thought it might come in handy.'

Gerard handed the screwdriver over and re-positioned the working lamp above the box. Tremayne worked on the lid and eventually managed to open it. A piece of cloth, discoloured with age covered something. He lifted the cloth to reveal the box's contents. The contents of the box sparkled when the light hit them. Tremayne stared into the box, astounded. It took him another minute before he told Helen to take a look. She moved forward, bending over the box as Tremayne stood aside. She stared open mouthed at the contents, and then looked up at Tremayne.

'Look familiar?' he asked.

'These,' she gasped in surprise, finding it hard to find her breath. '…these look very much like those we found in Mickey Edwards' place.' She paused to think. 'I'd lay bets on them being from the same haul.'

'Absolutely, I was just thinking the same thing. Okay constable. If you've taken photos, then this place can be closed down.' Tremayne said. PC Mike Gerard said he had, from the very beginning. After a few more questions Tremayne satisfied himself that the place had been searched from top to bottom. He decided that there was no need to continue working in the battery.

'Okay constable, when you've got all your stuff out, contact the beach rangers and tell them it's all theirs now.' He and Helen left the bunker. As they moved away, he glanced back at the grey concrete with its small square entrance, laughingly he said to Helen. 'They might want to turn it into a tourist attraction?' Still laughing they walked back to the patrol car and were driven back to the pub car park.

Tremayne and Helen Machin arrived back at the station carrying the old metal ammunition box.

'Allie, would you mind getting your jewellery out of the safe?' Tremayne asked her as he put the box onto a table.

'An old ammo box?' Martin remarked, puzzled. 'What's in that then boss, I hope it's not what it says on the label? Look at the date, nineteen forty two.'

'No, it's quite safe Martin.'

'Do you suppose that's been lying in there all this time, full of priceless objects?' Helen said to Tremayne.

'More than likely.' Tremayne replied. Allie arrived with the box of jewellery from the safe. By now the contents of the ammunition box had been laid out on the table. Allie gasped as she approached; she placed the box she carried next to the now empty ammo box. She opened her box, lifted out its contents and uncovered them.

'Snap.' Tremayne said with a laugh, as the two lots were compared. 'So where did all this lot come from then?' He said thinking out loud. No one answered. 'We can assume, as Mr Meyer told Allie, that they might have been taken from Jewish families during the war. We must assume that Carter found them, then got them back here, then divided them.' They all stood looking at the array of precious items on the table. 'There is a substantial value attached to these; I have no doubt about that. I think we need to have another word with your jeweller Allie. But I wouldn't suggest you carry them around outside. Give him a call and ask him to come into the station. We just need him to confirm, what they are, their origin and approximate value and I think we know that they are all part of the same hoard Carter brought back from Norway.'

Allie made an appointment for Leonard Meyer to be picked up in an unmarked car and brought to the station later that afternoon.

Leonard Meyer was shown into Tremayne's office just after four thirty, he was offered tea, but he declined the offer. Allie was not surprised having been shown his hospitality with the full silver tea service and fine porcelain china. The plastic tea from a vending machine must be anathema to Leonard Meyer.

'Well Chief Inspector Tremayne what is it that you are so keen for me to look at?'

'These...' Tremayne said removing the cloth uncovering the jewels. 'I'd like your opinion on these.' Meyer looked at them, remaining in an upright position in the chair.

'It had crossed my mind Chief Inspector, when your young officer showed me those other items, if there might be similar come to light; and so there are I see.' Leonard Meyer studied the new collection. He altered his position, drawing closer to the desk. He picked up each piece up in turn. He made no comment about any of them. After examining the last item he remained silent for some time. At last he spoke. 'Yes, I would suggest that these are all from the same collection. They are not all by

73

Fabergé of course.' He indicated those that were. 'He not only made exquisite boxes and of course the renowned Easter eggs, of which I dare say you are familiar. He made all kinds of things but not this type of jewellery.' He indicated other items. 'Although, I would suggest that these were undoubtedly made by master jewellers of that same period.' Meyer paused a moment. 'Yes, perhaps in Moscow, Paris or Berlin, yes, yes very fine work indeed.'

'You told DC Stewart that those first items you saw were made in the eighteen eighties or eighteen nineties, I take it these are also from that period?'

'Yes, yes, I would say that they are. You can tell by the style and the cut of the diamonds in particular. Since then the way in which diamonds are cut has changed, it's just a matter of fashion'

'You suggested that these items were stolen from Jewish families during the Second World War, and I take it these also?'

'Oh yes absolutely; undoubtedly.'

'Do you think there might be any way of tracing an owner or where they came from?'

'No, no I don't think so.' He said slowly, shaking his head. 'Although the Germans were meticulous record keepers, if these were stolen in the first place, then I should think it unlikely that they ever got onto an inventory. So no, I don't think there is any chance of tracing their origin. As I've already mentioned Inspector, they were made in Moscow or Paris during the late nineteenth century and are quiet exquisite and valuable, as I imagine you already know. I should think that whoever took these in the first place intended for them to be kept by him…as a little nest egg for after the war. They would have kept them in considerable comfort I should think, if he ever decided to sell them on. It would have had to have been to a private collector though, no questions you see.' He said knowingly. 'They could not have been sold on the open market, they would be recognised as special, and the auction house would have asked questions. They may of course, have been broken up and refashioned, now that would have been sheer vandalism.'

'Well thank you once again Mr Meyer, you have been most helpful. I'll get the officer to take you back home now. That was very enlightening and interesting too, for me personally.'

'No trouble Chief Inspector, don't hesitate to call again if necessary.' The two men shook hands and parted company. Leonard Meyer was taken home in the unmarked car. Tremayne returned to his office and tried to contact Redfern Sutcliffe, again. This time he got an answer to his call.

'Nice to hear from you Rufus.' said Sutcliffe 'What can I do for you this fine afternoon? Fancy a quiet aperitif somewhere?

'Yes, we need to talk…where?'

'How about the Monet hotel in say…half an hour?'

'Okay, half an hour then.' Tremayne hung up He tidied up his desk before making his way to the Monet hotel and his rendezvous with Redfern Sutcliffe. He phoned Sophie and told her that he was going to see Sutcliffe. He arranged to meet her in O'Brien's restaurant which was close to the Monet. He also remembered to ask her to book the table.

Tremayne settled himself into one of the many sofas scattered around the large reception area of the hotel; choosing one from where he could observe the door. A waiter attended him, minutes after he sat, but Tremayne sent him away saying he was waiting for a colleague and would order presently. Tremayne was getting a little anxious when Sutcliffe had not arrived after twenty five minutes. He looked at his watch, thinking if he's not here in ten minutes I'm off. However Sutcliffe walked through the door a few minutes later. He saw Tremayne, apologising profusely for his lateness.

'The phone rang just as I put my hand to the door handle. It's fatal you know to answer such calls Rufus, I am sorry. There's a cocktail bar on the first floor, shall we…?' Redfern said indicating towards the short curving flight of stairs.

Tremayne ordered a gin and tonic, while Sutcliffe, typical New Yorker, ordered a vodka martini. No sooner had they settled themselves into the seats, Tremayne was quickly onto the subject of the newspaper cuttings.

'Tell me Redfern, why did you give me those newspaper cuttings? What on earth did you expect me to do with them?'

'I thought you'd be interested.'

'Now why would you think that?'

'Simply because you're a typical nosey cop…and I assumed you'd like a mystery?' Redfern said in his New York accent heavy and distinctive in this English hotel bar. One or two people close by turned their heads to see who this loud American was. 'So naturally, when those papers came into my hands I obviously thought of you Rufus.'

'Well that was very kind of you Redfern, but why would you be so interested in old murder cases. Do you know that one of them is sixty odd years old for God's sake, carried out during the war? Come on Redfern you're keeping something from me; and to use one of your American expressions…now spill the beans.'

Redfern took a sip of his Martini, licking his lips 'um, not bad. These guys don't know how to make one as we like them in New York, but this is a good enough attempt.'

'I'm pleased to hear it. Perhaps we should send him over to the Waldorf to learn?' Rufus joked, laughing. 'Now come on Redfern quit stalling. If you were a journalist I'd say there was a story in it for you, but as you're not…then why the interest eh?' Rufus cocked his head upwards asking for a straight answer.

'Okay…okay Rufus. Look, I got hold of those cuttings out of a box. It belonged to my Grandma, on my mom's side. You see my grandma was English, my grandpa was a GI. He was stationed over here during the war and they met up. He was a mechanic on airplanes, stationed at some place called Burtonwood. But when he died she had a desire to move back…to the old country, so to speak. You know how these old folks are? But why she had these old cuttings, I truly do not know. Maybe she knew the guy, the navy guy…Simon Carter; he was a Chief Petty Officer in the British Navy.'

'Yeah that's the man, Carter…Simon Carter. I'm working on him; well I've got someone doing the research.'

Redfern Sutcliffe laughed. 'You see…I knew you'd get sucked in…' Redfern nodded and smiled knowingly. 'A little bit of intrigue, a bit of a mystery and you are in there. Look I've lived over here for some time now…you know what they call cops round here…bizzies…comes from busy bodies, you know poking their noses in where they are not wanted. You know I like that name…bizzies.' Redfern attempted a Liverpool accent but couldn't quite get it, it came out more Irish. 'So Rufus what have you found out?'

'To be honest, I've not found anything; too involved in a more recent murder case. So I took them, the cuttings, to a friend of mine, who is a journalist, editor of the local paper. He put the research onto a young woman called Frankie Bolton. Now, she's been quite an industrious young lady and has found out quite a bit actually. She traced two men who served with Simon Carter on a mission to Norway sometime in nineteen forty four. Just before he was found as it happens. One of these men said Carter was a bit of a fly-boy, not that he flew, but meaning he was sly…'

'Yeah, I know the term Rufus.'

'Oh right. Well, when they landed in Norway, they went to some house that was being used by the Germans officers on R&R by the sea, but actually used for other purposes also. Carter apparently mooched around, on his own and only reappeared when the call came to return to the beach. Frankie Bolton spoke to Davy Cox an ex commando. He said Carter looked furtive when he got back, looking around him, as though he was watching the others. He said that he'd hung back as they made their way down to the beach. Now I have a little theory. I think he may have found something. He was hanging back just to make sure it was well secured and hidden in his rucksack.

'So you think he found something valuable in that house. Like what…money, gold?'

'I've no idea, possibly money, possibly jewellery or precious stones, or small gold items.' Tremayne paused, watching Sutcliffe's expression. But saw none. 'But it must all have been very portable. However, some items of value have come into our hands. Two lots, in actual fact. One lot came from the house of a murder victim; the other from an old wartime gun emplacement on the shore.'

'So, you're saying that he found some jewellery and got himself murdered for his trouble?'

'Something like that yes. The newspaper cutting said that Carter was found dead in the sand dunes, close to the disused anti-aircraft battery. By that time in the war, I believe some of the smaller ones had been closed down, this was one of those. They were never demolished, too expensive to waste money on them. They had more important things to do. Like finishing the war and then re-building the country. We uncovered that same battery in our search of the area where a body was found recently.'

'So why was this Carter guy murdered?'

'To be honest I've no idea. You think up a scenario and you'll be as near the mark as I am.' Tremayne said grinning.

'There was also another cutting about a murder sometime in the sixties. What about that, are you any further with that one?'

'No, I don't think Frankie has even looked into that yet. Give the girl a chance, she's still talking to the men who were about in the forties. You've another twenty years to wait for that one' Tremayne said laughing.

'Very witty Rufus, so what about these jewels then, what are they, bags of diamonds?'

'Oh no, they are exquisite pieces made by some of the best jewellers of the time. Some were even made by Carl Fabergé in Moscow, others were made in Paris. We had a master jeweller look at them. He confirmed that they were late nineteenth or early twentieth century.'

'Wow! You don't say? So how did they come to be in some house in Norway.'

'We believe that they were stolen from Jewish families by the Nazis. I believe they were being hoarded ready to disappear with some high ranking general as the war ground to an end. There may have been a group of them, laying down their little nest egg.'

'Ah…so the murderer may well have been a Nazi general, who sneaked in and was trying to get his little nest-egg back.'

'Nice one Redfern, I meant if you could think up of a realistic scenario you'd be as far as I am.'

'Well it is possible…isn't it?'

'In this game anything's possible.' Rufus sighed, thinking Redfern was just messing him about.'

'Well, I'll work on it Rufus.' Sutcliffe looked at his watch and finished his Martini. 'Well Rufus, I'll have to go now. I'll call you. Bye for now.' Sutcliffe half got up, but then sat down again. 'Tell me Rufus, that's not a usual Brit name, where did you get it.' Tremayne looked at him briefly.

'It's just a nickname; I got it at University, where I studied history, Norman history, there was a Norman King called William Rufus, he was nicknamed that because of his red hair,' Tremayne touched his head. '…and it's stuck, you see my name's William and so…'

'Yeah, I get it, very good, okay Rufus I'll be seeing you, bye.'

Sutcliffe grabbed his coat from the chair back and walked away; he paused at the top of the stairs, waved and disappeared. Rufus checked his watch, left the Monet hotel and strolled along the road to meet Sophie.

Tremayne paused outside O'Brien's, a favourite restaurant of his and Sophie's. It was their number one choice when in that part of town. Martin O'Brien, originally from Dublin, had worked worldwide learning about food and styles of cooking and had now settled in Liverpool. His restaurant was especially well known for its Irish-cum-French cuisine, with seafood to die for. Rufus looked up and down the street, but there was no sign of Sophie. He walked into the restaurant, sat in the bar, and ordered a G&T., but he'd hardly wet his lips when Sophie walked in. He jumped up and kissed her and asked how she was, while the waiter took her coat and asked what she would like to drink. 'A Kir,' she said tiredly and plumped herself into the soft sofa.

'How's your day been?' she asked, and then she remembered and leaned forward and said. 'Oh you were meeting Redfern Sutcliffe didn't you...what did he have to say for himself?'

'That he'd passed the cuttings on to me because he said...in his New York drawl,' That Rufus tried to imitate. 'Simply because you're a typical nosey cop...and I take it you like a mystery? We then talked about what I'd found out, well what Frankie had found out, and really that's about it. He did say though that his grandmother was English, his grandfather was a GI stationed over here during the war, which is how they met. He was at Burtonwood Airbase, which is now under one of those massive retail parks. He said that she'd probably kept the cuttings for some reason, but what? He couldn't or wouldn't say.'

'Bit vague, do you think he knows more than he's saying?'

'Oh yeah, absolutely; he's as cute as a cart load of monkeys. I've no doubt he knows more about this than he's letting on. Anyway, enough of Redfern Sutcliffe; I'm starving. What do you fancy?' But before she could answer the unmistakable Irish lilt of Martin O'Brien rang across the room.

'Rufus, Sophie how are you both; it's lovely to see you. I was beginning to think I'd cooked you a duff meal, you've not been in for...what...two weeks, is it. Or are you going to tell me that you've so much work on that you've no time to eat. You've surely not been relegated to takeaways, now that would be criminal.'

'You said it, Martin. But we're here now and we're looking forward to something special.'

'Special is it...well.' O'Brien paused, thinking deeply. 'Well, you like fish, of course, I know you do. Well I've just got hold of some fantastic young turbot or turbotin as the French call them. Now I thought that I'd braise them lightly with a garnish of different mushrooms and shrimps with a sauce Bercy with a little truffle essence and meat glaze. How does that grab you?'

'It sounds first-rate Martin; and I suppose you're going to tell me that this fantastic dish has a fancy name?'

'Oh certainly does, it's called Turbotin Kléber, it's a classical dish. I came across it in an old college book of mine called the Repertoire de la Cuisine, which is a sort of French culinary dictionary. It was written by a guy called Brunet. I think my copy in English was published way back in nineteen fifty.'

'Okay Martin, you've sold us your Turbotin we'll leave it entirely in your hands.'

They ended their meal with the lightest crème brulé ever. Sitting with coffee and cognacs afterwards Sophie brought up the subject of Redfern Sutcliffe again.

'What do you think Sutcliffe is going to get out of this investigation into a cold case almost six decades on, well two cases actually?'

'Your guess is as good as mine Sophie. As I said earlier, there has to be something in it for him. Otherwise he wouldn't have started down this road in the first place. You know he never does anything if there's no good reason. But obviously I haven't yet found that crucial element. Maybe when Frankie gets onto the other victim she'll turn something up.'

'Well it's certainly intriguing?'

'You can say that again. Would you like another cognac?' They had more coffee and the second cognac.

They left the restaurant and Rufus and Sophie walked slowly along the street enjoying the night air; looking into the brightly lit shop windows. The night was fresh and it brought them alive again. After such a good meal they liked to walk. The streets were not too crowded, but there were people about making their way home or towards another pub or club. Finally they hailed a taxi for home.

8

Helen and Allie, exited yet another pub irritated. Their attempts at finding Mickey Edwards' girlfriend was drawing blanks and creating weary feet. They returned to the Café Antoinette, hoping that either Angie or Jilly might, by chance, be in there but no such luck. Becky said that she'd not seen them in the café bar for a few days. This news didn't improve their mood.

'I think we'll try a large glass of white wine Becky. We've had it and my feet are killing me.' Helen said. They settled into a seat near the window, each with a chilled glass of chardonnay. Rethinking their plans and watching for signs of the two girls they were looking for. Hoping they might pay a visit to the Café Antoinette, but they weren't going to be so fortunate. Forty minutes passed quite quickly, reluctantly they left the comfort of the café-bar and continued their trawl through the pubs and clubs. After checking her watch, Helen suggested that enough was enough.

'I'm up to here with this, it's bloody futile. I need a drink and something to eat; especially if we're to keep this up for the rest of the night.'

'Where do you suggest then?'

'I know a nice little pizzeria, something spicy and a glass of wine will see us through.'

'Sounds good to me.' Allie said enthusiastically. A good hour sitting in the pizzeria and a couple of glasses of wine fuelled their ambitions. Helen called Clive, telling him to join them in their search. At around ten o'clock along with Clive they commenced their slog around the late night watering holes.

They checked out the *Wild Orchid*. They didn't go inside. Heavy-handed Harry said that neither Angie or Jilly were working that night. He suggested they might try the *Blue Jasmine*.

The doorman at the *Blue Jasmine club* was having words with a couple of lads. They'd had a few drinks too many and were getting a little boisterous. Clive knew the doorman, who said he could handle them. Inside the club the lights flashed and the music blared. It wasn't too crowded; after all it was a week day. They made their way over to one end of the bar from where they could watch and where the noise level wasn't too bad. Helen nodded towards the girls on stage. Almost inaudible to Allie who was only inches away from her ear shouted.

'Do you think any of them is Angie or Jilly?' Allie simply shrugged her shoulders and raised her hands, and shook her head.

'I'm going back stage' Helen mouthed, pointing towards the door just behind the stage and close to where they were standing.

Allie shouted back in similar fashion 'WHAT?' To which Helen shook her head and grabbed her arm dragging her along, until she realised what her intent was. Clive watched them go, but remained at the bar. Helen flashed her warrant card at the ugly looking guy standing security at the stage door. His crooked nose and cauliflower ear, along with his hefty eighteen stone, demonstrated to anyone foolish enough to attempt entry backstage, that they should seriously think again. Reluctantly he moved aside, allowing them barely enough room to manoeuvre, they had to press themselves against him as they passed. He sneered at them. Helen glared back, thinking, you do that again pal and I'll nick you, you ugly bastard. Back stage was grubby; boxes and beer barrels from the bar were stacked against the walls of the passage, black bin bags waited to be consigned to the yard and eventually to the tip. And judging by the number of them it'd been a long time since anyone had made that trip. They could hear chattering and laughter coming from a room further along the passageway. The door was open, inside there were five girls all in various stages of undress. A brunette was seated in front of a mirror applying her make-up. The others were lounging around on the few chairs that were provided.

'Hi girls, I'm Helen Machin and this is Allie Stewart.' Helen said cheerily. 'Do any of you know any dancers called Angie or Jilly?'

'Or are any of you Angie or Jilly?' Allie chipped in.

'Are you police?' The girl in front of the dressing mirror asked, pausing applying her makeup, and glared at the two officers. 'I might have known.' she said sarcastically. They all carried on with their chatting and lounging, but none were very forthcoming as to whether they knew the two girls Helen had asked about. Helen went on trying to settle their scepticism.

Then Helen was quick to emphasise 'They're not in any trouble if that's what's worrying you. It's just that the boyfriend of one of these girls had been murdered and we'd like to talk to them about him. About his last movements and so on. So if you can help us out here, we'd be grateful. We might even be able to pick up the scumbag who killed him.'

'What was his name…the one who was killed?' One of girls asked, nonchalantly, not sounding concerned either one way or the other.

'Mickey Edwards, do you know him?' She just shrugged and muttered 'Nah!'
'Does anyone know him, have you heard his name…just mentioned in passing maybe? What about Angie or Jilly…those names ring any bells?'

'Well…' said the now blond girl, who had been applying makeup and was combing her blond hair, the sudden change had surprised Helen for the wig had been put on so deftly that she hadn't noticed the change, her face lit up by the array of bulbs surrounding the mirror. 'If you say she's not in any trouble.'

'No, I promise you they are not in trouble from us.'

'Then, yes, I do know them.'

'And your name is?'

'Jo.'

'So where are they now Jo?'

'Well, today being Thursday they should be dancing in the *Wild Orchid.*'

'The *Wild Orchid*, are you sure?' replied Allie quizzically, having been told earlier by Heavy-handed Harry that they were not in the club.

'Oh yeah…Tuesday, Wednesday, Thursday they do the *Wild Orchid*. Friday, Saturday they are in here. And Sunday and Monday, well that's their days off, unless they get a bit of extra and do a couple of hours of a Sunday lunchtime. Most clubs are shut Mondays anyway.'

'Okay thanks for your help' Helen and Allie returned to the bar where Clive was engrossed watching the show on stage.

'Sorry to spoil your entertainment Clive.' Allie shouted, smirking at him and shaking her head. 'But we need to leave.' She shouted, nodding her head towards the door. They extracted Clive away from the show before making their way back to the *Wild Orchid* club. Helen was by now not in the best of moods.

'Heavy-handed told us earlier that the girls were not in the *Wild Orchid* tonight. But one of the girls here told us that they should be dancing there. So I think we'll go and rattle a few cages, and give Heavy-handed a piece of my mind while I'm at it.' Helen explained to Clive.

'He might not have known who was working in the club'

'Didn't know, they work there all the time, so don't you stick up for the big shit, of course he knows. He's knows everything that's going on in that bloody club; who the punters are, who the girls are, who the good tippers are and who to keep out. So now he's got a few questions to answer.

'Do you think we ought to inform the boss? I mean going into Tony Franklin's place?' Clive questioned.

'We're not raiding the joint Clive, so you can calm down. We're only looking for a couple of dancers, with whom we're going to have a nice friendly chat, that's all. We're not even going to see Tony Franklin.'

'You can bet your bottom dollar that he'll know we've been in though. And what's the boss going to say about that?'

Helen glanced at Clive through the driver's rear-view mirror. 'Don't panic Clive, he's not going to say anything. This is just a simple, nice friendly chat we're going to have with a couple of the girls…that's all. Anyway, why would you think the boss wouldn't like us going into this club? Has he said something to you? To my knowledge he's never said don't go in there. We're not busting Tony Franklin…are we, eh?'

They pulled up alongside the kerb, just up the road from the brightly lit doorway of the *Wild Orchid*. They remained in the car and watched punters entering and leaving the club. Groups of them were quite boisterous, singing and weaving all over the road. A marked patrol car drove slowly past the club, the observer looked into their car intently, but he didn't recognise the car, nor those inside it. One group of young men shouted at it as the patrol car passed, they waved their arms, obviously shouting something derogatory at the police car, but it didn't stop. They didn't want the bother confronting half a dozen drunken lads. Allie watched the patrol car, in her driving mirror. It made a three-point turn a couple of hundred metres further down the road. Then made its way slowly back towards the club and the group of revellers.

'They'll have them later.' Allie said

'More than likely,' Replied Helen 'come on, let's go and have a word with Heavy-handed Harry, then we'll see what's happening inside shall we? Clive you stay here and keep an eye on that bugger on the door. We'll go and have a word with the girls.'

Helen and Allie got out of the car and made their way slowly towards the club. At the same time another couple of lads suddenly appeared behind them, having quickened their pace, after seeing them leave the car.

'Hello girls, looking for a good time eh?' one of them whooped as he grabbed his crotch and made of couple of thrusting gestures.

'Piss off; we don't go out with boys.' Allie said calmly.

'Stuck up bitch.' the lad shouted as they hurried towards the club's door laughing. They nodded to Heavy-handed Harry and vanished into the club.

Helen and Allie watched them on their way but held back until they entered the club. When no one else was around they walked up to Harry.

'Hello again Harry, you know I've reason to believe that you were telling us porkies earlier?' Helen said coolly.

'Porkies, I don't know what you mean Detective Sergeant Machin, honestly I don't.' Harry said all innocently 'Why would I tell you porkies; anyway what lies am I supposed to have told you then?'

'Think back Harry, about three or four hours, now that's not a long time. I asked you about two girls…namely…Angie and Jilly. You told me that they were not in here tonight? Now I was told that they always work here on Tuesdays, Wednesdays and Thursdays. And being a detective, I concluded that today being Thursday…they would be here. Now what have you to say to that?'

'Sarcasm is the lowest form of wit DS Machin. Now I told you that these girls were not in the club tonight and that is because…they are not. Yes, they should have been…but they aren't. Mr Franklin is not too pleased either.'

'Well personally I don't give a shit whether he's pleased or not…but never mind eh. Okay, so they're not here…why?'

'Oh I've no idea Sergeant Machin.'

'Where do they live Harry?' Helen asked as politely as she could.

'I'm not sure Detective Sergeant.'

'You're not sure?' Allie butted in sharply 'You get taxis for the girls don't you? So where do you tell the driver to go…politely?'

'The girls tell the driver. I'm not here to run round after them; I've got my own jobs to do.'

'And what are those jobs Harry?' Allie asked, with a cynical tone.

'Never mind her.' Helen cut in. 'What we want to know is where those girls live. Come on Harry, stop messing us about, where do they live? Now you wouldn't want us to get…er, unhappy now would you?'

'All right, if you're going to get stroppy. They live at 36 Western Road. I think they are in flat 2…satisfied now are we?'

'Thank you Harry, now why didn't you say that in the first place instead of all the theatricals?'

Western Road was a typical street close to Sefton Park with large Victorian town mansions. These were huge buildings that at one time housed not only an extended family but a whole hive of live-in servants. Clive commented that it wasn't right, people having to work as servants.

'We're all servants Clive, don't you kid yourself we're not.' Helen rebuked him saying. 'We're no different and they were housed and fed, the alternative at that time was pretty grim, there was no social to go running to if you lost your job. So I think they would tell you that they thought they were better off than some.' Helen looked at Clive, who wasn't convinced with her argument. 'Right then, let's see if they're in shall we?'

They walked up to the big front door that was set back in a vestibule with a black and white patterned tiled floor. At one time it had been closed off from the outside by a double glass door that kept the wind and rain off people as they waited for the inner door to be opened. Allie pushed the door, it opened easily. The hallway was large, there were three doors leading off it and a wide staircase led to the first floor. Only one of the doors had a number screwed to it, number one. They assumed the others led towards the back of the house, or to the caretaker's room. The house was well maintained and the garden tidy.

'Flat two, Heavy-handed said, and for his sake I hope he's right. Two must be upstairs?' They arrived on the upper landing. 'That's it.' she said, moving towards the door and knocking on it, nothing, she knocked a second time. After a minute the door opened a couple of inches, secured by a chain, allowing only enough for an eye to peer out at the visitor.

'Yes, who are you?' the voice from behind the door asked.

'Police...I'm Detective Sergeant Machin' said Helen showing her warrant card. 'This is DC Stewart and that's DC Fraser. Is your name Angie or Jilly?'

'Jilly...' the voice said. She closed the door and Helen could hear the chain being removed, the door re-opened, a little more this time. 'What do you want?'

'We need to speak to Angie. It's about Mickey Edwards, I believe she knew him?'

The girl looked at Helen inquisitively, 'Knew?' the girl said picking up the past tense. 'What do you mean...KNEW, what's happened to him?' The door was now opened fully, revealing a tall, slim and shapely brunette; she was wearing a slinky, silk night dress, the dressing gown she wore over it was open down the front, showing off her well-rounded figure.

'May we come in?' Helen asked politely.

'Oh yeah sorry.' She said, stepping back into the flat, allowing the three officers to pass. Clive eyed her up and down, he smiled at her; she smiled back, pulling her dressing gown together. 'Please go through.' She said pointing to an open door at the end of a short hallway. She closed the flat door and followed them into the living room. It was a clean, comfortable, but sparsely furnished with an oldish, yet presentable three piece suite. There was a low coffee table fronting it, a dining table with two chairs and a large, wide screen TV furnished the room. A glass vase stood on the table containing a bunch of slightly wilted flowers. There were framed paintings on the walls. 'I like those.' Helen said, moving forward for a closer look.

'They're mine, I'm an art student' said Jilly. 'The dancing pays for my studies and I don't want any debts.'

'Good thinking, you hear so much these days about student debt problems.' Helen said.

'If everything goes well, I'm off to study fine art at Uni' next year, so I need every penny I can get.'

'They're very good. I like that one of the market place?'

'Yes, it's my impression of a market. We were studying the French impressionists and I thought I'd try something. I was trying to instil the flavour, colour and atmosphere of the place. It's for sale if you like it that much.'

'Maybe…' said Helen 'yeah, I like that, really nice.' Helen paused, before continuing. 'But I'm afraid we need to get down to business. Is Angie here, it's her we really need to speak to?'

'Yes, but she's not too good, that's why we're not at the club. I bet that old bugger Tony Franklin is fuming.'

'No doubt, but never mind him. Is Angie well enough to talk to us.'

'Probably, she's got a really bad cold. I'll get her, just a mo.'

Jilly returned after a couple of minutes. 'Angie'll be through in a minute; just putting something on.' She said smiling.

'Tell me' Helen began 'Did you know Mickey Edwards?'

'Vaguely, met him a couple of times with Angie; she'd been going out with him for a while. He lived here for a bit, well a couple of weeks.

Said he needed a new scene, whatever he meant by that?' she said scathingly. 'Anything for nothing, grasping little toe rag.'

Suddenly a croaky voice announced the arrival of Angie. 'He wasn't grasping, I loved him.' She said, sniffing and blowing her nose into a tissue, Angie stood, just behind her friend; dressed in a silky dressing grown similar to the one Jilly was wearing. She held it tightly around herself, as though trying to keep warm. A box of tissues clasped under her arm. She looked drawn and pale; her eyes were red and puffy. She was obviously suffering from the effects of a nasty bug.

'Sorry you're not feeling well Angie. We won't keep you long; I'm Helen by the way. First, can I just confirm one or two points with you? We'll talk to you again when you're feeling better though.' Angie nodded. 'Can you tell us your names, just for the record; I take it that Angie and Jilly are just stage names?'

'Well sort of; my name's Angela, Angela Thompson…Angie is what I'm usually called, so...'

'And you…' Helen said turning to Jilly.

'Jacqueline Lloyd, I'm usually called Jackie by my friends, Jilly is a stage name, yes.'

'So, tell me about Mickey?' Angie moved towards a vacant easy chair and flopped onto it as though her legs couldn't support her weight any longer, tucking them beneath her as she settled into it. She took a long deep breath, trying to get sufficient air into her lungs. She sniffed and pulled another tissue from the box and put it to her nose. Blowing noisily.

'Sorry…' she said, Helen smiled saying 'It's okay'.

'Mickey and I had something going. I loved him, I really did. I thought he was special. I've not seen him for such a long time. I've tried his mobile, but there's never any answer.' Angie pulled a couple of tissues from the box, but this time she used them wipe her eyes as a tear ran down her cheek. 'I was worried, I thought he'd run out on me, without so much as a by-your-leave. I was angry with him and ready to give him a piece of my mind when I saw him again...'

'So he hasn't contacted you since you last saw him. In any way at all…emails, text, not even a note or a post card?'

'No nothing! You'd have thought he would though…wouldn't you. I thought he loved me. He just disappeared. So, where is he, is he in the nick?'

Helen took a deep breath, she hated this sort of thing. She knew all too well what was going to happen and no matter how often she had told people bad news it never got any easier. 'I'm afraid I've got some bad news for you both. Mickey has been found…'

Angie realised what Helen was about to say and cried 'No, no he can't be…'

Helen nodded and held out her hand in a gesture of compassion. 'I'm sorry to say this, but he was found dead...'

Angie and Jilly gasped with the shock at this news. Angie's hands automatically went to her face and the sobs could be heard through her fingers. Jilly got up to comfort her. She turned to the detectives and asked.

'How did he die, was it an accident?' She looked at Helen who shook her head slowly. Jilly's face turned pale as the realisation sank in, with the thought that he'd been murdered. 'Was he killed…murdered?' the word was hard to get out, it was almost inaudible.

'I'm afraid so' said Helen 'He was discovered more than a week ago, we've been trying to trace anyone who knew him.'

'But why…why, who would want to do such a thing to Mickey. I know he was no angel, but this…'

Helen quickly changed tack and attempted to get some answers to her questions.

'When was the last time you saw him?'

'Oh I don't remember…' said Jilly 'it must have been a couple of months ago. That's why Angie's in such a state. She thought he'd just walked out on her, never realising...'

'So,' continued Helen 'Mickey used to drive for Tony Franklin?'

'Yeah he used to do odd jobs for him. He'd clean the club if the cleaner didn't turn up, he'd stock the bar, take out the empties and the rubbish. He'd drive the girl's home at night…pick them up during the day, anything really for a few quid.'

'Do you know if he was involved in anything else? Did he do…other little jobs for Tony Franklin, you know, other than just general odd jobs.'

'Other little jobs?' Jilly said not quite understanding Helen's question. 'I'm not sure what you mean?'

'What she means is…'Angie cut in sniffling and grabbing another tissue, to mop her tears and blow her nose again. '…did he get involved in Tony's underworld activities? That's what you mean isn't it?' She looked at Helen closely. 'Come on Jilly you're not that naïve not to know what Tony Franklin is, the real business he's in?'

'Do you know if he got involved in Tony Franklin? Angie?'

'He never talked about anything. I got the idea that silence was the best policy where Franklin was concerned. But he did flash more than a few quid about now and again, you know what I mean.'

'What do you mean by a few quid…a lot more than he usually had, I take it?'

'Oh yeah, just before he…left, he took me out for a fancy meal. He certainly flashed it about then. He must have had, oh, I don't know. How much is a wad of twenties this thick?' She said holding her thumb and finger like a pincer showing the thickness of the wad of notes that Mickey had. 'He said he'd got more, and that we would go on holiday together. He said we could go to Majorca, or Greece, or even Florida he said. It never struck me at the time where the money came from, is that me being naive?'

'So you think he'd done a job for Tony Franklin, and been paid a lot of money?'

'Well…it's possible I s'pose.'

'But you've no idea what?' Helen asked, but answered her own question. 'No of course you don't. If you hear anything, anything at all no matter how trivial it sounds. Will you let me know? Here's my number.' Helen said passing Angie her business card.

9

Tremayne and Nick Chandler sat talking about what they understood so far.

'This Mickey Edwards business bothers me Nick; you know what bothers me most? Where in hell's name did he get hold of all that jewellery? It's not just jewellery though is it…what would you call it? Art treasure. It'd fetch millions in auction, surely. And he had it tucked up under his bed, in a suitcase, all packed and ready to do a moonlight flit. Then there's that stuff we found in the anti-aircraft battery. And what about the cuttings Redfern Sutcliffe gave me, where in God's name, does that fit in?'

'Do you really think there's some kind of link between Mickey Edwards and those other cold cases? You don't think it's stretching the imagination just a little too far. What's ol' beardy chops going to make of it all?'

Tremayne laughed 'I don't know Nick, I honestly don't know. I'll bet it'll be an interesting conversation, don't you think? Would you fancy sitting in?'

'Yeah, I would…but on second thoughts, maybe not. He's all yours Rufus.'

'Thanks a lot pal.'

Martin had been sitting at his desk for over an hour and he was not happy. He had been trawling through the national police database of art and jewel thefts, but he could find nothing that matched. There were no reported the thefts of anything even remotely resembling what they had in their safe. The same question went through Martin's mind as was going through Tremayne's. Where had Mickey Edwards got it all from?

Tremayne was exasperated speaking to Nick Chandler, Martin tapped on the door and walked in. Tremayne could see the look of frustration on his face.

'How far did you check back, Martin?' Nick asked.

'Years, more than eight, but I just drew a blank. There have been no reported thefts of anything remotely resembling any of that stuff; nobody, no gallery, no museum, no jeweller, absolutely zilch anywhere in the country, in all that time.' He said throwing his hands in the air. 'It's as though it just appeared as if by bloody magic, never owned by anybody. I just don't get it, it's a bloody mystery.'

*

Tremayne strode into the outer office and called for everyone's attention. Nick and Martin close on his heels. He looked at the incident board for thirty seconds before settling on the edge of a desk. He folded his arms and stared into the distance, in deep thought. He heaved himself off the desk and stood with his back to the incident board and without turning he rapped loudly on the board with his knuckles.

'This lot,' he said angrily '…is not getting off the ground. ACC Pearsall has made it absolutely clear that if things don't begin to move, he'll want to know the reason why…we need to crack on with it.' He paused, tapping on the board with his knuckles again. Martin, what about that lorry driver?'

'I've finally tracked his firm down boss. His name's Roger Brookes he's in Germany just now. He'll be back Thursday, I'll go and talk to him then.'

'Fair enough. Helen, what's the story so far with finding Mickey's girlfriend?'

'We've found her boss. She lives in a flat, part of big house; sixteen Western Road. Her real name is Angela Thompson, she lives with her friend Jacqueline Lloyd. They are both art students doing a bit of moonlighting as pole dancers in the *Wild Orchid* club. They are known as Angie and Jilly as far as the club's concerned.'

'Tony Franklin's place eh!' Tremayne said, his voice rising a couple of octaves. 'That name seems to be cropping up annoyingly frequently just lately. That's too much of a coincidence for my liking. We need to keep our eye on him and his minions, especially Trendy Smith. Remember, Trendy is bad news, and dangerous, I'd do anything to see him go down. I want something that will stand up in court that would put him away for a long spell.'

'I got the impression that neither of the two girls really knew what Mickey was up to.' Helen stated, 'But…Angie did say, that he'd flashed a bit of money around just before he vanished. He even told her that they'd go on holiday together, somewhere nice in the sun. She said he talked about going to Florida.'

'Florida! What did she think of that; did she not question where the money was coming from all of a sudden? He wasn't exactly known for having wads of cash in his arse pocket, now was he?'

92

'They both thought he'd done a job for Franklin and he'd had a big pay-out.'

Tremayne shot a question into the room. 'She never thought what sort of job pays out that sort of money? I don't recall anything about a big job occurring lately?' He paused momentarily, and continued, more thinking out loud. 'Not round here or anywhere for that matter, that Franklin might be involved with?' Silence, no one spoke, everyone knew, including Tremayne, that there had not been any big jobs recently. If there had, they would have known about it. 'The big question is; where did Mickey Edwards get his greasy little paws on thousands of pounds-worth of jewels? Ladies and gentlemen…I look forward to your input.' Tremayne looked anxiously at the faces of his officers.

'What's intriguing boss is that the jewels we got from his flat are the same as those we got from that place on the beach. Mickey hadn't been in there. That place had not been disturbed since the end of the Second World War. Yet his body was found near there, almost on top of that gun emplacement; coincidence or what?' Helen said puzzled.

'Now listen,' Tremayne continued 'A few nights ago, Sophie and I were dining in a restaurant.'

'Nice meal was it boss?' Clive commented.

'Shut up Clive and listen.' He snapped at the feeble comment. 'A man called Redfern Sutcliffe came into the restaurant and handed me a document folder. In it were a couple of old newspaper cuttings. One dealt with a murder from nineteen forty four, the other was about a murder from nineteen sixty three.

Helen nodded; the look on her face mirrored the confusion of the rest of the team.

'It is my guess, that there's a link between the cold cases and those jewels, and…somehow Mickey Edwards. Don't ask me how or why, it's what we've got to find out. What we have to do is get back and go through every bit of information we have. Copies of the cuttings I handed over to Tony Clayton, a journalist friend of mine, and he's having a look through their archive, actually he's got a young journalist to do it. You met her the other night in the pub, Frankie Bolton.' Tremayne went on to explain all about CPO Carter and the mission to Norway. 'Is it possible that this guy Carter found the little hoard of looted treasure and looted it for himself? He managed to get it back here. He may have then split the hoard just to safeguard it and…I think he got himself killed for his trouble.

'What about this other bloke, the one from the sixties. Where does he fit into the equation?' Helen asked.

'I'll give you my honest opinion Helen,' Helen nodded, in anticipation. '…I haven't the foggiest. I'm hoping that Frankie will be able to dig something up about him. Obviously this is all a side show, our concern is Mickey Edwards.'

'So, this lorry driver I've been chasing, is he a suspect or am I just eliminating him from the inquiry?' asked Martin who'd had to endure the harsh tongue of Anne Barrett, the HR manager of the Transcontinental Logistics haulage company and wasn't keen on meeting her again.'

'You'll find out when you've talked to him in person.' Tremayne said shrugging his shoulders. Nick Chandler reached behind him and picked up the phone that had just rung.

'DI Chandler' He listened for a few moments. 'Thank you, someone'll be round shortly. There you go Martin, speaking of the devil, that lorry driver, he's just returned; early.'

'Right Martin, get round there and have a word with him. Clive, go with him.'

'We might just get another piece into the jigsaw.' Tremayne said as the two headed for the door. Martin on the other hand was thinking of Anne Barrett again, he was not looking forward to meeting her. Twenty five minutes later they pulled into the Transcontinental Logistics' depot. He and Clive walked into the reception and asked to see Anne Barrett, saying that they were expected. The receptionist got up from her desk and showed Martin and Clive into her office.

'Hello again Ms Barrett.' Martin said cheerily. '…you telephoned to say Roger Brookes was back?'

'He is…why do you want to speak with him, may I ask?' Anne Barrett said haughtily.

'I'm afraid I can't discuss that with you; police business, you understand. But I must emphasise that he is not in any sort of trouble…no traffic offences so you need not be concerned.'

'I'm not concerned young man; I just don't like our employees being visited by police officers, that's all.'

'I understand.' said Martin 'So, where can I find him?'

'I'll call him for you, and you can use Mr Johnson's office.' Ms Barrett said indicating a door at the end of her office. Five minutes passed before a short, stocky man, with at least a day's growth of beard entered the office. Dressed in jeans and a grubby T shirt with the logo *I survived the Munich bier fest* emblazoned across a frothing giant beer stein. *I bet you did too*, thought Martin looking at his beer-belly.

'Mr Brookes, I'm DC Wilcox this is DC Fraser. Thanks for agreeing to talk to us.'

'You can use this office.' Anne Barrett said opening the door for them. The door closed behind them as they entered. They sat on the chairs fronting the desk. Roger Brookes looked a little concerned.

'I must begin by assuring you Mr Brookes that you are in no trouble at all.' 'Oh thank God, you had me worried for a while there. I couldn't afford to lose this job.'

'No, it's nothing to do with driving Mr Brookes. It's about a neighbour of yours, Mickey Edwards, I believe you know him?'

'Yeah that's right. I live in number 3, and Mickey lives in number 4. Why what's this about? I've not seen him for a while. Mind you I've been on the continent for a few weeks, in Munich, in southern Germany.'

'That's a good run?'

'Yeah, certainly is, just over eighteen hundred miles, round trip.'

'So Mr Brookes why we're here really is to tell you that, I'm afraid that Mickey Edwards was found dead.'

'Whoa…how…when?'

'He was found a couple of weeks ago. Can you tell me, when was the last time you saw him?'

'Well…now you're asking something. As I said I've been away for a few weeks, this jaunt wasn't just to Munich, I picked up and dropped off in several places. You know, Mickey Edwards and I, we weren't exactly bosom buddies, although we did have a few pints together now and again in The Wheatsheaf. You could ask Denny the last time he went in there, spent a bit of time drinking there he did, well when he had any money that is.'

'Who's Denny?'

'Oh sorry, he's the barman. Denzel la Croix is his name, quite a mouthful eh? But he prefers to be called Denny. He's Jamaican, used to play football, he now coaches a kid's team. He was quite good in his day, not premier league but good nevertheless.'

'So…the last time you spoke to him…do you remember how he was?'

'How d'ya mean?'

'Well did he seem concerned about anything, worried, on edge you know?'

'I don't know really. I seem to remember that he was talking about going away somewhere…on holiday like, you know. Which I thought strange, I'd never known him go on holiday before, not even to Blackpool for the day. Well, he never 'ad any money did he. I stood him a few pints on more than one occasion; he got to be a bloody nuisance at times. Sometimes I'd notice 'im walk in, so I nipped into the gents and then walked out sharpish you know. I know it's not friendly but there were times when I definitely thought he was taking advantage, well you can take *friendship* too far don't you think.'

'Right…so, you thought he might have come into some money then? That's interesting. By the way, did he have a job as you know?'

'Job!' Roger Brookes laughed. '…Mickey Edwards work, you must be joking. He was allergic to work; never did a decent day's graft in all his miserable life. He was a crook, so if he did have money then he'd nicked it.'

'Yeah well we know he had form. But what bothers us is that we found…well, I can't say really.'

'Yeah I know what you're saying, and I can read between the lines. So I take it his death was not exactly…accidental, or you wouldn't be asking such damn fool questions?'

'Yeah…I'm afraid he was found murdered. He was found by a dog walker, half buried on the beach in the sand dunes.'

'In the sand dunes?' said Roger Brookes in disbelief. 'What was he doing there then…bird watching?' Roger Brookes laughed 'If he was he wasn't watching seagulls.'

'Ah well we don't know. So, if you've nothing more to add Mr Brookes we'll leave you in peace. But if you do think of anything, you can get hold of me on this number.' Martin said handing his card to him. 'Thanks for your help.'

Martin and Clive drove straight round to The Wheatsheaf in the hope of finding the barman Denny la Croix on duty. They were not too hopeful that he would be able to shed much new light on one of the punters who frequented the pub. As Martin pulled into the pub's car park he commented to Clive. 'This place looks just a bit too upmarket for the likes of Mickey Edwards, don't you think?'

'Yeah, far too posh for the likes of Mickey. Do you think he came in here to spot likely marks?' Clive replied as Martin pulled into a parking place.

'Maybe he just used this place after he'd made a few quid on one of his little escapades.'

The Wheatsheaf stood detached, surrounded by gardens and car park. The large double door stood imposingly central in the long curved frontage, along with a big colourful sign, suspended above the ground floor windows, advertising the food they had on offer – *'Steak nite Thursday'* - it looked more like a restaurant than a pub.

'I suppose they think that's clever do they, spelling night like that?' Clive said sarcastically.

They noticed the tables with large umbrellas around the side and to the rear garden. Be nice here on a summer's evening commented Clive. Martin agreed, we should give it a try one night, he said. They walked in, pausing just inside the door, just moving to one side to let some people out, and weighing the place up.

'Nah, I can't see Mickey Edwards in here.' Martin said, to which Clive agreed. They moved to the bar and ordered a pint of lager each. After weighing the place up, and savouring their drinks, Martin called the girl who had served them.

'Excuse me, but is Denny la Croix here?' he asked.

'Who wants him?' she said haughtily.

'Detective constables Wilcox and Fraser.' Martin said to her quietly but firmly. Her eyes stared questioningly; *I wonder what he's done.* Clive quickly added 'he's not in trouble; we just want to have a word about someone he may know, a punter who drinks in here, that's all. Now is he in or not?'

'He is in somewhere; he's not on duty just yet. I'll see if I can get hold of him for you.'

They both turned and leaned with their backs against the bar, looking around the room and they waited, as barmaid spoke to someone on the phone.

'I've asked him to come and talk to you both. He won't be a minute.' She said as she went to serve the customers who had been waiting patiently. Martin checked his watch; they'd been waiting fifteen minutes before a tall, black guy arrived at his side. Long dreadlocks touched his shoulders, his wispy beard confirmed Martin's idea of a Jamaican hippy, a hint of Bob Marley about him.

'Hi man, you looking for me?'

'Denzel la Croix?'

'Yeah that's me man, but it's Denny if you don't mind. Now what can I do for you?'

'I'd just like to ask, if you remember a guy called Mickey Edwards. I believe he comes in here on occasions?'

'Yeah, he comes in here from time to time.'

'When was the last time you saw him?'

'Oh I don't know man; it was a while ago now, a few weeks, maybe a month or more.'

'And…on his last visit, would you say he was flashing the cash?'

'Hey man…I just said it was months ago when he last came in here, how do you expect me to remember. We get very busy in here…know what I mean.'

'Yes I realise that. I just thought that with a guy like Mickey Edwards…it might have seemed unusual for him to be flashing a lot of money about. Only I was told he was usually broke. Scrounging drinks off so-called mates.' Clive said, inclining and nodding his head in a knowing manner.

'Sorry man, I just don't recall him flashing large amounts of money about in here. Yeah, I remember him all right and if he'd had cash I'd have remembered. I remember he came in with some guys, you know, but they paid for his drinks. There was one guy yeah, you know, he looked a real cool dude you know what I mean…sharp suit, expensive. Totally alien to Mickey's usual…mates, yeah, you know what I mean.'

'I don't suppose you know who this guy was, the one in the sharp suit?'

'No, I'd never seen him before or since…and I wouldn't want to either, you know what I mean.'

'Okay Denny thanks. But if you remember anything give me a call.' Martin gave Denny his card. They finished their drinks and headed back to the station.

Tremayne called Allie into his office, he asked her to trace any living relatives of Simon Carter.

'I know Frankie Bolton is looking into his service record, but I want to know if there are any living relatives. I suggest your first port of call, if you'll excuse the pun, is to speak to naval records or go on-line. No, you call them, never mind all this internet searching. This is a murder inquiry. Find out where he came from, they must have his last address, and then you can go through the electoral roll of the time. I'll leave the rest to you.'

Just as Allie left the office, the phone rang. Tremayne picked it up and listened.

'Hello, Detective Chief Inspector Tremayne, this is Frankie Bolton.'

'Oh hello Frankie, I hope you have something, for I sure need it.'

'Well Chief Inspector, I think I might be on track with our missing bank manager.'

'Please Frankie, call me Rufus, no need for such formality. So who is our mystery bank manager then?'

'Well…Rufus, what's taken me so long is that the bank he worked for has changed its name three times since then. But the best part is…I don't think he was born in England, he might have been born somewhere else in the Commonwealth perhaps; well Empire then wasn't it. So, I'm not sure where he came from just yet. I have been through the records at the National archive at Kew, in London. I looked at all the records of births of all the Masons, who gave birth to a son during nineteen o-eight. I've checked all the Masons in the country who named their son Richard Gilbert. I found seven Masons, but their sons were called Richard George, of which there were three, or Richard Gordon or Richard Graham or Richard Gerald of which there were two. But none of them christened their son Richard Gilbert.'

'So, what's your next tack?'

'I'll see if I can trace him through the bank's records. Although, as I said, the bank he worked for was taken over, the parent company should still…I hope, have records of previous employees. And if it turns out good, I'll see if I can trace him back to his origins.'

'Well Frankie I don't envy your task but good luck with it anyway. What was the name of the bank he worked for?'

'During the sixties it was called Williams and Glyns, they're easy enough to trace, but as I said finding an employee from forty odd years ago. Well that might prove difficult. Anyway, that's where I'm at just now. I'll give you a call as soon as…'

'Okay Frankie I appreciate all your work, I'll speak to you soon, bye for now.'

Tremayne sat back in his chair and reflected on what Frankie Bolton had just told him. *So not English, eh!* Nick Chandler entered the office breaking Tremayne's thinking. Almost immediately, before Nick had chance to say what he'd come in for Tremayne was there. Telling him what Frankie had said.

'I've just had an interesting little snippet from Frankie Bolton. That bank manager who was killed in nineteen sixty three, she thinks he might not have been English, which I assume means he wasn't Welsh or Scottish either.'

'Right, so what does that prove?'

'To tell you the truth Nick I haven't the foggiest. So what have you got?'

'Nothing really, but I thought we might invite one or two of Mickey's friends in, having them in here for a quiet chat might just freshen their memories, loosen their tongues.'

'I don't know Nick, we've talked to some of his so-called mates and where has that got us – nowhere. No I don't think that's a starter. What else have we got?'

'Well there's always Tony Franklin.'

Tremayne leaned back in his chair, he kicked himself off against the edge of his desk and swivelled round, coming back to face Nick. 'And what line of questioning will we throw at him?

'How about jewels and then Mickey Edwards?'

Tremayne said nothing, he swivelled around in his chair again, and he spun round a second time. He came to a stop, and stood up. 'I think we need something more Nick, we don't have enough to worry Franklin, you know what he's like. He'll have an answer for everything.' Tremayne paused. 'Well not just yet anyway. I think that those jewels are the key to Mickey Edwards' demise as well as those other two guys…Carter and Mason. This is a fifty-fifty case half new, half cold and we are in limbo, up shit creek without a paddle.'

'Yeah I know what you mean, and to use a Naval term, the sun's well over the yardarm and I would suggest the pub beckons.' Nick gave Rufus a knowing grin and they walked out of the office, announcing their destination. The others quickly finished what they are doing and followed on.

10

Frankie Bolton was not the only one to be phoning the National Archive at Kew in London. Allie Stewart had been detailed to trace any family of Simon Carter, living or dead, maybe just to get a handle on an address no matter how old, just to give them a jumping off point. The answer to her telephone conversation was that to trace a name from that time she should try their website or visit the archive in person. Despite Allie's protests to the effect that she was involved in a criminal investigation; she was firmly, yet politely, told that they had staff shortages. They were terribly sorry but that was how it was. Allie searched through their website but it didn't give her what she wanted. Frustrated, she leaned back in her chair and stared at the ceiling. She was thinking of a trip down to London, would she be allowed the expense of travelling anyway, but she lived in hope. *Budgets are tight* she could hear Tremayne saying. He was always saying that, because it was all he heard from Chief Superintendent Pearsall. So why should her request be met any differently. Suddenly she sat upright, saying to herself *Frankie Bolton of course.* She reached for her phone, then put it down again, *number?* Tremayne gave it to her and so Allie was now listening to a ring tone. After what seemed an age a voice answered.

'Hello, Frankie speaking.'

'Hi Frankie, this is Allie Stewart, I work with DCI Tremayne…'

'Oh yes, I met you briefly in the pub that night.' They passed a few girlie comments. 'So, what can I do for you Allie?'

'I'm trying to trace any relatives of Simon Carter. During your search did you find out where he came from, or where he was born…whether he has relatives still living?'

'I'm sorry Allie, but I've not really gone down that route; I've only looked at his service record relating to his mission to Norway you know. He was born in nineteen o-nine, in Liverpool which I worked backwards from what Davy Cox told me. Sorry I can't be of more help. But listen, I'm going down to the National archive at Kew tomorrow, why don't you come?'

'I was hoping I might get a trip to London, but I've not asked yet. Oh! what the hell, if you're going. I'll see the boss now; treat it as a girl's day out. Listen, I'll check it out with the boss and get back to you.'

Allie requested her visit to London and much to her surprise it was granted. She met up with Frankie bright and early for the train from Liverpool Lime Street to London Euston and from there via the tube to Kew.

Allie and Frankie settled themselves into their seats. Each had a takeaway coffee, which they drank through a little hole in the lid of the paper mug and a bacon sandwich from the station buffet. After the usual pleasantries and a bit of a chat, their conversation got onto business.

'Why do you think DCI Tremayne got my editor, who then got me involved in researching these old murders from way back? It's not that I mind, in fact I rather enjoy the research, but shouldn't the police be doing their own investigations.' Frankie asked, thinking she wouldn't receive a proper answer.

'Well yes, under normal circumstances we would, yeah. But the boss seems to be treating these cold cases as a personal thing. I don't know why really. He told us that he was given this folder with the old newspaper cuttings from some guy called Redfern Sutcliffe…you heard of him?'

'No, I can't say I have.'

'Well after Sutcliffe gave the boss the old newspaper cuttings, he suddenly seemed to link the murder of Mickey Edwards to those cold cases.'

'Why, is there a link?'

'To be honest I don't know.'

'Oh come on Allie you must surely have an idea?'

'I shouldn't really.' Allie remained silent for a long minute before answering Frankie. 'Now can I trust you to treat this in absolute confidence?'

'So you do know something?' Frankie said with a journalist's eagerness to know more.

'Can I trust you, this mustn't go any further.' Allie repeated her earlier question, but wondering whether she was right to bring a journalist into her confidence. 'In the end you might get a story out of it, but the boss has to give his say so.'

'Yes, yes you can trust me on this. I promise I'll keep it to myself.'

'Look, it's only my own hunch, now can I rely on you not to take this any further?'

'I've just said, I promise really, I promise it'll go no further.'

Allie hesitated, thinking to herself *Am I doing the right thing here, the boss'll kill me it any of this gets out...but I could always say I was delving for info.* 'Tell me Frankie what do you know of the case concerning Mickey Edwards?'

'Well my editor Tony Clayton, who is apparently a friend of your boss. Well he told us that he'd been found in the sand dunes, battered to death and something about the beating was designed to hide his identity.' Frankie gave a visible shudder at the thought of it. 'He told us that you had been digging in the area and had come across an old gun emplacement or something left over from the Second World War,' Frankie paused and looked keenly at Allie. '...and there was a hint that something had been found. So was the thing you found the link between Mickey Edwards and those cold cases?'

'You're very astute...' Allie said sounding quite surprised.

'We are in a similar line of business you know Allie. We both have to make assumptions. Create them out of little bits of knowledge. I have to write an article, and you have to convict someone, but basically it works out the same in the end. So what was it you found? Come to think of it...you found something in his flat too, didn't you?'

'Well yeah, but I'm not sure I should say, but we did find something in both places. And there is...probably...maybe...a link, tenuous though it may be. But believe me I can't tell you what it was.'

'So now you're off down to Kew to research Carter's family. D'ya think he has any?'

'I've really no idea. He obviously had a family, but whether any of them are still living...well? This is just...grasping at straws. So, why are you going to Kew?'

'The bank manager Richard Gerald Mason...well he's a bit of a mystery, quite a big mystery actually. I have a hunch that he wasn't born in Britain. I've checked. He wasn't born in England, or Scotland or Wales or Northern Ireland, come to that. He may even turn out to be foreign and I don't mean born in the Commonwealth, but foreign.'

'Not English or anything; what makes you say that?' Allie said rather surprised at the suggestion.

'Well I checked through all the records for births for nineteen o-eight. I know he was born then from the newspaper cuttings. I looked for families called Mason. I could find no record of a boy being born and christened Richard Gilbert. So I asked myself either he was born elsewhere, somewhere in the British Empire, like India or some African country, Australia or New Zealand, there's loads of places. Perhaps records weren't as thorough then in some of those places. Or…he was born somewhere else, Europe possibly and he came to England and changed his name for some reason.'

'Changed his name…why would he do that?'

'You're the detective, you tell me. His name wasn't English or English sounding so he changed it.' Frankie said with a laugh, as though expecting a sensible answer.

Their conversation lulled. Allie's brain was in overdrive, thinking frantically about what Frankie had just told her…*Mason not English; changed his name…but why would anyone do that. He's got form, he's in hiding…from an outraged wife…or girlfriend…who? Interesting.* Eventually she returned to the real world.

'Fancy a coffee?' Allie asked

Standing, swaying to the motion of the train; sipping their coffee through an annoying little hole in the lid of the carton; Frankie suddenly said. 'Apart from going to Kew I had an idea of visiting the headquarters of the Royal Bank of Scotland, if they are even in London; it could mean a trip to Edinburgh, I don't know. I want to check through their records of staff. You see, Mason was working for a bank called Williams Deacons at the time of his death in nineteen sixty three. That bank then became Williams and Glyns before finally being taken over by the Royal Bank of Scotland. So I'm hoping that they still have records dating back to the fifties and early sixties. But I still just want to check if there are any immigration records at Kew. Trouble is, they might not have him down as Mason so it's a long shot but I do have a theory, I'll tell you about it on the way back, if anything comes of it.

Helen picked up her phone and dialled Frankie Bolton's mobile number. Tremayne wanted to know if she had come across any friends or colleagues during her trawl through the paper's archives. '…and if there are, find out their addresses and then you might go and have a chat with them. See what you can find out about our mysterious banker friend.' He said as Helen dialled the number.

Helen listened to the ring tone; pencil poised over her notebook; after a few rings Frankie answered. Helen asked her question and made a note of her answer. 'Okay thanks Frankie, bye.' She walked into Tremayne's office saying 'There's only one possibility boss. Frankie found a name mentioned in the original report. The reporter at the time spoke to someone in the bank called Graham Wilson. He was a trainee then, but Frankie says she hasn't got round to tracking him down.'

'Right, you do it, off you go…good luck.' Tremayne said with a broad smile on his face. Helen returned a weak grin, thinking; *yeah, thanks boss.* Before she left the office she looked hard at Tremayne, saying.

'Are you sure there's a link between these old cases and Mickey Edwards?'

'Look Helen, it's all a bit tenuous I know but…I think there is. No local villain would go to all that trouble to brutalize a face unless, oh I don't know. Look…Mickey's too well known locally, we know him, and the local villains know him…so yes I think there is a link. We'll find it sooner or later…sooner I hope, before ol' beardy chops upstairs gets the figures for our little escapades. So see what you can find Helen, if he's still in the area he could push you towards something.'

Helen sat at her desk and stared at her computer screen. She picked up the phone again and redialled Frankie's number.

'Sorry to bother you again Frankie, but what was the bank this guy Mason worked for?'

Frankie gave her the information. 'Thanks Frankie. The boss has asked me to track the guy mentioned in the original report, so don't think I'm poaching your territory will you?'

'No, no not at all, I'm glad of the help. I'm in London just now. I'm just off to the National Archive to try and trace Simon Carter's siblings if there are any still alive or even their children.'

Helen keyed into her search engine *<Royal Bank of Scotland>*. It didn't give her what she wanted so she phoned their headquarters and asked to be put through to, if such a department existed, personnel archives. After a few minutes a woman with a soft Edinburgh Morningside accent spoke.

'Hello, Muriel Hamilton, how may I help you?'

Helen explained who she was and what she wanted, but followed on with an apology for even expecting records of staff to still be in existence and from a bank that ceased to exist more than fifty years ago.

'That's no problem at all Detective Sergeant, even if he worked for Williams Deacons he'll still be listed and since you know his name it should be…ah yes here he is…Graham Wilson. He joined the bank from school as a trainee manager, good A-levels too, Maths, English and History. He attended a school called Merchant Taylors Grammar School.

Joined the bank in nineteen sixty two aged eighteen. He did well; he ended up as manager of our large branch in Liverpool.

'Can you give me his address Muriel?'

'You'll understand, but I'm afraid I cannot let you have it over the phone, you could be anyone. I know you say you're the police but you understand my position.'

Helen thought for a minute. 'Muriel, if I give you my number, you'll be put through to me via the police switchboard; would that satisfy you?'

'Yes I think that would be a good idea. Just to keep those upstairs happy, you know how it is.'

'Of course, I understand, so my number is…'

Muriel Hamilton was back speaking to Helen after a few minutes. 'Thank you Muriel, this'll be a great help.'

Helen had written down Graham Wilson's details as quoted by Muriel Hamilton. She walked into Tremayne's office. 'I've got the name and address of someone who might remember Mason. He was a trainee in the bank at the time of Mason's death. He was interviewed,' Helen said wagging two fingers like inverted commas. '…by the press after Mason's body was discovered. His name is Graham Wilson; he's retired now, but he still lives in the area. He lives in Aughton near Ormskirk, I've got his address, and I'll give him a bell and go and see him.'

'Okay good work.'

'I'll do that now, but I don't hold your breath; he was only eighteen at the time.'

'Yes but he may remember something about him, Mason's personality, his manner, how he spoke or behaved, where he lived. Anything at all about the man Helen, go and speak to him, be nice. Exploit your feminine charms.' Tremayne smiled, a broad grin developed, 'Okay off you go.'

Helen telephoned Graham Wilson and after convincing him that she was from the police and this was a serious matter, an appointment was agreed for the following day.

Allie and Frankie sat at a table, patiently waiting for an assistant to bring them the records they had each requested. Their wait was soon over, when a young lady arrived and told them that a microfiche was now available for them and the fiches detailing their request were loaded. The assistant showed them how to use the equipment and said if they had problems, just to ask.

Allie soon found a death certificate for Simon Carter. She read,

Name of deceased: *Simon Carter, Chief Petty Officer RN.*

Date of death: *23rd September 1944.*

Cause of death: *Head trauma caused by severe beating caused by person or persons unknown.*

Next of kin: *Henry Charles Carter, father. Alice Margaret Carter, mother.*

'Very helpful.' Allie said.

'What is?' Frankie asked.

'Oh nothing really, this doesn't tell me anything that we didn't already know.'

'Yes, research is like that. You always seem to discover more about what you already know than what you don't.' Frankie moved across to look at what Allie was reading.

'Ah, Carter's death certificate, yeah just the cause of death on that, no great detail. Well, of course you already know that, don't you? It does give you his next of kin though. You need to see if you can find a birth certificate. Do you know when he was born?'

'Yeah nineteen o-nine, you said. But where, now that's another question all together.'

'I'll go through all the Carter's for nineteen o-nine.'

'There'll be thousands. Best go through naval service records and work it back.'

'Are they here?'

'You should be able to access them from here, if you get onto one of the computers.' Frankie said before she went off to do her own bit of research.

It took Allie quite some time to sort through the naval service records and trace Carter back to his birthplace. She made copious notes, she almost copied every detail. She ordered a photocopy of his service record, his birth certificate, and a marriage certificate too, which surprised her for no apparent reason other than, that she never thought of him as being married. Allie closed down her terminal and left the building to phone Tremayne. He was pleased she'd made some progress, but then he gave her other questions to answer.

'See if you can find out what the mission to Norway was all about, see if you can get some details. The guys Frankie spoke to were not privy to everything, they just followed orders. I believe they went to a house of some kind, find out what that place being used for, was it an official German HQ or what?' Allie listened to Tremayne's instructions. She then rejoined Frankie.

'Ah there you are,' Frankie said 'Where've you been.'

'Just to give the boss a ring, now he wants me to find out what Carter's mission to Norway was all about, and he wants to know what the place was used for where they went.'

'Oh right, no problems then.' Frankie said laughing.

'Helen,' Tremayne said as he entered the incident room 'Allie's found Carter's birth certificate. His full name is Simon Peter Robin Carter. He was born in Crosby. So I imagine there's not too many called Robin there, so that should narrow your search a bit. Get one of those two to help you out' He said nodding towards Clive and Martin who were engrossed in a conversation regarding Liverpool and Everton football clubs.

'Hey you two, I've a little job for you, so I'm terribly sorry to disturb your football.' She said with a wicked grin. 'Allie has just phoned in with details about Carter. She said he was born in Crosby. Family Carter, father's name Henry Charles, mother Alice Margaret, nee; Robinson. Carter's full name is Simon Peter Robin. That's just general info. What I want you to do is go through police records again for both Carter and this bank manager Mason. Pick up any little detail; and see who the investigating officers were and if any of them are still around go and have a chat. Obviously those from nineteen forty four won't be…but they might have kept a diary perhaps so contact their families…but that's a long shot. I'll leave it to you. Helen knocked on Tremayne's office door. 'Boss, I'm off to speak to Graham Wilson, the guy who worked with Mason the bank manager.' Tremayne gave Helen a quizzical look for a moment before he realized who she meant. 'How long ago is it since they worked together?'

'Forty seven years.'

'Right, well I hope he has a good memory. But what I'm hoping is that he'll remember some peculiarity about him, an accent, a particular mannerism in his speech or behaviour; a funny pronunciation of a word, did he pronounce a 'W' as a 'V' for instance, you know the sort of thing. See you later.'

Allie and Frankie sat in front of the microfiche terminal, squinting at the almost illegible handwriting in the immigration registers of the early nineteen hundreds.

'We'll just have to make an educated guess as to when he might have come into the country. It could have been any time after he was born. Just skip through all the Masons, but his name might not have been Mason then.' Frankie said.

'We could be in here forever at that rate; they'll find our bleached bones sitting here, empty eye sockets staring blindly at this screen through a curtain of cobwebs. Anyway, you're only guessing that he was an immigrant and where from? The whole world's out there; millions wanting to get into the country. There have always been loads of people entering the country. Ah – it's an impossible task.'

'Look I'll just do a search of countries in the British empire…'

'You're wasting your time. There'll be no record. He was white; and to all intents and purposes he was English he was a British subject. Now if he was a foreigner and changed his name when he got here, that's more likely; but how do we go on to track him down then? I'm telling you it's bloody impossible.'

'Maybe you're right' Frankie said sighing deeply and feeling disappointed at what she thought had been a wasted trip.

'Come on, we'll pack it in and head back. A couple of drinks might go down well. I'll take it up with the boss tomorrow.'

Helen drove slowly along the quiet wooded lane; a man walking his dog, stopped to watch her suspiciously as she drove past. A wide grassy verge separated the road from the tall hedges that lined the road and hid the properties. This was the realm of premiership footballers, Helen thought, not retired bank managers. From the car she could not see any signs of a house. But every so often the grass verge and hedge were punctuated by a gated driveway and a sign giving the house's name, the only indication that habitation lay beyond the green screen. *Well this guy's done well for himself working for a bank, bit of embezzlement?* Helen cynically thought. She stopped the car and read a small sign – 18 ACER COPPICE. She reversed a little and turned into the driveway. Tall trees towered above her; a forest of Japanese Maples had been planted below them. The drive was long, the house came into view, standing squarely to the drive; it impressed Helen with its elegant façade. In front of the house there was a circular flower bed, a sort of roundabout making it easy to turn and drive back out onto the road. She saw no other cars, and assumed there must be garages elsewhere. She stopped the car just to one side, where another vehicle, if necessary, could get past. Helen climbed the two steps, and just as she lifted her hand to ring the doorbell, the door opened. Facing her was a tall man, casually dressed in light trousers and golf shirt, with its crossed gold clubs logo and the name of a club, which she didn't recognise.

'You must be Detective Sergeant Machin. I'm Graham Wilson, please do come in.'

She entered a large square entrance hall; a curving staircase ran to the upper floor. Four closed doors led off the hall into other rooms. Helen was shown straight through to the rear of the house and into a large conservatory overlooking the garden. It was furnished stylishly with wicker furniture and floral cushions. The four wicker chairs surrounded a low glass-topped coffee table; the whole was set on a large Chinese carpet. Various pot plants in elaborately painted containers adorned the conservatory.

'May I offer you something Sergeant Machin, tea, coffee, something soft and cool?'

'Thank you; a long cold drink would be just the thing.'

Wilson busied himself with the drinks. Carrying them over, he placed them on the low table, before sitting opposite her in one of the chairs.

'Now sergeant, you intrigue me, you said you wanted to know about Richard Mason.? Now there's a name I've not heard in many a long year.'

'Yes that's right. You see, during a recent investigation, his name came to our attention. I was hoping that you might be able tell me something about him, anything at all you might remember.'

Graham Wilson leaned forward to take up his glass, he took a sip; putting it back down on the glass-topped coffee table; he leaned back, remaining silent for a short while, obviously in deep thought. Helen did not like to break his concentration, she sipped her drink and watch him.

'You must understand Detective Sergeant,' He said at last. '…that it's been almost fifty years since his death, and to be honest I haven't thought of him in all that time. I don't know where to begin, surely your records would tell you about him?'

'The reports aren't all that thorough, and they don't answer all our questions. So if you could perhaps remember something about the man. For instance did he have any particular, er…mannerism or way of speaking…or …'

Wilson sat in silent thought again, obviously trying to come up with something. He made a few hesitant beginnings of a sentence but then just mumbled a word.

'No,' he said sighing. 'It was my first job with the bank, Mason was the manager. I didn't really have anything to do with him. You can understand that as a junior, one didn't. In those days the manager was second to God, if you know what I mean, you certainly wouldn't pass the time of day with him. It would have been a polite good morning, after that you spoke when spoken to and that's all.'

'You were interviewed by a newspaper, that's how we traced you.'

'Really, very clever. Yes they interviewed me, they spoke to everyone, I was no one special, I didn't know anything.' Wilson suddenly put his hand onto his chin; he half closed his eyes and tightened his brow as though in deep thought. 'Now that you mention it, I seem to remember that if he was agitated by something, or worried maybe…he used to pronounce certain words strangely. But I can't remember which in particular, it may come to me later, but there is something at the back of my mind…I'm sorry Sergeant, I just can't remember.'

'Do you think he may have been foreign?'

'Foreign!' Wilson said surprised. 'Oh, I've not thought of that before. I don't know…it's…possible I suppose. It's something that's never crossed my mind; he might have been South African, but I couldn't really say for definite. He seemed to me to be the archetypal Englishman; he was like Captain Mainwaring from Dad's Army. Always immaculately dressed, I can see his bowler hat in his office, but I can't really remember ever seeing him wearing it. Funny the things you remember when something's triggered in your mind.'

'I don't suppose you remember him being visited by foreigners.'

Wilson shook his head and chuckled 'No…sorry. After all he would have seen many people conducting all kinds of business.'

'Do you remember anyone else who worked there, when Mason was manager, someone who worked closely with him, a secretary maybe who might be able to help us? Presuming they're still with us.'

'I can't say that I can, fifty years is a long time you know. We all get old. Most will be dead by now I should think, or very old. I was a young trainee then and I've now retired. But I'll give it some thought. What might be of interest you is, I have a few archives of my own relating to different periods of my career. There might be one or two still alive and kicking. If I come across anything that I think might be useful to you I'll give you a call.'

They said their goodbyes and Helen set off back to the station. The man with the dog eyed her again as she pulled out of the gateway. She pulled up, wound down the window. 'It's all right Sir, I'm a police officer not a burglar, but it's nice to know people watch out what's going on.' Helen smiled at him and pulled away, through the rear-view mirror; she could see the man was still watching her.

Tremayne was the first to ask how she had got on with Graham Wilson.

'Nothing definite, but he is going to go through his papers, diaries and stuff. He said there might be other people who could possibly remember him, if they're still alive that is.'

'Good, at least it's a start. When Allie gets back we can begin to put two and two together.'

'Yeah, but what if two and two make five?'

'Very funny Helen, let's just be positive eh. I know there's a connection here somewhere. I know the water's a bit murky just now, but it'll clear – trust me.'

'Oh I do boss, and just as you say things can only get better.'

Allie leaned back in her seat rubbing her tired eyes. She had been staring at the computer screen for what seem like hours. She had found what she sought, thankfully the freedom of information worked in her favour. The mission to Norway of which Carter was part, was not too top secret a mission, and its details were released soon after the war ended. Allie read the report written by the RN captain in command.

> *0600 hours Tuesday 24th July 1944. Scapa Flow, Orkney.*
> *Weather fair, light rain, sea slight to moderate, wind force 4.*
> *The passage was as scheduled, arrived off Norwegian coast Wednesday 25th July 1944 0600 hours. Weather and sea conditions still good. No ships seen on route, no vessels in sight on arrival,*

no activity on shore. Landing party put out at 0730
hours. The landing was scheduled to last until
0930 hours.
Signal from shore party 'landed; all clear;
proceeding as planned.'
Gunfire heard at 0752 hours.
Signal: 3 German guards engaged all killed;
proceeding.
Signal received every fifteen minutes; nothing
reported.
Final signal received 0925; returning to ship. One
man injured.
Sea boat returned with Norwegians, returned to
Scapa Flow. 1400 hours Thursday 26th July.
Signed: Ralph Benedict,
Captain.

'But what the hell happened on shore.' she said to Frankie.
'That's what I want to know. Davy Cox told you that Carter
was acting suspiciously, hanging back, he was the last to rejoin
them when the whistle sounded for them all to assemble on the
beach and return to the ship.'

'He found something, yeah?' Frankie said innocently.
Allie said nothing, but Frankie could see in her eyes, in her
expression, she knew more than she was letting on. 'He did
find something didn't he…What was it, something valuable?
You know don't you?'

'I can't say Frankie, honestly I can't,' Frankie eyed
Allie with a knowing look and began an assessment of her
thoughts on the subject.

'Okay, let me see…how's this for an educated guess.
So, he found something, something valuable, he pocketed it
and he wasn't seen by anyone. On his return he thought he'd
profit from his ill-gotten gains, but something happened with
the deal and he was bumped off for his trouble. How's that for
an assessment of the situation. I think that's pretty sound, don't
you.'

'I'm not saying you're wrong, but neither am I saying
you're right…' said Allie trying to be non-committal.

'So I am right, well in the right part of the ball park anyway. '

'But we need to link it all together. That's why I'm here, wasting my bloody time if you ask me.'

11

Tremayne and Helen Machin sat at the bar of The Royal Oak waiting for Denzel la Croix, or Denny to his friends, to finish serving a young couple.

'Mr Tremayne, what can I get you and your friend?' Denny asked.

'I'll have a glass of Fitou…Helen?'

'Same.'

'This by the way is Detective Sergeant Machin.'

'No kidding…hi, how ya doin' Denny poured their drinks. Tremayne shot a few questions at him as he did so.

'You told one of my officers that Mickey Edwards used to drink in here?'

'Yeah man, that's right an' I also told him that he hadn't been in here for quite some time. He asked me if Mickey was carryin' like money, know wha' I mean? I told him I didn't recall him showin' off with loads of dosh.'

'And of course you'd remember if he was. A guy like Mickey, bit fly, with a lot of cash, you'd surely remember.'

'Yep, just as I said, he wasn't flashin' cash about. No buyin' doubles or cognacs or buying rounds. Nah, I don't think he had a lot of cash on him.'

'Okay Denny thanks. Oh by the way do you know a character called Jockie Jackson? He might have been in here with Mickey.'

'Jockie Jackson…Jockie…Jockie, yeah, if he's the guy I'm thinkin' of. Came in here quite a bit with Mickey, not what you'd call regular, but often enough. Is this guy smallish, thin; slightly built; pointy features, weasely lookin'?'

'Yeah that's him. Was he in here with Mickey the last time you saw him.'

'Yeah I think he was. I'm sure they were sittin' over there in the window. They were deep in conversation; you'd have thought they were plannin' somethin' big, the way they were goin' on, almost head to head, gesticulatin' with their hands. Yeah, they were really goin' some.'

'Why didn't you say this before?'

'Hey now listen man, you only reminded me when you mentioned this Jockie guy just now. I see a lot of…'

'Okay Denny, forget it. Do you know where he drinks other than in here?'

'No sorry, and he only came in here with Mickey.'

'Right Denny thanks. You've got customers I see, I'll see you again, nice wine by the way.'

Tremayne and Helen chatted as they finished their drinks.

'What do you make of that then boss?'

'Oh, he's probably right. Denny has no axe to grind; he's straight as a die; reliable too.'

'But if we don't know where this Jockie guy is…'

'Ah well there you go Helen…no one said we don't know where he is.'

'You do know where to find him?'

'Oh yes, I know where he is all right.'

'Well come on we might be chasing around a bit?'

''No we don't need to rush. Fancy another glass of this fine Fitou?'

'Yeah…and are you going to tell me where he is?'

'Oh, yes he's in Walton gaol…six months for burglary.'

'Oh nice one, then I will have another glass. Oh Denny, when you're ready, two more glasses of Fitou please.'

'When we've finished these I think we'll pay Tony Franklin a visit. I have a feeling he knows more than he's letting on about our corpse.'

'Good trip?' Nick Chandler asked Allie as she walked in to the incident room on her return from London. 'Shopping good was it?' he said with a broad grin on his face.

'Very funny I'm sure, but not a bad trip. I'm not really sure we're all that far along with finding relatives of Simon Carter. Although I did discover that he was born in Crosby, so I'm off to the town hall to check out the electoral rolls. I'm hoping that his family, well some of them, still live in the area.

Allie telephoned the records office, telling them that this was a murder enquiry and what she wanted. That she'd like to check through the electoral rolls, to see birth certificates and any records with reference to Simon Peter Robin Carter, late of the Royal Navy.

An hour later, Allie announced herself to the receptionist at the records office of the town hall. She followed her to the registrar's office, knocked on the glass-fronted door that had the name C. B. Wilkes. Senior Registrar, written across the frosted glass panel in bold black letters. A voice answered *'come in'* Allie was greeted by a woman of about forty, smartly dressed in a grey tailored skirt, with a white blouse and a light blue silk scarf which was fastened loosely around her neck. As she rose to greet Allie, her jacket, which was over the back of the chair fell to the floor, *'oops'* she said as she stooped to pick it up.

'Sorry...I'm Carol Wilkes, senior registrar, you must be Detective Constable Stewart?' She said extending her hand in greeting; Allie reached out and shook it.

'Yes Allie Stewart, Good morning, pleased to meet you. I'm here about Simon Carter.'

'Yes, of course, please have a seat. Joanne is bringing the files through in a minute. May I ask...what interest you have in Mr Carter? I glanced at his death certificate; he died during the war didn't he?'

'Yes that's right. He was in fact the victim of a murder and his name has been linked with a more recent case, which is puzzling. And that's the reason I'm doing a bit of research about him. What I'm trying to find out is if there are any relatives still living in the area.'

A knock on the door stopped their conversation and Joanne, a young girl of about twenty entered the office carrying a buff-coloured document folder. Mrs Wilkes thanked her, Joanne left. Carol Wilkes opened the folder and took out a thin sheaf of papers.

'Well, here's his birth certificate, it confirms his birth place as Crosby, in the district maternity hospital; his death certificate...oh yes, sounds nasty, beaten to death.' Carol Wilkes said, Allie noticed the visible shudder at the thought. 'There's also a marriage certificate too...'

'Oh good; I only found out recently that he was married, does that say who to and when they got married'

'Yes, it was in nineteen thirty two; her name was Elizabeth Lindsey Fitton...'

'Is there anyway of finding out whether she's still living?'

'Yes, if she remained in the region.' Mrs Wilkes picked up the phone and asked Joanne to search for Elizabeth Lindsey Carter nee Fitton.' It wasn't very long before there was a light knock on the door that announced Joanne's arrival.

'Here she is; but I'm afraid she was killed during Liverpool's blitz.' Mrs Wilkes thanked her and she left.

'Well that solves that then.' Allie said, feeling that yet another door had shut in her face. 'So, where do I go now?' she said half thinking herself and half asking Carol Wilkes for her help. 'Would you have records of any children of their marriage?'

'We will, but it would take time for us to search. The best thing I can suggest, and it might be quicker, is for you to go through the Crosby electoral rolls and births, marriages and deaths archive and then follow it through. I know it'll be a slog, but there can't be many Carters around at that time who called their son Simon Peter Robin.' Allie's heart sank at the thought of going through archive material again. *I hope this is all worth the trouble, back and forth to London, now here, if anyone mentions archive to me again I'll scream.*

Allie thanked Carol Wilkes and walked to the office where the archive she needed was kept. She sat herself down in front of yet another microfiche machine and searched through the electoral rolls. A couple of hours later she exited the town hall feeling very pleased with herself; She punched the air with pleasure – *got them YESSS., GOT THEM.* The afternoon had drawn on; she checked her watch and made her way round to the Golden Lion.

'You're looking very pleased with yourself.' Steve the Golden Lion's barman said to her, as he poured her a glass of Chardonnay.

'Too right, I've had a good result today. D'ya know I was down in London yesterday, then back up here, and I've just been sat in the bloody town hall going through thousands of records, but it came good. I'm telling you, it was doin' my 'ead in, but now I'm going to enjoy this and most likely a couple more besides. Yeah, I am feeling pleased with myself. She took a big gulp from her wine glass and looked around the room. She saw Tremayne sitting with the rest of the team in their usual spot. She drained the glass, got a fill up and made her way over to them and sat down, still with a big grin on her face.

'Well,' quipped Helen, laughing 'cat got the cream or what?'

'Well yes, I have got the cream actually; I've had a good result. I've found a relative of Simon Carter.'

'That's brilliant, who…where?'

'His brother, he lives in a nursing home, he's ninety six though, but still with us. His name is Charles Patrick; he's in the Avon Nursing home in Formby. I've given them a ring, the matron said he's got all his marbles and I've arranged to go and have a talk to him tomorrow.'

'Good work Allie, good work.' Tremayne said, sounding very delighted. 'Any luck with Mason, the bank manager chappy?'

'I'm not sure. Frankie Bolton was still digging into his background when we last spoke. We went down to London together; she may have something by now. She said she'd give you a call when she had something positive.'

'Right, we'll just have to be patient then. Clive how about another round?' Clive jumped up and ordered another round of drinks. Tremayne settled back into his seat, looking pensive; a far-away look in his eye. His brow furrowed, he seemed to be counting on his fingers, holding his hand open and moving each finger in turn as though counting off something. Suddenly he snapped out of his trance at the sound of a soft French accent. 'Rufus, are you with us?' He shot upright and smiled at Sophie, who was making her way to sit next to him as everyone shuffled about in a sort of musical chairs.

'How has your day been?' She asked.

'All right I suppose, but Allie here has had a good day. She's found a relative of Simon Carter, his brother. He's alive and well and living in a nursing home in Formby. She's off to see him tomorrow.'

'Well done Allie, you must be pleased?'

'Don't say that, she'll become even more insufferable, she'll be expecting promotion next.' Tremayne said grinning all over his face.

'Just ignore him Allie, go on you were saying, before we were rudely interrupted.' Sophie said nudging Rufus in the ribs with her elbow.

'Yes, it was a good result, it took time and a trip to London, but I got there in the end.'
'How's it going at your end Sophie?' aske Tremayne.

'I've been going through Mickey Edward's post mortem report and I've been looking at the samples taken from him at the time. I thought they might reveal something.'

'Like what?' Tremayne said suddenly sitting upright and jumping into the conversation.

'No idea, as yet. But if you think about it, someone seems to have gone to a lot of trouble over this killing. There were rope burns on his wrists, so he was tied up to something, a chair maybe, judging from the position of the marks on him, on the top of his wrists. There were minute pieces of gravel embedded around the toes of his shoes. At some point he was dragged somewhere, to a vehicle perhaps, across a road or paved area because the toes and sides of his shoes showed deep scratch marks, all in the same direction. The drag marks may have been before and/or after death. Most likely it was a road surface he was dragged across, because there were traces of bitumen on the stone or it may have been a car park. I would hasten to add that I think it was a side road because the main roads don't use that kind of surface with loose gravel. On main roads they used hot –rolled asphalt…no loose gravel. But what intrigued me most was…that under his finger nails, which were well manicured for a man of his type, I found some particles. So, I'm working on them. It might show us where he was killed. Would that be of use to you, by any chance?'

'Yes, it would.' Tremayne said enthusiastically. Clive arrived with the tray of drinks. 'I got you a Kir Sophie.'

'Oh very nice Clive, thank you.'

'Anything else to reveal from your little investigation, per chance?'

'Possibly, but I'll let you know in due course, tomorrow…maybe.' Sophie said, taking a sip from her Kir.

Allie pulled off the road and drove up a long tree-lined driveway to a large Victorian villa, now the Avon nursing home. Manicured gardens and lawns made the nursing home look quite palatial. Allie parked in one of the designated visitors spaces. At the door she pressed the buzzer; a voice on the intercom asked her business. The door lock clicked and Allie pushed the door and announced herself to the receptionist.

'I'll ring for Mrs O'Connell, please take a seat. I'm sure she won't be long.'

Allie checked her watch after she'd been sitting for a while; twenty to eleven. Then she heard hurrying footsteps on the parquet floor, and an out of breath voice saying, 'I'm sorry to have kept you constable, it is Constable Stewart? Bit of an emergency. If you'll follow me I'll take you to see Mr Carter, he's quite looking forward to seeing you. Oh, may I ask you your first name? They like to call people by their proper names.'

'Yes of course, it's Alison, but people call me Allie.'

Allie was shown into a largish room over-looking the gardens. People where sitting at tables playing games in groups or just chatting, or just sitting quietly reading newspapers or books. Mrs O'Connell led the way across the room, to where a man was sitting in a large easy chair, he was reading a newspaper, the Telegraph Allie noticed. He looked up as they approached. Charles this is Alison Stewart, she'd like to have a chat with you about your brother.' Charles Carter folded and put down his paper on the low table in front of him before rising, holding out his hand, Allie shook it saying good morning to the old gentleman.

'I'll leave you two alone then. See you later Alison.' The matron smiled and went off to speak to another resident who had waved to her.

'Would you like some coffee, Alison?' Charles got up and went off to a sideboard where he poured himself and Allie a coffee each. 'I've got some biscuits too.' He said as he arrived back to where Allie had settled herself into a big easy chair next to where Charles Carter had been sitting. 'Hope you like these, I'm afraid all the choccies have been snaffled, you've got to be quick round here.' He said laughing.

'Yes of course, I'm sure they're very nice.'

'Very nice, bit ordinary you mean.' He said, a wicked look in his eye. 'So Alison…'

'Please, my friends call me Allie.'

'Very well…Allie. What is it that you wish to talk to me about?'

'If you don't mind I'd like to ask you about your brother Simon.'

'Simon, well you are digging in the distant past aren't you. You know he was murdered?'

'Yes I know. I'm a police officer actually.'

'Umm, I thought as much. I used to be one too, a long time ago now. I retired in nineteen seventy four, then I worked doing odd jobs just to keep me active you know, bits of gardening. I used to volunteer for the National Trust at the nature reserve near here; they had a lot of red squirrels, cute little blighters. They even took nuts from your fingers, if you remained still and quiet. I enjoyed that.'

'How long have you been here?'

'Oh, just over five years now; I came here after my wife died, my lads thought it best. I'm not brilliant at cooking, and I like the company here, we have some fun and games.' Allie said something complimentary, but then moved onto the subject of her visit.

'So, what can you tell me about your brother Simon?'

'Simon…well. He was a bit of a jack-the-lad really, never quite conformed. How he ever got to become a Petty Officer, I'll never know. The navy must have been good for him, knocked some sense into him I should think. Good discipline. That was the place he first had to adhere to some.'

'Do you have any theories about his death?'

'Ah, the old brain box doesn't work as it once did, young Allie. I seem to remember though, he had come home, said he had a few days

121

leave and I was there for some reason, to see mum I suppose. He said he'd been on a secret mission to Norway or somewhere. I seem to remember him saying something about how he'd be all right after the war. I didn't know what he really meant by it, never gave it much thought actually. I assumed that he meant he'd get a good job being a Chief Petty Officer by then and all that. I thought perhaps he was thinking of staying in the navy. We thought he liked the life at sea, and he had only recently been promoted, Chief Petty Officer, I ask you, huh!'

'So did you not think he really was suited to naval life?'

'Well…you had to know our Simon; he was always a funny sort of lad. As a child he'd be off on his own, never really made friends, although he had a couple, but not what I'd call real mates, if you know what I mean.'

'Would you say he was capable of…'

'What criminal activities?'

'Well, I wasn't thinking that exactly, but what do you think?'

'Don't forget I was a copper. Giving it a little thought now though, yes I'd say it was likely. As far as I know he was never in trouble with the police. But, then maybe he was never caught.'

The lunchtime show at the *Wild Orchid* had been going for half an hour or so when Tremayne and Helen walked into the club. There were about a dozen or so workmen in having a liquid lunch. The music as usual was loud and blasted the ear drums, with the base level enough to make the whole building vibrate. Tremayne was about to say so, but thought better of it. He would have had to use a megaphone he thought. One of Tony's henchmen stood by the door to Tony's office.

'You're new?' Tremayne said to him politely. 'Are you going to open the door for us then?' The man glared at the two officers.

'Mr Franklin is busy.'

'I'm not interested whether he's busy or not – open the door or I'll nick you for whatever my fertile imagination can come up with.' Tremayne said calmly. The man's face remained unmoved, expressionless. But after a short while he turned the door knob and held the door open. Tremayne and Helen barged him with their elbows as they passed him.

'New man Tony?'

'What an unexpected pleasure Mr Tremayne and Miss Machin as well what an honour. Yes he is new; I hope he wasn't…er, rude in any way?'

'No, he just needs to learn who's who.'

'Certainly Mr Tremayne, I'll have a word with him later. Now what brings you to my establishment? I do seem to be attracting the constabulary quite a lot just lately, my new girls perhaps?'

'Mickey Edwards. And you know what bothers me Tony? It's why do I get the feeling that you know more than you're letting on?' Tremayne's eyebrow raised in a questioning manner, his eyes bore deep into Tony Franklin, demanding an answer.

'You've asked me about Mickey before, Mr Tremayne and I told you then, that he did the odd little job for me, errands, running the girls home, restocking the bar, that's all.'

'Yes I know, I remember. But it's the other little jobs that interest me Tony.'

'Other jobs? I'm sure I don't know what you mean Mr Tremayne. What on earth are you insinuating?' Just then Trendy brought in a tray of drinks. 'Now Mr Tremayne I know you like a drop of good…Vin. This is a wine I think you'll like Mr Tremayne, I understand you are a bit of a connoisseur. This is one of my particular favourites; Bordeaux, Château Margot.' Trendy placed the glasses in front of each of them, he poured the wine and left. Helen glanced at Tremayne, gauging the situation and doing as he did. He did not pick up the glass. Tony Franklin did. He made an elaborate play on taking in a deep breath through his nose to appreciate the bouquet, then swirling the wine around the glass, holding it up to the light and looking at the colour, before taking a sip and slurping in air loudly before swallowing. 'You really ought to try this, it's excellent.'

Tremayne rose to his feet, Helen followed suit. 'I know what business you are in Tony, and it's not just clubs. If I find out you're keeping something from me…well, we'll leave it at that…for now. I'm just not in the mood for fine wines just now Tony, another time perhaps.' The two officers walked out of Franklin's office. 'And who might you be?' Tremayne said to the big man standing outside Franklin's office.

'Donald Jenkins.' Was his surly reply.

'Donald Jenkins eh! How long have you worked for Tony Franklin?'

'Just a few weeks.'

123

Tremayne stared, eye to eye, then turned and walked away without another word. Sitting in the Alfa Tremayne quietly fumed, 'That bastard knows something. But time will tell. You know Helen he deals with fine antiques, that furniture in his office; it's not reproduction; and the bottles of fine claret. The art squad have been watching him for months, years perhaps. Give them a call and see what they can tell you. Tell them we're investigating a murder to which we think he's linked. If you meet them half way you never know what may come of it. Oh and check out that Jenkins fellow too, he's probably got form I shouldn't doubt. '

Tremayne arrived back at his desk still fuming about Tony Franklin. Almost before he'd opened his office door the phone was ringing. He glared at it, swore at it and took a couple of deep breaths before picking it up. It was Frankie Bolton.

'Nice to hear from you Frankie; I do hope you've got some good news, for I certainly could do with some.'

'Yes I think so. Is it convenient to call round, say in half an hour?'

'Yeah sure, see you soon.'

Tremayne called Helen and Allie in. 'Frankie Bolton's on her way, you might like to join us when she gets here; about half an hour.'

Helen got on the phone to the stolen arts recovery squad. She thought it a long shot but it was worth a call.

'DS Turner,' the cheery, male voice answered. 'How may I help you?'

'Hi, I'm DS Machin, Merseyside CID. I hope you can help me, we are currently investigating a murder and during a search we've come across some fine pieces of jewellery. Is that in your line?'

'Yeah sure, if it's old, antique, worth something and can be called art then yes I'm interested.'

'Tell me; what do you know about artefacts stolen by the Nazis during the Second World War.

'Now you're getting into a minefield. Museums, art galleries and private collections all had artefacts missing; and all of a sudden they were said to have been stolen by the Nazis. You see, after the war stuff turned up in all sorts of places. The private stuff was principally from Jewish families. Most of course, perished in the holocaust. But there are survivors, as you're more than aware, relatives, distant in some cases, but relatives nonetheless. Then they all made claims for their return of these items. Hundreds of claims began to be put forward. Some of the stuff was in museums and they were reluctant, to say the least, to hand them back. They wanted absolute proof, which is understandable really. So what is it that you have, a forgotten Rembrandt, a Dűrer perhaps?'

'No not paintings, jewellery, Fabergé and others.'

'Expensive I take it' Alan Turner said excitedly. '…but jewellery, that's not my field. I'll put you over to my colleague, Nicola Biancci, she's our jewellery expert. Hang on a sec'.'

Helen could hear Alan Turner call across his office, even though his hand was across the mouthpiece of the phone. A female, Italian accented voice answered.

'Allo, Nicola Biancci, Alan tells me you 'ave some jewellery?' she said with her attractive Italian accent.

'Yes that's right; I'm Helen Machin, by the way. We're in the middle of a murder enquiry and yes we have some jewellery that we think was stolen. We had an independent jeweller look at it and we were told that judging from the hallmarks it came from somewhere in Europe probably during the Second World War. I was hoping that you might be able to throw some light on the subject?'

There was a minute's silence, 'Well I can take a look at what you 'ave. I'll take some photos and compare them with what we 'ave on file. But I cannot guarantee anything. If no one has made a claim and they don't 'ave pictures or provenance then I'm afraid all you've got is a hoard of stolen jewellery. It could be put up for sale or placed in the care of the V&A for instance.'

'Right Nicola, that's the best I'd hoped for. When can you come over?'

Arrangements were made with Nicola to come to the station along with her file. As Helen finished her call, Frankie Bolton arrived. After the usual greetings Frankie told them what she had found out. Tremayne listened expectantly.

'This is all a shot in the dark.' She began 'Richard Mason is as elusive as the proverbial spirit. Helen told me that after speaking with Graham Wilson, who was a young trainee at the time. He couldn't say that Mason was not English. But, he's thinking about it and trying to…hopefully give us contact with someone else, which is why I say it's a shot in the dark. Anyway to be honest, after all this time the chances are slim. I've been through immigration records and that also led me up a blind alley.'

'So what you're saying is,' Tremayne interrupted 'that we may never discover who the hell he was, and he'll remain unidentified forever, under the pseudonym Richard Mason, English gentleman and bank manager?'

'Not entirely,' Frankie said, making the assembled officers take a combined intake of breath in surprise. Tremayne looked at Frankie with a questioning stare.

'So…have you discovered who he is?'

'Not exactly…not yet anyway. I've been working on the premise that he was not English, yeah?' She waited a second for them to nod an agreement. 'So this case revolves round the war or it starts during the war with that mission to Norway and Simon Carter…yeah?' Again she paused, again the nods of agreement. 'Well what if he was German?' Frankie watched the amazed looks cross the faces of the assembled officers. The whole room gasped, and the united buzz broke out - *German, German*…

'Okay, enough, let Frankie finish' Tremayne said calling for silence, but he threw in a question all the same. 'What are you getting at Frankie? That Mason was living in England…to do what exactly?'

'I could say he was a spy. But considering that the authorities at that time had an excellent record of catching German spies, and none of those who got here, really succeeded. No, Mason…I don't think he was an active spy. So I'm not sure what he was to be honest. Maybe he was a sleeper as they say in all good Len Deighton books. Maybe he was waiting for instructions? And all the time he was busying himself working in a bank. So I got onto the internet and keyed in his name and told it to find the nearest German equivalent to the name Mason. It gave me the name Maurer, which, as it happens, is German for a mason. Richard is the same in both languages, but Gilbert could be the same or he anglicized it from…to be honest I've no idea.'

'This sounds like an excellent piece of detective work Frankie. Is that as far as you've got?'

'Not quite. Taking my new-found info I went back to immigration records. This time I searched for Richard G. Maurer…there are fifteen records and so now the foot slogging begins.'

'Do you need any help getting into the German records?'

'I'll let you know. Well that's all I've got for now. So I'll leave you all to it. Bye for now.' Frankie left the police station to continue her search for Richard Gilbert Mason or was it now Richard Maurer?

'Okay' Tremayne said letting the word slide out as a long syllable '…so where does that leave us?' He continued, but he was met with a sea of blank faces.

'Well…' ventured Allie 'If this guy Mason or Maurer or whatever his name is. Why was he murdered and his body buried in the same place as Carter and Mickey Edwards?'

'Good question.' Tremayne replied. 'All comments would be gratefully received.'

Allie continued with her theory. 'Had he something to do with these jewels? Now…was he supposed to receive them from Carter...no, he didn't know Carter. Carter pinched them from whoever hid them in Norway. Should Mason have received them by some other route, I wonder? He could have kept them in the bank vault until needed. When they went missing from that house in Norway that would have set alarm bells ringing and begun a chain of events began that led to Carters death.'

Everyone was looking at Allie in silence. Tremayne leaned back in his chair staring at the ceiling in deep thought; after a while he sat upright again. 'Well Allie, that's either a fantastic piece of deduction, worthy of Sherlock Holmes or you have a very fertile imagination. But, nevertheless, I must say it does sound like an excellent piece of deduction to me. Work on it.'

12

Sophie Bouvier sat at the table in her lab; she peered down through the lens of her microscope. On the stage was a sample taken from beneath the finger nails of Mickey Edwards. Sitting next to the microscope in a small vial of ethyl alcohol was another sample also taken from beneath Mickey's finger nails. With these two samples Sophie was hoping they might lead her to the place or places where Mickey was held shortly before his death and to the place where he was killed.

She was asking herself, *what am I looking at here?* She sat upright on her stool and stared at the microscope. Sophie was thinking out loud, which she thought quiet normal in her isolated world. '*It looks like stone, or gravel, concrete maybe?*' After some minutes she went back to the microscope, peering intently down through the lens. *What the hell are you?* She sat upright again and began tapping her fingers on the bench, repeating out loud; *Concrete umm? Stone, no, no. Concrete, concrete, no, no…*' She stared out of the window at the buildings across the road from her laboratory. After a few minutes she suddenly put her hands to her head and screamed. *Of course yes…it's brick dust…yes, a particle of red brick. So has this come from a building site or a demolition site possibly?* She sat upright again and jotted in block capitals the words…RED BRICK DUST – BUT FROM WHERE? into her notepad and on a label which she stuck on the vial. *Yes where have you come from? There must be dozens of demolition sites around here, but since his death they'll be gone, new buildings on the sites. That's a non-starter.*

She took the brick sample off the microscope stage and replaced it with the sample from the vial. At first glance she said '*Ah, a seed, but from what? A raspberry seed was he picking his teeth just before he died, probably not? I'm going to need expert advice with this, so… botanists, who do we know?* ' Sophie replaced the seed into its vial and left her work bench, and walked into her office. She checked through her directory of specialists. She picked up her phone and dialled a number, it was answered after three rings.

'David, Bonjour, Sophie Bouvier.'

'Hello Sophie, how are you?'

'I'm fine thank you. I'd like you to take a look at something for me if you could.'

'Yes sure, what is it?'

'A seed.'

'A seed, what kind of seed, from where?'

'Well, that's why I'm calling you. I'm no botanist. Shall I bring it to you or…'

'If you could bring it over, I've got the references here, so that would be best.'

Sophie made her arrangements to meet Professor David Jenkins, a friend and research palaeobotanist. She put the single seed in its vial of alcohol into her handbag and she set off for the Department of Botany in the university. Before she did though, she replaced the brick sample under the microscope and took another look at it. She thought she could see something else; but it was too small for her to determine on the conventional microscope. She carefully placed that sample back into its vial, and she set off with both of them.

Tremayne called from his office. Martin and Clive jumped from their seats and hurried in. 'I want Tony Franklin watched' he began. '…and I want Malcolm 'Trendy' Smith watched as well. You two can take it turn and turn about. I want to know where they go, who they see, even what they have for breakfast, loose them and you're dead. Keep a close eye on Trendy. He may be the better bet on turning up something nasty. He'll be the one Franklin sends out on messages. He'll be thinking that no one would take any notice of old Trendy, but be careful, he's as slippery as an eel. He's not half as daft as he looks. He might dress like a tailor's dummy and behave a bit camp, but he can be vicious if he has a mind to be.'

'Right boss.' They both replied in unison. 'We'll be careful.'

'Good, I'm glad to hear it. Right get yourselves organised, oh and buy yourselves a flask; the coffee'll keep you awake.' He said with a grin across his face. 'You can make a start right now.' Tremayne was still laughing as they left the office. 'Keep in touch lads. And if you think you need to be in two places at once, call for backup. Is that clear?'

'Yes boss.' They said, again in unison. Forty minutes later they were parked up watching the front door of the *Wild Orchid* club. They hadn't been there long when Martin asked.

'Are there any back doors to this place Clive?'

'No idea, but I suppose we'd better take a look. You stay here and I'll go and nosey about'

Martin found his way round the back of the *Wild Orchid* club. A steel-barred gate secured the yard; it was not locked, although a chain and padlock hung from the large bolt. Martin did not enter the yard, he pushed the gate open a little, just enough to look inside. He was looking for security cameras and for any of Franklin's men lurking at the back door. He noticed a dark red Jaguar XJ6 parked close to the door, he assumed it was Tony Franklin's. He made a note of the registration number. He pulled the gate to and walked along the narrow back street that ran along behind the buildings. All was quiet. More or less opposite the club's gate was a vacant plot, where once stood a building, now the site was used as an *ad hoc* car park. Martin walked back and rejoined Clive.

'It's all quiet round the back.' he said climbing into the passenger seat. 'There is a back entrance and with Franklin's Jag parked up in the yard. It might be a good idea if we had another car so we could watch both ends. I took a note of the car's number.' Clive made a note of it. 'Just check with DVLA, but I think it'll be legit'' Clive checked the database and the Jaguar was registered to Franklin.

'A second car sounds a good idea. Shall we rope someone else in on this party?'

'Contact the boss and ask.' An hour later another vehicle pulled up behind them and Allie knocked on the passenger's window. 'I've brought a van, I'm not staying,' she said, as Martin wound the window down, sounding quite pleased at not having to sit on surveillance for hours on end. 'I might relieve you later. I'm making my own way back to the station. See you later boys – have fun.' She said laughing as she walked off down the street.

'Very FUNNY.' Martin shouted, but she either didn't hear or simply ignored them, probably still laughing. No one liked surveillance work.

Martin and Clive sat, each in his own vehicle, their radios tuned in to each other's so they could keep up a steady chat as they watched. As was usual on these jobs, nothing happened. A light rain began to fall. Martin was sipping the coffee he'd just poured from his thermos, it was just going dark and he noticed a light come on in the yard of the *Wild Orchid* club. He sat up and paid attention, but no one came through the gate. He thought it was just security lights coming on anyway. After a few minutes the gates opened. He downed his coffee and spoke into his radio. 'Someone's coming out. They're coming this way. I think it might be

Trendy, hold on.' There was a long pause. 'Yes it's him all right. He's on foot. I'm going after him.'

'All right,' replied Clive 'keep in touch.'

Martin got out of the van after Trendy had passed. He closed the door quietly and locked it. Then set off after him, keeping a good distance behind. He wasn't sure whether Trendy was aware of him or not, or whether he would check to see if he was being followed. Martin thought he hadn't noticed him. The streets were quiet so Martin's job was not easy. He was aware of the fact that he could easily be spotted should Trendy turn round and see him dodge into a shop doorway or act as though he's talking on his mobile or several other things one could do just to look innocent.

Martin had been following him for a mile or so. Trendy entered an office building. Martin got to the building. There was a polished brass sign on the wall adjacent to the door which read – *Franklin Investments.* Martin called Clive on his mobile.

'Clive, Trendy's come to an office Franklin Investments. I think it must be Franklin's housing business?'

'Yeah, most likely, I'll get someone to check it out. It's probably quite legit.'

'Yeah probably. Wait, he's coming out again, speak to you later.'

Martin continued his tailing of Trendy. He didn't return to the club. Martin followed him for another ten minutes. Eventually Trendy went into a pub. *Not the sort of place I would expect to find you in.* Martin thought. The place was more than a bit run down; the outside with its peeling paintwork and two boarded up windows. The inside was as Martin suspected, smelled of stale beer, the carpets shiny, dirty and worn by the many boots that had traipsed in and out. He poked his head round the door, he stood just inside and pretended to check texts on his phone, he surveyed the room as unobtrusively as he could. A huge flat screen TV hung from the wall in one corner. It was tuned into Sky Sport; but no one was watching it. It played silently, showing European cycling which obviously no one was interested in. Martin glanced around the room, there were half a dozen men; the great unwashed, the unemployed and the unemployable stood along the bar chatting to each other. Then he saw Trendy standing well away from the other men. He was talking to a big thick-set man who looked as aggressive as the Staffordshire bull terrier sitting quietly by his feet. The man held a thick plaited-leather lead in one hand and a pint of strong lager in the other. He was listening intently to

Trendy. Martin didn't recognise the man. He held his mobile to his ear as if making a call then quickly took a couple of photos of the two men. He then turned and left. He walked across the road from where he watched for Trendy to come out again. He didn't have to wait long. Trendy came out, and glanced at his watch. Martin followed as he walked away from the pub. The road they walked along soon joined a main road, where after a minute Trendy hailed a taxi, and jumped in, so ending Martin's surveillance. Martin phoned Clive to tell him Trendy had jumped into a taxi and was most likely heading back to the club. Martin told him he'd jump a taxi and back to him. Trendy's taxi pulled up at the club's front door, so Clive did not know of his return.

Clive had decided to move to the rear of the club. He thought that he'd have better chance of seeing Franklin leave via the rear entrance. His idea had paid off. He'd been sitting for half an hour when the gates swung open and the Jaguar pulled out and drove towards the main road. Clive followed. He called in to report that Franklin was moving and that Martin had been following Trendy until he'd jumped into a taxi. 'I think he's in the Jag with Franklin.' Allie said she knew. 'Martin has just sent me a text and a photo of Trendy and another man. We're running him through the database.' She said.

'Good, let me know who he is. It might be a good idea to tail him too. Then you too could join in the fun and games.'

'You're all heart, you know that Clive.'

Allie called Martin, telling him that Clive was tailing Franklin. 'He thinks Trendy is with Franklin.'

'Okay, I'll head back to the club and wait there. Call me if you need me.' Martin said.

'I've got an ID on the guy in the pub.'

'That didn't take long, do we know him?'

'Oh yeah, we know him all right. His name is Reginald Vincent Riley. He's on record for grievous and actual bodily harm, resisting arrest, causing an affray, shall I go on? He was arrested once for taking part in illegal fights, cage fighting stuff you know. Involved in dog fighting too.'

'Pleasant sort of chap then.'

'The boss said to forget the club and you're to go to the pub, see if Riley's still in there and follow him. But whatever you do don't let him see you and don't get involved with him.'

'Okay I'm on my way.'

'The pub by the way is called the Cherry Tree it's on Patterson Street.'

'I'll be there in five minutes, I hope our man's still in there.'

'Okay Martin, if he's not there, let me know.'

Clive called in as he was following Franklin. He gave the route he had been following. Tremayne was listening and said to Clive that he was most likely on his way home.

'He lives in one of those fancy warehouse conversions down by the old Sandon dock, over-looking the river. So if you end up passing the pier head then that's where he's going. But keep us informed Clive.'

'Okay boss will do.'

Just as Tremayne had said, Clive drove past the pier head with the Cunard and the Liver buildings standing dominating the river front. Clive followed Franklin along Great Howard Street. But he did not stop at the converted warehouse apartment building. He drove past and continued along the lower docks road. Eventually turning up onto the upper docks road and headed out of the city towards Waterloo and Crosby. Eventually he turned and headed towards Hightown, a suburb of Crosby, between there and Formby. Clive's mind was in overdrive.

'*Where the hell are you going Franklin?*' He said to himself. Clive followed him along a normal residential road that ran into farmland. They passed the last house in the road and continued for about half a mile. He eventually pulled off the road and into a disused builder's yard. Clive stopped just past the gateway but by the time he'd parked up and got out of his car, the gates had been closed. Clive walked quickly to the gates, but saw no one in the yard. He looked around. The place had not seen any building work done from there for some time. He could see an old rusting van laid up. Its tyres were flat, its doors hanging off and side bashed in. The windows smashed and the seats ripped out. It looked like it'd been the victim of a terrorist attack, but most likely was the victim of the local kids. There were piles of old bricks, no doubt the kids' ammunition for the raid on the van. An old rubbish skip blackened by fire stood testament, he thought, to other deeds of the local kids.
He called in to report where he was.

Tremayne told him to stay put and watch. 'I want to know who else is in there Clive, so be ready to snap off a few pics as they come out. But under no circumstances are you to go in – understand.'
Tremayne called Martin and told him to give up on Riley, and told him to get back to the station.

An hour later Clive walked into the office. 'I've got a few snaps,' he said and began to download them onto his computer. After a few minutes the team were pouring over the faces on the screen.

'So, who've we got then?' Tremayne said. '...well that's Franklin, obviously and Trendy in the jag.'

'Now, that's the guy from the pub, the one Trendy met up with, Reggie Riley.'

'Yeah, he means trouble, a right wicked bastard. If Franklin is employing him, I'd hate to be on the receiving end.' said Helen.

'Do you know him then?' said Allie.

'Unfortunately yes, and you'd need a battalion to subdue him too. The best thing to do would be to shoot the bastard on sight without a second thought.'

'Alright, let's concentrate here.' Tremayne said strongly, getting the team back on line. 'I want to know what they are using that yard for.' He tapped his fingers on the table. After a minute he continued. 'I think we might just go and take a closer look.'

'We'd need a warrant boss.' Helen said.

'For what reason? We've had a report of vandals in the yard giving the local residents earache with all their noise. You heard what Clive said about the van and the skip. A fire could spread to local houses and we don't want that do we?'

'A report?' Allie said surprised. Tremayne looked and smiled at her, before the penny dropped.

'Right then let's go and just take a look round.' The team followed Tremayne out of the office. Thirty minutes later five officers were standing, looking through the rusted iron barred gate. It was secured with a padlock and chain. 'Have a look round, see if there's a gap in the fence.' Tremayne said nonchalantly. Clive called to them, that he'd found the netting down. 'This seems to be where the kids get in.' He said as they walked up to where he stood. Allie looked towards the nearest house to see if the resident was watching over their fences to see what was going on, but all was quiet. They walked across the yard and into the building. They entered into a large room, a workshop. Boxes and old crates were stacked against the walls, cobwebs hung from everywhere. Footprints were visible in the dust on the floor. To the rear of the workshop were two rooms, one had been used as an office at one time, the other a mess room, on one wall hung an old calendar, and several yellowing copies of the Sun's page-3 girls. In the office was a table set down in the centre of the room, a chair had been place to each side of it. Two filing cabinets stood with their drawers open, great dents in the sides showing the efforts of kids testing their kick boxing skills against the defenceless steel cabinets. The expert eyes of Tremayne and Helen Machin scanned the room, its floor and walls.

Helen scrutinised the table and chairs, bending closely, her hands behind her back, careful not to touch anything. 'I think there's something here boss.' Tremayne looked to where Helen pointed. He thought quickly.

'Right Helen, call forensics get everyone outside.' She nodded a yes pulling her phone out of her pocket, and organising the scientific teams. 'I'll sort the paperwork. I'll speak with the Super; this has to be right Helen.' Tremayne said, his mind working fast. He knew they had no cause to be there; he needed a warrant and a good reason. 'I'll see you later,' He said heading for his car. 'When we've got this place organised, we'll go and have another chat with Tony Franklin. Martin, see if you can find out who owns this place. It's likely to be Franklin's, just check it out. Have a word with the local residents see what they know, if they ask questions tell them we're looking for stolen goods. Get uniformed here, they can help with talking to the locals and one can keep nosey neighbours away'

'Okay boss.'

Tremayne managed to persuade Chief Superintendent Pearsall as to the importance of the builder's yard. It wasn't long before several white-suited people began moving their equipment into the old workshop, to begin their painstaking work. Helen greeted Barry James, one of the forensic team, whom she'd got to know from previous jobs.

Helen followed them into the workshop and watched as they carefully moved round the building.

'The boss wants particular attention paid to that office Barry.' She said pointing to the room with the table and chairs. 'I think there are traces of blood in there, on the table, the chair and probably the floor too.'

'Right you are Helen, leave it with me.' Helen walked outside and phoned Tremayne, just to keep him up to date. She paced up and down outside in the yard waiting impatiently for forensics to find something and to give her the news. *Was this grubby little workshop where Mickey Edwards met his end?* Helen thought as stood in the doorway at the same time scanning the yard. She could hear the SOCO team busying themselves in the workshop. She then walked across the yard to take a look at the old skip. It had a lot of burnt debris in it. *Is this just kids lighting fires or has someone lit them deliberately to get rid of something?* Returning to the workshop she asked one of the SOCO team to make sure the skip was checked out when they'd finished inside.

'It might have something important in it.' She said and then went back to her waiting and pacing.

Tremayne picked up his phone and was greeted by a voice he knew and loved. Sophie answered him with news that she thought she's identified the place where Edwards had died.

'You have,' He said enthusiastically.'…well done, where is it?'

'It's on the river, a place known locally as the artificial beach. It's where they dumped the rubble, bricks and concrete after the bombing in the Second World War. Now, what's really interesting is…it has become quite unique botanically speaking. Not because the plants are particularly rare, they can be found along the north Wales coast. But because of the unique environment created by this rubble, certain plants have colonized this particular area, such as the Yellow Horned Poppy or *Glaucium flavum.* On this side of the River Dee wouldn't normally find these plants. So, putting two and two together; the seed and the brick particles I found beneath his finger nails, means that he could only have been killed on that beach at Hightown. Good or what?'

'Excellent news Sophie, you're becoming a right little Miss Hercule Poirot aren't you?'

'Yes, and I'll let you buy me dinner, just for that.' She laughed.

'Did you know this beach is close to an old builder's yard that we are searching at this very minute?

'Yes I had heard.'

'So… yes, this is very interesting Sophie, thanks a lot, you're a treasure. Listen I'll get back to you later. Just now I need to go over there and see how things are developing. And dinner sounds great, see you later, love you bye.'

Tremayne walked into the incident room and onto the large-scale OS map attached to wall, he marked the builder's yard, the artificial beach and the Wartime gun battery. Franklin's club and Mickey Edwards' flat were already pinpointed. *This is looking good, as long as we can find a link between the yard, the beach and…Mickey Edwards. Then…Tony Franklin.*

Helen was surprised to see Tremayne's blue Alfa Romeo pull up outside the yard so soon. She walked over to him as he got out. He stood and looked along the road towards the river and sea.

'Hi boss, what brings you back here so soon?'

'I've just had a call from Sophie. She told me that she thought Mickey Edwards was killed on the so-called artificial beach,' he said pointing along the road. 'It's only a couple of miles down there. She told me he had particles of brick dust under his finger nails...'

'Yeah, but there's plenty of that here.'

'Yes, agreed, but there was also sand and the seed of some sort of plant that only grows on that beach, on this side of the Wirral. I think he was here, before they took him to the beach. He was still alive then, he scrabbled about, clawing at the ground. Come on, we'll go and take a look at this...artificial beach.'

'Do you think SOCO could find anything there?' Helen asked. Tremayne thought for a moment.

'No, I wouldn't have thought so, not after all this time, anything would have been washed or blown away by now. I think all we can say is that he breathed his last on the beach. Our best chance lies here, in that workshop. They knocked seven bells out of him in there, before taking him to the beach. But I still don't understand why they took him down there and then to the dunes miles away.'

Tremayne and Helen Machin stood on the artificial beach; they looked along its length. At first glance it looked like an ordinary shingle beach, until one looked more closely. The whole place was made up of brick and concrete debris, worn and rounded by sixty five years of tides, wind and weather.

'I see what you mean. We could spend days looking along here and find nothing.' Helen said sounding disheartened at the thought of even beginning such a search. She knew he'd already told her, but she said it anyway. 'Tell me you're not thinking of searching this place...are you?'

'No, be waste of time. We might give it a walk over. No, our best bet is to concentrate on that builder's yard and I've no doubt it does belong to him. We have Sophie's findings. Now if we can find something substantial in there, backed up with what Sophie has, then, I think we can implicate Franklin. Come on, we'll get back there shall we? They might have something for us.'

137

Barry James was just walking out of the building as Tremayne and Helen ducked under the tape cordon, held up by the uniformed constable. Barry walked over to them, holding his hand out in greeting.

'Ah Rufus, 'he said shaking his hand vigorously. 'I've some good news for you. We have found traces of blood, well quite a lot really; on the chair, the table and on the floor around the chair, just as you suspected Helen.' He said smiling at her. 'There was also, what I think is some kind of fibre. It'll probably turn out to be fibres from the rope used to tie him to the chair. I'll give you a call when I've done a proper job in the lab. It'll probably be tomorrow morning, at the earliest, but don't hold your breath.'

'Tomorrow! This afternoon would be better.'

'Yeah, I dare say it would Rufus, but tomorrow is more likely, we're not all married to the job. Anyway these tests take time. See you Rufus, Helen.'

They got back into Tremayne's car. He turned on the ignition, put the Alfa into gear and drove back to the station. They arrived to find Sophie sitting in the incident room chatting to Clive, Allie and Martin.

'Glad to see you're all busy.' Tremayne said, with a degree of humour in his voice, but only because he'd been given good news by Barry James.

'How was it at the builder's yard boss?' Martin asked interested.

'I think we'll get some good results out of it. Forensics will get back to us tomorrow morning. It'll take as long as it takes, is all they'll say. Helen and I took a look at the beach, but I don't think it's worth bothering with. It's that yard, that'll provide answers. And I'm expecting forensics to come up with them.' He looked at the clock on the wall. 'I think a glass of something is in order.' They tidied their desks, grabbed their coats and walked from the office, heading for the Golden Lion. But before they'd reached the end of the corridor Chief Superintendent Pearsall came through the door and demanded to know what progress had been made. Tremayne told them to carry on, saying he'd catch them up. Tremayne then followed Pearsall up to his office. It was a large room; book cases along one wall, lined with a mix of law and police procedural books. Family photos and gifts from visiting police officers sat on other shelves. There was a long, dining-room type table that was used for meetings; it stood in the centre of the room and had six chairs round it. Pearsall's desk had its back to the window, a large leather office chair stood behind it and two upright chairs stood in front. To one side of the desk two maroon leather button-backed chairs were placed. Tremayne had always eyed these, thinking they were for the sole use of friends or special visitors. To his surprise, Pearsall indicated that Tremayne sit in one of them.

'Well, Rufus,' He began, seeming very friendly and cheerful, for a change. 'Where are we with this Edwards case?'

'As you know we are searching a builder's yard, traces of blood have been found, forensics will get back to us in the morning' Tremayne told Pearsall all they had up to date, before giving his thoughts on who killed Edwards. 'One of my team followed Malcolm Smith, you know him, Trendy.' Tremayne paused, Pearsall nodded. 'He visited a pub, the Cherry Tree, where he met up with Reginald Vincent Riley, a nasty piece of work…'

'Riley? Ah yes Reggie Riley, grievous and actual, robbery with…used to be a fist fighter as I recall?'

'That's him.'

'Why was he meeting him do you suppose?'

'I believe he was involved in Edwards' killing. He probably knocked him about and Trendy was there to question him. Now whether his death was intentional or Reggie just got too rough, I don't know.'

'Can you prove it, that's the rub – proof?' Pearsall said pointedly, a stern look on his face,

'Yes I know that Sir and I think we can. I think that Tony Franklin owns the yard where we've had forensics all afternoon. As I've said, they've found blood, probably Edwards. Samples from under his finger nails have been identified as having come from the artificial beach at Hightown.'

'What samples, what are they?'

'Particles of red brick; salt and a plant seed from a particular plant that only grows locally on that beach.'

'Are you sure?'

'I think so Sir, Sophie's not prone to rash decisions.'

'No I'm sure she isn't. All I'm asking is…there could be no doubt about what the samples are and their origin? I've said this many times, we need to get this right Rufus, as I'm sure you know without me going on about it.'

'No Sir, there's no doubt.'

'Very well Rufus, keep me informed. I'll not keep you. Good evening.'

'There is one other thing I'd like to discuss with you Sir.'

'And that is?'

These artefacts we've got in the safe. I'd like to send Nick Chandler to Norway…'

'Why…to what end?'

'Well Sir, I believe we need to discover their background, the place where they were found by the naval officer. It will help us answer many questions relating to the Edwards murder. I think there is a link between our current case.'

Pearsall considered Tremayne request, there was further discussion before he sanctioned the trip.

'You speak with the Bergan police and get Chandler to liaise with them.

'Yes Sir, thank you. Good evening.'

'Good evening Tremayne.'

Tremayne arrived at the Golden Lion and joined the team. Clive got up and got Rufus a glass of his current choice, a Fitou, a powerful meaty red wine.

'Thanks Clive.' he said, settling himself down. Clive asked him about the wine, which after a while he wished he hadn't.

'This comes from one of the oldest wine producing areas in France, the Languedoc Roussillon…'

'It looks very dark; it'd probably be too heavy for my liking.'

'You should perhaps try one of the Fitous from closer to the Med, to begin with, they're not so powerful, slightly lighter, but still good.'

'Yes boss, I might give it a try one day. I think I'll stick with my lager.' Tremayne shuddered at the thought.

'You ought to be a bit more adventurous Clive. That stuff all tastes the same. How can you taste anything if it almost frozen? Live a little.'

'Leave him alone Rufus, if Clive doesn't want red wine he doesn't want red wine.' Sophie said in his defence. 'Only joking, Clive.' Rufus smiled.

'What did the Super' have to say?' Nick asked getting him off the subject of wine.

'Oh, he just wanted to know how far we'd got with the Mickey Edwards case.'

'Do you think the builder's yards will reveal anything?' Clive asked, cutting in, keen to know whether they were just wasting their time tearing the place apart. Tremayne thought for a minute.

140

'I do hope so Clive, I do hope so, and I have every reason to believe that we will find something.' He took a sip from his glass. 'I also think that Trendy and Reggie Riley are mixed up in this and Trendy's weird enough to revel in a bit of roughing up, and Riley…well he'd do anything on Trendy's say so. Look, this is how I see it. They picked Edwards up for some reason, and took him to that yard. There they had a go at him, wanting him to tell them something. Whether they succeeded is anybody's guess. Maybe things got out of hand, which is likely where Reggie is concerned. They then took him to the beach, he was still alive, and they finished him off. Then for some reason, perhaps they realised it was too close to the yard, too close to home, they took him further along the coast and buried him next to that wartime bunker. I don't think they knew that it was there though, that's sheer coincidence. But at that place there was a path that led to the bunker and it's an easy way through the dunes, from where a vehicle could be parked. And there he lay; ready to give the old dog walker the shock of her life. As a straight forward murder goes, I'd be happy with that scenario.' Tremayne took another sip from his glass. 'But what still bothers me are those damn jewels. How and from where did Mickey Edwards get them?'

'Do you think that was what Franklin was after, the jewels?'

'I don't know, I've been thinking about that. To be honest, I'm not certain he knew anything about them. If he had known, they would be long gone. Surely you would have thought that Franklin would have sent Trendy to look for them. After all Allie found them under the bed in a suitcase, not exactly well hidden? And…it was a place owned by Franklin, he had a key.' Tremayne said confidently. Listen, just follow me on this. Mickey Edwards was a second rate crook, not overly intelligent. He burgled a place one night, and got his hands on the box of jewels. He took the box back to his flat. Thought his birthdays had all come at once. I think he would have been worried, what with such a haul in his hands. He would have been keen to get rid of them, but where? No one reported any burglary, which is strange in itself; very expensive jewels and nothing reported stolen?' He raised a questioning eyebrow. 'He talks to his girlfriend, tells her that they will go off on holiday, to Spain or Florida. I think the message got back to Franklin. On top of all this,' Tremayne lets out a short laugh. '…there's another box of stuff that we found in the anti-aircraft emplacement, so where has it all come from? Now, according to Meyer they appear to be from the same source, yeah, from a Jewish family during the war. What I mean is where did they come from *now?*'

141

Tremayne emphasised, tapping a finger on the table, meaning recently. So, we have two lots, obviously from the same hoard and split up by Carter…'

'An' Carter put one box in the battery for safe keeping, in the short term and the other…?' Helen suggested.

'I think that's a fair assumption, and the other part he sold.' Tremayne picked up his glass of wine and took another sip. He held the glass close to his lips, deep in thought and appreciating the aroma at the same time. It was a little while before he spoke again. He put the glass down and continued. '…coming back from Norway, he carried the jewels in a rucksack. He might have hidden them all in the gun battery at first. Presumably by that time, that battery had been closed down, otherwise soldiers would still be stationed there. Air raids had ended and the threat of invasion had passed, the allies had launched their European campaign after D-day. So the gun battery was deserted.

'So how does Redfern Sutcliffe fit into all this?' Sophie asked 'He gave you those cuttings for some reason, I find it all puzzling.'

'Puzzling! You can say that again. This is like an Agatha Christie mystery, its bloody Poirot we need. I can see I'll have to be having another word with Mr Sutcliffe.' Tremayne lifted his glass and emptied it. He then took out a twenty pound note from his pocket. Handing it to Clive he told him to get another round of drinks in.

'So what's our next move boss?' Allie asked.

'In the morning we'll get confirmation from forensics and depending on their results, we then make our move on Tony Franklin and his little empire.'

13

Nick Chandler walked out of the customs hall at Norway's Bergen airport. He stopped momentarily to scan the faces of people standing and holding small boards in front of them on which were written people's names. These people, they were mostly businessmen and women being collected to be whisked off to their various meetings in Bergen. Perhaps a high-powered business lunch before they were back at the airport, where they would catch their flights back to the UK; to be ready for another round of meetings the following day to report on the meetings they'd had the day before.

Detective Inspector Nick Chandler was being met by his counterpart in the Bergen police department, Police Inspector Henning Bjorgum. Nick spotted a uniformed officer holding a small placard bearing his name.

'Good morning, I'm Nick Chandler.'

'God Dag Inspector. I am to drive you to the police headquarters; Inspector Bjorgum will meet you there.'

'Thank you, lead on. Is it far into the city.' Nick asked the police officer.

'No, it is not far, only eighteen kilometres. It should take us about twenty minutes, half an hour depending on the traffic.'

Nick Chandler settled back and enjoyed the views of the Norwegian countryside slide past as he contemplated his reason for being there. Back in England he and Tremayne had decided that a trip to Norway might lead to some clues and reasoning about the wartime mission that lead to the deaths of two, if not three people. As the police driver had said, it didn't take long to drive from the airport into Bergen. They pulled into the police headquarters' car park and Chandler was shown up to Inspector Bjorgum's office. Henning Bjorgum was not the man Chandler had envisaged; he was not the Viking, the athletic-looking blond-haired Scandinavian. Inspector Bjorgum was dark-haired for a start and although tall, six feet and about mid-forties any sport had ended many years ago. The effects of good living were showing round his middle. He greeted Nick warmly.

'Good morning Inspector Chandler,' He said holding his hand out and grasping Nick's hand with a firm grip. 'Welcome to Bergen.' Nick reciprocated the welcome. 'Can I offer you a coffee?' Bjorgum poured two coffees from his filter machine and they sat in a couple of easy chairs. Nick thought they were obviously from IKEA. They sat drinking their coffee, and chatting, just breaking the ice. When Bjorgum offered Nick a refill, he also poured one for himself.

'Now Inspector I'm intrigued, tell me what brings you to our beautiful city. Wartime activities I believe, how does that bring a policeman from Liverpool to Bergan?'

'Yes sort of.' Nick took a sip from his coffee cup. 'The story begins here in Norway, in nineteen forty four with a Royal Navy mission to pick up Norwegian resistance people. They meet at a place not too far from here. The place I believe, is a quiet area, with a house, once used by German officers as a sort of retreat. A few German soldiers were stationed there; just as basic security. But during that raid a naval officer found what we believe to be stolen jewels, very expensive jewels in fact, some made by Faberge and by other master jewellers.'

'Intriguing indeed. Do you know the name of this place?' Henning Bjorgum asked leaning forward towards Nick, and very interested in the story.

'I believe it's called Mathopen, Grimstadfjordem. You'll forgive my Norwegian?'

'No that's good, excellent pronunciation; I know Scandinavian languages can be difficult. Yes, that is a region just south of here. There are a lot of summer homes there. We Scandinavians like to get out of the city in summer. To the coast or into the countryside to hike or to sail or just relax in the sun. It's a long winter here you know, and we like to make the most of our short summers. But I'm thinking it might be more difficult to find one particular house than you anticipate Inspector. Only because our coastline is a maze of little inlets; it would have been easy for boats to get in and out without being detected.'

'Would you think there might be any locals in the area who might know of such a mission? Better still there might be some people who belonged to the resistance.'

'To be honest, I don't know.'

'Well, if it's all right with you maybe I could go there and see what I can find?'

Henning Bjorgum thought for a minute, 'If that's why you're here Inspector you must do as you think fit. I think I can help you though. I can spare a driver for a few days. The man who drove you from the airport, I believe he knows that part of the country. He can speak good English, and obviously he can act as an interpreter. So tomorrow you can begin your quest. But now, let me show you around our beautiful city…what do you say?'

'That would give me a lot of pleasure Inspector, thank you. I would like that very much.'

'And please, Henning, call me Henning.'

'Right Henning and my name is Nick.'

Henning showed Nick around Bergen, explaining its involvement in the Hanseatic League of merchants and the trade that went on around the Baltic and to Britain. A lot of Norwegian timber went to a town called Kings Lynn in Norfolk, he explained. Nick was delighted to see the brightly painted buildings of the waterfront, shooting off several pictures. They had a walk round the waterfront, where Nick bought some of the smoked salmon from one of the stalls. After a day's sightseeing Henning invited Nick to his home for dinner that evening. Nick accepted gratefully and was picked up in a taxi from his hotel. Soon after he was being introduced to Astrid, Henning's wife and their children, daughter Vilda and son Tomas. Nick left his shoes at the door and stepped into a pair of slippers provided for guests. The house was furnished stylishly, polished wooden floors, plain walls, but with none of the wallpaper that Nick would have expected back in England. On the walls there were several oil paintings depicting the Norwegian countryside. Around the table questions were batted back and forth about their different countries.

'Tell me about Liverpool Nick a great sea port is it not? Henning asked 'that is where you are from, yes?'

Nick talked about Liverpool saying that there was trade between the two cities, as in the past. Many of the old docks had now closed and now everything comes in containers, as it does in any port worldwide. And that the warehouses had now been turned into fashionable and expensive apartments. The meal and conversation made the evening pass quickly, suddenly Nick realised it had gone midnight. He made his farewells and a taxi arrived to take him back to his hotel, from where Peder Silvertsen had arranged to pick him up at eight o'clock the following morning.

Peder arrived into the hotel's dining room at just before eight. Nick was just finishing his breakfast; he was ready, if not a little tired, for the day's drive out of Bergen and out towards the coast.

'I had a late night with Henning and his family,' he said yawning. He finished his coffee and they hit the road.

'We are travelling towards a small community called Klokkarvik; it's on a small island about forty minutes away. Many people have summer homes along the coast there. Our whole coastline has many isolated inlets and it's difficult to find particular houses, unless you know exactly where they are. The roads are very narrow; many just end by the sea. It was a good place during the war to get things in and out.' Peder said enthusiastically, excited at the prospect of a bit of unusual work. 'There's a hotel that will make a good base too, I took the liberty of booking a couple of rooms for us. Inspector Bjorgum said it was courtesy of the Bergan police. We can search the area easily enough from there.'

'Well that's very noble of the Inspector, and very thoughtful, that sounds like a good idea Peder. When we get there, I was thinking what we need to do is plan our days. Then after we've checked into a hotel, we can ask around. What we are looking for is a house that was obviously built before the war. During the nineteen thirties or earlier, and one that was occupied by the Germans. We might, hopefully be able to come into contact with people who were here during the war. Perhaps there is a museum that could help us.'

'Yes, that sounds good to me.'

They continued their drive, Nick sat back enjoying the Norwegian countryside, with Peder giving a running commentary and Nick making numerous requests for Peder to stop so that he could take a couple of photographs.

They checked into the small hotel and settled themselves into their rooms. They met up again fifteen minutes later and took a stroll around the town.

'Let's go to the museum and ask if they know if there's anyone still living in the town who was here in the war?'

They found the museum easily enough and made their enquiries. They were delighted at the result. The assistant told them that her grandfather worked for the resistance.

'My name is Elisabet Berkstrom; my grandfather's name was Sigur Thorsen. He was involved in some secret work. I don't know what it was, but he and some other men were taken to England for a few weeks before being brought back to carry out…something, I don't know what it was.' Nick's ear pricked up at hearing this. *Was this man one of those picked up on that mission involving Carter?*

'I hope you don't mind my asking but, I am a police officer from England. The case that I'm working on has led me here to Norway, via the war time activity of a Royal Navy officer, who is now dead. But I believe that this officer was on the mission that took several resistance people to England. So, after what you've just told me, one of those men is most likely your grandfather. What I'd dearly like to do is talk to anyone who was part of that resistance group. If your grandfather was one of them I really would love to talk to him. Is that possible do you think?'

'Oh how exciting. I don't know if he'll talk to you I'll have to ask my mother this evening. Can I telephone you and let you know?' Nick gave Elisabet the number of the hotel and his mobile number. They thanked her and left the museum.

'That was a stroke of luck Peder?'

'Yes indeed. If the old man will speak to us then we should be able to put in contact with the other members of the team that went to England. One of them might remember your Petty Officer Carter.'

'I hope so, I do hope so. Come on lets go and have a drink somewhere, I'm parched.'

Sitting with their beers, Peder asked Nick what the case was that had brought him all the way to Norway. Nick explained what he could about the murder of Mickey Edwards, about the finding of valuable jewellery that no one had reported stolen and the old newspaper cuttings given to Rufus Tremayne by Redfern Sutcliffe.

'It all sounds like a Jo Nesbo thriller.' said Peder. 'So you think that the old resistance men will be able to…what exactly.'

'To be honest with you Peder I don't know. I'm hoping that they will remember Carter and be able to shed some light on the man. One of them might have seen him poking around the house just before they were called back to the beach for their return to the ship. They might tell us where the house is. If so we might go and take a look.'

'And, you think that Carter found these jewels in the house?'

'Yes…'

'So these jewels belong to the owners of the house?'

'Er…no I don't think so. We were told by an expert jeweller that they were most likely stolen from Jewish families by the Nazis somewhere else in Europe. Maybe they were from Norwegian families; we have no way of knowing.'

'I see, so why do you need to find the house?'

'Oh you know police work. It's all just part of the investigation. I'd like to look around and get a feeling of the place and the area. The beach where they landed, the path they took up to the house. They encountered German soldiers and there was a brief fire fight you know, the Germans were all killed. But if I can understand what went on during those few hours they were here, then I'll be able to get a better picture of what happened since.'

'Even so, how many years has it been now – sixty…more? A long time.'

'Yes, I know it has been a long time. I'm not looking for new evidence. No, I just want to get a feel of the place and more importantly, and being able to speak to the men who were there. Now that's important.'

'Hopefully then, the girl's grandfather will agree to meet us.'

'Yes of course he will; these guys always enjoy reminiscing about their exploits. A young journalist, who is doing some research for my boss, said she met two of the men from that same mission. They were very keen to talk about it, so hopefully…'

'Well let's hope for the right answer when she rings back. What do you want to do now?'

'Well if it's all right with you, let us take a drive along the coast and see what we can find. We may be lucky enough to spot one or two old houses that fit the bill.'

Nick and Peder drove along the coast. Nick took in the ruggedness of the coastline, the myriad little inlets where men could have landed unseen to carry out sabotage and slip away again. Peder told Nick that lots of people had weekend places. His family had one just a little further north and that there were many more summer homes today. Back in the forties he thought there would have been far fewer, a smaller population too and not having so much disposable income as those of today.

'It's like this for hundreds of miles Nick. Do you want to go any further?'

'No I don't think we need to go much further. Turn around where you can and we'll head back. It'll be time to eat by then.'

Nick and Peder sat in the bar after dinner and waited for the phone call from Elisabet Berkstrom. They finished off several beers between them before the call came through. It was quite late and Elisabet apologised for the lateness, but that didn't matter when she said that her grandfather would be pleased to see them. Elisabet said that she would pick them up the following morning about ten o'clock to take them to her grandfather, she would act as interpreter for them. Nick said that his police driver could interpret, but Elisabet said that her grandfather did speak English, but she thought it might be better if she was present and interpreted. They agreed and turned in for the night.

Sigur Thorsen stood and held out his hand and greeted them as they were shown into the sitting room of the Thorsen family home. Sigur was a fit and healthy looking eighty seven year old as was his wife Elisabet. Young Elisabet made coffee for them all.

'I'm pleased that you agreed to see us Mr Thorsen.' Nick said sounding quiet formal.

'It's a pleasure,' replied Sigur, 'But please call me Sigur. Now, tell me, how can I help the British police?'

'We have been investigating a murder. But there are certain facts that seem to link the current murder to a murder way back in nineteen forty four.' Sigur looked interestingly at Nick as he spoke.

'You don't let things slip do you, murders from nineteen forty four and you still investigate?' said Sigur rather astonished. Elisabet returned with a tray of cups, a jug of coffee and some pieces of cake. She poured them each a cup and offered the cake.

'Well, not as such, but certain items of valuable jewellery are the link. And the fact that the man murdered in nineteen forty four came here, to Norway. A naval petty officer called Simon Carter. He was with the group sent to collect, I believe, you and some fellow resistance men.'

'Yes that's right. We were taken to England in order for us to be briefed about causing chaos, we know now that D-day had occurred and we were to keep the Germans occupied here. We were told to destroy anything of military value, cause havoc to the railways, and the roads just to make movement difficult. I think it was in May or early nineteen forty four.'

'So you were to meet up with the landing party at a house along the coast and the Germans were occupying that house…yes?'

'Yes that's right. We, that is: Bjorn Altman, Sigur Nilsen and myself moved towards the house during the night. We hid and watched. We saw the Germans patrolling around the house. I think there were no more than seven or eight of them. We did not worry. The naval and marine commandos that were coming would know to be watchful for trouble. They dealt with the Germans easily enough.'

'Did you notice a petty officer acting…shall I say suspiciously?'

'Suspiciously? I don't recall, it was a long time ago you know. As I said, we were hiding in the trees up behind the house. We saw the men moving towards the house. The Germans were not very cautious. Nothing ever happens here, was probably what they were thinking, despite orders, I dare say. Any way they were dealt with cleanly and efficiently. The landing party then moved quickly towards the house, some stayed outside on watch, while the others went inside to get papers and the like. I seem to remember one man moving around the house outside. I thought he was just guarding his comrades you know. He then entered the house through the rear entrance, but then, obviously I don't know.'

'That man may have been Carter. Did you then move down to meet them?'

'No not straight away. We had to wait for a pre-arranged signal. If we did not get that signal we were to remain hidden and carry on as before.'

'Ah, I see. So what was this signal?'

'It was a whistle. The letter X using Morse code. They would sound it three times Do you know the Morse code Inspector?'

'No I'm afraid I don't.' said Nick, slightly embarrassed in front of the old man.

'No I suppose not, not with all your technology nowadays, emails and the internet.'

'And…the letter X is…what? '

'It is dash-dot-dot-dash, so we would hear a long whistle, two short then another long. We heard that repeated three times and then we came down to meet them. Almost immediately the word was given to rendezvous back on the beach. We were moving quickly along the path. I heard something behind me and I turned and noticed an officer some distance behind.'

'Can you remember anything about him?'

'This is hard you know. The memory isn't what it used to be, I am eighty seven you know. But yes, I seem to remember he was the only one wearing a…I don't know the English, en ryggsekk. *Hva er det på engelsk?*' Sigur said to his granddaughter.

'My grandfather apologises, he doesn't know the English word, but what he means is the man carried a rucksack.'

150

'Takk Elisabet.'

'He's just saying thank you.'

'That man with the rucksack that must be our man. His name was Chief Petty Officer Simon Carter of the Royal Navy. I think he must have found the jewels hidden somewhere inside the house. But why weren't they locked in a safe? He may have found the key of course but, more likely they were hidden elsewhere; in the cellar maybe. Are there cellars in those houses Sigur?'

'I don't know. We did not go into the house. But I would say yes, there would be cellars I think, for storing foods in the winter and other things. Not that we Norwegians would be on the coast in winter, it's too harsh, too cold and the sea too stormy. Unless they lived there all the time, some folk are very hardy but it would be a difficult life.'

'Would the Germans have evicted the family, if they thought fit to do so?'

'Yes I think so. I do not think they would hesitate. If the family had other relations in Bergen then...they may have gone there, otherwise they had to rely on friends or neighbours for help.'

'I don't suppose you knew the family?'

'No I did not know them, but I do know their name.'

'You do?' Nick said excitedly. 'And that is?'

'Amundsen, the family is called Amundsen. During the war we had many groups. The groups were kept deliberately small then we could not reveal too many names if we were captured and...' Sigur did not finish his sentence. 'Ole Amundsen was taken prisoner, unfortunately he never returned. He had a wife and children, two sons I believe. Now his wife's name was...' Sigur thought for several minutes. 'Ah yes her name was Margretha, but I cannot remember their son's names. Regrettably I don't know where she lives.'

'No that doesn't matter, we can find that out if we need to. But tell me Sigur, where is the house?' Sigur asked his grandaughter to bring the large scale map of the region; He laid it out and searched for a minute, before pointing out the house to Nick and Peder.

'I am with all the modern technology Inspector, Elisabet can make a copy for you.'

They bid their farewell to the old resistance fighter Sigur, saying that they would go to the house tomorrow in the hope of meeting a member of the family there.

The following morning Peder was listening to his SATNAV and following the road as it wound its way round headland after headland. Nick remembered the children's complaint, *are we nearly there yet?* But thought better of it and remained silent. After what seemed an eternity Peder turned off the main road and drove up what was little more than a track. Although tarmaced, it did have a line of grass up the middle. At the top of the track they came to a large wooden-built house, painted white with a red roof, and a well-tended garden. Peder pulled up alongside another car. As they walked towards the front door someone called to them.

'God morgen, kan jeg hjelpe deg?' A man called who was working in the garden. Peder replied to the man and introduced Nick.

'Yes I hope you can help us. My name is Peder Silvertsen, I'm a police officer from Bergen and this is police Inspector Chandler from England.'

'From England really, I speak English, we can speak English.' The man replied, holding his hand out in greeting.

'You do, excellent. We are looking for a house in this area.' Nick said 'that was used by the Germans during the war, as an officer's retreat I think. It was at this house where some Norwegians were picked up by the Royal Navy and taken back to England. The family name then was Amundsen. Would you know of such a family and where their house is?'

'Oh yes, it is this house.'

'Really! Oh that's great. Do you know anything of what went on here during the war?'

'No, not really, but I think it was more than just an officer's retreat. I was told by my mother that German spies operated from here, but you know how gossip is. I'm not sure if that's true.'

'Well that is possible. The naval mission that came here, their brief was to collect papers, of what I don't know, they also came to pick up three Norwegian resistance men. Now this might sound strange to you but, what I'd really like to check out is. Do you know if there's a…a secret hiding place where valuables might have been hidden?'

'Well, I know for certain that there is nowhere in the house. My sister and I grew up here; we played in the house, the garden and through the woods. I've also repaired and worked on it many times since then.' Then man paused for a moment, his hand went to his forehead, remembering something. 'there is a place in the garden at the back of the house. Would you like to see?'

'Yes please, I would, if it's not too much trouble.'

'No of course not, follow me please. Oh, please forgive me, my name is Nils Amundsen. This house was my grandparent's house, since before the war. As you have probably guessed, the Germans requisitioned it and they had to live elsewhere.' Nick and Peder followed Nils around the side of the house and into the garden at the rear. It wasn't really a garden as such, the ground rose steeply upwards to the forest. The grass was short, Nils explained he had to strim the grass on the slope, it was difficult, but it kept it tidy. Nils stopped at the foot of a grassy slope, where the grass had been left un-strimmed; the bed rock was exposed in places. Nick looked at the bank but saw only the bare rock and vegetation.

'Here it is,' Nils said pointing at a grassy bank.

'Where?' Nick and Peder said simultaneously.

'Here, look, where this boulder creates a slight overhang. It is well hidden isn't it? We leave the grass deliberately long just here. My sister Torhilda, and I used it to hide our treasures in the tiny cave, as we called it. A secret hiding place our parents didn't know about. But of course, they knew about it, my father and his brother would have used it also, as do our children. So really, it was not such a good secret hiding place. Trouble was, we would put things in there and animals would come at night and drag everything out, they were looking for food, and in the morning we would find our 'treasure' exposed for all to see.'

'I think this is the place where he must have…' Nick began to say.

'Pardon, where who what?' Nils asked, intrigued.

'Well, back in England I am part of a team investigating a murder. But that doesn't affect you, obviously. No, it's what we found in the apartment of the murdered man and other things we found hidden in an old wartime gun emplacement that brings me here.'

'This sounds very interesting? Please let me offer you some coffee and you can tell me about this murder.'

The three men went into the house, Nils made coffee and they all sat around the kitchen table and Nick continued his story.

'So, as I was saying, it was what we found in the man's flat and in the gun emplacement that has brought me here. And that was a small bag and an old ammunitions box containing valuable jewels. These things are exquisite, some were made by Faberge. They would bring many thousands of pounds at auction.'

'Are you saying that these jewels were originally found in our hiding place? I was told that a German officer hid valuables in there to keep them out of sight when he went away for a few days. It could be. Maybe this German officer hid stolen artefacts in there ready to be moved when the time was right.' Nils said, astonished by Nick's story. 'Coming new to the house and finding the cave he'd think it was an ideal hidey-hole.'

'So if he went away for a couple of days there would be no danger even if is room was searched?'

'Not if he thought his secret was safe outside in that cave, no.'

'But it wouldn't be safe?'

'No. My sister put all her dolls in there once. She said they were going camping, but next morning they were strewn all over the lawn.'

'Yes, I can believe that. But that leads us to another murder, that of the naval petty officer who came here. We think that this man found the jewels in your garden and he took them. They may have already been in a rucksack and he simply put it on his back and returned to England. The rucksack they were in must have been disturbed by a fox or something, as you said they do, looking for food.'

'Intriguing?' Nils said, finding the whole episode fascinating, and what a story to tell his grandchildren.

'As you mentioned; we also believe that they were stashed here by a high-ranking officer, ready to be secreted away as the war drew to an end. The jewels are thought to have been taken from Jewish families during the course of the war. The jewels had probably been moved from place to place with the officer.'

'So, do you know who killed this man? Did the German officer find him and kill him? But if you found these jewels then this officer didn't get them back.'

'No, I don't think he did. And we don't know who killed him either. It's a very cold and long-forgotten case.' Nick paused and sipped appreciatively at his coffee. After a couple minutes he asked Nils. 'Tell me, would you know the path they may have used to get from the beach up to this house?'

'Yes of course it's the path we use all the time to get to the beach ourselves. We'll finish our coffee, and then I'll show you.' The three men finished their coffee and followed Nils out of the house and walked the hundred metres down the steep path. 'These new concrete steps have been put in since the war,' Nils commented. '…there would have been fewer steps then, just tree branches laid across the path in places. It was probably difficult to climb, but not impossible, it was supposed to be a path afterall.' They stood on the beach; Nick looked out to sea and up and down along the small beach, little more than a cove, with its rocky entrance. He was trying to imagine that morning long ago in nineteen forty four; with a Royal navy frigate off shore and several men on the beach all armed and watchful. Some then set off up the path they had just walked down, and sometime during the next hour or so Carter found his million pound prize.

'You said that your grandparents had this house before the war?'

'Yes, that's right. My grandfather died during that time. He was a member of the local resistance group, unfortunately he was taken prisoner one day and my grandmother never saw him again. She moved away to Bergen and she alone brought up my father and my uncle.'

'Do you know if there are any records, military records of that period here in Norway?'

'I'm sorry I don't know. I think your best chance of answering that is to go and speak with the museum curator, either in Klokkarvik or you may have more chance in Bergen or better still Oslo.'

They walked back up the path and Nick thanked Nils for his time and he and Peder drove back to their hotel in Klokkarvik. The following morning they returned to the museum to speak to Elisabet Berkstrom.

'Hello Elisabet,' Nick said 'I'm hoping you can help me again.'

'I'll try.'

'Are there any records that you know of…German military records naming officers who were stationed in this region and…what their activities were?'

'We have some, but I think you'll need to go to the regional archives in Bergen or maybe even Oslo. They're all in German of course. Do you speak German?' Elisabet asked.

'I don't really; do you speak German Peder?'

Peder said he did and so they began reading through the papers, which Elisabet had in store, relating to the Klokkarvik district. Nick made notes of the officer's names and anything that related to units stationed close to the Amundsen house. They had been flipping though piles of records and Nick was beginning to wonder if this was just leading them up a blind alley. 'They're not going to write down where they've hidden valuables are they?' Nick said. Peder came across the name of a high ranking general.

'This man was not in charge of any unit in the area, but was visiting. The record was May 19th 1944.' He pointed it out to Nick. 'This doesn't look official Nick; it's more like a brief note made by some duty soldier. But why did he bother to make a note of it.'

'Does he name the general?'

'Yes, his name was Manfred Hans Maurer. The note says that he was visiting the area while on leave. He actually stayed at the Amundsen house for a few days. That's all it says, funny sort of note don't you think.'

'Yeah, but it's the name I'm interested in. Can you make me a copy of this Elisabet? I think this is what I've come for…that name.'

That evening Nick Chandler phoned Rufus Tremayne telling him that he thought he'd got what he needed and that he'd be back the following day. Nick made his farewell to Peder Silvertsen.

'Give my thanks and kind regards to Henning.' Nick said as he shook hands with Peder at the airport.

14

'How was your trip Nick?' Tremayne asked as soon as Nick showed his face through the door, but really wanting to get the pleasantries over. He really only wanted to know what had happened and what he had found out.

'Good, very good; and it's a beautiful country too. You ought to go there one day.'

'Yes I might just do that. Now what were you saying over the phone about something useful coming from it?'

'Yes as a matter of fact, something very interesting.' Nick briefed Tremayne on everything he had done. About his meeting with the old resistance man Sigur Thorsen; and about travelling to the Amundsen house on the coast. 'Most interestingly though, when Peder and I were researching in the papers of Klokkarvik museum I came across the name of a German officer. A General in fact, his name was Manfred Hans Maurer'

'Now that's what I call detective work. Did you hear that Helen? He came across the name of a German officer. Remind me, weren't they occupying the country at that time?' Tremayne said a broad grin on his face.

'All right,' Nick retorted '…you know sarcasm is the lowest form of wit. So this General Maurer was not part of any unit stationed in that area of Norway. Apparently he was just visiting, a bit of R&R. Peder Silvertsen took me to the place where the group landed and I saw the house. I met the grandson of Ole Amundsen, who during the war was a resistance fighter. He built and owned the house. I mentioned the jewels to the grandson, Nils. He showed me a secret hiding place in the garden; he said as children he and his brother hid their 'treasure' in it. Now…what if this General had hidden his treasure in Amundsen's hiding place? Carter came across a rucksack, Nils said animals dragged out things that had been stashed. So he just threw it over his back and trotted off back to the ship. He stowed it. When they got back to Liverpool, he just walked ashore with it.'

'Well…that suggests where Carter got them from.' Tremayne said cautiously. 'But not how he came to be found dead on the beach. We still need to confirm this German general and ascertain if there's anybody he could have contacted here. Sorry Nick, carry on.'

'Right, so he stashed them somewhere ashore, in the family home or in lodgings somewhere. We know he divided the hoard. He tried to sell them...he got greedy...they got pissed off and they killed him.'

'Yes but who...well that doesn't matter now. What I'm more interested in is how the story develops from then on, through the bank manager and on to Edwards and Tony Franklin.' Tremayne said disdainfully.

'I know what you're saying, but this General Maurer, he wanted his jewels back...' Nick suggested half-heartedly.

'Yeah, I dare say he did; only he couldn't just pop over here, find the perpetrator and say "excuse me but you've got my looted jewels. Can I have them back please" yeah.'

'Full of wit today aren't we Rufus.' Nick said mockingly. 'There was someone already here. The General contacted him...or her; don't ask me how, but they were told to be on the lookout, make discrete enquiries.' He noticed Tremayne's expression. 'Alright, I know it's a long shot, but...'

'Okay, let's just say that he did have someone here...who?' Martin tentatively knocked on the door of Tremayne's office and marched straight in.

'Forensics on the phone boss.' Tremayne reached for his phone, at the same time saying 'Knock louder next time.' But Martin was gone. He put the phone to his ear and curtly called down the phone.

'What kept you, when can I get some results?' he said sharply, without knowing who he was speaking to and immediately questioning the delay between the search of the builder's yard and the results coming through.

'Having a bad morning are we?' A soft French accent answered coolly. He hadn't realised that it was Sophie calling. But the apology came quickly enough.

'Sorry Sophie, just a bit frustrated that's all, I do apologise. What have you got for me then?'

'We took a lot of different samples: blood, fibres, splinters of wood, and soil from beneath the table. We have ascertained that there are at least, three different blood types, there may be more they're still working on it; most too old to identify positively. There is a lot of blood splatter around the room too. If I was you I would say that this place was used to interrogate people…violently, it looks like a mediaeval torture chamber.'

'A WHAT!'

'I'll repeat, just so you understand. I think that someone used this place to severely beat people. We have found blood splatters everywhere and…traces of human flesh and teeth fragments. Yes…a right mediaeval torture chamber…for real.'

'I can't believe this.' Tremayne said shocked, he became quiet, he was deep in thought. He hadn't spoken for so long that Sophie called down the phone to see if he was still there. 'Yes sorry Sophie, I can't believe this. But what about Mickey Edwards, can you ID his blood group and DNA?'

'Mickey Edwards, yes you'll be pleased to know I can confirm that he was there in that room. His samples were the newest and we can prove that he was there.'

'Thanks Sophie, was there anything else?' Sophie said there wasn't. 'Okay I'll see you later then. Love you, bye.'
Tremayne leaned back in his chair, staring at the ceiling as he always did when thinking. He let out a deep sigh, quietly saying 'My God, I can't believe what she just said.'

'And what was that Rufus?' Nick enquired cautiously. Seeing Tremayne in deep thought, staring at the ceiling, the years had taught him to tread lightly.

'Sophie said…I still can't…' Tremayne shook his head and sighed deeply as he quickly moved into an upright position. 'She said that they have found several samples of blood and actual flesh and teeth fragments, in the room at the builder's yard. Do you know how she described it…as a mediaeval torture chamber?'

'Bloody hell,' Nick exclaimed, his mouth dropping open, and shaking his head at the same time. 'You're joking?' he quietly murmured, knowing full well that Tremayne was not. '…and who do you suppose is responsible for this then…Tony bloody Franklin?'

'I'm in no doubt it was, Nick, and we are damn well going to confirm it.' He said rising from his chair and walking out into the incident room, Nick close on his heels. .

'Helen I want you to find out if Franklin does in actual fact own that yard. I want to know when he bought it and from whom…I want to know everything, even if he bought a box of bloody screws just check it all out. We're going to secure a conviction on Franklin..'

'Nick, you don't think he'd be stupid enough to bury evidence in that yard do you?'

'I've no idea Rufus, but I'll go and find out. I'll dig the whole place up if necessary. I'll get all that rubbish cleared off the surface and see what's underneath.' Nick paused, thinking. 'Yeah it might be worth a punt, a friend of mine is professor of archaeology at the University. I've heard him talk about something he calls geophysics. I think they can locate stuff below ground without digging.'

'Really, that sounds a good idea. Okay then Nick, organise that, and if you get it done for free…student exercise, it'll make,' He pointed a finger to the ceiling, indicating the Chief Super's office. '…him happy.'

'And you'll organise the proper…paperwork in the meantime?' Nick said, raising his eyebrows as it asking for something out of the ordinary.

'Yeah fear not, I'll have it for you by the time you've organised your logistics.'

∗ Nick stood watching lorries leave the builder's yard after being loaded by a JCB. They were driving off to some tip or other. It didn't take them too long to clear the site. But Nick insisted that the contents of the old rusting skip be turned out and searched before that was removed.

'I want everything checked. Let forensics have anything at all interesting, bits of cloth, paper, and pieces of wood or metal that could have been used as a weapon. Look for knives, and other sharp objects. I want anything and everything analysed.'

The team of police officers, dressed in coveralls and wearing face masks and gloves set about shovelling and scratching through the debris that had been tipped out of the skip onto the ground. The stagnant water that had settled in the bottom of the skip, along with a couple of dead rats, stank. It made everyone gag at the horrendous stench. A white suited forensic scientist stood by to remove anything which they thought suspicious. It wasn't long before one officer stood and raised his hand calling the forensics guy over. The work stopped, they all stood back as whatever he'd found was picked up by a gloved hand and placed into a plastic evidence bag. Work then resumed. After about an hour they had been through all the debris. Pieces of wood and other bits of cloth had been bagged and were now on their way for analysis. The debris was all loaded onto a lorry and taken away. The site being now cleared, police and forensics stood back to watch as three people from the university's

160

archaeology department set to with their electronic equipment to carry out a geophysical survey of the area.

Nick watched as they quartered the site, up and down they walked, fairly quickly, which surprised Nick, he thought they'd move along much slower. It didn't take them too long to cover the area. Then it was another wait while their computer analysed the data.

'It's all clever stuff Jon.' Nick said to Jon Granger, the forensic archaeologist from the university.

'It is that Nick. The beauty of it is, we can locate a buried body without disturbing the ground. Traditional methods of archaeology are too destructive and time consuming. The old question was, where do you dig? That was always the million dollar question. With this technology we can survey a site quickly and pin-point the archaeology or, for you guys, the location of a buried corpse for instance. What they are using is GBR or ground based radar. The trick later, when the data is presented, is determining the difference between the target, which is what you want to find and the anomalies in the ground. But we'll do our best.' Half an hour later Jon Granger called Nick over to the van. 'We've located something Nick.'

'What is it?'

'A pit of some kind, possibly something buried…'

'A grave?'

'Possibly, I'm not saying anything.'

'Okay Jon, I'll give my boss a call.' Nick phoned Tremayne to tell him that a possible grave had been found by the geophysics team and should they dig.

'I'll come down,' He said 'do nothing till I get there.'

Tremayne and Helen walked onto the site after donning protective clothing.

'Right Nick, what's all this about a grave?' Tremayne said, thinking he didn't really want any more complications. 'The Super's going to go ballistic you know; buried bodies and newspaper cuttings from the past, it'll all be too much for him, it'll upset his budgets.'

'Well we're not a hundred percent sure just yet, but to be absolutely certain we need to dig. Have a word with Jon Granger; he's the guy standing by their gismo.' Nick said pointing over to the wheeled machine, by which stood a tweed-jacketed man with the university scarf wrapped round his neck. Tremayne approached the man stood by the GBR scanner.

'Jon Granger? I'm Rufus Tremayne. What's all this Nick's been telling me about a possible grave?'

'Yes, and that's all it is, a possibility.' He emphasised possibility. 'Come, I'll try to explain the read-out data.' Tremayne stared at the computer screen, beneath the raised tail-gate of the team's vehicle. To Tremayne it was just a jumble of waves of various colours, reds, yellows, blues and greens. He looked confused. Jon Granger explained the various parts and what they meant.

'I would strongly recommend an exploratory dig here. I'm not in the business though of stating categorically that something will be found. I can only interpret this data as best I can, nothing is a hundred percent. But…we do have a good track record.'

'Well put Jon, you'd make a good politician.'

'Yes, we all have our superiors to deal with don't we.'

'If you were a betting man what odds would you give me?'

'I'm not a betting man Mr Tremayne I'm a scientist, I deal in facts, but reading this data I'd say you have an eighty percent chance of finding a body. Now I think that's pretty good odds, don't you?'

Tremayne walked away from the university's vehicle to rejoin Nick and Helen. 'Okay Nick organise a dig, see what's there. I'm going to have a talk with the Super.'

'Nice, I imagine it'll make his day.' Nick said laughing.

'For that, you buy the first round later.' Rufus said as he walked away from them.

Nick organised the excavation of the area pinpointed by the GBR survey. He and Helen then stood back and waited. They first had to break through a layer of tarmac and hardcore. The forensic archaeologist was always on hand to stop proceedings if he saw something.

'That's the rubbish gone, and the subsoil's exposed, nice and clean.' Granger said to Nick. 'I would say that the ground there has been disturbed, you can always tell. Notice the colour change.' Granger pointed out the disturbed, backfilled soil and the undisturbed natural ground.

'Could you say whether that tarmac was recently laid down, or has it been there for some time?'

'I could say for sure, not without specialist analysis. The tar binding the stone will deteriorate over time, of course, but I'd need to check with people in engineering to give you an absolute answer. Finding a body though will give us all the answers we need.'

Tremayne walked into the incident room, Clive was immediately onto him.

'Oh boss, we're not sure if Franklin does own that yard. We've been to the town hall and checked in the register of local businesses. The yard was last used by a builder called Johnson. He retired in nineteen ninety seven, his son carried on until two thousand and two before he moved away. It was then bought by a company called QualBuild but they don't seem to have used it…not as builders at any rate. We've phoned local people in that road; we didn't like to disturb the investigation there. They told us that the yard's not been used as a builders for years; although, they say people have been seen coming and going on several occasions.'

'I've checked QualBuild through the business register' Martin continued 'There seems to be four directors, but none of them is Tony Franklin.'

'Right, you need to find out if this QualBuild can definitely be linked to Tony Franklin?'

'We are still checking boss.'

'Okay, I'm going to see the Super, keep up the good works lads.'

Tremayne knocked on the door of Chief Superintendent Pearsall's office. A brusque 'come in' greeted him. As soon as Pearsall saw Tremayne he asked pointedly.

'Well Tremayne what have you got? This investigation of yours dealing with some half-witted villain is in fact going a little too far.'

'Well Sir, we're moving towards Tony Franklin. We are in the middle of searching a builder's yard at this moment. Forensics' have come up with several blood samples…'

'Blood samples? What from builders who have cut their bloody fingers. Is that all?'

'No Sir, one of the samples has been positively identified as that of Mickey Edwards. There are others, we don't know who they belong to, forensics say they might be too old or contaminated to be of any value. I have ordered a survey of the ground surrounding the buildings. Several items were recovered from a skip and they are in the hands of forensics.

We are also carrying out a ground based radar survey…' Pearsall jumped in again and Tremayne thought his was about to go into orbit.

'Good God man, do you think this department is made of money?' Tremayne maintained his eye contact with his superior and carried on with his report, even though it was obvious that Pearsall wanted to interrupt and stop his investigation.

'We have found, what might turn out to be a grave, Nick Chandler is supervising the excavation at this very minute Sir. We think that the yard is owned by Franklin, Martin Wilcox is checking through the local business records. Most important though Sir, forensics suggests that one room in the building has been used to…interrogate or people…in a rather vicious manner, you might even say torture.'

'TORTURE…my God Tremayne, what are you saying man? This is getting worse by the minute.' Pearsall became silent; he rose from his chair and paced around the room. 'All right Tremayne…I'll leave it with you, carry on.'

Tremayne walked back to the incident room, he felt better than he did before speaking to Pearsall. He felt he could now concentrate on bringing down Franklin and his little empire.

'Any news from Nick yet?' he asked Martin.

'No nothing yet boss.'

'So, how are you getting on with linking Franklin to the builder's yard?'

Tremayne asked.

'Slow boss, I'm going through the list of local businesses just now.' Martin replied.

'You said the yard is owned by a company called QualBuild?' He didn't wait for an answer. 'We know that it's not been used as a builder's yard since the original owner closed his business in two thousand and two. It is my view that the yard is just a cover; it's where he interrogates the misfortunate bastards who cross him. We need something that will put that yard fairly and squarely in Franklin's lap. I'm just hoping that Nick will come up with something substantial. Right, say he bought the yard in two thousand and two or three that gives us a starting point. He might have forgotten that his name is tied up with it somewhere...no, unlikely. The council will want someone to pay council tax on it. Go and have a word with them.'

Nick Chandler stood watching the excavation; Jon Granger waved him to come closer.

'We've found something Nick.' He said.

'Good, what?'

'I'm not sure just yet but it is a bone fragment.'

'Human?'

'Now hold on a minute, it's a bit too soon just yet. It is only a fragment; it'll take a little time before we can say for sure. I'm sending it back to the lab. We really need to find a larger piece for positive ID, a skull would be nice.'

'Okay Jon, I'll leave you to it.'

Nick watched as the forensic archaeologists painstakingly scrape away the soil in the 'grave'. It was frustratingly slow work. Half an hour came and went, an hour passed, it was more than two hours before he called to Nick again. He held a small, gardener's seed tray, lined with kitchen paper and in the tray, a bone rested.

'Well…' asked Nick 'is it human?'

This has just come back from the lab, and yes, it is human. It's part of the ankle. We are continuing to excavate, hopefully by this evening we'll have the whole skeleton. But I'm not promising.'

Nick thanked him and walked away. He turned and looked at the building where the forensic people were still busy. He decided to go in; he didn't know why, he'd just a mind to.

'Hello Nick…' said a familiar voice, he turned and saw Sophie standing at the doorway to the room where most of the blood samples had been taken. 'What are you doing here?' she asked.

'I've been round the back watching the excavation of the grave. I was just wondering whether it's another of Franklin's victims.'

'It's possible, but why would he bury them on his own premises. I presume that it will turn out he owns this place. So burying a victim on site, bit risky isn't it.'

'Yes I suppose it is, if it's not a murder victim, then who the hell is it?'

'We may never know. You'll need to get the archaeologists to date it.'

'Yes, I expect we will. You know, I don't know why I came in here, but a thought just struck me. If Franklin does own this yard,' Nick said thoughtfully, turning slowing and scanning the room. '…then there might be something here to tie it to him. I don't know what, but there must be something.' He turned back to Sophie, who was watching him inquisitively. 'I take it you've not come across anything?' Nick asked half knowing what the answer was going to be.

'No…not really. What were you thinking of, we've got the fragment of cloth out of the skip. This is not TV forensics Nick this is real life, we don't suddenly find that elusive piece of evidence and exclaim eureka! He's banged to rights.' She said trying to imitate an American accent.

'No, of course not; but I think I'll have a look round anyway if that's all right with you?'

'Yeah sure, help yourself. We've finished here, so unless you miraculously find something, we'll be off soon.' Sophie turned and went back to carry on packing her equipment away. Nick wandered around. He looked at the walls, the ceiling and the floor. He took out his mobile and dialled.

'Boss, I'm in the workshop at the builder's yard. Listen…I had a thought…do you suppose there's anything nailed up behind the walls? What I'm asking is, can we tear this place apart?'

'What do you hope to find?'

'I don't know exactly. Maybe something that can tie this place to Franklin.'

'Okay Nick, carry on.'

Nick searched around and came across an old tool box, the dust of eight years encrusting the lid. Inside it were some old rusty tools. '*Just what I need.*' He thought. Inside were a couple of big screw drivers, a hammer and wood chisels. He began knocking on the walls with the hammer, he levered panels loose and peered behind them.

'What on earth are you doing Nick?' Sophie said as she came running in, on hearing the banging and creaking of wood as another board came loose.

'I'm looking for hidden treasure.' He said smiling.

'Hidden treasure, surely you don't think there's more jewels?'

'No, I don't think there are any jewels here. Franklin never had them. I don't think he knew about them or we wouldn't have found them in Mickey's gaff. No I'm looking for…well I don't actually know what I'm looking for to be honest with you. But I have this strange feeling that there might be something here, something hidden that'll give us Tony bloody Franklin. You know I really hate the fucking man, and he's due for a long spell out of circulation. Right now, I'm going to rip this place apart…'

'On your own?' Sophie said laughing

'Nah, the boys'll be here soon. Let demolition begin.'

Clive began to search through the local business directory. First he typed in Johnson and sons (builders) 45 South Beach Road Hightown. He pressed return and waited. The screen flashed for a second and then he read, jotting down the details. *Business owned by Arthur Johnson, transferred to Norman Johnson (son) in nineteen ninety seven. The business closed permanently in two thousand and two.*

'So who bought the yard then?' he thought. He scrolled down the screen – Builder's yard, 45 South Beach Road; Hightown, bought by QualBuild two thousand and four. *'But who the hell is QualBuild?'* He typed in the name in a search, and hit return – nothing. He sat staring at the screen, slightly fuming at the lack of information. Tapping his fingers on the table, much to the annoyance of those nearby.

'Give the drumming a rest Clive, some of us are trying to work.' someone shouted.

'Sorry guys...' he said. He suddenly thought of *'Companies House'* he brought up their webpage and searched it for QualBuild. There was a list of directors, which he wrote the names. There was nothing else so he closed it down and re-read his notes.

'Martin I think I've got some directors for that QualBuild firm.'

'Go on let's hear them.'

'There are four. They are Benjamin Frank Lindsay; Patrick Stewart O'Malley; Daniel Daylew and Peter Paul Maryon.' Martin pondered the names Clive had just read out. He asked him to read them out again.

'Let me see those.' Martin said as he and half the office descended on Clive. They read the list over his shoulder, but said nothing. After a minute, one of them laughed. Martin looked at him. He whispered into Martin's ear. 'Nah, you serious, they're a joke.' He nodded; then Martin burst out laughing.

'Okay guys, what so funny, my flies undone or what?' Clive said rather put out by the sudden outburst of hilarity.

'Read the list again Clive, but…slowly this time.' Martin said stifling another outburst of laughter.

Tremayne walked into the office and demanded to know what the joke was and why they were all round Clive's desk.

'Clive's list of directors for that QualBuild firm boss, someone's pulling our plonkers.'

'All right Clive read them out, let's hear them.' Clive read them out loud.

'Read them again Clive…slowly …words of one syllable okay.' Martin said.

Clive started with the first name. 'Benjamin…yeah. Frank…yeah' Martin nodded. 'Lind…sey. Ah, I see now Benjamin Franklin…very funny. Yeah Patrick Stewart, Daniel Day…Lewis; Peter Paul Mary…on?' Clive shook his head, they've lost me on that one, sorry.'

One of the older guys said. 'Yeah I know who they mean; a sixties folk group Peter Paul and Mary.'

'Right…' said Tremayne 'so he's playing games is he. We'll have to dig a little deeper won't we. There must be something out there that has his bloody name on it. AND I WANT IT FOUND Okay.' Everyone gasped at Tremayne's sudden outburst. 'All right guys…and girls; let's just carry on digging shall we.'

Later that afternoon Nick arrived back in the office, a great beam on his face.

'Well you look pleased with yourself, won the lottery or something?' asked Helen.

'You might say that' replied Nick. 'I thought that there might be something hidden behind the walls in the ol' builder's yard. And look what I found.' Nick dumped a filthy wooden box and a leather brief case onto a table to one side of the incident room. 'Get the boss Clive; he'll be interested in this.' While they waited they pulled on latex gloves, Nick handed Tremayne a pair.

'So, your bit of searching showed results then Nick. Let's see what you've got then.' Tremayne said coming out of his office. The box was opened first, a collective gasp went round the room as they saw the contents; a stash of bank notes.

'Whoa, would you just look at that. There must be thousands there. And what's in the cloth?' Helen said.

Tremayne reached over and picked up the roll of cloth, half knowing what he would find within. 'Ah, as I thought. That's a nice little toy. Find any ammo Nick?'

'No, not as yet, we're still re-designing the place.'

'If I'm not mistaken, this is a Smith and Wesson, nice piece, used by police in the States. Best let ballistics take a look at this Nick. They might be able to pin it down to something. So, what have we in here then?' He said tapping his finger on the briefcase. The contents were tipped onto the table. Inside were mostly papers. Tremayne pushed the case across the table.

'Check for inside pockets…and the lining Martin.'

Martin took the briefcase, opening it wide he felt inside the various pockets, then felt around the lining. I don't think there's anything in here boss…'ang on, I don't know, yeah, I think there is something. Anyone got a knife or something sharp?'

There was a deal of hunting through desk drawers; finally Clive came up with a pair of scissors. 'Will these do?'

'Yeah, just right.' Martin took the scissors and began cutting the lining. 'Here we go…' he said as he pulled out an envelope. 'Feels like a CD…now this could prove interesting?' Martin opened the envelope. 'It's a CD all right; let's see what on it shall we? Let's hope it doesn't need a password to get in it.' He took it over to his desk and placed it into his computer and waited for it to load. Tremayne got Clive to take the automatic pistol to ballistics. At the same time Helen was checking through the pile of papers that now resided on her desk. After a couple of minutes she let out a whoop of delight and punched the air.

'YES…' All eyes turned to her. 'Here we are boss…Mr A. D. Franklin. Apartment 4, Sandon Warehouse.' She read out the name and address on a headed sheet of paper. 'He's obviously forgotten about this…now what else is here? It's like Christmas this…'

'Stroke of luck,' Clive said. '…no code needed. I've got the data up boss.' He called out louder. Tremayne pulled up a chair, leaning forward to get a better look at the screen as Martin explained. 'There are several files here, imaginatively named business one to business seven. Okay let's go for the first one.' Martin clicked on the file icon, 'It's a simple Microsoft excel spreadsheet. We've got columns with headings and a list of figures, some sort of code. I mean what the hell does A.97.gn, H.97.4.26 or Nm. 97.6.15 mean? I'll have to come back to this later boss.' He closed it and clicked on the second file '…another list of figures.' The next couple of files were the same. 'Okay number five…Ah…pictures, bit of porn. Do you think vice might like to take a look at these?'

'Never mind vice Martin, just find me something that WE can use. If I feel generous later then they can have a look. But only after we've got that bugger Franklin.' Tremayne said forcefully.

'Right boss, understood. So number six…is a database file, *Microsoft access.* There are several different files here. They're named with what appears to be dates, but they're a few years old now though. They're more than ten years old, so he must be finished with them and they've been hidden away and forgotten about.' Martin opened one of the files, the most recent first. 'Right here we are…dated the twenty third of October, year two thousand. There's a lot of data here boss, it'll take me some time to fathom it out. If these figures relate to money, then there appears to be some large sums passing from one place or account to another. If these are names' he said pointing to the column down the left hand side of the screen. '…they're all in some sort of code.'

'Okay Martin…' Tremayne sighed with an audible blowing of air. 'Go through them as quickly as you can. See if there's any mention of a name or a reference in plain language, relating to something we might get to grips with. Otherwise we'll have to just have to turn it over to the tech wizards and see if they can make sense of it all. We can't waste time wading through dubious computer files. So find something worthwhile or quit and get it passed over. I'll give you a couple of hours.'

'Okay boss, a couple of hours it is.'

Martin stared at the screen, he swore at it and then he began whipping through each of the files. But after ten minutes he realised there was nothing in plain text. Everything was written in some sort of code.

'Helen, has that briefcase been dusted for prints, or that CD or anything else for that matter?' Tremayne asked her.

'No, not yet boss; but now that we've looked through it, I'll whiz it down to forensics. The CD will have to wait until Martin's finished with it. What about the cash?'

'Right, Helen you sort those, get the numbers checked out with the bank, okay. Nick, the place where this stuff was found, would you say that it was nailed up behind the wall for some time and forgotten about or…do you say they kept going in and out of it in order to put more stuff in or take stuff out?'

'Well…er…come to think about it, I would say it's been opened on infrequent occasions. I think the screws had been in and out a few time, they were quite loose. But I don't think anyone had been into it recently, not with the layer of dust and cobwebs over it. No, I'd say it had been undisturbed for a while.'

'What, weeks, months, years?'

'Ah, now you're asking, you'd better check with forensics, how long does it take a spider to spin all those cobwebs? No, I don't do speculation.'

'Hello, DC Stewart.' Allie said answering the phone. She listened and ended the call. 'Boss that was ballistics, they'd like to see you; they say they've something interesting about that gun we sent down.'

'Thanks Allie.' Tremayne replied hurrying out of the door. An hour later he was back. Almost immediately he called for everyone's attention. Everyone was keen to hear about the pistol, all except Martin who had taken himself off to a quiet office to ponder the codes on the CD.

'Right folks, I've just come back from ballistics. They've been doing a few tests on the hand gun, as we know it's a Smith and Wesson SW 1911 a point forty five calibre semi-automatic pistol. It holds eight plus one rounds. As a weapon it's used by many police departments throughout the United States and by the looks of it, by the likes of Franklin. Now what's interesting is…it has been used and they've found a victim of that very same gun.' Tremayne paused while that sank in. 'The gun was used in a botched post office raid back in two thousand and three. A customer was shot, not fatally thankfully. The bullet was extracted and it's in ballistics' safe keeping. So when they got our mystery gun they tested it and compared it with their database *et voila*…that is the weapon used.'

'Any prints boss?' Clive asked hopefully, expecting a name he knew.

'One partial, they are working on it.'

Martin sat back in his chair holding a print out from one of the *access* files. He swivelled his desk chair in slow circles as he tried to think. Suddenly he stopped pulling back to the desk. He picked up the phone and dialled a number. He didn't have to wait long for it to be answered.

'Roger, Martin Wilcox how are you?'

'I'm good, I've not heard from you in a while. What you up to?'

'Oh this an' that you know. But listen, we're working on this case, I've got some database stuff, now with your knowledge of codes.'

'Don't beat about the bush Martin, what do you need to know?'

'Well as I say, we're involved in this case and I've come across a CD with what I think are names. But they are in some sort of code. I was hoping that you might take a gander at them for me?'

'Yeah sure Martin, can you bring them round or shall I come to you?'

'It'd be good if you could come here.'

'Fair enough, I'll see you soon.'

Martin went to speak to Tremayne. 'Boss, I think I'm on to something with that CD, but I've had to call someone in to verify my thinking.'

'Who?'

'Well he's a friend of mine, he works in the university. He's a lecturer of history, but he is also a cryptographer, a code breaker. If I just show him the list of names…the coded names, he doesn't have to see anything else.' Tremayne thought quickly.

'Okay Martin, carry on.'

Forty minutes later Roger Benson arrived; they sat in the empty office that Martin had commandeered for himself. Benson had a copy of the print-out containing the coded names from the list. He studied them for a while, before Martin asked. 'Well what do you think Roger?'

'Well, my guess is that it's a substitution code. You know where one letter is changed for another. The trick however, is finding the…substitution. So…you think that these are names…of people?'

'Yeah.'

'That might make it a bit more difficult to decipher. If this was a page of text then we'd begin by looking for all the repeated letters. We start with the most frequently used letter in the English language, which is E, followed by T. The least used are letters such as Q, J, X and Z. But with names, well I'm not so confident. We'll give it our best shot. Right, we've got plenty of plain paper. Do you want to leave it with me for a while?' Martin left Roger alone to concentrate on the list.

Allie stared at the pile of banknotes. 'Where do we start with this lot then?' Allie asked Helen as they began counting and stacking the notes from the box found by Nick Chandler.

'We sort them, twenties, tens, fives, we count it, we get the numbers recorded and sent to the Bank of England. We can also check for counterfeits, but I think these will all be good.'

Helen and Allie set to, they spent the next two hours checking, sorting and counting.

'I don't think I've ever handled so much cash, certainly not from my bank account.'

'Yeah me too.' Helen replied.

'So, how much have we got?'

'Forty seven thousand six hundred and eighty pounds.' Helen sat back in her seat, her brow furrowed, thinking deeply.

'Something wrong?' Allie queried.

'I don't know…' Helen paused for short while, at last she said. 'There's something about these notes, but I can't just put my finger on it.' She continued to stare at the piles of notes. She picked one of them up; she examined it before putting it down and taking another. 'I don't know what it is Allie. These are all genuine, yeah, there was no funny money, but there is something about them…I don't like.' After some time pondering she left the table and went to her own desk. She took her purse from her handbag and removed a couple of notes. Allie, she called 'Whose picture do those tenners have on the back?'

Allie picked a ten pound note from one of the piles. 'er…Charles Darwin, why?'

'Just a minute, right, now look at one of the twenty pound notes.'

'Someone called Adam Smith.'

'Have you got a fiver on you?' Allie walked over to her desk; she looked for a five pound note in her purse. 'No.' she said.

'…anyone got a fiver, I just want to know whose picture's on it?' Helen called round the office.

Someone called out, Elizabeth Fry, the prison reformer. Allie said thanks and returned to where Helen stood peering at the piles of notes.

'I thought there was something strange, there you are, look at those. They're different and I think they might be out of circulation, if I'm right, then these are valueless.' Helen laughed 'Almost forty eight thousand pound's-worth of duff notes.'

'What all of them?' Allie said sounding quite shocked. 'No, not all, just the twenties. But why would they keep old notes?' Helen pondered.

'To be honest, I've no idea, but I'd say that for some unknown reason they've been forgotten. Their records have not been kept up to date and these have been missed during a check that should have shown them they were due to be moved on. It's only the twenties that are out of circulation, the others I think are good, the twenties make up the bulk though. So the stupid sods have still lost out, well they've lost it all now, we have it.' Helen's face lit up, she let out a raucous laugh, saying 'Brilliant, that's made my day. Still funny though, why they were left hidden.'

15

Frankie Bolton sat at her desk, scribbling into her notebook as she read from the website displayed on the screen of her computer.

'What are you on with?' asked Jenny a friend and colleague.

'Oh I'm researching the German spy network in England during the second World War.'

'You're doing what!'

'Yeah, it's part of an investigation for Inspector Tremayne. Tony Clayton asked me to do it.'

'Sounds intriguing, what's it all about?

Frankie explained how she'd become involved and where she was in her research.

'What I've been trying to do is find the background of a bank manager called Mason. He was killed and his body was found in the sand dunes back in nineteen sixty three.'

'So…this man Mason…was he a spy?' Jenny asked.

'I don't know really. All I do know is that he worked as a bank manager up until nineteen sixty three when he was found dead in the dunes.'

'How about this for an angle; if he was a spy and he was German…then that English name Mason,' Jenny said tapping at the name in Frankie's notebook. '…could be translated into German as Maurer.' Frankie looked up at Jenny astonished.

'Yes, of course, I never saw that, an' I'm supposed to know German. And obviously you do too?'

'Yes, I did Modern European languages at university and German was one of them.'

'Yeah right. So Mason is Maurer in German'

'It might be worth following up Frankie. Anyway, I'll leave you to it. I'll see you later for a drink yeah?'

'Yeah sure, usual time and place yeah.'

Frankie began to think that Mason might have been in the German army at some time, so she keyed in >*German military records*< into her search. She found a site and searched for officers with the surname Maurer. She made a note of the first half a dozen names.

175

'*I'm not sure this is going to lead me anywhere. I'm not even sure that this guy Mason is German at all*.' She thought to herself, before pushing away from her desk, cursing and saying out loud that it was damn infuriating. After a few minutes she calmed, rolled back to her desk, picked up the phone and dialled. She listened to it ringing for almost a minute.

'Chief Inspector Tremayne…' He answered briefly.

'Hi, Frankie here, have you got a bit of time to talk?'

'Oh Hello Frankie not just now I'm afraid. How about seeing us in the Golden Lion later, say about six-ish?'

'Okay, I'll see you later then bye.'

Frankie arrived at the pub to find Rufus and Nick sitting together at their usual table, six empty chairs waited for the rest of the team. Rufus waved when he saw her and after getting her a drink he asked what she wanted to talk about.

'Well…' she began 'I'm at a dead end with this guy Mason, who might or might not be German. I really don't have a clue. I can't get anywhere with it, there's too many possibilities and blind alleys. All I've got is that the name Mason could be Maurer in German and if he was a German spy, possibly in the army, there were dozens of Maurers, it's as common a name there as here. I've checked military archives.'

'Maurer…?' Nick said, suddenly more interested, leaning towards Frankie. 'I've come across that name recently…in Norway. Peder Silvertsen came across it on an informal note relating to a visit made by a General Maurer to that house Carter went to. Now what was his name…Manfred Hans Maurer, yes that's it. If you speak to Peder, he might be able to give you a bit more information which might connect him with your guy Mason.'

'Oh thanks Nick that's really helpful. That's given me fresh incentive.' She took a long draught from her glass of lager and slumped back into the chair. Looking more relaxed than she had been when she sat down just five minutes earlier.

The following morning Frankie was back at her desk with renewed vigour, busily searching for a General Manfred Hans Maurer in the German military archive. It didn't take her very long to locate him, especially because of his rank.

'Ah…there you are, Herr Maurer. Manfred Hans Maurer born Hamburg in 1910; attended military college, served with…' She read on. 'No mention of his family though, bugger!' Frankie sat back to gather her thoughts. 'Talking of family, Mason might have had a wife possibly.' She pushed her chair back, grabbed her jacket and headed for the door. A few minutes later she was standing at the counter of the paper's archive section where she asked for the newspapers for the 23rd June 1963 and for the following few weeks hoping to find reports about Mason's death.

She flicked through the pages and after short time found what she was looking for; the write-up about Mason's body being found in the sand dunes. It was written by a journalist called Danny Baron. She read his report, but it didn't tell her anything she didn't already know.

Back at her desk she phoned Julia Rimmer the paper's archivist, if she didn't know Danny Baron, then nobody would.

'Hello Julia, Frankie Bolton. Just a quick query. Do you know a reporter called Danny Baron?'

'I met him on many an occasion. You'll come across his name referenced to many a good story. He retired in two thousand and two, why?'

'Do you think he'd talk to me, if he's still with us?'

'Oh he's still with us all right. He lives in…' Frankie wrote down the address. 'Best give him a bell first though, he's still active, sends us the odd story now and again.'

Frankie tried Danny's number a few times that day but to no avail. She succeeded the next morning. She asked him about the Mason murder, but he told her he'd have to check through his personal records. He told her to meet him in the journalist's watering hole at lunchtime.

Frankie walked into the pub just after twelve thirty to find Danny Baron sitting on a bar stool, with a pint of bitter in front of him. Frankie introduced herself, Danny got her a drink and they moved to a table by the window.

'So, you're looking into the Mason case are you…why's that then?'

'As a favour for Rufus Tremayne.'

'Rufus Tremayne! You want to tell him to do his own research.' Danny laughed.

'You know him then?'

'Do I know 'im? There's not many round here that don't sweetheart. He has a very pretty little French girlfriend if I remember rightly.'

'Yes, her name's Sophie, Sophie Bouvier, she's a forensic pathologist.'

'Yeah, I remember her.' Danny took a long draught from his pint, before continuing. 'So, what do want to know about our body in the dunes then?'

'Basically just one question; did he have any family, a wife for instance, children maybe? And, do you know where they live?'

'He did have a wife and I believe there was a son too.' Danny pulled a notebook from his pocket and flicked through it 'You, should always keep your notebooks young Frankie, you never know when some bright young thing needs your help. Here we are, yes he did have a wife and a son. Her name was Mildred; their son's name was Richard, same as his father. They used to live at 258 Montagu Park Avenue. I believe she's died since. I don't know if the son still lives in that house though. I think it might be worth a visit just to check.'

'Yeah I will. What else can you tell me about Mason, anything?'

'Well you probably know he was a bank manager, that's in my piece of course. But what I didn't write was my suspicion that he wasn't English.' Frankie sat bolt upright, her eyes opened wide, she gasped 'Why?'

'I don't know what gave me that impression. But I seem to recall something his wife said. I managed to get an interview from her shortly after the coroner's inquest. I don't think she intended to say anything really, now what was it?' Danny took another swig from his pint and was obviously in deep thought. 'I know…she said his brother, cousin or some relative or other, lived in Germany. We were idly talking about family, I said I had a brother living in Australia and she just said "Oh Richard had family in Germany." I thought that's interesting, but I didn't take it any further; filed it away in the old memory, just in case.' He said smiling knowingly at Frankie.

'Funny you should say that, I've said that I thought he was German. It was something that Graham Wilson said. He said he used to swear in a foreign language if he got really uptight…'

'So you've spoken to Graham Wilson too have you, you're a very resourceful young lady, you'll go far in this business.'

Half an hour later Frankie turned into Montagu Park Ave and drove very slowly past number 258. She turned her car around further down the road and pulled up opposite the house. It was obviously still lived in, lawns mowed into stripes and neat flower beds adorned the front garden. The garage doors were open; a BMW 5 series 520i was parked inside. The house itself was semi-detached. *Four, perhaps five bedrooms*, Frankie guessed. *Must have a reasonable job especially with a new car like that. Shall I go and ask if Richard Mason lives there?* Frankie thought to herself. She'd been watching the house for several minutes, when a little girl came out, aged about seven, *a grand daughter perhaps*, Frankie thought. She was followed by a man, obviously retired, about seventy maybe. *That's him I know it.* Frankie got out of her car and walked across the road; she just aimed the flip key behind her as she crossed the road to lock her car. As she got to the gate, she called 'Excuse me, my name's Frankie Bolton from the local paper. May I ask if you are Richard Mason?'

'Yes I'm Richard Mason, why do you ask?'

'I was wondering if I might ask you about your late father.'

The little girl's grandfather was obviously, and momentarily, taken aback. He said to the little girl to take her bike around to the back garden and that he'd join her in a minute.

'What's this all about?'

'Well…I have been asked to research some old reports, murder cases, from a couple of newspaper cuttings. These had been given to Inspector Tremayne, and your father's death was one of them. He thinks there is a link with your father's death, a murder during the war and a more current death…'

'Hold on, you are saying that the police think there is a link between my father and a current murder. You realise he was killed over forty years ago, how is this possible?'

'Yes I understand it's awkward but it all began in nineteen forty four…oh this is difficult. Could we arrange to meet somewhere and I can explain it all to you. I can see you're busy with your…grandchildren.'

'Yes I am a bit. Look, give me your phone number and I'll check my diary. I could perhaps manage one lunchtime perhaps.'

'Yes that would be great, thank you Mr Mason I appreciate this.'

Frankie walked back to her car; she glanced over to the house when she'd got in. Mason had walked away from the gate but had turned to watch her. Starting the engine she waved and drove off.

179

Tremayne sat at his desk, idly toying with a pen, tapping it on the desk top. He sat up and studied his doodles, a sort of spider-graph he'd made on a sheet of paper; Carter, Edwards, Mason, jewels, gun battery, old news cuttings, Mickey Edwards, Redfern S, and in big bold capitals, which he'd gone over several times making the words thick and heavy he'd written WHERE THE HELL DOES ALL THIS GO??? He pushed himself away from the desk and spun the chair round, kicking off from the desk's side, spinning a couple of times, he stopped and got up. He walked into the incident room and studied the board; Helen glanced up from her work and watched him. He stood with his hands in his pockets. He took a couple of steps back, his brows furrowed and his eyes narrowed.

'This is all a fucking mess.' He said angrily. Spinning round his gaze locked on Helen. 'Well what have you got to say for yourself sergeant?'

'Boss…' Helen said in reply, rather shocked at the suddenness and aggressiveness of Tremayne's question. 'The briefcase has been with forensics they say that the prints are too smudged for a positive ID, but there's a partial one. I've just had this memo from them. It says there's an eighty percent probability that it belongs to a Malcolm Smith…'

'Malcolm Smith eh, excellent, Trendy, Trendy, Tren...' Tremayne let out a sneering sort of laugh. 'I knew that bastard would be behind that place, Franklin's gopher and getter. How good is this print, strong enough to have him in?'

'Eighty percent they say, it doesn't say any more. But I can go and have a chat with them if you like.' As she got up to go, Tremayne asked where Martin was. 'He's tucked away nice and quiet working through that CD, the one that came out of the briefcase.'

'Good, let's hope he comes up with something good.'

Frankie got the result she wanted; Richard Mason had agreed to a meeting. He told her that he and his wife would be in town the following day. Frankie phoned Tremayne to let him know. 'I'll come along,' he said, 'if I'm not queering your pitch? But I think this needs, if you'll pardon me, more than a young journalist.' Frankie said she didn't mind. In fact she'd appreciate it.

Frankie and Tremayne waited in the lounge bar of the Monet Hotel. They hadn't been in there long when Frankie saw Richard Mason. Dressed in a rather swish tailor-made suit, the lady with him, Frankie presumed, was his wife. She dressed more casually, but very elegantly nonetheless. Frankie walked over to them as they stood and scanned the room. She welcomed them, saying that she hoped they didn't mind but someone else was with her. They walked over to the table where Tremayne waited, he rose as they approached.

'This is Chief Inspector Tremayne.' Frankie said to Richard Mason. Mason shook his hand saying '…my wife Alison.' They all sat and Mason was quickly in with his questions.

'Well Chief Inspector, this is all quite a surprise after all these years. Will you please tell me what all this is about? Miss Bolton here told me it concerned my father?'

'Yes, but I'm not entirely clear how. Can I get you both a drink?' Tremayne called the waiter and asked him to bring four glasses of Chablis. 'Let me tell you how all this has evolved.' He continued. 'Several weeks ago, I was presented with some old newspaper cuttings…' Tremayne related the whole story as far as he could. 'Recently Inspector Chandler, my second IC went to Norway, whilst there he came across the name of a German army general. His name was Manfred Hans Maurer…' Tremayne paused and questioningly looked at Richard Mason. 'does that name mean anything to you, Mr Mason?' There was a long silence before he replied.

'Well I don't suppose it matters anymore. The man you've just mentioned was in fact my father's younger brother.'

'Really!' Tremayne exclaimed. 'Can you tell me how your father came to be in this country?'

'Originally he was sent here to be educated and he simply never returned home. Especially with Hitler coming to power in the late thirties; he didn't approve of the Nazi politics. He also managed never to let his true nationality be known. He simply vanished into the country, he had the job with the bank and that's where he stayed…well until…' Mason's face suddenly appeared sad; his eyes had a far-away look for some moments, obviously thinking of his father.

'Yes quite, so, obviously he was never arrested as an illegal alien and interned?'

'No, fortunately for him; he worked right through the war; he wore glasses you see so his sight let him out of military service. Somehow he managed to remain with the bank.'

'And no one suspected his origins?' Again the answer was 'No.'
'Have you ever researched his murder, asked why he was killed?'
'I haven't, no.'

'So you wouldn't know if he was involved in other…extracurricular activities, so to speak?'

'Such as what Chief Inspector?' Mason said surprised and somewhat shocked. '…I'm afraid I don't follow your reasoning.'

'Well there's no other way to put it…did he act as a spy?'

A SPY…Oh…well you astonish me there Chief Inspector. To be honest with you I've never really thought of that possibility. I, I er, I don't think so, but there again I really don't know.'

'No I don't suppose you do.' Tremayne paused. 'Tell me, what do you know about his brother Manfred?'

'I've learnt that they were born in Hamburg. My mother kept a lot of his papers and correspondence in a locked box, which she kept out of our way. She wouldn't speak of it, nor would she let us look into it, which as you can imagine intrigued me greatly. It lay in the attic for many years. Only after her death when we began to sort through her things did we venture into the attic. There, I once again came across that wooden box which was still padlocked. My curiosity was obviously renewed. It was only after I'd opened that box Chief Inspector did I found out my father's origins. Up until that moment I had no idea, I never in my wildest dreams thought that he was not English, why would I? I was to put it mildly; somewhat shocked and taken aback to discover that in fact he was German. I don't know why I should have been? Not that that makes any difference now, but back then…' Richard Mason stopped speaking. He was shaking his head still disbelieving the facts and realising that he never really knew his father.

'So obviously he spoke without any hint at all of an accent?' Tremayne said breaking the spell.

'No none; he didn't really have an accent at all. Probably because of the school he attended.'

'Is there anything else you can tell me about your uncle?'

'All I know is, that he was at a military academy. He graduated with good grades, if that's the term for soldiers. He then joined his regiment, he retired from the army at the end of the war. But after that I've no idea what became of him.'

'Well thank you for your time Mr Mason, I appreciate what you've told me. I hope it's not been too upsetting for you, bringing up memories of your father all over again. The information, I'm sure will prove helpful to us.'

'Well Chief Inspector I'm glad I could be of help, and no, it's been good to talk about him.' Richard Mason and his wife shook hands with Tremayne and Frankie and left.

'Was that helpful to you?' Frankie asked after they'd gone.

'I'm not entirely sure, but it's given us plenty of answers. We've confirmed that Richard Mason senior is in actual fact Richard Gerhard Maurer, that he had a brother Manfred Hans Maurer who was a German army General. We know he stayed at the house in Norway. And we can assume that he…was the 'owner',' Tremayne said indicating with his fingers, exclamation marks. '…of the jewellery that Carter found. The next question to answer is…then what happened?' Frankie stared at Tremayne; they both sat in silence. Tremayne looked at the empty wine glasses; he called the waiter for two more Chablis'. They were brought; Frankie picked up her glass and took a sip, still holding it she said.

'Was part of the jewellery ever moved on or sold. You said you found part of the hoard in the old gun emplacement and another part in the flat of the guy who was murdered…'

'Mickey Edwards, yeah that's right. Just going back though; we know Carter brought the jewels back here. He then split it all into two lots. He hid one lot and possibly, he sold the other lot. Now, perhaps the person to whom he sold them killed him during a heated argument over…the price say, or maybe he didn't want to pay at all…anything could have happened, we'll never know. Anyway, wherever they ended up, many years later Mickey Edwards got his hands on them.'

'Yeah, but who killed him?'

'Oh I think he crossed Tony Franklin. He might have made some deal with him and welshed, then Franklin sent Trendy and Riley to have a 'word' with him, and we all know the result of that conversation. Now if it was about the jewels, Franklin must have thought they were safe enough in his flat, after all Franklin owned the place. But we came along and started sniffing around. Now we've found his so-called builder's yard and found a lot of interesting things there.'

'What…what have you found?'

'Ah, the journalist coming out eh? Sorry Frankie you'll have to wait in line with the rest.'

'Ah, can't you give me something ahead of the pack? After all…' Tremayne looked into her eyes and smiled.

'I'm sorry Frankie but I can't say anything just yet, But I promise, you'll be the first to know anything, I promise. Another drink?'

Martin Wilcox sat at his desk looking very pleased with himself having worked with Roger Benson continually for a day and a half on the CD with its coded headings and lists of figures. Impatiently, he almost ran into Tremayne's office.

'I think we've cracked the CD boss.'

''bout time too, take a seat.' He said nodding towards a vacant chair. 'Let's hear all about the secrets of the compact disk.' Martin put his notes onto Tremayne's desk, but declined the seat.

'I'll just load this into your computer if I may?' Tremayne pushed back from his desk allowing Martin to get in and load the CD. During the time it was loading they positioned two chairs in front of the screen. They watched for a short while, and then Martin began.

'These I'm sure,' Martin said tapping on the screen with his pen '…relate to horse races. The codes are simple enough, once you've looked at them for hours. For instance A 97gn is the Grand National at Aintree in nineteen ninety seven, H is Haydock, Nm is Newmarket, Y is York and so on. The numbers relate to the dates of those meeting. There are others but you get the drift.' Martin didn't wait for Rufus to acknowledge, but continued. 'The figures are almost certainly amounts of money. I think they are betting takings, but whether they are legal or not, I can't say. There's certainly a lot of money changing hands here; it goes into the millions.'

'Good work Martin. Now what about the other files?'

'Well those are very interesting. I had to work with that friend of mine, Roger Benson. You'll remember I mentioned him to you?' Tremayne nodded. 'He's an expert on ciphers and breaking them. All he saw was the headings, so he's none the wiser to what it's all about…'

'I'm glad to hear it.' Tremayne said firmly. 'Okay Martin, carry on.'

'Well, the headings, also in code, are what Richard called a substitution code. This is a code that substitutes one letter for another and these are a five letter substitution. Richard said it was a very easy code to crack. But your average villain who happened to see it open on Franklin's computer would be none the wiser …well most are pretty stupid anyway. Roger cracked it fairly quickly though. He just had to work through the possibilities. Several of the words are repeated; and they all turned out to be…names…'

'Whose...whose names? Do we know any of them?' Tremayne said, a little impatient.

'I don't as yet, they're all punters most likely. That's my next job. I'll put them through our database and see what comes up. They may be on other force's books, who knows? Here's a few though...' Martin read the first five or six names, but Tremayne said he didn't know any of them. 'As I said, they may be just punters who were on Franklin's list.'

'More than likely Martin, but let me know what you come up with.'

As Martin retrieved his CD, Tremayne walked into the incident room and wrote the new details on the board. He stepped back, his hands in his trouser pockets and read it all again, for the umpteenth time.

A phone rang; no one answered it for several rings. Just as Tremayne was about to shout: is someone going to answer that bloody phone? Allie picked it up. She listened, put the phone down and said 'It's ballistics with a confirmation of the partial print on that gun.'

'Well whose is it? I hope it's someone we know?'

'Yes we do boss, and I think you'll like it too. It belongs to Reginald Vincent Riley. They say that he must have had a small hole in his glove, the print was quite good actually.'

'The stupid bugger,' Tremayne laughed. 'I always said he was as thick as a brick, dangerous but thick...'

'Do we pick 'im up now boss?' Allie asked.

'No not yet, we'll just wait until they've gone over that briefcase thoroughly and Martin has finished with that CD. Then I think we can invite them all in for a little chat.' Tremayne paused briefly. 'Oh but sod it, we can't wait forever, I'm going down there.' He said and headed for the door, disappearing through it. Not long after he arrived in the science lab.

'Hello Rufus, we don't see you in here very often...only when you want something that is.' Sophie said with an inquisitive smile. 'What is it this time?...ah! I know, the old briefcase...'

'Well have you got anything?' His voice rather hard.

'A polite Bonjour would be nice.' She said in her quiet French manner.

'Sorry...Hello Sophie.' He said, looking at Sophie apologetically.

'Thank you' she replied 'As a matter of fact...we do have some prints...'

'I thought there were none, too smudged?'

'The outer parts of the case had been handled by more than one person. And yes, we didn't get any from it, but here.' She indicated the folds in the leather at the ends of the case. 'We've managed to get a couple of reasonable prints, protected when the case was closed. They are, at this very minute being analysed. We should have a result pretty soon. Would you like a coffee while we're waiting?'

Rufus and Sophie sat in her office, a demitasse of coffee freshly made through her fancy coffee machine, as Rufus called it.

'Umm, nice,' he said, sipping the dark liquid. 'I do like this blend what is it?'

'A Colombian coffee, yes it is nice isn't it?'

'Not French then?' Sophie shook her head and squinted at Rufus through narrowed eyes, thinking you know damn well it's not.

'What are you doing here Rufus, this is not one of your usual ports of call, I didn't think you liked it down here? What do you want; you're not just chasing finger prints?'

'I just needed to get out of the office for a while, get some air…'

'Really, so you thought the path lab was a good place eh. I would have thought the park more suited? And stop fiddling with that.'

'Sorry.' He said and paused for a moment. 'What do you know about spiders?' he said suddenly, surprising Sophie with such a question.

'SPIDERS? What on earth do you want to know about spiders for?'

'I'm interested in knowing how long it takes to accumulate a certain amount of cobwebs.'

'Spiders, cobwebs, what's this all about Rufus?'

'The briefcase and a box of cash were found walled up in the builder's yards…'

'Yes, I know.'

'Well, I was just interested to know how long it was since anyone last went into the little hidey-hole, that's all.'

'Quite a while I should think, but I'm no expert. Maybe you ought to go and find an entomologist.'

'Yeah very helpful but I don't suppose it matters really.'
They finished their coffee and went to see if the results were up on the fingerprints from the briefcase.

'Ah yes, here we go. Do you know anyone called Malcolm Smith and Bernard Alexander?'

'Do I, I'll say I do, particularly Malcolm Smith…or Trendy to his friends'

'Trendy, who is he?'

'He's a rather nasty piece of work, real name Malcolm Smith also known as Trendy. He follows Tony Franklin around like a lap dog and does his bidding without question, usually along with another nasty bugger called Reggie Riley. Trendy gets his nickname because of the clothes he wears; all the latest fashions, spends quite a bit of money on them by all accounts. But don't let that fool you; he's as likely to… Well you know that you said about the builder's yard…'

'Yes.'

'Well Trendy is your inquisitor'

'Ah! Okay, do you have enough to charge him?'

'We may have, now we've got conformation on the briefcase prints…anyway thanks for the coffee, do we have this at home?' Sophie looked at him through narrowed eyes again. 'Okay, right, I'll see you later then.' He kissed Sophie and headed back to his office.

All eyes turned to him as soon as he entered the incident room; there was a minute's silence before Helen asked if he'd had a result.

'Result I'll say, Malcolm 'Trendy' Smith and Franklin's accountant, Bernard Alexander. Sophie found prints and good ones for them both.'

'So what now then boss?' Helen queried enthusiastically.

'I think we'll have a talk to them Helen. You and Clive go and ask Mr Alexander if he wouldn't mind coming in to answer a few questions. You'll find his address in our database. Nick, you and Martin can have the honour of collecting Trendy.'

'And…it'll be a pleasure too. Come on Martin, I'm going to enjoy this.'

16

An hour later, Nick arrived back in Tremayne's office to say that Trendy and Mr Alexander were sitting comfortably in interview rooms one and three. Tremayne thanked him.

'Are they saying anything?'

'Only complaining like mad, especially that accountant; he admits he does the accounts for Franklin from time to time but denies all knowledge of the builder's yard. Trendy is trying the soft soap ploy.' Nick gave an impression of Trendy. "Why Mr Chandler, what's all this about, you know me, honest as the day is long." and all that guff. He makes me vomit, the bastard.'

'Right, we'll leave Trendy to stew for a bit. We'll go and have a word with Alexander. We should go easy at first, just to test the water so to speak. Then we can put pressure on depending how he goes. But I don't see any problems with him. You and Helen work on him Nick; I'll watch his reactions from the observation room.'

'Okay, we're on our way.' Nick left Tremayne's office, picking up Helen on he went to the interview room.

'What's he like this accountant?' Helen asked as they walked along the corridor towards the interview room where Bernard Alexander sat waiting nervously, constantly shifting in his seat, biting his finger nails, and touching his hair.

'When we picked him up he was shocked, said he couldn't understand why we would want to talk to him. He did admit though having worked for Franklin from time to time.'

As they pushed the door of the interview room open, Alexander almost rocketed from the chair, the uniformed officer went to force him to sit again but Nick stopped him. Nodding and saying quietly, he's okay, leave him.

'Hello Mr Alexander, please take a seat. We'd just like to have a little talk with you if that's all right?'

'Yes of course, but I've no idea what it is that you want to talk to me about?'

'Yes, well we'll get to that in due course. My name is Detective Inspector Chandler and this is Detective Sergeant Machin. This is just an informal chat. We'd like to clear up one or two things and we believe that you might be able to help us.'

'Very well…I take it I won't be needing my solicitor then?'

'Why, do you think you may need legal representation? As I said this is just an informal chat.'

'Fair enough then Inspector Chandler, what is it you want to ask?'

'First of all, tell me about your dealings with Tony Franklin?'

'Tony Franklin…the property and club owner? Well I've done his accounts for several years, for the *Wild Orchid* club and for his property company *Franklin Investments.*'

'How many years exactly?'

'Well…it must be at least ten; I'm not exactly sure off hand.'

'What do you know about a property at 45 South Beach Road Hightown and a company called QualBuild?' Alexander looked straight into Nick's face, then he turned towards Helen for a second or two, and then he looked down at the table top. He said nothing for a minute.

'QualBuild?' Alexander repeated, sounding puzzled at the name. 'I'm sorry Inspector but I don't recall ever having come across that address or that name in connection with Mr Franklin's business interests. As I said I've only…'

'Yes, yes, you just said. Mr Alexander, do you, as part of your association with Mr Franklin have dealing with any of his staff…Mr Smith, Malcolm Smith for instance?'

'I know the name of course but I don't really deal with his staff. No, I receive any paperwork directly by post or by courier, I work through them and return them. They are just normal accounting protocols.'

As Tremayne was listening to the conversation with Bernard Alexander, Clive came and told him that Sophie was on the phone and could he call her back because she'd found something that would be of interest.

'Thanks Clive I'll get back to her shortly.' Tremayne continued to listen to Nick questioning Alexander. He then went to look at Trendy as he waited in interview room one. He was sitting quietly; someone had brought him some tea, the mug sitting on the table in front of him, his fingers wrapped round the mug. He stared straight ahead as though thinking of answers to the questions he would be receiving in due course. Tremayne watched him for five minutes; suddenly he remembered Clive and the phone call he had to return to Sophie.

'Hi Sophie, sorry to keep you, we're interviewing Malcolm Smith and an accountant who does work for Franklin.'

'Well it's in regard to Smith that I've phoned. Do you remember the pieces of cloth which were found in that burnt-out skip in the builder's yard?'

'Yes of course.'

'Well, that cloth is not just any old oily rag one would expect to find in a builder's skip. It is quite exclusive material. It's a mix of fine wool and cashmere, the type of fabric you'd find in a bespoke tailored suit. Now, perhaps that material came in a bag of old clothes from a charity shop, but I doubt it. It looked too new, too clean, there was no oil on it. There were signs of it having been burnt though; someone was trying to dispose of it. But they didn't do such a good job; natural materials don't burn as easily as man-made fabrics.'

'That's very interesting. So, you're saying that this piece of cloth is from an expensive article of clothing?'

'Oh yes definitely, and very expensive too I should say.'

'Who would make clothes using that type of cloth around here or would it have come from London?'

'No, not necessarily there are plenty of bespoke tailors in the city.'

'Right…can you let me have it along with a description of its makeup?'

'Yes, I'll have it brought round.'

'Thanks, that's brilliant, love you bye.'

'Martin…let's go and keep Trendy company for a bit. He might be getting lonely; he's been stewing in there for a while now.'

Tremayne, followed by Martin walked along the corridor towards the interview room where Trendy sat waiting. Tremayne pushed the door open and strode in; Trendy looked up giving Tremayne and Martin a cursory smile of acknowledgement.

'Hello Trendy,' Tremayne said 'How've you been keeping?'

'Mr Tremayne, I don't know why I've been brought in here but obviously there's been a grave mistake.'

'You said it Trendy and you've made it.'

'I don't know what you mean Mr Tremayne.'

'Do you not? Before we begin I must warn you that this interview is under caution' Tremayne said leaning forward towards Trendy and staring him straight in the eye. Nick Chandler read him his rights. Trendy was now sitting upright in his chair, his hands lay flat on the table, he seemed to be totally relaxed as though this was a regular occurrence and he'd not a care in the world. 'Well let me enlighten you Mr Smith. I think that you and your employer Mr Franklin, along with Reggie Riley…where is he by the way?' Tremayne deviated, trying to take Trendy off guard. He waited for a reply.

'I've no idea Mr Tremayne; I've not seen him for yonks.'

'Really, my information is that you've spoken to him in the last few days or so.'

'No,' He said shaking his head slowly. '…whoever told you that was obviously mistaken.'

'All right…tell me about QualBuild?'

'Qual what…what's that then when it's at home?'

'You don't know…I am surprised. It's a so-called building firm…address 45 South Beach Road, Hightown. An address which I believe you know quite well?'

'No…you have me there Mr Tremayne, I don't think I know of such a firm, not had much use for a builder recently and I'm not familiar with Hightown. I live in a managed apartment building you see, where all that sort of stuff, maintenance is taken care of…all in the management fees you know. It's all very convenient I don't have to worry about…well you know.' Trendy said innocently with total unconcern in his voice. 'Where is all this leading, if you don't mind me asking Mr Tremayne?'

Tremayne didn't answer, going straight onto his next question. 'What do you know about Mickey Edwards?' Tremayne said harshly, suddenly leaning very close to Trendy, staring him straight in his eyes. Trendy flinched a little and moved away slightly, sitting upright, his back straight with the chair.

'I'm sure I don't know what you mean. Why should I know anything about him?'

'Because you…' Tremayne cut his sentence short.

'I don't think I'll answer any more of your questions Mr Tremayne, not without a lawyer, Mr Franklin said…'

'Mr Franklin said did he…and you of course do everything Mr Franklin says…don't you Malcolm?'

The sudden change in Tremayne's voice and the use of his proper name startled Trendy. 'I don't know anything about Mickey.' He said and clammed up. He would not answer any more questions and so Tremayne got up to leave the interview room. 'Get him a cup of tea and a sandwich constable. Just stay with him Martin, till he gets back.' But just as he reached the door he turned and casually asked.

'Oh and if you don't mind me asking Trendy, where do you get your suits?'

'Samuel Cohen, they're in town.' Trendy said straight out. Not expecting such a question.

'And that suit,' Rufus continued 'the one you're wearing…is made from what…wool?'

'Oh not just wool Mr Tremayne, it's a blend of the finest wool and cashmere, very expensive Mr Tremayne…I don't think on a police Inspec'…' But Trendy shut up, suddenly puzzled, perhaps concerned. He was going to say that on a police Inspector's salary you can't afford this quality. But he thought better of the comment. Tremayne left.

Tremayne was back in his office waiting for Sophie to arrive with the piece of fabric. It was more than half an hour before she appeared, but Tremayne was happy enough to let Malcolm 'Trendy' Smith sit in interview room number one and stew.

'Here it is Rufus, one piece of rather expensive fabric.'

'You know you're the second person to say that to me in the last hour. Mr Malcolm 'Trendy' Smith, as near as damn it, virtually told me that on a police Inspector's salary I couldn't afford such tailoring. He also told me that the suit he's wearing is a wool cashmere blend too, and made by Samuel Cohen bespoke tailors.'

'Well here it is.' Sophie handed Rufus a plastic bag containing the large piece of cloth. 'If you take this to the tailors I'm sure they'd tell you if it was theirs.'

'That's just what I intend to do.'

As Sophie was leaving, Nick and Helen walked in. 'We've let him go boss. I don't think he knows much. I would say he knows nothing about Franklin's other business interests. I would say he's a kosher accountant.'

'Oh and talking of kosher. I've a little job for you both. Take this and have a chat with Samuel Cohen. He's the tailor who makes Trendy's suits. This is the piece of cloth they found in that skip of yours Nick. I think, no, in fact I know it came from one of Trendy's suits, we just need to confirm it. I'd also lay odds-on that he got blood on it. In trying to get rid of it, he tried to burn it in that skip. Unfortunately for him it didn't all go up in smoke. He's just told me that the suit he's wearing is made by Samuel Cohen and it's a wool cashmere blend…'

'Oh very natty I'm sure.' Nick said sarcastically.

'I'm sure it's a very nice suit.' Helen dryly commented, sniggering.

'What about Trendy then?' Nick said as they were leaving.

'What about him?' Tremayne replied raising his eyebrows. 'He's not going anywhere. But I wouldn't linger, or his brief will be in and he'll be gone, just get me an answer and quick. Then we can nail him good and proper.'

Nick pulled up outside the tailors address. 'Not much of a shop.' Helen said as they got out of the car and stood looking up at the façade of the building in which a bespoke tailor worked. To each side of the single, green painted doorway were a mix of boarded-up shops, two Chinese takeaways; long gone was the traditional 'chippy', a betting office and a small supermarket boasting low prices. Screwed on the wall to the right of the door was a small brass plaque that read S. Cohen bespoke tailor. There was a small intercom below it. Helen pressed the button; a crackly voice answered 'Yes?' Helen replied 'Mr Cohen, I'm a police officer may we have a word please?'

'Oh, yes…come up.' There was a clicking noise and Helen pushed the door, it opened and they climbed the stairs to the first floor. At the top of the stairs, was a single door with a frosted glass panel with black lettering that read the same as the brass plaque. They entered a workshop that probably covered the area of three shops below. It was divided into a large workshop with a long wide bench along one wall, and a rack running down the opposite wall containing rolls of cloth. Just to the side of the entrance was a small office, outside of which, was a table and four chairs. Obviously, this was where Mr Cohen conducted his business.

'Mr Cohen? I'm Inspector Chandler and this is Sergeant Machin.'

'Good afternoon, what can I do for you, a new suit perhaps?' Cohen said smiling.

'No thanks, not today. I'd like you to look at this for me. Do you think you could say whether it's a piece of your fabric and to whom you sold it, probably as a suit or a jacket perhaps?'

Samuel Cohen took the plastic bag offered. 'Can I remove it from the bag?'

'Oh yes of course, but if you wouldn't mind...' Nick said proffering a pair of latex gloves. 'DNA, you know.'

Cohen put on the gloves and took the piece of fabric from the bag. He held it close to his eyes, then up to the light. 'David,' He called to a younger man working further along the table. 'Please look at this for me would you, my eyes aren't what they were. Is this ours, I think it might be?' The younger man also donned a pair of latex gloves before taking the fabric to examine it.

'I'm getting too old for this you know, my eyes don't allow me to do the fine stitching as my work demands.' Cohen said. 'David here does most of the fine work nowadays. I'm all right with the measuring and dealing with my clients, I enjoy that.'

David handed the fragment of cloth back to Samuel Cohen. 'Yes I believe it is one of ours, just a minute I'll get the file.' He disappeared into the office, returning after about five minutes carrying a large sample book, and balanced on top was a red document file. He opened the fabric sample book at a page he'd marked. 'This is it…' He placed Nick's sample on top of his example, 'See identical. It's a fine wool cashmere mix. We have only a few clients that have suits made from it, yes a few, not many…'

'And of those people who have had suits made from this cloth, is one of them a Mr Malcolm Smith, by any chance?'

David opened the document file and read through the short list of clients. 'Yes here he is Mr Malcolm Smith. Here is the order for a suit.'

Nick had Cohen photocopy the order and receipt for the suit made from the very same cloth. He also got Samuel Cohen to write a brief statement to the effect that Trendy had the suit made and the type of cloth used. He thanked Mr Cohen for his help and they left.

'What a result. I think we can safely say we've got that slimy toe rag.' Nick said gleefully and got back into the car feeling rather pleased with themselves. They walked into Tremayne's office; great beaming smiles on their faces.

'We've got it boss, this piece of cloth,' Nick said waving the plastic bag containing the fragment. '…has been identified by Samuel Cohen as being his material. He said he doesn't have many clients that choose it, it's rather expensive. And, we have a copy of the order and the receipt for a suit made for one Malcolm Smith also known as Trendy, scum bag of these parts.' Nick said sneering at the name. 'And we also have a signed statement confirming that this fragment is from a suit made by Cohen for Trendy.'

194

'Brilliant, now we might get somewhere. I think this should wipe the smug grin off his face.'

'Has he called in his solicitor yet?' Nick asked.

'Oh yeah too right and he's a smug little bugger too, also paid for by Tony bloody Franklin. Right then, let's go and have a word with Mr Smith shall we.'

Opening the door to the interview room the solicitor was immediately there with his comments.

'Really Chief Inspector this is too much, do you know that I've been kept waiting here for over an hour. I'm not in the habit of waiting on your beck-an-call. Now can we get on?'

'I'm sorry about that Mr Allen-Hyde, but I had to obtain confirmation and further information on a piece of evidence relating to your client Mr Smith.'

'Very well,' Allen-Hyde said contemptuously. '…have you charged my client yet?'

'No not yet, maybe we will after this meeting.'

'Very well, get on with it then.'

Nick reached out and switched on the recorder.

'Mr Malcolm Smith I must warn you that this interview is being recorded and what you say may be used as evidence should charges be brought. Now, for the recording Mr Smith would you please state your name, address and occupation?'

'Malcolm Smith, I'm the personal assistant to Mr Anthony Donald Franklin, and I live in apartment 46 Regency Gardens, Petersfield Ave.'

'What do you actually do for Mr Franklin; you say you're his personal assistant, would you expand on that a little more?' Tremayne asked.

'I do all sorts of things, I'm not a secretary as such, I don't take dictation or write letters you know. As his personal assistant, I er…'

'Personal assistant? That sounds rather a grand title. It's what you do to assist him with, that's what I'm interested in, as if I didn't know?' Tremayne said cynically.

'Chief Inspector my client will not answer questions that are not specific to your enquiries.'

'Oh I assure you these do relate to my enquiry.' Tremayne paused briefly. 'Very well Mr Allen-Hyde.' Tremayne nodded to Nick, who produced the plastic bag from his folder. He placed it in front of Trendy. 'I am now showing Mr Smith exhibit 1, a fragment of cloth. Now Mr Smith, do you recognise this piece of material?'

'No.' was all Trendy said, barely looking at it.

'This was found in a rubbish skip, in the builder's yard, at number 45 South Beach Road Hightown. This builder's yard is owned by Tony Franklin, which you, as his PERSONAL ASSISTANT would know.' Tremayne stared into Trendy's eyes, who remained placid and expressionless. 'Are you sure that you do not recognise it?'

'Yes I'm sure. I've never seen it before.'

'Well that's funny, you know why?' Tremayne paused, he looked intently at Trendy. 'I'll tell you why I think that's funny? Because, this piece of cloth…has been identified and verified that it came from a jacket or trousers that you wore. This material is from a suit that you ordered and paid for and it was made especially for you by a tailor, a bespoke tailor might I add, Mr Samuel Cohen. Now are you still saying that you've never seen it before?'

'It was stolen.'

'Stolen, really?' Tremayne raised his voice, 'Stolen?' He repeated sounding very sceptical. 'Don't make me laugh.' Tremayne paused for a moment. 'Okay…I am now showing Mr Smith a briefcase which was also found at the builder's yard. Now Mr Smith, do you recognise this briefcase?'

'No.'

'Well there again I find that hard to believe because this briefcase…as you are no doubt aware…has your finger prints on it. Now what have you to say to that Mr Smith?'

Trendy looked at Tremayne, he glanced over towards Nick Chandler, whose face was staring daggers back. 'No comment.' Trendy said before leaning towards Allen-Hyde. 'Say nothing.' Allen-Hyde whispered to him.

'I'd also like you to look at this Mr Smith. 'Tremayne said as he placed the semi-automatic pistol on the table. 'Do you recognise this?' He said knowing the answer before it came.

'Whoa, I've never seen that before.' Trendy said raising his voice in a shocked tone. 'I don't do guns Mr Tremayne and you know it.'

'Chief Inspector, I don't know what you are getting at. My client has denied knowledge to all your questions. So I suggest you either charge him or release him. My client has said that he does not recognise any of the items which you have shown him.'

'Well Mr Allen-Hyde, I think that your client does recognise them and he knows most certainly about incidents at that builder's yard. I think my evidence is strong enough to make a formal charge.' Tremayne glanced over to Nick as he stood up and moved away from the table.

'Inspector Chandler charge him.'

'Malcolm Smith,' Nick began. 'I am arresting you for the murder of Michael Paul Edwards. You do not have to say anything but it may harm your defence if you do not mention when questioned something you later rely on in court. Anything you do say may be given in evidence.'

Tremayne returned to the table and sat down. He continued. 'Now Trendy…tell us what you know about these items.' Tremayne stabbed at each in turn with his finger. '…this piece of wool cashmere cloth, this briefcase and of course, this gun. A weapon, which we know was also used in a failed post office raid; a raid where someone was shot and injured.' Tremayne stared at Trendy, he paused; he then slammed his hands flat on the table, the sound echoing around the room. 'Right then, let's start again. We'll begin with this piece of cloth shall we? And don't give me any guff Trendy. I've got the order and receipt with your bloody signature. And I can see that the suit you're wearing is of a similar material, quite expensive tastes you have, according to Mr. Cohen.'

'All right, all right so it is from a jacket I once had…'

'So, why was it found in a rubbish skip? Why did you try to burn it? Such an expensive jacket; why did you not just get it cleaned?'

'I got oil on it. I don't like things that have been soiled so badly. So I burnt it.'

'Oil eh! Sure it wasn't something else?' Tremayne's gaze was intent. Trendy appeared to be unfazed and relaxed.

'Like what?'

'How about blood…Mickey Edwards' blood. You were there Trendy, along with…would you like to tell me who was there with you or shall I tell you?'

'Blood Mr. Tremayne! Oh no, not blood, I've just said it was oil on it. I was bloody annoyed I can tell you, that jacket cost me a lot of money.'

'Yes I know I've seen the receipt. But where did you get that sort of money? A suit like that made by a bespoke tailor, and of such a fine material; what did that set you back then? A thousand pounds, fifteen hundred. More…two thousand pounds perhaps…more even? Come on Trendy I don't think even Tony Franklin pays you that much. Where does he get his clothes from by the way, does he shop with Samuel Cohen or Marks and Spencer?'

'I've no idea Mr. Tremayne. Yeah the suit cost me a lot of…' Allen-Hyde was looking across at Trendy, amazed at what he was spending on clothes. He was thinking I wish I could afford to buy that sort of suit. Tremayne caught his eye, was he thinking this guy is as guilty as hell? But he'd agreed to represent him.

'Yes I know,' Tremayne said. 'As I said before I've got the receipts here. I just wanted you to tell us all, I'm sure Mr Allen-Hyde here would like to know. But never mind I'll tell you what you paid. You paid Samuel Cohen the best part of five thousand pounds for each and every suit you've had from him. I wonder what he thinks you do for a living Trendy.' Tremayne gave him a questioning look, his eyebrows raised and his mouth slightly open. 'Now if I had paid that sort of money out for a suit and had something spilled on it…I think I'd do my best to get it cleaned eh? I don't think I would have burnt it. Yes, I would have cleaned it as best I could and given it to a charity shop, if it bothered me that much. Now come on Trendy tell me why you burnt such an expensive suit?'

'It was a very bad stain, I didn't think I could, I didn't think it'd come out, it would still have shown. Not even a charity shop would have taken it.' Trendy said. There was a tremor in his voice that Tremayne noticed, his whole demeanour had now changed, and he was beginning to look very nervous.

'You do talk bollocks Trendy. All right forget the suit for now. Let's talk about this briefcase shall we. Now, it's got your dabs on it, pretty good ones too I might add. Now there's no way you can tell me that you've never seen it before. You can also tell me why it was found boarded up in a wall and not in a safe…where any normal person would put it and why in a disused builder's yard, well disused for building purposes anyway; but not for other proposes eh Trendy.'

Trendy did not reply. He looked at Tremayne, then to Nick Chandler and then to his solicitor. Allen-Hyde whispered something to him before turning to Tremayne.

'Chief Inspector I'd like some time with my client alone if you don't mind.'

'Very well,' Tremayne said. 'Ten minutes.'

'I'll let you know when you can speak with my client again inspector.' Allen-Hyde said authoritatively as they left the room.

Tremayne, Chandler and the uniformed police officer left the interview room. They stood outside the door for a few seconds. Stay here Tremayne told the uniformed officer. Tremayne and Nick walked down the corridor.

'I'd like to know what those two buggers are cooking up.' Tremayne said to Nick as they walked away back to their office.

'We might get a confession out of him, if his brief thinks we've got him banged to rights.'

Tremayne smiled with a little laugh. 'You never know your luck Nick; you never know your luck.'

They arrived back into the office; Tremayne poured himself a coffee from a filter machine on their mess table. He stood sipping it, he glanced towards the incident board for some time.

'Okay Nick I think it's time we talked Riley. You and Helen go and pick up Reggie Riley. Oh, and I think you might take a little extra weight with you. I'll ring downstairs and organize that for you. Clive said he hangs around in the Cherry Tree pub in Patterson Street.'

'Yeah, I know where that is. And you might be right about extra weight. A battalion of the Gurkhas might be the best thing.' Nick laughed as he and Helen left the office.

Half an hour later Nick and Helen were at The Cherry Tree, Nick poked his head round the pub's door just to see if Reggie Riley was still in there. He was standing by the bar talking to an equally rough looking guy. They turned and went to sit in their car just along the road from the pub and waited for their back up. The first car arrived after ten minutes, shortly followed by two others, and then a security van. The eight uniformed officers were briefed by Nick Chandler.

'I don't know if any of you lot know Reggie Riley.' Two men nodded. 'But this guy is bad news,' He continued, with some of them looking bemused. These men thought they could handle the likes of Reggie Riley, afterall they were local coppers, but Nick wasn't sure whether they'd met the likes of this giant. Nick went into the pub alone. He walked the length of the bar. Riley was not to be seen, maybe he was in the gents. Nick was about to ask the barman where Reggie Riley was, when he heard shouting. An argument had broken out over the result of a game of pool and Reggie was the one shouting. He went over to the pool table. He spoke firmly.

'All right Reggie that's enough. Would you mind stepping outside with me, quietly that is.'

Riley glared at Nick. Helen was standing just inside the door and could hear everything that was going on. She turned and looked at the assembled group behind her. 'Get ready lads, any minute.'

'Fuck you.' Riley shouted at Nick.

'Now don't be like that Reggie. You know me. Now I just want a quiet word. I'd like to ask you about a mate of yours Malcolm Smith, Trendy.'

'Fuck you I said. You fuckin' deaf?' Riley made a move towards Nick. He moved quickly for a big man. Helen by now had taken a few steps into the pub; the uniformed men were still outside. She heard Nick shout something and saw him duck, narrowly avoiding a good right hand. She winced at the thought of it connecting. She looked towards Nick and decided it was time. She pulled the door open. 'NOW' she shouted and the eight uniformed officers rushed into the pub, Helen stood back and watched the unfolding scene. Riley was taken by surprise but that didn't mean he was taken easily. He kicked and punched leaving two of the uniformed bloodied. Amid shouts and orders he was quickly, but not easily, dealt with. After a few minutes scrummaging, he was handcuffed and was being dragged out of the pub much to the entertainment of the cheering onlookers, and all of them shouting abuse at the police officers. Soon he was being dragged along the footpath towards the open doors of the waiting van. An officer standing by the door, ready to close them quickly once Riley was inside. Still he kicked and struggled the whole time and still the shouts of the officers offering advice on how to control this wild beast of a man. Before he could be gotten into the van he'd lashed out with his feet and he'd booted and dented the open door of one of the police patrol cars. A baton was produced and Riley slumped slightly, he dropped to his knees momentarily, but rose up like a demon possessed, a raging bull. He lashed out with his feet, an officer jumped, narrowly avoiding a painful kick in the groin. Another was bloodied, his nose erupted as Riley made contact with his head. The officer's hand went to his face and he slumped. Six men now tried to subdue Riley, a writhing mass of bodies fought on the ground. 'Grab his legs.' Someone shouted. Two officers sat on them while a third tied them with a cable tie, a second one being secured in the same place for good measure. But this didn't stop him writhing and struggling. He was eventually pushed and pulled into the back of the van, and the inner cage door slammed shut. A great sigh rang out as the outer door was closed. Ten officers stood, breathing heavily, gasping, backs bent and hands on knees. Helen was now tending to the man with the bleeding nose.

'Get him away quick and locked up even quicker.' Nick said to PC Greg Wood. 'Right, everyone follow Greg, he'll need all the help he can get at the other end with that bugger.'

'You never said we had to catch a bull guv. Who the bloody hell was that?'

'That, my friends, was Reggie Riley. You should be stood a few pints tonight for that bit of effort.' They all laughed. The van was driven away and the street became quiet again. The conversation in the pub was probably police brutality.

Riley was safely locked in a cell, he was still shouting and cursing. Nick thanked the lads and they went off back to a quieter duty. Tremayne had arrived in the cell section to have a look at their prize. He peered through the Judas hole.

'We'll leave him in there for a while. He'll calm down soon enough. But on no account must that door be opened without backup. He's strong, so a taser might be available, just in case.' Tremayne said to the duty sergeant as he turned away from the door.

'Oh no fear of that Sir,' said the sergeant. 'I know Reggie from old, he's a thick as a brick, but as strong as an ox. There's no way I'm going in there without twenty men with me.' Nick and Rufus laughed before disappearing back to the quiet of the incident room.

'Right, that's got Reggie safe and sound. A few hours in the cell should quieten him down. Then we'll have a chat with him. Have you seen Trendy while I've been out?'

'No, we're still waiting to be summoned by Mr. Steven Allen-Hyde.' Tremayne shook his head with annoyance at the audacity of the solicitor and him having said I'll call you. It takes me all my time to be polite to the...' He was interrupted by the uniformed constable who was with them in the interview room.

'Excuse me, Chief Inspector Tremayne. Mr. Allen-Hyde asks if you would have a word with him.'

'Is he still in the interview room?' The constable said he was. 'Come on Nick this might be interesting.' They hurried along to the interview rooms; Allen-Hyde was waiting.

'Ah Chief inspector; now that I've had a chance to speak with my client. He has agreed to answer all your questions fully and truthfully as to the best of his knowledge.'

The three men entered the room, Allen-Hyde sat down next to his client and Tremayne and Chandler seated themselves opposite. Nick switched on the recording machine and said to Trendy. 'I must remind you that you are still under caution.'

'So, what is it that you want to say Trendy?' Tremayne asked, his voice calm.

'Okay Mr Tremayne that bit of cloth was off my jacket...'

'And you tried to dispose of it...because?'

Trendy remained silent for a long minute. 'All right it did have blood on it. I poured petrol on it, threw it into the skip and chucked a match in. It went up like a rocket, I singed my eyebrows...'

'Oh dear me, what a shame. Carry on.'

'Well I thought nothing would be left of it...anyway people used to dump their rubbish in it, it got covered. And to be honest I forgot all about it. I thought it had been incinerated.'

'What about Mickey Edwards. Did you kill him?'

'We were only meant to rough him up a bit. Mr. Franklin was pissed off with him; he welshed on a deal. So Mr. Franklin said to teach him a lesson. But things got out of hand. We'd waited for him to come out of the *Wild Orchid*, it was late, early hours of the morning. I think he was the last one out. I think he knew we were outside waiting, he was asked to leave in the end probably. We saw him come out, staggering he was, more than a bit pissed. We were in Mr. Franklin's jag...'

'Whose we?' Asked Nick.

'Reggie...Reggie Riley. We took him to the yard, tied him to a chair. Reggie hit him too hard, too much, you know what he's like, he's uncontrollable at times.'

'Yeah, tell me about it.' Nick commented. Trendy looked at him, not really understanding what he meant.

'We took him down to the beach, just down the road. Questioned him some more. We were going to leave him there. But Reggie hit him again, he collapsed. I was annoyed at Reggie. I called him a stupid bugger among other things. He blamed me for pushing him. Well, when we realized we'd killed him we panicked. We were more worried about what Mr Franklin would say. We took him well along the beach, into the sand hills and we dumped him. We tried to cover him up but...'

'Yeah, then the wind uncovered him and a lady walking her dog came across your handiwork. Anyway, what was this deal he had with Franklin?'

'Some stuff he'd nicked; jewellery I think. I never saw it. Mickey said it was worth squillions. Make us all rich he said.'

'Then what happened?'

'Well he got mouthy didn't he, gabbing to all and sundry in the club, I ask you. He'd had a few too many see. He talked about this stuff he had. Well Mr Franklin couldn't have that could he? His rivals could move in and he has enemies…'

'Yes I know,' Tremayne said raising his voice '…ME for one.' Allen-Hyde stared at Tremayne. 'Inspector please if you don't mind.'

'All right Trendy carry on.'

'Well Mr Franklin said to me that he should be taught a lesson. He can't make deals with one person who then goes shouting his mouth off in public places; now can he? So we picked him up and took him to the builder's yard. It's quiet there. The nearest house must be a few hundred yards away…'

'And you've insulated the place as well, haven't you?'

'Yes I suppose so. Anyway we tied him to a chair and I chatted to him. I said that Mr Franklin was disappointed with him. And that he shouldn't go shooting his mouth off. Well he got abusive with me, said it was none of my business. Said he'd deal with the organ grinder and not his monkey. I'm sorry but that annoyed me. I nodded to Reggie and he hit him. He's a big lad, strong; he only hit him once, twice maybe no, more. Well blood spewed from his nose and mouth, I was close, my jacket got splattered. Then I thought we'd killed him. I thought Mr Franklin would be pissed off with us and kill us, so we dumped him.'

'But what else Trendy…you worked on his face…Why did you do that?'

'As I said we panicked. We thought that if no one could recognize him.'

'And you finished him off on the beach.' Tremayne gave him a knowing look, stared deep into his eyes. 'Trouble was…he wasn't dead when he got there was he?' Tremayne said softly. Trendy's face developed a horrified look. 'No…we found tiny grains of brick dust from that beach. Did you know that was where they dumped all the bricks and concrete after the blitz? And there was a seed, a tiny little seed; came from a plant that only grows there too. He clawed at the ground as you or Reggie pummeled him to death.'

Trendy's head was hung low; he said nothing more until Tremayne started on the next topic.

'Okay Trendy, let's move on. What about this briefcase, the money in it and the CD, which we found concealed all nice and snug behind the wall.' Trendy suddenly looked up into Tremayne's face. Tremayne could almost see the cogs whizzing round in his mind, thinking up an answer.

'I know nothing about that, Mr Tremayne. I've owned up to the killing of Mickey, but what the briefcase is I don't know, I swear.'

'So if I mention to you…fifty thousand pounds in used notes…and the fact that there's a nice print of yours on it. Are you still saying you know nothing about it?'

'Mr Franklin has two or three briefcases and I've handled them all. But this money you're talking about, nah…fifty grand eh! Well, I might wonder why that was hidden there myself?'

'When we talk to Tony Franklin later, I'm betting he wishes he'd moved it sooner. But…just to cheer you up Trendy, I'll tell you something about that money. A lot of it had been withdrawn from circulation, in fact, it's just a worthless pile of paper; It'd make fancy wallpaper though. What do you make of that then Trendy?' Trendy said nothing, but laughed quietly to himself.

Rufus sat with Nick in the office and discussed Trendy's interview. They concluded that although he was a nasty piece of work, when he wanted to be, he did seem to be telling the truth about the money.

'I think he was genuinely puzzled about the money. So, Franklin might just be keeping some things from him, not so much of a personal assistant eh?

Nick asked when they might go and rattle Franklin's cage. 'I'm really looking forward to that. Do you think he'll know that we've got Trendy in custody?'

'I'm not sure but the jungle telegraph might have told him by now, and we'll certainly be having a little chat with Mr Tony Franklin.'

'I've been looking forward to this for too long. Do we bring him in or chat to him there.'

'Oh no, the time for pleasant chats is over. This will be under caution, here. So you can have the honour of escorting one Anthony Donald Franklin to interview room one.'

'Thank you very much…' Nick turned called to Clive. 'We've a nice little job Clive, come on.' They headed out of the office, a broad smile on Nick Chandler's face.

An hour later Nick walked into Rufus' office to announce that Franklin was sitting quietly in interview room one.

'What did he say when you arrived?'

'Well surprisingly nothing. He just grabbed his jacket and quiet as a mouse, which makes me smell a rat, he walked out to the car with me. Clive drove I sat in the back with him and he never uttered a single word all the way back here.'

Tremayne pushed open the door to the interview room, made for one of the chairs and sat facing Tony Franklin. Nick sat next to him and glared at Franklin, who ignored him.

'My lawyer will be here presently.' Franklin said matter of factly. 'Until he arrives, I'm saying nothing Mr Tremayne; any chance of a cup of tea?'

'Okay we'll come back when he arrives. Get him some *tea* constable.' Tremayne said and walked out of the room. 'That bloody man, he really gets my goat, for two pins I'd wipe that supercilious grin off his face.'

'Sorry boss, there's a queue.' Nick said laughing. Fifteen minutes later Tremayne got the message that Franklin's lawyer had arrived.

'Who is it? No, let me guess, Allen-Hyde again?'

'It is.' Nick replied. They returned to the interview room.

'Hello again Mr Allen-Hyde, we meet again so soon.'

'You seem to be having some kind of vendetta regarding my clients' Chief Inspector.'

'*Vendetta* Mr Allen-Hyde? Not at all! If your clients were not villainous scumbags they wouldn't be in here in the first place.' Allen-Hyde said nothing. He just gave Tremayne a hard look, knowing Tremayne spoke the truth about his clients.

'Well Chief Inspector what is it this time? Mr Franklin is a respected business man…'

'Ah well, be that as it may Mr Allen-Hyde. But what sort of business, and as for respected, well, that's debatable.' Tremayne nodded to Nick, who switched on the recording machine. 'Right then, talking of business let's get down to some.' Tremayne looked sternly at Tony Franklin and without preamble read his caution. 'Anthony Donald Franklin I must warn you that this interview is under caution and as such you do not have to say anything but it may harm your defence if you do not mention when questioned something you later rely on in court.

Anything you say may be given in evidence. So, Mr Franklin seeing that we were talking about business, tell me about yours?'

'You know very well Mr Tremayne, I own a club, and a property investment company…'

'And a builder's yard…but I'm puzzled as to what you do there. I didn't know you were a brickie as well Tony, man of many talents eh?' Franklin remained silent for a minute before answering.

'Shall I repeat the question Tony or do you need more time to think of an answer?'

'Yeah…the builder's yard, oh yeah they use it to store stuff to repair my properties.'

'Bollocks, I've been to your properties. I've been to the place where Mickey Edwards lived; that place has never seen so much as a lick of paint for donkey's years, and it smells musty too. You really should take better care of your houses Tony. Anyway we've been in there too…in the yard. I'm afraid it's in a bit of a mess just now, but a good joiner will soon have it back in shape. We found a couple of interesting items there…hidden, I might add.' Tremayne paused. He looked deep into Franklins eyes, they were cold and calculating. Tremayne thought that Franklin will take a bit of knocking off his perch, not as easy as Trendy. 'Would you like to know what we found, Tony?' Tremayne said calmly lifting his voice.

'No, not particularly, but I have the feeling that you're going to tell me. So go on then…enlighten me.' He said sounding quite bored and uninterested in the whole proceedings.

'Amongst other things…we found some money. Fifty–thousand–pounds…to be exact.' Tremayne said, pausing between and emphasising each word, letting them sink in and all the time he looked into Franklin's eyes. 'Fifty k Tony…FIFTY K. Now what do you suppose that was doing in your builder's yard eh?'

'Well that's certainly a lot of money Mr Tremayne, fifty thou' yeah. I imagine somebody would miss that, no mistake.'

'You know Tony the interesting thing is…is that we found Trendy's prints on the briefcase that held the money. Now how do you suppose they got there?' Franklin said nothing. Eventually he spoke

'He must have nicked it. I'll bet he nicked it from me, you wait till I get my hands on him, the bastard must have hid it there. I certainly don't know how it got walled up in my yard.'

'I never said where we found it.'

'I guessed, must have been hidden somewhere.' Franklin said, his voice still calm and non-committal.

'Okay, we'll move on. We also found this.' Tremayne opened a cardboard box-file and took out a plastic bag containing the semi-automatic pistol. Franklin looked at it. Tremayne said nothing. After a minute Franklin spoke first.

'What's that?' He said poking the pistol with his finger.

'It's a Smith and Wesson semi-automatic pistol. We found it in your builder's yard too.' Tremayne paused, with an intense look at Franklin. 'So now, we've got fifty thousand pounds and a hand gun…'

'What next…a cuddly toy?' Franklin remarked.

'Don't get smart with me…' Tremayne forced himself not to get into a tirade of abuse. 'No…not a cuddly toy, a CD, not one, there are three altogether. And on two of them there seems to be reference to an awful lot of money changing hands. Was that fifty k part of some sort of dealing you had going?'

'I told you Mr Tremayne that I know nothing about any briefcase, fifty k, or that gun. If Trendy's dabs are on that case then it's all down to him…not me.' Tremayne again remained silent for a few minutes. 'Tell me Tony…' he said 'How did you know this lot was *walled up* in the yard?'

'Er…you said'

'No, no; I never mentioned where or how we'd found it. Perhaps Mr Allen-Hyde would like to check the tape.' Tremayne said pointing at the tape machine.

'I assumed…I thought that's what you said.'

'Assumed, never assume Tony.' Tremayne said shaking his head. 'Now come on, spit it out, what's all this money, the CD and this gun? All found on your property, so come on, let's hear it.' Franklin played for time. Tremayne knew he was desperately trying to think of excuses. 'So Tony, let's talk about this CD, shall we. I have the feeling that it deals with some kind of betting scam. The amounts of money detailed total hundreds of thousands of pounds. I wondered how you could afford such a fancy apartment down by the docks. That club of yours doesn't bring in that kind of money, now does it.' Franklin remained silent. He just stared into space, listening but saying nothing. 'The money in the briefcase. Was that betting money? You know Tony, something bothers me about it. I get the feeling that it's been hidden for some time. Forget about it did we? That was foolish, wasn't it?'

'And what makes you say that Mr Tremayne?' Franklin said, sounding unconcerned by the whole proceedings. Tremayne was also thinking that Franklin was a contemptuous bastard who deserved what was coming to him. Then he said with great delight.

'Because Tony…and I don't know whether you realise,' A big grin spread across Tremayne's face. '…It's all out of circulation, it's old money, it's been superseded by new designs…in fact Tony,' Tremayne laughed '…you had walled up in your yard fifty k of duff notes…it's all worthless. All those twenty pound notes…valued at, what was it Nick, yeah…forty seven thousand pounds, to be exact. Now it's little more than toilet paper. I bet you've always wanted to wipe your arse on twenty quid notes eh Tony. What've got to say about that Tony?'

'Well somebody must be pretty well pissed off I would say.'

'Yeah I bet they are. And d'you know what Tony. I think that person is you…isn't it Tony? That's your money…that's your gun, and the CDs, well they're yours as well. Oh, and did I mention that ballistics have determined that this gun,' He said tapping the plastic bag containing the handgun.' '…was used in a crime?' Franklin suddenly looked anxious; he leaned towards his lawyer and whispered something. 'Oh and another thing there are prints on it too. Very careless some people. Any comments Tony?' Tremayne paused, Franklin remained silent. '…and would you like to know whose prints they were Tony?'

'Not really, but I get the impression you're going to tell me.'

'An employee of yours…'

'An employee of MINE…who?'

'Reginald Vincent Riley, ruffian of these parts.'

'I don't employ Reggie Riley.'

'You don't? But he's been seen talking to Trendy, and Trendy admits…' Franklin cut in.

'Look Mr Tremayne, everybody knows Reggie, and they also know to stay out of his way.'

'So tell me Tony. Why are his prints on a gun that was found on your property along with other items belonging to you, and all nicely hidden behind a wall?'

'I don't know.'

'All right, we'll come back to that…tell me about Mickey Edwards, Tony?'

'What about him…I told you ages ago he did little jobs for me, that's all.'

'Yeah I remember you saying. That he ran the girls home. Who then, as payment, let him get into their knickers. But what I want to know is…what about the little earner you negotiated with him?'

'What little earner…I don't know what you mean Mr Tremayne?'

'The little earner involving rather expensive jewellery…worth something in the region of…well I was told any one individual item could have been worth in excess of…a million pounds…ring any bells Tony? Come on Tony, that's serious money in anybody's language.' Franklin remained silent; again he turned towards his lawyer, who simply shook his head indicating to Franklin to remain silent. 'Trouble was Mickey didn't deliver did he Tony? He welshed on the deal, so you had him killed, you gave the order…that's what happened wasn't it Tony? You, Trendy and Reggie Riley, you're all involved…thick as thieves? I'll give you time to reflect on your next move. Interview suspended. Tremayne checked his watch and quoted the time.

17

Settled on their huge sofa Sophie lay comfortably against Rufus' chest. Music played softly in the background, Vivaldi's Four Seasons. Two drinks sat on the small table close at hand. Enjoying each other's company without talking, they were just being close together, alone, warm and snug in each other's arms. Rufus reached out and took a sip from his gin and tonic, it'd been there for some time, the ice melted away diluting the flavour. 'Let's go out for dinner?' he said to her out of the blue. 'Where do you fancy?'

'Yes, why not, what a lovely idea. I'd like that.'
An hour later they were walking into their favourite restaurant.

'The last time we were in here that man Sutcliffe began all this nonsense about cold cases and hidden treasure.' Sophie said remembering how Redfern Sutcliffe had spoilt her evening.

'I know,' Rufus said apologetically. 'I don't think it'll happen tonight.'
They ordered their meal and settled down to enjoy it.

'I know I've just said that I hated Redfern's interruption,' Sophie began 'but are you any closer to solving the…mystery? I mean it's been a few weeks now.'

'Well we've concluded the case of Mickey Edwards, I hope. But we still don't know where Mickey got those jewels, nor are we any closer to relating Carter and Mason. Did I mention that he was German, Mason that is?'

'No I don't think so.'

'Well yes he was. He also had a brother, a general no less, in the German army. Nick went to Norway and to the same house where the naval mission went. He spoke to the son of the family that had owned the house since before the war. It was in the garden of this house where Carter found the jewels. So, he just picked them up and walked off with them. Manfred Hans Maurer was the bank manager's brother's name. We think he'd been picking up these artefacts, looting them from the poor unfortunates of war for himself. He'd taken some leave in the area and for some unknown reason he decided to hide the artefacts in the garden. Nils Amundsen showed Nick where he and his sister hid things when they were children. It was a sort of mini cave in the rock, hidden by long grass, just big enough for a rucksack. He said it wasn't very good, as animals dragged anything out they put inside. So I imagine that's what happened for Carter to find the bag they were in.'

'I bet that annoyed him.'

'That has to be the understatement of the year Sophie…annoyed, he'd have been incandescent. I think he must have suspected that a member on that mission took them. Somehow, I think he must have alerted his brother, and told him to be on the lookout for them. But how do we prove that he wrote to his brother…well, I'm at a loss. How could he do that anyway?'

They continued their meal in silence for a while. Then Sophie said 'If he posed as a refugee, he could have been able to get a message, via the Red Cross, coded most likely, to his brother. What do you think?'

'Yes, good thinking, it is a possibility. I'll check it out.' Rufus said taking a sip from his glass of wine.

'What puzzles me though is,' Sophie said. '…even if Carter managed to get this stuff back without being seen, why did he divide the haul. But, did he sell half of it? There might be a bank account somewhere with a large amount of unclaimed, unused money in his name?'

Rufus lifted his glass to his lips, he took a sip; his eyes became distant in deep thought for a moment. 'You know,' he said eventually. 'I'd never actually thought of that. You're very astute at times, you know. Yes, It might well be worth a look, it could lead us to a buyer; well a buyer's name anyway, but he's probably long dead by now.'

Tremayne listened to the ringing of the number he'd just dialled, a couple of minutes passed before it was answered. He didn't recognise the voice. 'Hello, I'm trying to reach Frankie Bolton.' He said.

'Hold on I'll get her for you.' The female voice said. Tremayne could hear a cacophony of voices and noises in the newspaper's office. 'Hello Frankie Bolton' She answered. 'Oh Hello Rufus, what can I do for you?' They discussed progress so far and then Rufus talked about checking out various banks.

'Have you tried to get your hands on a possible account?' He asked.

'Well it did cross my mind, but as yet I've not done anything. I'm not sure that I'd be given access though…but a serving police officer might; especially when such valuable stolen artefacts are concerned.' She said. Tremayne agreed with her saying he'd put someone onto it.

'If and when I've got anything, Frankie, we'll get together and collate our findings.' They agreed. Tremayne replaced the phone. He picked it up again. He called Helen Machin.

'Helen, I'd like you to check something out for me.' He said. 'See if you can trace an old bank account. It may or may not still be active but I think we might find quite a bit of money in it. And I've a feeling it'll be from the sale of those jewels we found in Mickey's flat.'

'Sorry…whose account are we talking about?' Helen said.

'Simon Carter's.'

'Simon Carter's? How do you come to think of this then?' she said astonished.

'I think Carter did get the jewels back, in fact we can be absolutely certain he did. He divided them; one half we found in the bunker, the other we found in Mickey's flat…right?'

'Yeah…' Helen said still not quite following Rufus' train of thought.

'Carter did sell part of his haul. It must have been to someone in the area, where the jewels remained. Otherwise Mickey would never have got his hands on them. So, unless Carter spent it all, which I doubt. He didn't have time did he? He was found dead not long after the mission to Norway, only three months if I remember rightly.' Helen agreed. 'So in that time he must have put the cash somewhere. Either in a sock under the bed or…in a bank account and that's the most likely. He had no reason to be on the lookout for anyone.'

'Okay, so you want me to check with the bank?' Helen asked, as if she didn't know.

Tremayne had said that she should start with someone at the Royal Bank of Scotland as that was the bank that took over Williams and Glyns, which took over Williams Deacons, which was the bank where Richard Mason worked as manager. Helen walked into the regional head office of the Royal Bank and asked to speak to the duty manager. She sat on one of the chairs in the banking hall and waited. She watched people coming and going, paying in money, poking cards into the ATM, and hurrying off to spend it. She watched the queue at the information desk, and the expression of the assistant, as she explained the complexities of whatever. Eventually a uniformed young lady approached her and said the duty manger was free. She apologized for the wait.

'Good morning I'm Detective Sergeant Helen Machin.' She said to Thomas Adams, showing him her warrant card at the same time. After they had greeted one another she asked him if and where she might gain access to archive accounts dating back to the Williams Deacons era. He looked at her astonished.

'Well…' he said 'that's some time ago, the bank has been through another name change since then.'

'Yes I know.' Helen said. 'But is it possible for me to go through your archives in order for me to locate these accounts. It is possible that one of these may well still be active.'

'What are the names you're looking for, just out of interest?'

'One is for a man called Simon Carter, he was a naval officer during the war, and he died in nineteen forty four. The other is a Richard Mason or possibly Richard Maurer. Now he worked as a manager for Williams Deacons. He died in nineteen sixty three. Both these men died in suspicious circumstances and that's why I need to trace the bank account.' Adams looked inquiringly at Helen, but got no response. After a minute he spoke.

'Very well Detective Sergeant Machin, I'll introduce you to our archivist Annette Wade.'

Thomas Adams escorted Helen into an office and introduced Annette Wade. 'Annette can give you access to all that you need. I'll leave you in her capable hands, good bye.' Helen half said good bye but Adams was quickly out of the door and gone. She turned to the middle-aged lady, who by now had walked round her desk to greet Helen.

'Hi, I'm Helen Machin.' Helen briefed Annette. 'Right Annette where do we start?'

'Who are we looking for and when?' she asked. Then the two women began their long trawl through the archive.

Nick walked into Tremayne's office. 'I've just had a Richard Mason on the phone. Said you spoke to him about his father, the bank manager. If possible could you go along to his house he has something to show you.'

'Oh good, he spoke only briefly the last time we met. He must have found something since then; umm, could well be?' Tremayne picked up his phone and made arrangements to go and see Richard Mason junior. A couple of hours later Tremayne was on his way. The anticipation made Tremayne almost feel like a kid again, on Christmas morning.

Richard Mason watched the Alfa Romeo pull into his driveway before going to the front door to welcome his guest.

'Sorry to be so insistent that you come here Chief Inspector but I've something to show you. Please do come in.' Tremayne followed him into an elegantly furnished room, antique furniture and quality Wilton carpets. A young woman, who was introduced a Sally brought in a tray of coffee. She said good morning to Tremayne, and smiled as she put the tray down and left them alone.

Sitting on the table in front of them was a wooden box. Tremayne thought it must be the infamous wooden box that Richard Mason had mentioned during their last meeting, the very one that his mother had threatened him not to touch.

'So this is the box you mentioned?'

'This is it…the box of secrets and intrigue.' Mason began. 'After our last meeting Chief Inspector, you re-established my curiosity. And to be honest I'd forgotten much of what was in it, so on returning home; well a few days later, I got it down from the attic. I read through everything, I looked at every photo, read every letter and note. I had emptied the box, but I had found nothing of great interest, well not to you anyway. I was placing it onto the floor and as I did, I tipped the box sideways. I heard a sound, like a…a sort of knock. I looked inside but the box and as I said, I'd emptied it. I shook it and there was something, something loose in the bottom. I thought that maybe it had a false bottom or something, a secret drawer as sometimes these things have; a place for the young ladies to keep their secret love letters. Well I took the box into the garage and I took a screwdriver to it. I discovered the false bottom…real James Bond stuff what?'

'And you found…what?'

'These…letters,' Richard Mason pushed them towards Tremayne. '…as you see they are written in German. But look at the date Chief Inspector…nineteen forty four. They are from my father's brother Manfred, unfortunately I don't read German.'

'Neither do I, but if it's all right with you, may I take them? On second thoughts, no. But if you could copy them for me, I can get them translated. If I need the originals at any time I know where they are.'

'Yes of course, my computer's in the study. I've got a scanner, I'll just be a minute.' Mason went off to copy them. Rufus looked through the other items from the box. There were family photos and letters, all from before the war. Rufus noticed the dates on some. He was looking at the photos when Richard Mason returned.

'Those are people I don't know Inspector; family from Germany perhaps but these two men, that's my father,' he said pointing to one of the figures. '…and this I think is his brother Manfred.' The two men looked at the photos for a minute before Mason handed over the copies. 'Here're the copies of the letters for you Inspector.'

'Thank you Mr Mason. I appreciate this.'

'It's a strange business Chief inspector Not only finding out that you have unknown family in other parts of the world. But this intrigue, you know it's hard to believe that one's father was perhaps mixed up in something…shall I say criminal activities.'

'Well I'm not absolutely sure he was; intrigue maybe, criminal activities well…that's not proven. So don't think too badly of him.'

'You'll let me know what the letters say, I'd like to know.'

'Yes of course. Now I think I must go, much to do. And thanks again. Good bye.' Tremayne headed back to the station.

Tremayne phoned Frankie Bolton. 'I've a favour to ask Frankie. None of my lot is of any use. But do you speak German by any chance? I seem to remember Tony Clayton saying you did languages at university.'

'Yes I do, why?'

'I need a couple of letters translating, if you wouldn't mind. You'll need to do it here, okay.'

'Yes fine, when do you want it doing.'

'As soon as you can actually.'

'Right then, I'll come round now. I'll see you in about an hour.'

Tremayne looked round the incident room. 'Is Helen not back yet?' somebody shouted that she wasn't. It was a couple of hours later that she eventually arrived, and by that time Frankie was busy translating the two letters that Richard Mason had found in the bottom of his mother's old wooden box.

'I've been ages in that archive,' said Helen as she walked into the office. '…the archivist Annette Wade was extremely helpful. Anyway we managed to find accounts for both Simon Carter and Richard Mason senior.'

'Right then let's hear it.' Tremayne said enthusiastically.

'Attached to Simon Carter's details there was also a letter, brief but nonetheless informative. It said that he had just inherited a sum of money from an aged aunt and that a large sum would be deposited in due course.

That was obviously to avoid suspicion of course. Now I think we are safe in saying that was the money he received from the sale of the jewellery. Look here,' Helen said pointing to a place on the statement…he is making a very large deposit on the twenty second of August, that's four weeks after the mission to Norway. See five thousand pounds which was an awful lot of money then. I've looked on the internet and you could have bought a good house for fifteen hundred. I've converted it; have you any idea what that would be worth today…' A few volunteered a figure ranging from a hundred to five hundred thousand. 'I'll tell you, be ready to be amazed…over a million.' The office rang with astounded voices.

'A million pounds, my God; so where's all that money now?' Tremayne asked.

'No idea,' Helen shrugged her shoulders. '…it's not shown in his account now. But it was moved; it was withdrawn; wait for it…on the Friday before Carter was found dead on the Monday. The withdrawal was counter signed by the bank's manager…one R. G. Mason.'

'Richard Mason countersigned the withdrawal, so where did it go?'

'If I was a betting woman, I'd say to Mason's brother. He may have given his brother, bank manager Mason, a sizable sum, just to see him right. But there were no amounts of money paid into his account, nothing unusual anyway.'

A knock at the door disturbed their conversation. 'Come in' Tremayne called, the door opened. Frankie stood there waving a bundle of papers.

'Here we are then, my translation, want to hear it, it's good, you'll like it.'

'You bet we do.' Tremayne said enthusiastically, in unison with Helen. Tremayne called Nick in to hear what Frankie had got. 'Okay Frankie we're all ears.'

'They are addressed, obviously to Richard Mason from Manfred Hans Maurer. He didn't use Mason's German name you notice. So the first letter is dated the thirty-first of July nineteen forty four. That was just a few days after the mission landed in Norway. So what he is saying is that some valuable items have been stolen from me and that they must have been taken by one of the allied sailors who landed near Klokkarvik. He goes on to say. It is imperative that you make urgent enquiries to determine the whereabouts of these articles and take all necessary steps to retrieve them and deal with the perpetrator. It is simply signed MHM. It's very short as though it was written down as a message. Judging by the language used it's not a letter as such, it is a curt message, an instruction even, telling his brother to do what he asks.'

'So,' Tremayne said. '…do we think that it was received via a radio and taken down verbatim? Which would mean either Mason had a receiver or someone else did and passed the message on…yes? I wonder if his son remembers a radio like that when he was a boy. Sorry Frankie, carry on.'

'The second letter or message is dated the second of October, which is twelve days before Carter was found dead…'

'And nine days before the withdrawal of that money.' Tremayne commented. 'Sorry again Frankie, please'

'What withdrawal?'

'I'll tell you in a minute.'

'So, this is received on the second of October. This is a very short message too, in fact just a couple of words; it simply says, deal with it. There may have been a message sent back to Norway and this is the reply. But what it means…I've no idea.'

Tremayne leaned back in his chair and stared at the ceiling; everyone else just sat and waited, but said nothing. Tremayne came forward after a minute.

'I think I do,' he said. '…let me try to wrap it up. What we have is Carter returning from Norway with a rucksack full of precious artefacts. He quickly finds a buyer or he knew someone in the first place. Possibly it was prearranged that if he ever came across anything of value…then he was safe and he could move it quickly. He sells it, well half of it anyway. He then deposits the five thousand pounds in a bank account. He tells the bank manager that he has inherited a fortune from a wealthy aunt. But…unbeknown to him, the manager of the bank is the brother of the man who Carter had nicked it all from and he's a bit pissed off.' Tremayne chuckled at the thought. 'Then he got the message from his brother in Norway or somewhere. Mason put two and two together, he realised who Carter was. A message was sent back and this final message was returned. Not long after that Carter is found dead.' Tremayne paused to think. 'I would suggest that Mason used some of the cash to pay off the assassin…well as his brother had said 'deal with it'. The money was withdrawn from Carter's account on the Friday. The signature forged by Mason, but he has no worries as he's the manager, so he thinks he can cover any queries. Carter is found dead on the Monday. Nobody knows anything about jewels. He's in the clear.'

'Okay, so where's the money now? There'd still be a sizable amount left.' Helen asked.

'No idea, maybe it got back to Mason's brother after the war. Maybe they split it between them, but now it's long gone. Those other pieces we've got; well they'll, go up for sale no doubt.'

Tremayne thanked Frankie for her efforts. 'When I get the word you can write your story perhaps.' She left, saying 'One day maybe, might make a novel, what do you think?'

'Good idea.' Tremayne said. Frankie Bolton left police headquarters.

'So, that's that then, but what about those three buggers downstairs?'

'Yes, I think we've got a tight enough case to put them away for a while. But I'd like to get to the bottom of that betting scam they were running. If we can do that, it might just put the last nail in their proverbial coffin.'

'If it was a scam.' Nick commented.

'Of course it was a bloody scam, fraud or blackmail there's something in there. Come on Nick can you honestly see Tony Franklin doing anything above board? Because I can't. No, there's something here and it might just be that final nail in his coffin and we can bury the buggers. We need someone to look at it who is expert enough to spot something.'

'Okay we'll let the fraud guys take a look at it.'

Nick left Tremayne's office. He asked Martin how he was getting on with the CD. He said he'd got as far as he could. 'I've deciphered the names but as for the figures well...I'm not sure.'

'Boss says to let the fraud guys take a look.'

'Okay, fair enough...but I'd like just a little while longer. Can I keep it till... tomorrow?'

'Fair enough Martin, sure you want to be bothered?'

'Yeah I'll just give it another look see.'

Martin reloaded the CD and brought up the *Microsoft access* files. He stared at the columns, the coded names, which he could now decipher. He picked up his pencil and began to write down the top few names from the enormous list.

All right, the headings, six columns; interesting one in red, okay. Now what did Roger say, E is the commonest letter. Martin checked all the words, counting off the commonest letter used, substituting this for the letter E. *Ah, a double E here, interesting. Now if this is about betting then...this might be the meeting, yeah abbreviated to meet.* Martin carried on working through the coded words, guessing some but coming up with the goods. The names were trickier, but Roger Benson said they would be. He then turned his attention to the figures in the columns. He'd worked out the headings. He wrote down: Name, of punter; meet meaning the race meeting, the date followed, then the figures, headed bet, odds, pay out, and owe in red, he guessed that that meant money owing. *These suckers have borrowed; they were on a losing streak. Some owed rather large sums too, several thousands of pounds. There must be another file with addresses.* He thought. *Now if it's on this disk, where the hell...maybe there's another disk?* He searched though the files, but came up with nothing. *If I could...then we'd really have them banged to rights.* He pushed his chair back and walked over to Nick, 'Are they still pulling the yards apart Nick?'

'Yes, they're giving it a real once over.'

'Have they found anymore CDs?'

'Oh I don't know; is it important?'

'Possibly yeah, I think I've cracked that one,' he said nodding towards his desk. 'It seems to be related to betting, they're names, dates, bets made, the odds and the pay outs but there's a column in red. I think it refers to monies owing, they've borrowed from Franklin, some to the tune of several thousand pounds.'

'Jesus, Franklin's the last person you want to be in debt to.'

'Yeah, But what I'm looking for are addresses, there're no addresses on that one. I think they must be on a separate disk. They might be on one in his office at the club?'

'Well we can shoot off down to the yard if you like.'

'Yeah why not.'

Nick pulled up outside the builder's yard. There were still several white suited forensic people busy poking around. They arrived at the gate and where issued with clean suits. Inside the building were three other people.

'Have you come across any CDs Rachel?' Nick asked.

'Yes we have actually, yeah. They are in a box in the van, one CD's Van Morrison.' she said laughing.

'Yeah and another I suppose is the Yard Byrds.' Nick and Martin walked over to the forensics' vehicle, calling to a guy nearby to let them see the box containing the CDs they'd found.

'Are these all the disks you've found?' Nick was told they were, so far. 'We'll need to take these, we'll be careful.' He said as he tucked the box under his arm and walked off site; dumping their clean suits with the bored looking constable standing by the gate, keeping the nosy neighbours and journalist at bay. But their interest had wavered, leaving the constable with nothing to do. 'Just a couple more hours.' Nick commented as he handed over his white protective suit.

As Nick drove back to the station, Martin donned a pair of latex gloves and had a quick flick through them. Several were music CDs as the forensic officer had said. 'You'll not believe this Nick, this one is Van Morison.' He laughed. 'But these others, they look promising...coded titles.' Martin said. 'If not, I think we're up shit creek without the proverbial paddle.'

Martin was able to discard some of the CDs straight away, having quickly put them through his computer; they were just unlabelled music and crap music at that,' He said 'but nonetheless music.' The others looked more interesting. He came across more data files. He called to Tremayne, who was standing by the incident board.

'I think these might be what we've looking for boss.'

'Good, let's hope you can find something useful.'

'I'll give it my best shot, boss.'

By now Martin was getting better at seeing through the substitution code. He could now spot the frequently used letters quickly and with the odd guestimate, he usually came up trumps. He worked away for a couple of hours before he called into Tremayne's office. With a deep puffing out of air, inflating his cheeks he said with relief

'I think I've cracked it boss.'

'Excellent, let's see what you've got. Nick, Helen' he shouted. '...want to see this?'

Nick and Helen entered the office and stood behind Martin, straining their necks, trying to get a clear view of the monitor.

'What we've got on this disk,' Martin said tapping the computer screen 'Is a list of punter's names, along with race meetings, the dates of those meetings and money changing hands, bets, the odds and most importantly money owed, see, these in red. Now on this one,' He continued, changing the CDs. 'I think we have the addresses of the punters who laid bets and those that took out loans from Franklin. I just need to recheck my findings but...yes, I sure that's what we've got.'

'Excellent; what's on the others Martin?' Tremayne asked.

'This is the roll-over prize…'

'How do you mean, roll-over, why, what's on it?'

'I'll show you.' Martin took out the disk they'd just looked at and replaced it with another. The officers watched for a few minutes before realising what was going on. The disk was a movie showing a couple having sex. The picture was shaky, not entirely focussed and a bit grainy, certainly not a professional porno, but the man in the picture was clear enough. 'What we are looking at is a honey pot scam. The guy caught…on film, is then blackmailed. The girl will be a local tart who would be well paid, she wouldn't care who the guy was as long as the money came in. He was probably a bit pissed when she came on to him, an old guy and a young girl…well. There are ten short films on this CD alone. But what makes me laugh is this disk…it's amateur night and I don't mean just the quality of the picture. No, it also includes all the details, in plain English.' Martin snorted. 'I don't know why they didn't destroy this lot. What do you think boss, do we contact these guys?'

'Yes I think we might have to, but they might not want to talk especially if their wives are unaware of their…extramarital activities. However our job is to put away scumbags like Tony Franklin and this is as good an opportunity as we'll ever get.' Tremayne said. 'I'm going to speak to ol' beardy chops. Give me a while and then I think we can move on it.'

'If we can find just one who's prepared to talk to us boss, shall we go through the list?' Nick suggested. Tremayne agreed and told them to proceed.

Tremayne arrived in Chief Superintendent Pearsall's office, who as it turned out, was enthusiastic about removing Franklin from the streets for a few years.

'I don't want any comebacks with this Tremayne, softly-softly, right? If this goes pear-shaped and someone makes a complaint…well you know the consequences.' Pearsall paused for a minute or two. Tremayne sat watching his fish swim around his aquarium. 'Alright Tremayne carry on, but remember Tremayne…do it right and put Franklin and his hoodlums away.'

'Yes Sir.' Tremayne said as he left Pearsall's office. He walked back down to the incident room, not exactly over the moon but confident that he could bring Franklin and his empire down. He spoke to his team, emphasizing what Pearsall had just told him. 'He wants a softly-softly approach and that means we only speak to the victims if they agree to it.

We do not pressurize them…understood. We'll phone first as you suggested Nick. We verify the person involved before going further. We arrange a meeting, only if they are prepared to take things further. Maybe some of these guys are single or divorced. They might be our best chance. Helen, Clive, I want you to take this on. And remember our necks are on the block with this…all of us remember. But you understand we also need to nail Franklin. Okay off you go.'

'These betting scams or whatever they are.' Martin said 'Many of them are clearly none starters. It looks like they've paid up as there are zeros next to their names, but others are more promising, since they're large sums. Now I know they are a few years old, but these punters may still be in the grip of Franklin. The whole thing might still be on-going. So I'll try and decipher them and run them through our database. We'll see what appears.'

18

Tremayne sat at his desk, oblivious to the bustle going on in the incident room beyond the closed door of his office. He thought about all that had gone on in the last few weeks. *Perhaps I should contact Redfern Sutcliffe*, he said to himself. He was the man who started this whole damn wild goose chase off in the first place. Was it all worth it? Tony Franklin apart; Nick's trip to Norway, finding and excavating a wartime anti-aircraft battery, linking Mickey Edwards' murder into it all, and a million pounds worth of precious jewellery to boot. Suddenly he was snapped out of his daydreaming by Martin knocking on the door.

'I think you ought to see this boss, on my computer.'
Tremayne followed Martin, pulling up a chair to his desk, he sat down and looked at the screen.

'Okay Martin what've you got?'

'This CD with the list of names; well I managed to decipher them. I then ran them through our database and a few of them cropped up. I'm not sure they're all worth chasing though. Anyway, I went through the first few on the list who still had outstanding debts. These debts range from fifteen hundred pounds to almost five grand. I was able to phone two of the three.' Martin pointed to the names. 'Those two live locally. The third name is dead; he's marked up as suspicious. He fell or maybe he was pushed into the Albert Dock and drowned. Post Mortem report said he must have been semiconscious when he went in. There was bruising on his face, his chest, and long wheals on his back, injuries that do not coincide with falling into water. It looked as though he'd taken a beating first. And he had a lot of alcohol in his bloodstream; if he'd been breathalysed he'd have been six times over the limit. So what do you think; Franklin's handy work? Obviously the investigation at the time didn't have this CD, now if we shove this in front of Franklin's nose it might just tip the balance.

'Yeah,' Tremayne said, but not enthusiastically. '…sounds like he missed a payment or most likely several. Who was he?'

'Er, he was…Raymond Jonathan Davidson.'

'Right Martin, get what you can about him, then we'll go and have another word with Mr Franklin.'
Martin worked through the police database, typing Raymond Jonathan Davidson into the search. He came up with the name of the senior

investigating officer, DI Terry Stearn. Martin picked up the phone and spoke to him.

'Yeah, we worked on it for a few weeks, but the trail ran cold, there was no evidence, well nothing we could build a case on anyway. He'd only been in the water overnight. He was found by one of the cleaners going into work at about half past six. He'd obviously been seen to elsewhere and then taken to the dock. We were puzzled why he was dumped there in such a prominent place. They obviously intended him to be found quickly. But why, that's anybody's guess.'

'Did you ever find out where he might have been taken to before hand?'

'No, could have been anywhere…waste ground, empty warehouse, garage, you know as well as I do there's loads of places. Have you come across something…well you must have done, otherwise why would you be interested?'

'Yeah, we're investigating the murder of Mickey Edwards. And he's been linked to Tony Franklin and we've come across this builder's yard, it's owned by Franklin and this is where his thugs worked on debtors. I'd lay bets that this guy Davidson spent some time there.'

'Where is this yard?'

'Hightown, why?'

'Where exactly?' Martin explained where the yard was. DI Stearn asked him hold a minute.

'Yeah, I know that place. We were tailing a guy once, a big guy, looked like a cage fighter. He drove to that yard with another bloke. This other guy…well they were like chalk and cheese, complete opposites if you know what I mean. We took a few piccies of them. Would you like to see them?'

'Would I! I'll be round, see you soon.'

Martin returned with an envelope containing the pictures that DI Stearn took. Martin excitedly rushed into Tremayne's office.

'I've just been to see DI Terry Stearn at Grosvenor Street boss. He had some interesting photos. Take a look, you'll like them.' Tremayne emptied the envelope onto his desk. Sorting them the right way up, he studied them for less than a minute. 'Would you look at this – Trendy and Reggie Riley and the man himself…' Tremayne jumped out of his seat and shouted through the open office door. 'Nick, Helen come and give yourselves a treat.'

'Gotcha bastards…let's see you squirm out of this Tony.' Nick was delirious with joy, as were the rest of them. 'Good work Martin….nice one, the drinks are on me.' The photos went into Tremayne's desk drawer, he locked it. The celebration started early that night in the Golden Lion. The following morning Franklin was back in the interview room.

Franklin was sitting alongside his solicitor, Steven Allen-Hyde, when Tremayne and Nick Chandler arrived, they sat opposite, and Nick turned on the recording machine.

'I must remind you Mr Franklin that you are still under caution.' Tremayne began with the usual formality. 'Right Tony, some new evidence has come to my attention.'

'What new evidence? There's no new evidence I'm squeaky clean and you know it.' He said boldly, assuming very confidently that Tremayne had nothing whatsoever on him.

'Well, for a start there are these CDs. They were found in *your* builder's yard. DC Wilcox has gone through them and do you know what he found? I'm sure you do although I've a feeling you'll say you don't.'

'You're doing all the talking, Mr Tremayne. I'm saying nothing.'

'Video's…little films, not long…but long enough.'

'Chief inspector, are you going to prevaricate all day or are you going to get on with it. I'm a busy man and I'm not here for theatricals.' Allen-Hyde said sternly.

'All right, these are videos used for blackmail purposes. They show men *in flagrante delicto.* You're quite a Cecil B de Milne Tony. Then you make your appearance, you confront these men, or do you send Trendy? You treat the unfortunate fellow to the premier performance, he would be shocked and irate no doubt and then you demand money…with menaces…or you tell them it goes on general release. How much did you make out of these Tony? Was it a one-off payment or were there instalments?' Tremayne stared at Franklin who remained impassive and cold. 'I've not finished yet though…not only are there videos, there's this other file. Now on this there is a list of names, in code I might add. But unfortunately for you we've cracked it. It wasn't a difficult code, just a five letter substitution code.' Tremayne smiled at Franklin, but he remained silent. 'The database is divided into six columns headed: name, meet meaning a race meeting, the date of that meeting, the bet placed and the odds given and in bold red letters is money owing.' Tremayne paused after naming each heading, for effect and allowing it to sink in. 'Are you following this Tony?'

'Yes. But I don't know what you're getting at.'

'Bear with me, you will. From the list DC Wilcox picked out those names with the largest sums owing, many thousands of pounds; in excess of twenty k in some cases. There were three names he picked out in particular; we've spoken to two of them but the third person unfortunately died. We learned from police records that he was found floating in the Albert Dock. Post mortem report said that he was not dead when he went into the water and that he had injuries most likely the result of a beating...' Tremayne stared hard at Tony Franklin, who returned the stare with his blank, cold expression. 'Looks like your handy work Tony, well more likely that of Trendy in association with Reggie Riley, but under your orders. The two people that DS Machin has spoken to have named you as the one with whom they had dealings. So it looks like you are well and truly banged to rights; anything to say Tony eh?' Franklin remained silent and expressionless as he'd been for the whole of the interview. He had made few comments and neither had he spoken to his solicitor Steven Allen-Hyde. 'Oh, one last thing Tony. Do you remember me asking you about a builder's yard?'

'Yeah, vaguely...I said that I don't remember any yard. It must be one used by my builders to repair my properties.'

'Yes that's what I remember you saying. Well, I'd like you to look at these. For the tape, I am showing Mr Franklin some photographs. Take a good look Tony, they're quite good, these fourteen megapixel cameras give fine detail when blown up. For the tape the photographs I am showing Mr Franklin show Malcolm Smith, known as Trendy, an employee of Mr Franklin, with him is Reginald Vincent Riley known as Reggie...and the third man... is that not you Tony? Anthony Donald Franklin. You are all about to enter the said builder's yard at number 45 South Beach Road Hightown. The same builder's yard which you said, not five minutes ago...you knew nothing about.' Tremayne paused. 'Do you wish to alter any part of your verbal statement Mr Franklin, anything at all...Mr Franklin.' Franklin said nothing.

Tremayne then read him the charges, and had great pleasure in doing so.

'Anthony Donald Franklin I am charging you with the murders of and being implicated with the murders of Michael Paul Edwards and Raymond Jonathan Davidson, also using blackmail and using threats of violence to obtain money, illegal gambling and betting. You do not have to say anything but it may harm your defence if you do not mention when questioned something you later rely on in court. Anything you say may be given in evidence.' Franklin remained silent. 'Do you have anything more to say Mr Franklin?' Steven Allen-Hyde leaned towards Franklin and whispered something, Franklin replied quietly. Steven Allen-Hyde spoke.

'My client has nothing more to say at this juncture Chief inspector Tremayne. My client will make a statement in due course, but only after I have had the opportunity to consult with him fully.'
Tremayne and Martin Wilcox stood, as did the solicitor and Tony Franklin. Tremayne told the uniformed officer to take Franklin to the cells. Tremayne and Martin Wilcox followed the constable and Franklin out of the interview room closely followed by Allen-Hyde. Tremayne returned to the incident room, from where he issued instructions to charge Trendy and Reggie Riley the same.

Tremayne returned to his office where he had a quiet word with Nick Chandler.

'We need to make this water tight Nick or that slippery bugger will be loose again.'

Tremayne stood and walked to the incident board, Nick followed. After looking at the board for a couple of minutes then turned to Martin.

'Martin, didn't you say to me that there were two punters on your list who still live locally?'

'Yes boss, as yet I've not spoken to them.'

Tremayne continued to stare at the board. 'Well…I think it's about time we did.' Remembering Pearsall's words softly-softly, no mistakes, no complaints. 'Does that man want us to put these bastards away or not, you can't make an omelette without breaking eggs. 'Bollocks to this…Martin give them a ring; see if you can get them to talk, cautiously mind, I don't want them scared into silence. If necessary arrange a meeting somewhere quiet, maybe not here. We need them in the witness box.'

'Okay boss, I'm on it.' Martin returned to his desk and found the two names from Franklin's list. He'd got phone numbers too. Then he dialled them. The first person he called was Mr Peter Mitchell. Martin listened to the ringing of the phone for sometime. Before an answering service could cut in he put the phone down. He picked it up again and dialled the second number. It was answered after a couple of rings. A man's voice; success thought Martin.

'Mr Brown, Robert Brown?'

'Yes…' he said suspiciously thinking it was another cold call trying to sell him something.

'I'm sorry to bother you, my name's Wilcox, Detective Constable Wilcox. I believe you are acquainted with a man call Franklin?'

'Er, vaguely, why, what's this about?'

'Now I understand your hesitation, but do you think it would be possible for you to speak with us? This can be done quietly, anywhere you choose, a pub or café…anywhere, your home if you like?' There was no immediate reply, Martin, eventually said 'Mr Brown. Are you still there?'

'Yes, I'm not sure I can help you constable. You see…'

'I understand your worry Mr Brown but this is important. Franklin and his thugs can be sent down for a long time but we need witnesses to testify against him. We have plenty of evidence but what we really need is…people like you who have been taken in by him. Please Mr Brown…will you not reconsider my request?'

'Let me think about it…I'll get back to you constable.'

'Wait Mr Brown I'm pleading for your help here. Your name does not have to be publicized; you can give evidence *in camera.*' The line went quiet again. Eventually Peter Brown spoke.

'All right Constable Wilcox, I'll meet you.' Martin breathed a sigh of relief and made his appointment. He then tried the first number again, with success this time.

'Mr Mitchell, my names Wilcox, Detective constable Wilcox. I wonder if I might have a word with you about a Tony Franklin?' Unlike his previous call, Mitchell was the opposite of Brown. He was instantly there with his accusations against Tony Franklin. 'So Mr Mitchell, can we arrange a meeting to discuss this?'

'Damn right you can, I'll give you my address.' Martin thanked him, putting the phone down. 'Boss, result; I've made arrangement to go and speak to these guys. One guy is very keen on the idea. The other, Robert Brown is a bit nervous though.'

'Okay Martin, take Allie with you when you go, and remember softly-softly; they are witnesses after all not villains.'

Tremayne watched Martin leave the office, thinking this is almost over. His thoughts were broken by the sound of the phone ringing in his office. He picked it up and listened. Yes, I'll be pleased to meet you Mr Meyer, where and when…'

Less than an hour later Martin and Allie drove up to Peter Mitchell's house. It was a large detached house in a leafy suburb; a circular lawn fronted the house with a Greek-style statue in the centre of it. The house was double-fronted; an ornate porch stood centrally leading into the house. The house was accessed via a semi-circular driveway around the lawn through one of two gates, one in; one out. *Very flash* Martin thought.

'Looks prosperous don't you think?' Martin said to Allie as they waited for Mitchell to answer the door. He greeted them warmly and showed them through the house into a conservatory that opened onto a large garden boasting well-tended herbaceous flower beds, a pond with water lilies, and lawns. Other Greek-style statues half hidden amongst the trees and shrubs, peered out as though intrigued by everything going on around them.

Peter Mitchell appeared the archetypal business man, successful in his job, which puzzled Martin as to why a man like this would even need to get involved with gambling, illegal gambling at that. *Why would a man like you not just go into the high street to a bookmaker's office or have an account on-line.*

'Can I offer you a drink of some kind, tea, coffee, or something stronger maybe?' Mitchell made a pot of coffee before settling down. Then he sat facing them, the coffee tray on a low table between them, which also had on it magazines such Country Life, Shooting Times and Trout and Salmon magazine and a Top Gear mag'; all male orientated. *Likes his leisure, this fellow, expensive leisure too* Martin thought. Allie was also taking in the surrounds and looking for the little touches that a woman might bring, but she could see none.

'Thank you for agreeing to see us Mr Mitchell.' Martin said.

'It's a pleasure. If you can help put Tony Franklin away then I'll do all I can to help.'

'If you wouldn't mind, will you tell us how you came to get involved with Tony Franklin?'

'Well, it was some time ago now; a few years in fact. I was running a successful business then; I was happily married with two children. Then,' he laughed cynically at himself. '…on a business seminar weekend, I was introduced to Tony Franklin.' Mitchell let out a sharp breath, an angry Huh! 'He was everybody's friend, everybody's long-lost buddy, so full of himself, OTT had nothing on him. He was part of the group in no time at all. He told us about his clubs, his business successes and his failures, but how he always rose to the top again…smelling of

229

violets of course. Everyone was taken in by his charm, his manner, he was so friendly it was impossible; you couldn't help but like him. The drinks flowed; he bought more than his fair share of rounds. I should have smelt a rat then. And…of course on the Saturday night we were invited into one of his clubs with the pretty girls, drinks and…of course the gambling. We were sucked in, hook line and sinker, played in like…the trout,' He said stabbing his finger on the fishing magazine that lay on the coffee table. '…and once hooked…well…end of story. There's no disgorger to get you off.'

'So you gambled and eventually lost….by how much?'

'Almost seven grand.'

'So, did you go back to the club?'

'Oh yeah, though my next visit was a couple of months later. But then it became more and more frequent. Then it got really addictive, a real problem. My business started to go downhill. My wife at first was sympathetic. She tried to help me, she had therapists round here…they sat there where you are now, but nothing came of it. Finally the ultimatum was issued…not long after that she and the children left.'

'And that was when?'

'Oh…eight, maybe ten months ago.'

'And since then, have you visited the club?'

'I did after my wife left. I was feeling bitter and angry at her. Then after a couple of weeks of being on my own, maybe a month or so, I began to realise what was happening to me, what a stupid bastard I'd been and what I'd become. So, I went back to the therapist. Only this time…I listened. She booked me into a gambler's anonymous group and they really helped. I was amazed at how it helped talking to people in a similar situation and I've not been back since, to the clubs that is.'

'Tell me what was your business?'

'IT, I did anything associated with computers, built them, serviced them, built websites for businesses and individuals, I even ran courses. I now have the chance to rebuild, both my business and my life.'

'What about your wife, have you been in contact with her?'

'Yes…' Mitchell went quiet. Martin and Allie watched him.

'And…' Allie prompted.

'She said she might…and she emphasized the might, consider coming back but only when I can guarantee…that the gambling has ended permanently. Otherwise she said I would never see her or my children ever again. Now that is a very real incentive DC Wilcox. And I'm well along the road to re-building my business again. I've got some good contracts going just now.'

'And you still owe Tony Franklin…how much?'

'At my last reckoning I was still in debt to the tune of five thousand pounds.'

'Quite a bit of money.' Martin said raising his eyebrows. 'Could you afford to repay him…should you have to?'

'I can now, as I've just said I've restarted my business and it's going really well. Yes I could repay him, but would I have to; him being a criminal and a conman to boot.'

'To be honest, I don't know, I shouldn't think so. But you did tell me on the phone that you would be willing to stand up in court and testify that he made threats towards you.'

'Yes, absolutely, I'm prepared to give evidence. Hopefully after that I'll get my family back and we can put all this behind us. I'm now even offering advice to others in the gambler's anonymous group, so that's another indication to my wife that I am serious about this and gambling is well and truly a thing of the past.'

'Well thank you Mr Mitchell. DC Stewart will get you to sign a statement to that effect and we'll leave you in peace.' Allie had been writing notes as they talked and half an hour later they had their statement and were heading back to the station.

There was a scribbled message waiting for Martin when he got to his desk. It was from Mr Robert Brown. *Ah good… thought Martin. Maybe he's willing to talk now and then we should have Franklin well and truly trussed up.* He picked up his phone and dialled. After several rings the call was answered.

'Hello Mr Brown; Detective Constable Martin Wilcox here. I was…'

'Ah yes Detective Constable Wilcox.' He paused briefly, as though not really wanting to talk, but he continued, hesitantly. 'I have considered what you asked, and I er, have spoken to my wife who…after some discussion…I will agree to meet you.'

'Thank you Mr Brown, I appreciate this and how difficult if is for you. Now where would you like to meet?' They arranged a meeting place, and time.

Martin waited in the foyer of the Western Hotel. He'd already drunk two cups of coffee and consumed almost forty minutes. He was beginning to think Robert Brown was having second thoughts and was not going to turn up. He then noticed a man standing nervously by the door. He watched him step to one side to let a couple out carrying suitcases. Martin took in his manner and appearance. He stood nervously looking around the hotel foyer. Dressed conventionally, his clothes, although not dishevelled had seen better days, thought Martin, certainly not like Peter Mitchell; this man did not give the appearance of a prosperous man at all. In fact Martin thought he was possibly strapped for cash. The man himself was clean shaven, about five foot eight, balding and in his late fifties. Martin got up and walked over to him. 'Mr Brown? Martin Wilcox.' The man anxiously said yes and Martin directed him over to the table where he'd been waiting.

'I was beginning to think…'

'Yes I'm sorry,' Robert Brown said. 'I must admit that I was beginning to have second thoughts. This whole business is…to say the least, worries me.'

'Of course it is Mr Brown, that is why I need you to tell me about Franklin and then we can do something about him.' Peter Brown remained silent. Martin could read the signs, a worried man, his whole manner, he was a bag of nerves; his hands were clasped together as though it gave him comfort. 'Would you like a drink, tea, coffee…something stronger?'

'Thank you, a whisky if you don't mind.' Martin called a waiter; he ordered a whisky for Robert Brown and a small beer for himself. Martin chatted to him trying to get him relaxed. The drinks arrived and Brown took the whisky in one gulp. Martin asked him if he'd like another but he declined. 'Now Mr Brown what can you tell me about Franklin, how you became involved with him'

'Well…It began over eighteen months ago. I had been out with friends, I don't know how it began but we ended up in a gambling club. I've no real problem with gambling, I've played the gee-gees most of my life. I first went into a betting shop as a lad, my dad took me in. But I've always been able to cope with that. I would place little bets here and there just a few quid you know, maybe something more on the big races like the National or the Oaks, the Cheltenham Gold Cup that sort of thing. But never anything out of hand. But that night, after going into that club I don't know what came over me. I've never seen anything like it. The roulette, the blackjack, even that dice game from America…craps. Well I must have had a few drinks, had a few smiles from the pretty girls, maybe they even flattered me a bit. I've never had women flaunt themselves towards me before, not even my wife. Their provocative clothes and low necklines showing all that cleavage and the heady perfume, well…I'd never experienced anything like that before. My wife and I are…conservative to say the least constable. I'm a simple man, I work hard and…now look at me. I've lost all our life savings, nearly six thousand pounds…'

'I take it that you were approached by one of Franklin's people to settle your debt?'

'Yes… at first they said I could settle up quickly if I paid them a hundred pounds a week. I thought that wasn't too bad. But then I got behind again and that's when the real threats began. I missed another payment and they picked me up as I walked home from work…I was terrified constable, I thought they were going to kill me or break my legs or something equally horrible.'

'Where do you work Mr Brown?'

'I'm an electrical maintenance supervisor at the Albert Dock.'

'So what happened when they picked you up? Do you know where they took you?'

'I don't know where it was, but they took me to what looked like a builder's yard. I don't think it'd been used for any building work for a long time. Anyway, they forced me into an old office and into a chair. At first they spoke calmly enough but even so I was scared to death. After some time they said if I didn't settle up by the end of the month, this will happen. That's when the punches flew; I think he only hit me once. I've never hurt so much in all my life. I thought they'd kill me.'

'Can you describe these men Mr Brown?' Robert Brown looked at the empty glass sitting on the table, Martin indicated to a waiter for another whisky. He took a deep breath, closed his eyes trying to regain his nerves and courage.

'The one asking the questions, and doing all the talking was well dressed, yes very smart. You would have taken him for your archetypal businessman. The other was a big brute of a man. He always stood just behind me. He looked like a heavyweight boxer, only cruder. His…smile was grotesque. He looked as though as he was enjoying every minute of it…yes, I think he enjoyed inflicting pain on people…I saw the man facing me give a slight nod…and that's when I reeled with the pain.' Robert Brown was visibly distressed by the telling of the events. He remained silent for a minute or two, he sipped the whisky; his hands shook as he held the glass. Martin could see that the trauma Reggie Riley and Trendy had caused this quiet, foolish man. Foolish for getting involved with Franklin, but Martin was not there to judge, he was there to get him to testify in court.

'Thank you very much Mr Brown. We know who these people are. I can tell you that they are in custody now and have been charged. So, if there's nothing more you want to tell me I've no reason to detain you any longer. And thank you once again; I appreciate how hard this is for you. We'll be in touch Mr Brown.'

Martin entered Tremayne's office feeling over the moon with what he'd been told by Mitchell and Brown.

'So, what have you learnt Martin?'

'That the two of them owe Franklin several thousand pounds, Mitchell is seven grand and Brown is five grand in debt to him. Brown said he was taken to the yard and received a severe beating...'

'Don't tell me from Trendy and Riley?'

'Yeah.'

'And they are both willing to stand up in court?'

'Yep.'

'I'm pleased to hear it Martin, very pleased. Well I think we have enough to take this to ol' beardy chops and then to the CPS. Good work.'

'Thanks boss.'

19

By seven o'clock there was a party atmosphere with Tremayne buying the drinks in the Golden Lion, thanking his team for all their hard work.

'I'd just like to clear up one or two things though before we settle down.' He said getting their attention. All eyes were now on Rufus Tremayne. 'Two interesting things have just occurred, the first is that I've just given Redfern Sutcliffe a ring, I'm going to see him in the morning, tell him what we know.' Rufus said.

'And the second thing?' Sophie asked.

'This is very interesting, earlier today I got a phone call from Leonard Meyer, the jeweller. I went and had a chat with him. What he told me, even now, I can hardly believe myself.' Everyone shuffled about, to get into a better position to hear. Tremayne smiled and looked at the intent faces. 'He apologized profusely at first. I thought he looked very worried, concerned even. We met in the Monet Hotel, he said nothing for quite a while, he just, stared into his glass, but eventually he emerged from it. He said that when Allie placed the jewels on his desk, and he first set eyes on them, suddenly his heart was in his mouth, he said…he recognized them, and not just because of what they were or the maker even. He said that they had been in his house,' Tremayne paused for effect. '…and, that they were bought by his father, who was also a jeweller.' Tremayne saw mouths opening wanting to throw questions at him but he raised his hand to silence them. 'All your questions will be answered, just wait a minute. He said, that he had always known about these items. His father had bought them a long time ago, during the war, but he didn't know from where or from whom. He said that they were on display in the house and were a great source of pleasure for his father and he never failed to miss an opportunity to show them off to the family. When he died though, they were not declared, and so death duty was never paid. When they were stolen Meyer did not report the theft. He said he didn't report them stolen for that reason. So, they'd sat in Meyer's house from nineteen forty four up until the night when our light fingered Mickey went a-calling.'

'So, that clears that up, we now know where Mickey Edwards got them from. But, what do you think Redfern wants from all this?' Sophie asked.

'As I've said before, I really don't have a clue. I mean honestly why should he be interested in a forty year old murder case? It has me beat. But, I'll bet you he has some ulterior motive. He's up to something. Redfern Sutcliffe does nothing if there's no profit in it. He's like one of those aliens on Star Trek. You know, the ones with the big ears for listening to all the gossip, hoping to pick up a tit-bit or two and then make a profit from it.'

'Ferengi?'

'What?'

'The aliens with the big ears, they are called Ferengi.' Sophie said to him.

'Really and how do you know so much about Star Trek?'

'Oh you'd be surprised at what I know.' She said with a wry smile. Rufus shook his head in disbelief. Then he picked up the bottle of Fitou and refilled their glasses. Rufus had asked Steve the barman to have some sandwiches and nibbles for them, they were celebrating. He picked up a plate and handed it round. Sophie asked if he'd got enough evidence to convict Franklin and his cronies.

'Yes I think so. We had the best break ever when Martin discovered a CD that had some names on it. When we interviewed them they agreed to stand up in court and give evidence.'

Tremayne stood impatiently on the steps of the Monet Hotel waiting for Redfern Sutcliffe. *Is that man ever on time for an appointment?* Tremayne fumed. Fifteen minutes had passed before a taxi drew up and Sutcliffe jumped out. He saw Tremayne and beamed, hurrying forward the half a dozen paces with hand out in greeting and full of apologies for his lateness.

'I'll buy you a watch for Christmas, Redfern.' he said a little sarcastically. Redfern simply smiled, 'Okay, sorry Rufus.' They settled into a couple of seats in the foyer and ordered coffee. Chatting generally, Rufus waited for Sutcliffe to make the first mention to the cuttings that had sent Nick Chandler all the way to Norway; and, had given Frankie Bolton hours of research work. Eventually, after finishing off his second cup of coffee, Redfern said, 'How's my little puzzle performed Rufus?'

'If you mean those newspaper cuttings, they've caused more than one person many a bloody headache.'

'Yes…I thought as much. But…what conclusions have you made?'

'To begin with, after we'd got into them, I saw a possible similarity, a link even, though tenuous, to the current murder case we were working on. The victim, as those from the past, was found in the dunes, but that turned out to be mere coincidence.'

'Okay, so then what?' Redfern asked trying not to sound too enthusiastic.

'I could not devote any time to those cases, that is, to your little puzzle as you put it. Too old, too long dead you understand, my bosses would never have gone for any investigation. So, because it was simple research, I asked a journalist friend of mine to do a bit of digging. He said he was too busy to go digging into them, but he did have a new journalist, a young lady called Frankie Bolton, fresh out of university and keen as mustard to get her teeth into a bit of research.'

'Okay, so you've made your excuses, so what did she dig up?' Tremayne ignored his sarcasm.

'By the end she uncovered quite a bit actually.'

'Sounds fascinating…go on.' Redfern looked at his watch. Raised his hand and ordered a couple of glasses of Manzanilla, a dry sherry full of life and zest. 'Not many places serve this, it doesn't keep well once opened. I'll offer to buy the bottle afterwards. Do you like dry sherries?'

'Yes, very much.'

'So this girl Frankie Bolton, you were saying she uncovered…what?'

'She found two members of the team who went to Norway, alongside Simon Carter, the man found dead in the dunes back in nineteen forty four. At that time she was pulling at straws. But to cut a long story short, she discovered who he was; she also discovered that the bank manager Richard Mason was in fact not English but German.'

'Interesting' Redfern picked up his glass, took a long sip savouring the bouquet and flavour. '…not English eh?' Tremayne looked at him and thought. *You know more about this than you're letting on, you bugger.* 'So who was he?'

'Well I got intrigued, so much so that I sent Nick Chandler to Norway on the pretence that my current case had some sort of link, a slim tenuous link at that, with these old cases.'

'And…'

'That mission during the war went specifically to a house near a place called Klokkarvik. There Nick met the current owner of the house. It turned out that the family had owned the place for many years; the current

237

owner's great grandfather built the place. But during the war the Germans requisitioned it as an R&R retreat,' Rufus said making quotation marks with his fingers. '…for officers. Soon after their return the Chief Petty Officer Simon Carter was found dead in the dunes. Coincidentally at or damn close to the spot where twenty years later the bank manager Richard Mason was found and then another fifty years passed and Mickey Edwards was found in almost the same spot.'

'So, are you saying there *is* a link Rufus?'

'Possibly,' Tremayne said coolly 'But tell me Redfern, what do you know about all this? I've got a nagging feeling that you know more than you're letting on.' Rufus said raising his eyebrows, staring intently at his friend.

'Go on with your story Rufus.' Redfern said without elaborating or answering Rufus' query. Tremayne continued relating the story to Redfern. But he was still uncommitted about knowing anything at all about anything. They had been in the hotel so long Redfern offered Tremayne lunch, which he accepted. *I've got to find out what he knows, even if it means sitting in here all day.* He thought.

During lunch Tremayne learnt nothing from Redfern, the talk was general; little was mentioned of murders, old or new.

'So Rufus' He said at last. '…collating all this information, obtained by Nick Chandler and this young journalist…what conclusions did you come to?' Rufus was taken aback by this sudden enquiry, after so long eating and idle chatter.

'Well, there did seem to be a link between Carter and Mason. Frankie discovered that Carter deposited a rather large sum of money into the bank where Mason was manager.'

'This money…did you determine where he got it?'

'No not really.' Rufus said, evading what he actually knew.

'How much did he put away?'

'Quite a bit actually…five thousand pounds, which by nineteen forties standards was a sizable sum.' Redfern sat back into his seat, took up his glass and took a sip, obviously reflecting upon the amount of money deposited. 'The money was deposited, in mid-August. It was withdrawn on the eleventh of October nineteen forty four, a Friday as it happens. Simon Carter was found dead on the following Monday.' Tremayne watched Redfern's reaction to this snippet of information. He thought he could see a twinge of anger in his eyes, but he did not respond verbally. 'You look like a man who was expecting to hear something more

Redfern. Is there something else?' The conversation was a cat and mouse affair, Tremayne trying to get information out of Sutcliffe and him not giving it. 'Tell me Redfern what might that be?'

'What did Frankie Bolton find out about the bank manager Richard Mason, you said something about him not being English…was there something more about him that you've failed to mention?'

'Ah! Then there is something that you've not told me…isn't there Redfern?'

'Maybe; tell me about Mason.'

'Well as I said it was suggested that he wasn't English. Frankie followed the trail though the National Archive and discovered that he had been married; his wife was killed during an air raid. But his son survived. And like a true detective she traced him. Both she and I have spoken to him…'

'Really…and what did he say?' Sutcliffe said, suddenly alert and eager to hear what this man had said to Tremayne. But Rufus realised this and decided to play Sutcliffe along, play him as a trout on a line. Reel him in little by little, attempting to get from him that last piece of knowledge he was keeping close to his chest.

'Well he talked about his father. He was sent to England to be educated, long before the war. Hitler began to rise to prominence and he stayed. He'd got a job with the bank. He rose through the ranks and ended up as manager of a branch of Williams Deacons Bank. He died in nineteen sixty three, killed by person or persons unknown.'

'Now come on Rufus, that's just a report. You're not reading to me from a sheet verbatim, tell me what he SAID. You must have learnt something more than just that. We know all about how he died and where he was found.' He said tapping the cuttings that lay open on the table. 'I need the *inside story*, what you read between the lines.' The two men smiled knowingly at each other.

'He said his mother, she was Mildred Spencer, had a smallish wooden box in which she kept her personal papers. Richard Mason junior was never allowed to look into it. She kept it under lock and key.'

'An' she's alive and still not letting him in on the secret.' Redfern suddenly smiled, laughed. 'Surely Rufus the old lady must be long gone by now and you're saying he doesn't know what's in that box. Come on Rufus you're pulling my leg. What did he say?'

'He told me that there were family photos many of people he didn't know and…'

'Yeah and Christmas cards from my Auntie Jo and letters from God knows who. You're stalling Rufus.'

'No more than you Redfern, come on we've been sitting here for hours, we've had a good lunch and we've drunk good wine. Now it's your turn. You tell me what the hell this is all about. You're not simply interested in old murder cases just for the hell of it. There's something more isn't there? Something deeper…is there money involved per chance?'

'Money, damn right there's money and a hell of a lot of it too.' Redfern suddenly became animated, as his voice rising a few decibels that diners nearby turned to see what the trouble. Redfern realised this and smiled benignly as he looked around apologetically.

'Ah now we're getting somewhere. So let's stop fishing shall we. What is all this about Redfern?'

'Okay Rufus, okay, you'll remember I said my mom was English and that she married a GI?'

'Yes.'

'What I didn't tell you was that she was Jewish. At that time her family still lived in Amsterdam Holland. The war had been raging for just over one year. In February nineteen forty-one the deportations began and they were never seen again. They were a wealthy family, successful business people, merchants, had been for generations apparently. They had an art collection worth…well God knows how much.'

'And you're going to tell me that this, art collection, was taken by the Nazis when they took your Grandparents and the rest of their family?' Tremayne said enquiringly.

'Yep and I think that there is something connecting this guy Carter, the banker Mason and my family's fortune. Now am I correct?'

'Yes you are. But what I don't understand is, what made you link these cuttings to you family?

'Ah! You see Rufus this is not my first attempt at trying to sort this. I've had these cuttings for some time. I knew about Carter's trip to Norway and I knew that Mason was a bank manager, well that's there in the paper's story. I found out about the Kraut General and that he was Mason's brother, that Maurer was in Norway, and when I found out Carter went to Norway, I simply put two and two together. That Maurer had the jewels, Carter found them, but after that…well…I came to dead ends…but you seem to have tied it all nicely together. So, go on.'

'You'll recall I said that five thousand pounds had been deposited into a bank account in the name of Simon Carter?'

'Yeah.'

'Well we believe that money was the cash he received from the sale of certain artefacts that he found at the house in Norway.'

'I see…so it's all gone then?' Redfern said shrugging his shoulders dejectedly, sighing deeply. Tremayne did not reply immediately. *Do we really have the property of this man?* He thought, looking at the expectant face of the man sitting opposite him. Redfern Sutcliffe stared back, his mouth moved as though he was about to blurt something out, but he remained silent. Then Tremayne broke the silence.

'No…I don't believe they are all gone.'

'NO…so what…what are you saying Rufus?'

'We have recovered some artefacts.' Redfern looked at Rufus, astounded, speechless. 'We found, two lots in fact. The first was in the flat of a guy called Mickey Edwards, a known petty crook. The other lot we found in a wartime anti-aircraft battery, abandoned after the war, ultimately covered by the sand and lost. We were looking for evidence for a murder and came across it by chance.' Tremayne paused. 'I can tell you, that both these lots now reside in our safe, in the station.'

'You're telling me that, you have found my…' Sutcliffe paused speechless. '…some in a crook's flat and some in a wartime gun battery…this is incredible Rufus.'

'Yeah, I'm amazed that those in the bunker remained there all that time actually. They were in an ammunition box. And by stroke of luck, no one went into the emplacement and found it. As time passed the whole place disappeared under a sand dune and was forgotten. They were never demolished, just left to rot and disappear. I think it was mere coincidence that the bodies were found in that area, almost on the same spot in the dunes. As we were searching for clues to Mickey Edwards' murder we came across the concrete roof. One of my officers found the hatch. We thought that maybe something was hidden inside. After a bit of digging and poking around – *voila* we found the box containing the jewellery.'

'I'm amazed Rufus. Can I see it? More to the point can I have it back?'

'Not so quick Redfern. We'll need proof; we're not in the habit of handing over valuable items not without proof and provenance of ownership.'

241

'Yeah sure, I understand that, no problem. I can you provide you with al the proof you need.'

Tremayne looked astonished, his mouth open slightly, not believing Redfern Sutcliffe. 'You have proof of ownership?'

'Yeah sure, what do you think this is amateur night? Too right I have proof. I have a written description of all the items and photos too. There is also proof of purchase, receipts even. And…how much was paid for each piece and where they were bought, everything.' Redfern leaned back in his chair, his arms open, palms towards Tremayne expressing sincerity. 'You see my grandfather was a very astute and meticulous businessman, although a bit naive. That naivety cost him and his family their lives. He stayed put. He thought he'd be all right…but…well as we all know now. But yep, he catalogued every single item that he bought. He sent the list, for some unknown reason, and all other details to my mom. He also sent a few small items to keep her…well, financially sound should the need be. I have those pieces, she never sold them, never would.'

An expectant Redfern Sutcliffe sat with Tremayne in his office. They were waiting for DC Allie Stewart to fetch the boxes containing the jewels. Tremayne told Sutcliffe that Allie had taken them to a respectable jeweller and that he had confirmed the authenticity of them. And that Leonard Meyer had said the maker of some of the pieces was the renowned Carl Fabergé. Redfern simply nodded, but said nothing. Tremayne assumed he knew this. Eventually Allie arrived carrying the old green ammunition box, its yellow markings still quite legible. Balancing on top was the bag that came from Mickey's flat. Allie first opened the box. The items had now been wrapped in tissue paper. As she lifted each item out and unwrapped it Sutcliffe's face opened, his mouth dropped and tears emerged from his eyes.

'You didn't say why this guy Mason died Rufus?'

'The two letters I mentioned.'

'Yeah?'

'They were written in German. They were from Mason's brother who was a general in the German army. He told his brother that these had been stolen, from him. He said to his brother to be on the lookout for them. When Carter suddenly arrived and deposited a large amount of cash, he became suspicious, although Carter had a letter explaining where the cash had come from. He did a bit of asking around; he discovered that Carter had recently been to Norway. So putting two and two together, and when the money was deposited in his bank…well he thought all his chickens had come home to roost. Mason now had the money in his bank, but he didn't know where the jewels were. He sent a message back to his brother, who replied with a note that simply said 'deal with it'. So he had Carter killed. The money was withdrawn, probably using a forged signature. This wasn't a real problem as he had a genuine signature to copy. No one questioned him. What happened after that? Obviously something did, because Mason himself was eventually killed, but why…I don't know and probably never will. Maybe he tried to pull a fast one on his brother; who was maybe a greedy man and vindictive. Maybe he didn't believe that Mason didn't have the jewels tucked away somewhere. So the brother had him murdered.'

'Well I'm sorry I was so mysterious to begin with Rufus. But I didn't think you'd want to get involved with a mere treasure hunt. You had to feel it was a cold case or something. But I'll be eternally in your debt for finding these. And thank all those involved will you.' Redfern Sutcliffe walked from the police station, knowing he was about to be reunited with his family's property as soon as the provenance was verified.

'So that's that then.' Nick commented, walking into the office as he saw Redfern leave. 'He seems happy enough. Did he tell you why he gave you those old cuttings?'

'He thought there was some family connection.'

'And…was there.'

'Yes, but he needed a bit of research doing and he thought that I could…well never mind. Anyway Nick, I've had enough of treasure hunts. In future, I deal only with plain simple murders.' Nick left the office and settled down to finish off his reports. Tremayne leaned back in his chair and stared at the ceiling.

Some weeks later he learnt that Redfern Sutcliffe had returned to the United States. Rufus himself received a thank you letter and a cheque for…well, services rendered, as a gift of course.

Rufus Tremayne, Nick Chandler and Helen Machin sat in the witness waiting area of the crown court, nervously awaiting the jury's verdict on Tony Franklin and associates. They didn't wait long and soon after that, drinks were flowing in the Golden Lion.

Lightning Source UK Ltd.
Milton Keynes UK
UKOW05f1546051213

222401UK00001B/83/P

9 781782 998730